Red-Hot Cowboy

A Blazing Collection

VICKI LEWIS THOMPSON
DEBBI RAWLINS

MILLS & BOON

CONTENTS

Cowboy Untamed

Vicki Lewis Thompson

A passion for travel has taken *New York Times* bestselling author **Vicki Lewis Thompson** to Europe, Great Britain, the Greek Isles, Australia and New Zealand. She's visited most of North America and has her eye on South America's rain forests. Africa, India and China beckon. But her first love is her home state of Arizona, with its deserts, mountains, sunsets and—last but not least—cowboys! The wide-open spaces and heroes on horseback influence everything she writes. Connect with her at vickilewisthompson.com, Facebook.com/vickilewisthompson and Twitter.com/vickilthompson.

Books by Vicki Lewis Thompson

Thunder Mountain Brotherhood

Midnight Thunder
Thunderstruck
Rolling Like Thunder
A Cowboy Under the Mistletoe
Cowboy All Night
Cowboy After Dark

Sons of Chance

Cowboys & Angels
Riding High
Riding Hard
Riding Home
A Last Chance Christmas

All backlist available in ebook format.

Visit the Author Profile page at millsandboon.com.au for more titles.

Dear Reader,

Oh, those Magee brothers! In *Cowboy After Dark*, I fell in love with Liam and figured his younger brother Grady couldn't possibly be as endearing. Was I ever wrong! Please don't ask me to pick my favorite Magee brother. I doubt you'll be able to, either, after you meet Grady, the cowboy turned metal artist. I guarantee he's hotter than a blowtorch!

Like Sapphire Ferguson, I have a weakness for creative men because they're creative in...well, everything they do, if you get my meaning. Grady's sculptures of majestic creatures like eagles and wolves are crafted with recycled metal, which makes him both artistic and ecologically aware! Not only that, but he gets hot and sweaty doing it. Sculpting, that is. What did you think I was talking about?

Okay, I don't blame you for going there. The minute you get a glimpse of this tall cowboy with his muscles and slightly shaggy haircut, you'll be ready to trade places with Sapphire. And when you find out Grady's plan to make a sculpture for Rosie, his foster mom, your heart is gonna melt.

Welcome back to the Thunder Mountain Brotherhood! This amazing band of men each experienced a tragedy that landed them in foster care, but they were all lucky enough to find a home with Rosie and Herb at Thunder Mountain Ranch. Their days at the ranch taught them the cowboy way and forged an enduring bond, although love doesn't come easily to guys with emotional scars. Join me for another story featuring the awesome cowboys who call themselves the Thunder Mountain Brotherhood!

Creatively yours,

Vicki Lewis Thompson

To visual artists—dedicated souls who enrich
our lives by allowing us to see the world through
their eyes.

1

A WYOMING SUNSET tinged the horizon pale orange, reminding Grady Magee of the Dreamsicles he used to crave as a kid. But thoughts of adult pleasures nudged out childhood nostalgia as he parked his truck in front of the Sheridan Art Barn next to a grape-colored pickup, the only other vehicle in the lot. It likely belonged to Sapphire Ferguson, the woman who'd been on his mind during most of the long drive from Cody.

Three weeks ago during a visit to Thunder Mountain Ranch, he'd come by here with his foster brother Cade to pick up some local art for Cade's new cabin. Sapphire, a talented potter, had been minding the store. He'd barely recognized her.

The quiet girl he remembered from high school had morphed into a confident woman with a smoldering glance that set him on fire. When she'd asked him to headline a charity event featuring artists creating work on the spot, he'd set aside his packed schedule and agreed without finding out what the charity was. Didn't matter.

Hauling his tools and materials from Cody and setting up a studio in a corner of this renovated barn was a pain in the ass. He didn't care. Sapphire had his attention. While honing his welding skills in Alaska and dreaming of making a living with recycled metal art, he'd also dreamed of the kind of woman he'd want to share his life with.

She'd be a self-starter, imaginative, bold and sensual. Good looks wouldn't hurt but sexual chemistry was more important. Getting both would be a bonus. In short, the woman of his dreams was a lot like Sapphire Ferguson. Maybe his first impression would turn out to be wrong. Or maybe she already had someone in her life.

His gut told him she didn't. She wasn't wearing a ring and she'd acted as fascinated with him as he'd been with her. Since then, they'd communicated only through brief phone texts because they'd both battled crazy deadlines. He could be imagining the hum of sexual energy underlying those texts, but he didn't think so.

He climbed out of his truck with that same energy fizzing in his veins. She'd agreed to meet him and help him get his stuff unloaded, but he hadn't counted on being alone with her. Eight other artists were part of the co-op Sapphire had organized, each claiming one of the renovated stalls as both a work and display space. He'd expected some of them to be around.

Apparently, they weren't as manic about working as he was. He put in long hours, both because he loved it and because the commissions kept coming and he didn't like making customers wait. His brother Liam had reminded him that building a successful career in less than three years was unusual and few artists made a living, let alone a good living.

Grady believed him, although he didn't have much to go on. He'd used the nest egg he'd saved during his pipeline job to keep him afloat while he followed his dream. His first sculptures had sold like hotcakes and after that he'd been so busy keeping up with the demand that he'd had no time to hang out with other artists.

Spending time with Sapphire was his primary motivation for doing the charity event, but he also looked forward to conversations with other creative types. Not to say he was disappointed that he and Sapphire were alone tonight. Fraternizing with the other co-op members could wait.

He'd started toward the double-door entrance when he heard a woman's soft voice coming from somewhere to the right of the barn. He couldn't make out the words, but from the sound of it she really liked the person she was talking to. He paused to listen. Maybe he had this all wrong and the grape-colored pickup had brought two people here—Sapphire and her boyfriend. That would suck.

Standing very still, he listened for a response, a deeper murmur that would indicate she was with a guy. Nothing. He edged closer so he could make out what she was saying.

"Come on, Fred," she crooned. "You know you want this."

Dear God. If Sapphire was about to have sex with someone named Fred up against the side of the barn, he did *not* want to be here. Yeah, he'd arrived a little earlier than planned because he'd broken a few speed limits on the way. She might not be expecting him for another hour.

"You liked it last night, remember? Don't be shy."

Grady squeezed his eyes shut. This couldn't be happening. He'd pinned his hopes on Sapphire being available, yet he'd had no proof of that. If he stayed here much longer, he'd find out exactly how misguided his assumptions were.

Better to quietly climb back into his truck and slowly exit the parking lot. If they were about to get busy, they wouldn't hear him drive away. He'd grab a cup of coffee in the diner.

"There you go. Isn't that nice?"

Yikes. He took a slow step backward, then another.

"Such a good boy. Such a brave kitty-cat."

Kitty-cat? He froze. No man with an ounce of self-respect would let a woman call him *kitty-cat.* And now that he thought about it, no straight guy would need coaxing in order to have sex with a woman like Sapphire.

He crept to the corner of the building to take a look and discovered Sapphire crouched in the dry grass, the golden glow of the sunset igniting sparks of fire in her long auburn hair. She'd placed several bowls in a semicircle around her and he counted eleven cats munching away. Instead of having sex, she was feeding strays.

He sighed in relief. The sound wasn't loud but it caught everyone's attention. Sapphire and all eleven cats looked at him. A black cat with white markings backed away from the dish. "Sorry," Grady muttered.

She kept her voice low. "You're early."

"Traffic was light."

"You'd better not come any closer. I'd like Fred to eat some more."

"Fred." He swallowed so he wouldn't laugh and spook the cats.

"Fred Astaire. The tuxedo. He's the most skittish of the bunch but I'm making progress with him."

Grady had never heard anyone refer to a cat as a *tuxedo* but it was a great description. The white patch on Fred's chest made him look as if he'd dressed for the Oscars.

All the cats went back to eating except Fred. Hunkered down, eyes wide and pupils dilated, he stared at Grady. His whiskers, white to match his chest, trembled.

"He won't hurt you, sweetie." Sapphire's voice dripped honey as she spoke to the cat. "The food's yum-yum-yummy, kitty-cat. You know you want some. Come on, come and get it."

Her words seemed to have no effect on Fred but they were having a definite effect on Grady. After three weeks of erotic dreams featuring her in the lead role, he was a hot mess of raging hormones. Listening to her woo the cat was initiating action below his belt. She'd told him to stay put but that could prove embarrassing if she kept up this seductive murmur. Sure, she was addressing a cat, but he had no trouble imagining her using that same tone during sex. The longer he stood there, the larger his problem grew, so to speak.

He couldn't very well tell her that. "Maybe I should move

so Fred can't see me." He hoped she hadn't heard the telltale huskiness in his voice.

"That might help." Fortunately, she didn't glance over at him. "I'll be finished in a few minutes."

"I'll meet you out front." He began a slow retreat, wincing at the pressure of his zipper against his pride and joy.

"Okay." She went back to sweet-talking Fred.

He did his best to block the sound as he ducked out of sight and made the painful journey to his truck. Bracing both hands on the hood, he took several deep breaths. Anyone would think he was some horny teenager.

Normally, he didn't have this issue. He thought back to the last woman he'd dated and was shocked to realize they'd broken up more than a year ago. Time flew when you were making art. She'd never understood his preoccupation with his work and they'd fought about it enough times that they'd decided to call it quits last July.

Okay, so he hadn't been in bed with a woman for a long time and now he'd found someone so hot that he'd fixated on her for weeks. That could explain his sudden stiffy. He felt a little better about his reaction, although he'd have to watch himself to make sure he didn't come across as sex starved.

Turning around, he leaned his butt against the truck and adjusted himself. Better now. He repositioned his new Stetson so it sat more firmly on his head. Liam had talked him into buying it to fit his image as a celebrated Western artist and it was the most expensive one he'd ever owned—black with a silver-and-turquoise hatband. Naturally, Liam had insisted such a hat deserved a new pair of boots, also black, with fancy stitching. Grady had worn them to make a good impression but he'd brought his old scuffed ones to work in.

He had two projects in mind. First he would put together a nice sculpture for his foster mom, Rosie Padgett. She and his foster dad, Herb, had welcomed Grady and Liam to Thunder Mountain Ranch ten years ago when their mom's car accident had left her unable to care for a couple of rowdy teens. Last month Rosie had hinted to Liam that she'd love a sculpture, and Grady had come up with a great idea for the design.

Creating Rosie's gift would help him settle into the workspace, so he'd be ready to put on a performance for the charity night. He'd come up with a sketch for that one, too, and it was a piece he could finish within the three hours allotted to the event. Sapphire planned to have a silent auction for his contribution and she hoped to raise a lot of money.

He really should find out what the charity was. His sculpture should relate to the cause in some way, and just because he liked the cougar he'd sketched, didn't mean it would work with the evening's theme. He'd ask Sapphire about that when she finished feeding the stray cats. It was possible she'd told him and the information hadn't registered, because he'd been so focused on her.

Nudging his hat back with his thumb, he gazed up as the first stars blinked on. They weren't as bright in town as they were out at the ranch. Much as he'd love to stay with his foster parents during his time in Sheridan, it wasn't practical.

Thunder Mountain Academy, a new venture that involved teaching high school kids about everything related to horses, was in its last week of the summer session. The cabins that had once housed foster boys were now filled with teens enrolled in the program. Grady would only be in the way, so he'd accepted an offer to stay in town with Ben and Molly Radcliffe.

Ben had made saddles for just about everyone Grady knew in Sheridan, including his foster parents. Molly was Cade Gallagher's cousin, although Grady hadn't quite worked out the details of that connection. It had something to do with the well-known Chance brothers in Jackson Hole. In any case, Molly and Ben were part of the Thunder Mountain Ranch extended family and they were happy to let him use their guest room.

He'd warned them he didn't know when he'd show up. Unloading his equipment and materials had to come first. At least, that was how he'd rationalized stopping at the Art Barn to meet with Sapphire. Technically, he could have driven over to Molly and Ben's tonight and brought his supplies here in the morning.

Yet when he'd suggested stopping by tonight to drop them off, Sapphire had readily agreed. Her eagerness had fired up his imagination, and discovering that she was here alone added to the anticipation. He wondered if she'd had dinner. He ran through the restaurant options and decided to suggest his favorite bar because it had live music and a dance floor.

"That takes care of that." Sapphire rounded the corner of the barn holding a stack of bowls. "I thought I'd be done before you got here."

He pushed himself away from the truck and walked toward her. "No worries. Do you feed them every night?" She looked even prettier than he remembered—wavy auburn hair pulled back on one side with an elaborate silver comb, exotic earrings that dangled to her shoulders, a low-cut peasant blouse and a brightly patterned skirt that reminded him of gypsies.

"We feed them every night and every morning. We rotate weeks and this happens to be mine." She tipped her head toward the double doors at the entrance. "Come on in. I need to wash these and then I'll help you unload your equipment."

"Thanks. That would be great." He caught the spicy scent of her perfume, the same one she'd worn when they'd met three weeks ago. He breathed it in and all his hopes and dreams came flooding back. "So everyone pitches in to feed the strays?" He wondered if she liked to dance. Even if she wasn't much for dancing, they could get out on the floor and do the shuffle-and-sway routine to a slow tune so he could hold her.

"They're not exactly strays. Can you please catch the door for me?"

"Sure thing." He hurried to do it, berating himself as he slid the barn door open. He'd been so busy making plans for tonight that he'd forgotten his manners.

"You can check out the new pieces on display while I wash these."

"You have a sink?"

"During the renovation we put in a small bathroom and a tiny kitchen." She gestured toward the row of stalls. "Go ahead and look around. I left on the lights so you could see the new stuff. Everyone's getting ready for the big weekend. Lots of good work."

"Sounds great, but I'd be glad to help you with the cat dishes." Even in high school he'd been fascinated by her turquoise eyes. He'd never asked her out, because he'd been busy denying his own artistic leanings. He'd had a feeling she could see who he really was and he hadn't been ready to acknowledge that yet.

She smiled. "It's a one-person job. Go ahead and browse."

"Okay." But he sure hated to leave those eyes and that smile. He thought about both as he walked down the aisle between the stalls. Although he glanced at the artwork along the way, all he really cared about tonight was Sapphire's pottery.

Three weeks ago Cade had bought a vase of hers that Grady would have given his eyeteeth for. But the trip had been for Cade and so he'd scored the vase. Grady was curious as to what else she'd added to her collection since then.

Her display was conveniently located next to the large stall that would be his for the next several days. He stepped into the space and sucked in a breath. During his first visit here he'd noticed the sensuality of her work, and the newest pieces were even more dramatic, especially her dinnerware set.

The saturated colors and undulating lines of the single place setting made him wonder what sort of orgy the two of them could have with food served on these dishes. Picking up a red bowl with a dark purple interior, he cradled it in both hands and ran his thumb over the pebbled rim. The bowl was a tactile and visual feast.

Her potter's wheel stood in the corner ready for the next project, and he wanted to be there to see if her expression while creating was as passionate as the work itself. If she'd had an erotic nature back in high school, he'd totally missed the clues.

Not surprising. He'd been an insecure idiot back then, but he'd changed and so had she. He'd embraced his true calling and had finally realized that testosterone and art weren't mutually exclusive. Obviously, she'd grown out of her timid phase.

"That collection's new."

He turned to find her standing in the opening that used to be the stall door. He'd been absorbed in his plans and hadn't heard her footsteps. "It's sexy."

"You're not the first person who seems to feel that way." Her gaze met his and for a moment there was a flash of heat. Then she looked away and studied the colorful dinnerware. "I put that place setting out yesterday and I can already tell it startles people."

"Why?" His blood warmed as he registered the interest he'd seen in her eyes. This could turn into an excellent evening.

"The colors seem to make them nervous. They're also thrown for a loop when I explain that each place setting's slightly different. Most people expect their dinner dishes to match. It'll take a certain kind of customer."

Like me. But buying her pottery right off the bat might brand him as a suck-up. He would get some eventually and, if everything turned out the way he'd like it to, they'd enjoy a meal together, preferably naked.

He gestured toward the wheel. "You obviously work here."

"Yep. I visualized this as a combination studio and gallery from the beginning. Not everyone spends as much time here as I do, but I love it. The concrete floor is easy to clean and nobody cares if it gets stained. I have a kiln out back. Best conditions I've ever had."

"The venue makes a difference." He glanced at the large stall where he'd be setting up. "Looks like we'll be neighbors."

"Uh-huh. I like being in the back. Earlier this summer I considered moving into what'll be your space but I didn't, which is a good thing. Ready to unload your truck?"

"You bet." He set the bowl down with great care. His work was nearly indestructible but hers could be a victim of gravity. He didn't want that on his conscience.

He hauled in the big stuff—odd pieces of scrap metal and unusual gears and machine parts that he scavenged from anywhere he could find them. The hunt was part of the fun, although he didn't have as much time for it as he used to. Friends had volunteered to comb junkyards for him and Liam was always on the lookout for interesting finds.

Sapphire carried in a box of welding equipment. "Where do you want this?" She stood in the middle of the spacious stall with her arms full.

"In the corner's okay for now. I'll set up everything tomorrow. Have you had dinner?"

"Um, no." She put the box down and turned back to him. Instead of looking eager, she seemed wary. "But I'd planned to head home and catch up on some paperwork."

Not the response he was hoping for. "How about taking some time to grab a bite with me at Scruffy's Bar? There are a few things I'd like to discuss."

Her expression remained guarded. "I guess I could. I'll meet you over there, but I can't stay long."

"That's fine." It wasn't fine at all. Where was that spark he'd seen a moment ago? He'd pictured her falling right in with his plan. They'd have a few drinks, dance a little and explore what he'd hoped would be a mutual attraction.

Maybe she had mountains of paperwork and really did need to finish it before tomorrow. "Listen, if you don't have time, we can take a rain check."

"No, it'll be okay. I'm grateful that you agreed to be part of this."

Oh, great. Now she was joining him out of a sense of obligation. "I'm happy to do it. Please don't feel you have to keep me company while I eat. We can talk in the morning."

"No, let's do it now." She gave him a quick smile. "I'll lock up and be over there in a jiffy."

She clearly didn't want him hanging around while she took care of that. "See you there, then." He touched the brim of his hat.

Damned if that gesture didn't light up those amazing eyes of hers. Not for long, but this time he knew he wasn't mistaken. She was attracted to him. But for some unknown reason, she didn't want to be.

2

ONCE GRADY LEFT, Sapphire leaned against the nearest wall and groaned. How the hell was she supposed to get through tonight, let alone all the days and nights to follow, without jumping his bones? She'd hoped at least one of the co-op members would show up, but as much as they all wanted to meet Grady, every blessed person had other things going on.

She'd have to deal with his high-octane sexiness all by herself. Her hope that he wasn't as gorgeous as she'd remembered from their meeting three weeks ago had died the minute he'd appeared beside the barn. He possessed a lethal combo of cowboy charm, good looks and creative talent that spelled trouble in neon lights. He was her particular brand of kryptonite and she'd agreed to have dinner with him.

Refusing would have been rude, even though he'd given her a way out. He'd put his own work on hold and driven up here because she'd asked him to support the charity event. Although he was staying with Ben and Molly Radcliffe, he apparently wasn't expected there for dinner—another piece of bad luck.

Or maybe he'd been vague about his arrival time so he'd be free to ask her to dinner. They'd sparked off each other three weeks ago and self-preservation should have stopped her from asking him to headline the event. But her love for the kitties and gratitude to the shelter had overcome her misgivings.

She had no one to blame for this mess but herself and she'd do it all again considering how many guests and potential donations he'd pull in. She'd just have to exercise restraint whenever they were alone together and make it clear that she wasn't interested. If the little voice in her head suggested that this man would be different, she wouldn't listen.

She had a weakness for creative men. But after four failed relationships with artistic guys, she'd finally admitted that she didn't belong with that type no matter how much they intrigued her. Some fatal flaw always turned up and doomed what had started out as something wonderful and promising. She was through taking chances.

After locking up, she drove her purple truck over to Scruffy's, a bar known for good food and live country music. The smell of barbecue made her mouth water as she climbed out of her pickup, tucked her keys in the pocket of her skirt and started for the door. The parking lot was full, as always, so at least they'd have plenty of chaperones.

"Hey, there." Grady walked toward her from the other side of the lot.

"Hi." She paused, captured by the sheer beauty of him. Ignoring that for the next few days would be impossible. The waistband of his Wranglers sat easy on his lean hips and his yoked Western shirt emphasized the breadth of his shoulders. She imagined sliding her palms up the soft material and feeling his muscles bunch beneath her hands. His wavy brown hair, worn collar length, would feel like silk between her fingers.

His smile brought her attention to his mouth. She could write an essay on the sensual contours of those sculpted lips. Men like Grady had usually perfected the fine art of kissing. His lips would be like velvet as they—

"Ready to go in?"

Great. She'd been caught ogling. She cleared her throat. "I thought you'd already be inside."

"I waited for you."

"Thanks." She risked looking into his brown eyes and her heart began to pound. Even shadowed by the brim of his hat, his gaze was hot. When a man looked at her that way, he had more than dinner on his mind—but she should talk after the way she'd checked him out.

The evening was taking on a familiar pattern. First they'd share a cozy booth and enjoy a meal along with some beer, which would loosen her inhibitions. Scruffy's casual atmosphere made it a great place for shedding inhibitions, especially on the dance floor. She could hear the music from here and it got louder every time someone went in or came out. Grady would ask her to dance to a slow tune and they'd rub against each other until they were both ready to combust.

After that she'd suggest heading to the little house she rented with her sister, who was conveniently out of town. They'd spend most of the night having amazing sex and the game would be on. She'd vowed never to take that path again with an art-making man.

Accepting his dinner invitation had been a bad idea. Yet changing the plan now would be a delicate operation. She hoped the excuse she was about to give him would do the trick. "You know, I hate to do this, but on the drive over I continued to think about all the paperwork I have waiting at home. Dinner would be lovely, but I really need to take a rain check."

"I see." He nudged back his hat, which allowed the light from the building to illuminate his square-jawed perfection.

"I'm really sorry, Grady. Organizing the event put me behind." True enough, but he didn't seem to be buying it.

He gestured toward a spot away from the entrance and out of the glare of the lights. "Let's step over there for a minute, where it's not so loud."

"All right." She followed him into the shadows.

He paused and faced her, thumbs hooked in his belt loops. Sexy stance. "Sapphire, I'm interested in you and I get the impression you're interested in me. But if there's another guy, just say so. These things happen."

"There isn't anyone." Not for lack of trying to find a non-artist whose company she enjoyed. She'd dated an insurance adjuster, a dentist and a systems engineer. She hadn't clicked with any of them.

"Then why not have dinner with me?" He moved a little closer as his gaze held hers and a smile brought her attention back to his tempting mouth. "You have to eat sometime."

"I know, but...let's be honest." She took a deep breath. "It's not just about dinner, is it?"

His eyebrows lifted. "You want dessert, too? I dunno, Sapphire. That might stretch my budget." His grin faded. "No, you're right. It's not just about dinner, but if you don't have a boyfriend, what's the problem? Am I wrong that you kind of like me?"

"You're not wrong." God, he was potent. Being near him fried her brain cells right when she needed to be alert. "But it'd be better if we just leave it at that."

"Why?"

"What if it didn't work out? That could make this week very awkward."

He smiled and drew closer still. "If that's all you're worried about, there's no problem. It'll work out."

"You seem pretty sure of yourself." Too bad she found that hot as hell.

"Normally, I'm not, but this time I have my reasons. We've had chemistry from the minute we laid eyes on each other three weeks ago. I've seen the way you look at me."

Heat sluiced through her. "Sorry. I'll stop doing that."

"Please don't stop on my account. I look at you the same way. Finding you at the Art Barn that day was a revelation. From what I can tell, you've allowed your true self to shine

through and that turns me on. You make the sexiest pottery
I've ever seen."

She laughed because he was the first person to say it out
loud. No one else had dared. "Thank you."

"No, thank *you*. Holding it is quite an experience. I picture
the way your hands molded each piece and I—"

"Um, right." If she let him go on in this vein, they'd never
make it back to her house. They'd end up doing it in the back of
a pickup, either hers or his. She'd thought their mutual attraction would be manageable. She'd never been so wrong.

"Lady, you and I generate a lot of heat. You can head home to
catch up on paperwork but that's not going to change anything."

"Maybe not." She shoved her hands in her pockets and
clutched her keys as a reminder that she was leaving. Just because he thought her surrender was inevitable, didn't mean he
was right. But she could feel that heat he was talking about
melting her resistance. "I need to go." She started to turn away.

"Hang on for a second." He lightly touched her arm.

The contact sent fire through her veins. "What for?" She
turned back to him and saw the intent before he spoke the words.

"A kiss."

"No, that would be—"

"Only fair. I've been imagining kissing you ever since I drove
away three weeks ago. If you don't want to take it beyond that
point, I'll abide by that decision." He smiled. "What's one little kiss?"

A mistake. "I guess that would be okay."

"Not a very romantic answer." He drew her into his arms
and lowered his head. "But good enough."

The velvet caress of his mouth was every bit as spectacular
as she'd imagined. If she stuck to her guns, this would never
happen again, so it seemed criminal to waste a single second of
kissing Grady Magee. She hugged him close as he worked his
magic. She'd figured the man could kiss, but she hadn't known

the half of it. He started slow, tormenting her with gentle touches that made her ache for more.

When he finally settled in, she opened to him greedily, desperately wanting the stroke of his tongue. Kissing him was exactly what she'd been trying to avoid, but when he cupped her bottom and drew her against the hard ridge of his cock, she forgot why she'd been so reluctant.

Wouldn't a woman have to be crazy to reject this man? Wrapped in his strong arms and teased with his hot kisses, she craved the pleasure he promised.

Taking his mouth from hers, he continued to knead her bottom with his strong fingers. "Still think we should nip this thing in the bud?"

Speaking of nipping...she wouldn't mind some of that, too. She gulped. "You've paralyzed my brain."

"Good." His mouth hovered over hers. "Maybe you think too much." And he delved deep again as he coaxed her to respond.

She didn't need much coaxing. With a low moan, she slid her arms around his neck and arched against his solid body. He answered with a low growl of pleasure and locked her in tight. She'd completely lost her mind.

In no time she'd thrust her tongue into his mouth. Somehow her hands moved from around his neck down to his firm butt cheeks. When his muscles flexed, she whimpered in frustration. There was only so much that could happen in the shadow of Scruffy's Bar and they'd reached the limit.

Breathing hard, he lifted his mouth a fraction from hers. "Okay, we're stopping now. But this isn't over."

She was incapable of speech, let alone an argument on that point.

Slowly he released her and backed away. "What time are you opening up tomorrow?"

She swallowed and frantically tried to remember. It finally came to her. "Seven."

"I'll be there. Take care, Sapphire." He touched the brim of his hat.

She turned and fled. If she didn't get out of there, she was liable to hurl herself back into his arms. Tomorrow she'd be stronger.

AFTER GRADY FINISHED his sandwich and beer at Scruffy's, he headed over to Ben and Molly's place. Although it seemed strange to be with them instead of at Thunder Mountain Ranch, they soon made him feel right at home. He had a chance to admire Ben's new saddle shop adjacent to the house and talk with Molly about her teaching job at Sheridan Community College and her curriculum planning for Thunder Mountain Academy. He also made friends with their golden Lab.

He found out from Ben and Molly that the charity benefiting from Sapphire's art event was the Fabulous Felines Cat Shelter. Fortunately, he was able to discuss the event and its organizer without letting his thoughts drift to that explosive kiss. But once he bid them good-night and stretched out on their comfy guest bed, he could think of nothing else. Holding her had been even more perfect than he'd imagined.

They fit together as if designed for the passionate lovemaking she claimed they shouldn't have. Her soft breasts, her perfectly rounded ass and her supple lips taunted him relentlessly as he lay aroused and sweaty in the Radcliffes' guest room.

Maybe she really believed that getting involved would compromise their working relationship this week, but he hoped to change her mind. He fell asleep thinking of all the ways he could do that. Kissing would be a major part of the plan.

The next morning he dressed in his old scuffed boots, well-worn jeans and a faded chambray shirt. Leaving the black dress hat on the dresser, he picked up his everyday brown Stetson and left the Radcliffes' house after politely declining breakfast. They'd offered to fix him some, but that would have made him late.

He figured she'd be feeding the cats at seven. Ben and Molly had called it a feral cat colony. Although he wasn't familiar with the term, he could figure it out. The cats living in the woods weren't completely civilized, but they weren't completely antisocial, either. He could relate to that. There were times he longed to retreat into his studio and never come out. Other times he craved human companionship.

He wondered if other artists felt the same. This week would be a great time to find out if he was crazy or not. He was very different from his brother, a guide for white-water rafting trips. Liam was extremely social and even after all these years didn't totally understand Grady's need for solitude.

Dew sparkled on the grass when he pulled into the Art Barn parking lot a good thirty minutes early. Sapphire's purple truck wasn't there, so he sat with the windows rolled down and waited. The air smelled great and he wondered how often these days he took the time to simply *be*.

The sudden fame had taken him by surprise. Within a year he'd gone from living a somewhat solitary life in Alaska to being the darling of the Western art world. He was a beer-and-barbecue guy thrown into a champagne-and-caviar crowd and he still didn't quite have his footing. Being in Sheridan for this fund-raiser offered him the small-town ambiance he liked, maybe even needed.

Sapphire drove in and his body tightened. He couldn't remember ever wanting a woman this much. Maybe her reluctance to become involved with him played a part in that—the old forbidden-fruit ploy.

Because she didn't know him that well yet, she might be worried that he'd take off if the two of them had a spat. Raising money for the shelter was very important to her and she wouldn't want to jeopardize that. He wasn't sure how to convince her that he wasn't the kind of selfish SOB who would ruin her cherished event because they weren't getting along. Besides, they would get along. Oh, yeah, they certainly would.

Grabbing his water jug for later, he left his truck and closed the door with a minimum of noise. This time of the morning, traffic was light on the road that ran past the Art Barn, so birds chirping and warbling provided the only soundtrack. He liked sharing this peaceful setting with her.

Yet when he joined her as they walked to the front door, he could tell she was nervous. She gave him a quick smile and a breathy "Hi," but her hand quivered as she tried to open the door. Today she'd worn embroidered jeans and a tie-dyed blouse. Her colorful glass earrings reached to her shoulders and they tinkled as she worked with the key.

"Let me." He took the keys and got the door open. He fought the urge to cup her earrings in one hand to quiet the music while he nibbled on her tender earlobe. He'd read somewhere that earrings were a sexual invitation and he was more than ready to accept.

"Thanks. I must have had too much caffeine."

He hadn't had a drop but he was as wired as if he'd mainlined a whole pot. "Speaking of that, if you'll show me the coffee routine, I'll make some."

"I'll put some on. I'm sure you want to start setting up your equipment." Her gaze met his and skittered away.

"How about if I help you feed the cats first?"

"You don't have to." She gave him another quick glance, this one more pointed, as if silently warning him to back off.

"Are you worried that I'll scare Fred?"

She opened her mouth and then closed it again. Her tiny sigh of resignation was almost too faint to hear. "If you come out with me and keep still, it should be fine."

"I can do that." He wasn't about to stay away from her, even though that was clearly what she thought she wanted. "Since they're the reason I'm here, I'd like to get better acquainted."

Her smile said she didn't quite believe that, but she nodded. "You can make the coffee while I fill the food bowls."

"Sounds like a plan." He followed her into the small space.

Close quarters, which made it a great spot for a seduction, but he wasn't going to attempt one. He could feel the tension radiating from her. If he remained patient, she might surrender to it and seduce him, instead. Not this morning, but maybe before the week was over.

"The coffeepot and coffee are down there at the end. It's a basic model."

"Good. I like basic." He filled his water jug before making the coffee. He'd need the hydration once he started welding. "Ben and Molly said to say hi."

"They're good people." She got out the bowls and opened a bin of fishy-smelling dry cat food.

"They think the same of you. They're excited about this event to generate donations for the shelter."

She smiled at him. "Glad to hear it." She began scooping food into the bowls.

"Did you get your paperwork finished?"

"What paperwork?"

"You know, the paperwork you rushed home to work on last night."

"Oh...yeah." Her cheeks turned pink. "I didn't finish but I made a sizable dent in it. Thanks for asking."

He started the coffee perking and turned to watch her. "Actually, I didn't know until last night that the event is to raise money for the cat shelter and the work they do with feral colonies. Ben and Molly filled me in."

"I didn't tell you?"

"You might have. I wasn't focused on that aspect."

She paused and looked over at him. "Are you saying you only agreed to be here because of me?"

"Yes, ma'am." She might as well know it.

She groaned. "I didn't mean to give you the wrong idea."

"Or maybe you gave me the right idea. Three weeks ago I glanced in the rearview mirror as I was driving away from here and you were standing there watching me go. I extrapolated from that and figured we might have a good time when I came back." He held her gaze. "I still believe we can."

Her breath caught and desire shimmered in her turquoise eyes. He'd bet good money that if he tried kissing her again, she'd let him. They weren't in a public parking lot anymore, either. He imagined lifting her to the counter and unbuttoning her blouse.

The image was followed by thoughts of openmouthed kisses and intimate caresses as he sought the moist recesses of her trembling body. By the time he was finished loving her, they'd have bowls and cat food scattered everywhere and a mess to clean up. The cats still wouldn't be fed.

He took a calming breath. "We need to feed those cats."

3

SAPPHIRE COULDN'T DECIDE whether she was relieved or disappointed that Grady had passed up the chance to kiss her. Her thoughts had run in circles all night long, but one intriguing concept kept coming back around. What if they could have sex without any emotional entanglement?

The idea had merit. He lived in Cody, after all, and he was a very busy guy. She'd made the mistake of becoming emotionally invested in those other men and that had seemed to bring out the worst in them. If she didn't allow that to happen with Grady... Yeah, getting involved with him would still be somewhat of a risk, but he could be worth it.

She was touched that he'd wanted to interact with the cats this morning and that he'd taken it seriously enough to give the job priority. He'd clearly had other things on his mind a moment ago. Yet here he was helping her carry bowls out to the same spot where he'd found her the night before.

He glanced at her as they set the bowls in the grass. "Couldn't you just use a couple of large bowls?"

"I could, but some cats might be crowded out and not get their fair share. This way I know everybody gets a decent helping."

"Must be tricky hauling them all out here by yourself."

"A little. I've learned to manage it."

He crouched down beside her, which meant she was able to breathe in the scent of his aftershave. Whatever he used had a smoky, seductive quality that suggested an activity involving hot bodies and soft sheets. Rolling around in the grass sounded like a good alternative. Being with Grady was a party waiting to happen.

If she didn't concentrate on something else, she'd be fighting the urge to grab him the entire time they were out here. "Normally, some of the cats would be here waiting but we're a little earlier than usual."

"So you're feeding them, but how does the shelter come into the picture?"

"The biggest contribution is medical." She kept her attention on the tree line as she looked for cats emerging from the shadows. "If we can get the cats into carriers, that's great, but mostly we have to trap them. Then they're either spayed or neutered, vaccinated and checked for any other issues. If the vet finds anything else, she treats it for the cost of the meds and supplies."

"Sounds like a great program."

"It is. The cats stay healthy but they don't keep adding more strays to the population."

"Have you figured out how the cats wound up here?"

She appreciated his interest. Questions about a topic dear to her heart made for a welcome distraction. "The first generation might have been barn cats when horses were housed in the stalls. Then the property was sold and the grain and the hay disappeared. Once the mice left, the cats had nothing to eat, so they likely moved to the woods and foraged for small rodents."

"And essentially became wild."

"They did." As she talked about the cats, her tension gradually eased. "But most of them seem to have retained a connection to people and to this barn. Fred's the least trusting. He joined the colony late and I don't think he liked being trapped and neutered."

"Do you blame him?"

She smiled at his look of horror. "We can't let them procreate."

"I get that and I'm all for population control. I just avoid thinking about the process."

"Are you squeamish?"

"Only when we're talking about cutting off—"

"Look." She pointed toward the trees. "Here they come."

"Where?" Squinting, he scanned the area.

"Over there, moving past the trunk of that big pine. Snow White's in the lead, as always. Grumpy, Sneezy and Dopey are following her." The little white female was always easy to spot, while the dappled shade camouflaged the others until they stepped out into the open.

"Okay, I see them."

"We're fairly sure those gray tabbies are Snow White's kittens because of the way she mothers them. And here comes Athena with her brood. They all got her butterscotch coloring except Persephone, the tortoiseshell. There's Fred, bringing up the rear."

"He sure does stand out."

"Yep. He was the hardest to catch. We finally got him in the trap using tuna as bait. I think the others would eat any flavor I put out, but I buy the fish kind because that's all Fred will eat."

"You're partial to him."

"I am. He's the smartest one and a survivor. He has several scars from the fights he's been in, but he beat the odds." She glanced at the approaching cats. "They seem a little uneasy about you being here. Maybe we shouldn't talk."

As they both fell silent, every cat settled down to eat except Fred, who stayed about six feet away with his green eyes fixed on Grady. Sapphire waited in hopes the cat would come forward on his own, but at last she decided he needed to be coaxed.

"Stay very still," she said, "while I try to sweet-talk him into coming over."

Grady gave a slight nod.

Leaning forward, she began crooning to the cat. "Come on,

sweet Freddie. This man isn't going to hurt you." She lowered her voice. "Freddie, Freddie, Freddie. You know you want some. Come on, kitty-cat. That's a good boy."

Fred crept up to the bowl and began to eat, his teeth crunching on the small pellets. But that wasn't the only sound Sapphire heard. The rhythm of Grady's breathing had changed. She knew that rhythm because she'd heard it last night after he'd kissed her senseless.

She couldn't imagine why he was reacting that way, unless… She had to smile as she thought of a possible reason. She'd probably sounded damned seductive just now when she'd lured Fred up to the food bowl. Having a man around who was that susceptible to her was flattering. And arousing.

The cats made short work of the food. When it was gone, some moved away from the bowls and began grooming themselves. Snow White and Persephone came over for some head scratches, but Fred grabbed up one last bite before turning and scampering back to the woods as if he couldn't wait to leave.

"I'm determined to pet him someday."

"You probably will." Grady's breathing was back to normal.

"I think I will, too, eventually." She gave Athena some attention before she began gathering up the bowls. "Show's over for this morning, though."

He picked up the rest of the bowls. "I'll help you wash these."

"That's above and beyond. I know you want to get your area set up." She didn't feel ready to share the small space with him again. Besides, one of the other co-op members could show up at any moment and she didn't want to take a chance on major embarrassment. "I'll do it."

He must have heard something in her voice, because he didn't insist. "Thanks for letting me come along for the feeding routine."

"You're welcome. Did you pick any favorites?"

"Either Snow White or Athena. I haven't decided which."

"The two mama kitties."

"Yep." He held the door for her and followed her into the tiny kitchen. "I'm a real fan of mothers who stick by their kids. Like my mom did."

She put down the bowls and turned to him in surprise. "But you ended up in foster care at Thunder Mountain Ranch."

"And consequently, people think she abandoned us. Instead she was in a car accident and Rosie offered to take Liam and me until Mom was on her feet. Once she was okay, we went straight back to her. She's terrific."

"Does she live here?"

"Not anymore. She's in Cody with her new husband. Liam moved there when he got the job with the rafting company. I'd left to work in Alaska, so Liam talked Mom into moving down there with him. She met John in Cody. It all worked out."

"I can see that." Her heart squeezed as she thought of how tough those years when his mom was laid up must have been. "I'm glad for you. When we were in high school, all I knew was that you and your brother were at Thunder Mountain. I figured the two of you had no parents, or at least none that were worth anything."

He grimaced. "That's the only bad thing about going there. People assume we were neglected. Rosie's tried to set the record straight, but it's not easy. Thunder Mountain boys are supposed to be hard-luck cases."

"And some of them are."

"Yeah, just not me and Liam." He walked over to the coffeepot. "I'll get a cup of coffee and move out of your way."

"Will you start work on the sculpture for the event?"

"No, I'm saving that for the actual night." He took a mug out of the cupboard and poured coffee into it. "But I need to get comfortable with the space. Liam said Rosie would love to have one of my pieces, so that's what I'm going to make first to test the setup."

"That's so sweet!"

"I'm a sweet guy." He grinned. "So if you need me, I'll be

in the back of the barn getting hot and sweaty." He picked up his coffee and left the kitchen.

Once he was gone, she took a deep breath before turning her focus to the bowls. She'd never washed those bowls so thoroughly. She scrubbed each one until her fingertips wrinkled while she tried to blot out the image of Grady's smile and his "getting hot and sweaty" comment. He wasn't going to let up on her.

Well, who could blame him? Last night she'd practically shrink-wrapped herself to his body. She'd barely escaped from the parking lot without begging him to come home with her.

She'd vowed on her way here this morning that this would be a new day and she'd keep her cool. That had lasted until he'd climbed out of his truck in his work clothes. He shouldn't have been as sexy in those as when he'd been dressed to impress, but apparently, it didn't matter what that cowboy wore. He had only to show up and she'd respond with a rapid pulse and damp panties.

Her lusty thoughts persisted even though he'd walked to the back of the barn at least fifteen minutes ago. The clank of metal and the hiss of a torch indicated he was working while she stood staring into space and wasting time.

Before his arrival yesterday she'd thought having him in the adjoining stall would be harmless fun, a chance to prove she could flirt without getting involved. Instead it looked as if she'd battle constant temptation with no relief in sight. She'd underestimated her sex drive, as well as his.

Swearing off artists had seemed like a piece of cake when she'd been smarting from the last humiliating breakup. Then Grady Magee had walked into her life. If the gods were testing her, they couldn't have given her a bigger challenge. He was better looking, sexier and more talented than any of the other four.

She had plans for today, though, and her wheel was waiting. Maybe once she immersed herself in the project, she'd forget that Grady was on the other side of the wall getting hot and sweaty. Yeah, right. Molding slick clay on a revolving wheel was a sensuous experience that would only make the situation worse.

One of the other co-op members was bound to come in shortly. She took courage from that as she walked down the aisle between the stalls. If she went straight into her work area without stopping by his, she might be okay.

The hissing of the torch stopped. "Is that you, Sapphire?"

"It's me."

"Could you give me some advice on this thing I'm making for Rosie?"

She could hardly refuse such a request. "Sure." Besides being flattered that he'd ask her opinion, she was curious about the design. He hadn't mentioned what he'd planned to create for his foster mother.

She felt the heat before she stepped inside the stall. He hadn't been kidding about the "hot and sweaty" part. His goggles hung around his neck and moisture had collected in the hollow of his throat. She wanted to dip her tongue into that depression and savor the salty taste.

Or maybe she'd comb his damp hair away from his forehead and unbutton the shirt that clung to his muscular chest. Booted feet braced apart and leather gloves tucked under one arm, he studied a sketch he'd tacked to the wall that separated his stall from hers. He'd laid an assortment of metal pieces on the floor beneath it.

She stifled a groan of frustration. Knowing he was the man who'd created the sculptures she'd seen in galleries had certainly made him appealing. Yet that was nothing compared to being in the same physical environment where he labored over his art. A visceral tug of longing almost made her reach for him. She clenched both hands and fought the impulse.

Something told her he wouldn't welcome a sexual advance right now, in spite of all the discussion they'd had on the subject. When he looked at her, his direct gaze was all business.

He was in work mode. "This won't take long, I promise. I know you have your own stuff to do."

"No problem." His change of mood might have insulted another woman, but not her. She understood it. He'd entered his creative zone and had channeled all his sexual energy there. As long as he was focused on sculpting, she wouldn't have to worry about this attraction between them. She hadn't counted on that, because it was a rare gift, but one she respected. It also might explain why Grady had achieved such a high level of success.

"I thought I knew what I wanted when I sketched this," he said, "but now I'm rethinking the configuration. It's wolves."

"I can see that. Nice." The sketch was more than nice. He'd captured maternal love so perfectly that she had no doubt it was a mother with her litter.

"I picked a female wolf for Rosie because wolves have several pups. I'll make a bear for my mom because bears only have two."

Talk about irresistible. Now he'd added a layer of tender consideration to his blatant sexuality. "I'm sure they'll both be thrilled. The concepts are brilliant."

"I don't know about the brilliant part, but they're logical."

Oh, and FYI, the guy was modest. His admirable traits kept stacking up. "Trust me, both ladies will think the pieces are brilliant."

He laughed. "They do have an embarrassing tendency to gush. Okay, back to these wolves. My sketch has six pups but I think five is plenty. Maybe I should drop it back to four."

"Hmm." She studied his drawing. He'd arranged the wolves so they were all interconnected and would form a cohesive sculpture. She loved the symmetry of it.

"On a practical note, I'm one short of the recycled pieces I need for the pups' noses. I'd have to go looking for another one if I keep six, but dropping just one doesn't feel right for the composition."

"I'd leave them all in. You've already figured out how to do it, so taking one out means redoing the whole arrangement."

"But what about the nose thing? I don't know the scrapyards around here the way I do the ones in Cody."

"Could you alter one of the poses so the pup has his paw over his nose?"

"Maybe." He stepped toward the drawing. "That one. I could move the paw up without compromising the design." He turned to her with a smile. "Great idea. Thanks."

"You're welcome."

"Yeah, that'll work. Great suggestion." He repositioned his goggles, picked up his torch and grabbed one of the pieces of metal from the grouping on the floor. He acted as if he'd forgotten she was there.

Fascinating. She'd imagined having to fight off his advances, but it seemed that when he was working, he wouldn't be making any. That alone separated him from the other artists she'd dated. All of them, she realized now, had been easily distracted and basically lazy. They'd expected success to come to them without a whole lot of effort. They'd had ability and she'd allowed herself to be impressed with that, but ability without discipline was useless.

But comparisons to her ex-boyfriends didn't matter, because if she did decide to have sex with Grady, that was all it would be about. She'd keep it pure so she'd never have to discover his fatal flaw and become disillusioned for the fifth time. Could she manage to enjoy the sex and keep her emotions out of it? Only one way to find out.

Walking into her cubicle, she stared at her potter's wheel. She already had a plan for her next project, a large bowl to hold fruit. The interior would be a cool lime green and the exterior would be pale orange. She might add some flecks of yellow if she settled on the right shade.

Yesterday she'd been excited about making it, but today her thoughts were on Grady instead of the new piece that had been

on the drawing board for more than a week. Several customers had said they'd buy such a bowl, so she'd already presold a
few. On the other side of the wall Grady's torch hissed, and the
air was filled with the acrid scent of hot metal.

Listening to those sounds galvanized her. She'd make that
bowl this morning and have a prototype for the others. Each
one would be slightly different because that was her hallmark,
but she had to create the first one in order to make variations
on that theme.

Generally, she preferred working alone in the barn, but having Grady there intent on his sculpting kept her at the wheel
longer than she'd intended. His energy seemed to penetrate the
barrier between them and she experienced design breakthroughs
that stunned her. The fruit bowl took on an unusual shape that
dipped on one side to leave room for a cascade of grapes or a
cluster of bananas. She could see that becoming a trademark
of her fruit-bowl designs.

She'd transferred the first one to the kiln and stopped by the
kitchen to get coffee when Arlene Danbury came through the
door. Arlene's watercolors of Wyoming landscapes had become
increasingly popular in the past year, but the income wasn't
enough for her to live on. She worked part-time as a nail tech
in a local salon to make ends meet. She reminded Sapphire of
a sparrow—always in motion and easily flustered.

This morning she was more hyper than usual. "He's here,
isn't he? I can smell hot metal."

Sapphire felt like the gatekeeper, but if not her, then who?
"He's working and I've learned he's very focused. We probably
shouldn't disturb him."

"I wouldn't dream of it. But he'll take a break sometime,
right? What's he working on? Is it the piece for the silent auction? I thought we were supposed to—"

"It's not for the silent auction." Sapphire had learned it was
best to interrupt Arlene when she launched a barrage of chat-

ter or it would go on forever. "He's making a sculpture for his foster mom. You know Rosie Padgett, right?"

"She's my client! I just did her nails this week. She'll be so thrilled. Is it a surprise? I'll bet it's a surprise, so I won't say anything. But if it's not a surprise, then she might think it's odd that I don't—"

"I think it's somewhat of a surprise but I didn't find that out. We'll ask him when he comes up for air."

"Okay. Let me get some coffee before I go back to my stall." She kept talking as she walked over to the pot. "I shouldn't have any more, because I'm already a little jumpy, but I work so much better when I'm sipping coffee. Wait, there's only enough for one cup. Did you want that?"

"Go ahead. I'll make more."

"If I'm the one to take the last of it, I'll make another pot. That's the way it always worked in my family. Maybe Grady wants some. Is he a coffee drinker?"

"I am." Grady appeared in the doorway to the kitchen. "But I can make it." Stepping through the door, he held out his hand. "Grady Magee, ma'am. Pleased to meet you."

For the first time in Sapphire's memory, Arlene was speechless. She stared up at the tall cowboy with her eyes wide and her mouth hanging open. After what felt like a very long time, she murmured, "You're beautiful." Then she pressed her hands to her pink cheeks. "Did I just say that out loud?"

Grady smiled. "If you think I look good, you should see my brother, Liam. He's the handsome one in the family."

"Then your mom and dad must be beautiful, too."

"Never knew my dad, but my mom is definitely beautiful." His gaze flicked over to meet Sapphire's as if to ask, *Who is this nutty lady?*

Since Arlene didn't seem aware that she'd failed to introduce herself, Sapphire decided she'd better do the honors. "Grady, this is Arlene Danbury. Her watercolors of the Bighorn Mountains are becoming quite popular."

Arlene's blush deepened. "Not as popular as your sculptures, Grady."

"They will be. I noticed your watercolors. Really nice."

"Oh, thank you! Pick whichever one you want and it's yours!"

He smiled at her. "You know I can't do that. I'd choose the best one and you'd be out a lot of money."

"I don't care."

"But I do. I'll buy one of your watercolors and be honored to have the opportunity. Now, how about if I dump out the dregs and make us all a fresh pot of coffee?"

"Okay." Still dazed, Arlene nodded and moved out of his way. Then she turned to Sapphire and mouthed, *Oh, my God.*

Sapphire struggled not to lose it. At least she wasn't the only one enthralled with Grady. Arlene gradually recovered her poise and began pelting him with questions about his work. Surprisingly, she gave him a chance to answer each one before she threw out another, but it was more like an interview than a conversation.

He took it in stride, as if this happened to him quite a bit. Sapphire didn't doubt it. She couldn't recall his being followed by a pack of female admirers back in high school, but he'd filled out since then. And he'd taken up sculpting.

She'd bet his career choice affected how women perceived him. It certainly had influenced her. In high school he'd been a cute cowboy like all the others who attended school there. He still had cowboy charisma going on but he'd added a layer of intrigue with his career in the arts. No wonder Arlene had been struck mute.

But Sapphire had picked up another tidbit thanks to Arlene's fan-girl moment. He hadn't known his dad. In talking about his mother and Rosie, he'd skipped over any mention of his father. He'd quickly dismissed the subject just now, too. Come to think of it, Grady and Liam wouldn't have lived at Thunder Mountain Ranch if their father had been around to help out.

In a way she wished she hadn't learned that. It made him

more vulnerable, more human and endearing. Because he hadn't elaborated, she didn't think the story was a pretty one. He admired his mother because she'd stuck by her kids and had raised them by herself, apparently, until the car accident had left her with nowhere to turn. That meant grandparents hadn't been on hand, either.

Yeah, she really didn't want to know that about him. Staying emotionally detached from a guy who looked like Grady and had the talent of an angel was difficult enough without finding out that he was fatherless, too. Herb Padgett, Rosie's husband, would have taken that role to some extent and maybe Grady's new stepdad had belatedly become a father figure. But during Grady's early years he'd missed out on having a dad for games of catch or afternoons spent at the nearest fishing hole.

"Coffee's ready. Who wants a cup?" Grady held up the pot.

"Me, please." Arlene stuck out her mug. "Thank you so much for making it. Have you ever heated water for coffee with a welding torch? I knew a guy who used to do that all the time, made me so nervous. I told him a million times not to do it but he thought it was a cool idea. In my opinion—"

"Fortunately, I don't do that." Grady held up the pot. "Sapphire? Coffee?"

"Sure. Thanks."

He poured it and tossed her a wink when Arlene started in on unsafe-welding-torch stories again. "If you ladies will excuse me, I'm gonna take my coffee and get back to work."

"Me, too," Arlene said. "I'll walk you down there."

"That would be great." Grady gave Sapphire a quick smile before leaving with Arlene.

Her voice drifted back as they started down the barn aisle. "Can I peek in on your project?"

"Not yet, ma'am." Grady sounded polite but firm. "If you don't mind, this is a very personal sculpture, so I'd like to make a lot more progress before I show it to anyone."

"Oh, sure, sure. I totally understand." Arlene must have realized she was being pushy. "I'll just stop off here at my stall, then. See you later!"

Nicely handled, Sapphire thought. Knowing he'd trusted her enough to seek her advice about the piece created a warm glow that she carried with her as she returned to her wheel. But her plan to keep her emotional distance wasn't working worth a damn. That could be a problem.

4

BY THE END of the day Grady had met five of the co-op members and made good progress on Rosie's sculpture. He needed another two days to finish it so he could take it to the ranch when he went there for supper. He'd sworn the other artists to secrecy and everyone had agreed to warn him if by some chance Rosie stopped in at the Art Barn.

He didn't think she would. The last week of classes for Thunder Mountain Academy was always a busy time and she'd be needed out there. His surprise should stay safe until he presented it to her. He'd get Cade to help him set it up while Rosie was busy in the kitchen. They could always move it later if she wanted it in a different spot.

Right now, though, he knew it must be about time to feed those cats and he wanted to help. Working all day had felt good and he wasn't as desperate to make something happen with Sapphire as he had been when he'd first arrived. Or so he thought until he walked into the kitchen.

She had the phone to her ear and her back to him as she pulled bowls out of the cupboard. His timing had been excellent for watching her unobserved. He paused to admire how her embroidered jeans hugged her ass. His palms itched to feel her muscles flex the way he had last night in the shadows at Scruffy's.

That remembered sensation triggered a replay of others—the warmth of her lush body, the heat of her mouth and the sound of her moans. They'd been so damned close to making the leap. He didn't want to get that close again unless he felt fairly certain they'd go the distance.

He'd outgrown the teasing phase of a sexual relationship a long time ago. Yeah, a certain amount of dancing around was fun, but eventually, he liked to know where he stood. With Sapphire he still wasn't sure. She was giving him mixed signals.

"I'm glad the gig's working out for you, sis." She opened the bin and reached for the scoop.

He rapped on the doorframe so he wouldn't scare her. When she turned, he entered the kitchen and took the scoop out of her hand. Then he waved her off and began dishing food into the bowls so she could finish her conversation.

"The event is looking good." She leaned against the counter and watched him work. "Having Grady Magee on board doesn't hurt." She listened for a moment. "There is? What's it of?" She held eye contact with him. "That sounds really cool. I'll tell him how much you like it. I'd better go. Time to feed the kitties. Love you!" She disconnected. "Thanks for doing that."

"I figured it was about time for the evening meal."

"You figured right." She put the phone on the counter. "That was my sister, Amethyst. Do you remember her?"

"Sure. She had the lead in the school musical one year." Amethyst had been the flashier of the two. Plenty of guys had lusted after Sapphire's younger sister, especially after she'd belted out "Santa Baby" during a Christmas choral program.

Sapphire laughed. "Everybody remembers Amethyst. You didn't ever date her, did you? She went out with so many guys that I lost track."

"No, we didn't date." Thank God. He and Sapphire had

enough obstacles without adding the weirdness of having dated her sister. "What's she up to these days?"

"Professional singer. She followed my dad's musical lead."

"Does he still have that jazz band?"

"The members have shifted around and the name's changed a couple of times, but yep—he loves it."

"That's cool. And your mom's still teaching art?"

"Absolutely. I asked her to be part of this co-op but she really doesn't have time. Maybe when she retires."

He enjoyed watching the love shine in her eyes as she talked. "Creative family you have there."

"Yeah, I feel lucky. Anyway, Amethyst mentioned that one of your sculptures is in the lobby of the Jackson Hole resort where she's performing for the next two weeks."

"I have a couple over there. Which one?"

"It's the waterfall fountain that goes into a pool at the bottom with a doe and buck drinking. She said it's huge."

"Twenty-two feet eight inches, to be exact."

"Wow."

He filled the last bowl and closed the bin. "I took it up there in sections and finished the welding on the spot."

"That must have caused quite a stir among the resort guests."

"It did. I offered to complete it in the middle of the night but the management thought it would be more dramatic if people could see the final construction phase. It was great PR but I'd still rather work in the privacy of my studio."

"Is our evening event going to be a problem for you?"

He gazed at her. "It's not my favorite way to create, but like I said last night, I wasn't concerned about the how. Only the who."

"I know." Her quick swallow betrayed her uneasiness.

"Forget I said that."

She gave him a rueful glance. "Not likely. But right now it's feeding time. We've tried to keep a regular schedule they can count on. It's part of building trust."

"Makes sense." He pondered that as he helped her carry out

the bowls. Trust was an issue between them, too. Whether she didn't trust him or herself wasn't clear, but either way, she expected bad things to happen if they gave in to this attraction.

"You can put the bowls down now. They're waiting."

"Right." While he'd been lost in thought, she'd stood waiting as the cats milled around at their feet. "Sorry."

"It's just good to put all the bowls down together so they each have one."

"Makes sense. But Fred's not here. Do we wait for him?"

"No. He'll be along. Sometimes he hangs back."

"Okay." He lined up the ones he carried, dropped to his knees and sat back on his heels. "Sorry for holding up the show. I got distracted."

"I've noticed that doesn't happen when you're working on a sculpture. You're incredibly focused."

He couldn't resist the opening she'd given him. "That's one of two activities that get my undivided attention."

"And the other is football?"

Kidding around was a good sign they were making progress. "Guess again."

Her breathing quickened. "You're too sexy for your own good, Grady."

"Too sexy for you?" He glanced over at her.

"I didn't say that." She kept her attention on the tree line as she watched for Fred, but her cheeks had turned a pretty shade of pink.

His pulse hammered. Maybe he'd built up a little trust, after all. "Any chance I can cash in that rain check so we can have dinner tonight?"

"I think— Oh, my goodness. Who's that?"

A large gray cat left the shelter of the woods and bounded toward them.

"You don't recognize it?"

"Nope. And he's not acting like a feral."

"How can you tell it's a male?"

"I'm not positive but he looks like a tom to me."

The cat marched right up to the food bowl at the end of the row, within arm's reach of Grady, hunkered down and began to devour the food. When Fred showed up, the bowls were all occupied. He surveyed the line of cats before sitting down and fixing his green eyes on Grady as if he might be to blame for this fiasco.

"Stay here." Sapphire slowly rose to her feet. "I'll bring out another bowl for Fred."

"Good idea. He's giving me the stink eye."

As she backed away carefully, Fred stood, arched his back and hissed. Then he retreated a few feet while the other cats continued to munch.

"She's going to get you food, bozo," Grady said. "Show some appreciation."

Fred sat down again and glared at him, but the gray cat looked up at the sound of Grady's voice.

Blinking, he studied Grady with eyes as blue as a midday sky. Then he went back to eating the last few nuggets in the bowl. Athena had taken the spot next to him and she still had food. He sidled over as if to grab some but she gave a warning growl and he retreated.

After searching his bowl for any crumbs, he gave up and stared at Grady some more. Then he made a noise low in his throat that was neither meow nor purr. Must have been a greeting of some kind, because he walked around the bowl and came over to rub against Grady's thigh.

"Hey, there." Grady gently scratched behind the cat's ears and was rewarded with a soft purr. "You're no feral, are you, buddy? You're somebody's pet." He noticed burrs and matted hair in what was otherwise a luxurious-looking coat. "Or were somebody's pet a while ago. What happened?"

In response, the cat tried to crawl into his lap. But Grady was kneeling, which meant the lap situation was never going to work out. Instead he scooped the cat into his arms. In midmotion he realized it could be a very dumb move. He didn't know this animal and he could decide to bite or scratch him.

That didn't happen. Purring even louder, the cat settled in and tucked his head under Grady's chin. Although his appearance suggested he'd be heavy, he was extremely light. All that hair disguised the fact that he was skin and bones.

"Wow, that's amazing."

Sapphire's murmured comment took Grady by surprise. He hadn't heard her come back, probably because he'd been involved with his new friend and she'd been moving as quietly as possible to avoid disturbing the cats as they finished their meal. He gazed at her over the top of the gray cat's head as he stroked its tangled fur. "What now?"

She set down the bowl for Fred, who came over with more enthusiasm than he'd shown the last two times. "We have to find out if someone's missing a cat. He obviously used to have a home."

"Yeah, but I don't think he's been there in a while. He's pretty thin."

"And his coat's a mess."

"But he's friendly as all get-out."

She smiled. "I noticed." She petted the butterscotch mama cat, who'd come over with her look-alike family. The others lounged in the grass, either grooming their coats or watching the interaction between Grady and the cat in his arms.

Fred finished his meal and moved away from the dish, but instead of leaving, he sat down and stared at Grady.

Sapphire watched the tuxedo cat. "That's a switch. He's never hung around after the meal before."

"Maybe he sees me loving up this one and thinks it looks like fun."

"I hope so. It would be great if I could hold him the way you're holding our newcomer." She sighed. "Not that I could take him home. My sister's allergic."

"You both still live at home?"

"No. By *home* I meant the little house we rent together. She's a perfect housemate except for the fact that I can't have a cat. She's offered to take meds so I can adopt one but I don't want to put her through that. Eventually, we'll each get a place and until then I can work with the shelter and the ferals. It's fine."

"How about having a barn cat?"

"We've all talked about it. Naturally, we'd want one of our ferals, but we can't split up the mamas and their kittens, which leaves Fred, and he's so not ready. Ah, there he goes." She stood. "Guess it's time to figure out a plan for this new guy."

"What are the options?" Grady levered himself to his feet and felt little pinpricks on his chest as the cat dug his claws into his shirt and held on.

"I should probably drive him over to the shelter. They can keep him for the night while we check around and see if anybody's reported losing a cat that fits his description."

Sensible as that sounded, Grady didn't want to do it. The cat seemed to have chosen him as a savior and he couldn't picture handing this skinny creature over into someone else's care, although the shelter staff was obviously capable.

"You're frowning. What's the matter?"

"I just… I want to keep him company until we find out what the story is."

"Oh." Her expression grew soft. "That's sweet."

"And impractical. I don't want to haul him over to Ben and Molly's. It's an imposition. We don't know anything about this cat, and besides, they have a dog who may or may not react well to cats."

"I agree you can't take him there." She gathered up the bowls. "Bring him into the barn and we'll figure something out."

"Hey, here's an idea. We probably shouldn't give him the run of the place, but I could make up a bedroll and stay with him in the office tonight." That plan screwed up his hope of having dinner with Sapphire, but he couldn't abandon this animal that had latched on to him, literally.

Cradling the gray tom, Grady followed Sapphire into the barn. Along the way he found himself talking to the cat and assuring him everything was going to be fine. It would be if Grady had anything to say about it. The members of the feral colony seemed satisfied with their life in the woods. But Gandalf wasn't suited for that.

Grady had named him without realizing it. Of course, someone had already given this cat a name but that person wasn't here to supply the info, so might as well come up with a new identity. Years ago Grady had seen *The Lord of the Rings* and he'd been fascinated with Gandalf the Grey. Gandalf's wand had seemed a little like a welding torch. Point it in a certain direction and stuff happened.

Sapphire led the way into the kitchen and dumped the bowls in the sink. "First I should check him for fleas."

"Gandalf doesn't have fleas."

Her azure eyes sparkled with amusement. "How do you know his name?"

"I don't, but we can't keep calling him *the gray cat*. I've decided his name is Gandalf."

"It's a good name. I watched those movies, too. But naming him Gandalf doesn't magically rid him of fleas or ear mites." She turned on the overhead light. "Hang on to him while I have a look."

Grady was treated to the sensual pleasure of holding a warm, purring cat while listening to Sapphire's sexy voice as she examined Gandalf for fleas. The combination had a predictable effect but he pushed those thoughts aside. The cat's welfare came first.

"We're in luck," she said. "He doesn't have fleas or ear mites. Did you happen to see if he'd been neutered?"

"Nope, didn't notice."

"Then shift him around so I can peek under his tail."

"Does it matter? It's not like we're going to arrange a hot date for him."

"It matters. If he's an unneutered male, he could decide to

mark his territory and that smell is nasty. Just move your arm so I can check. Oh, good. Nothing's there."

Grady leaned down and put his mouth next to the cat's ear. "Don't be offended, buddy. I'm sure you had a nice pair while they lasted."

"Oh, for heaven's sake." Sapphire rolled her eyes.

"Never mind. It's a guy thing."

"I'm sure it is, but Gandalf's better off without his equipment. It would only have gotten him into trouble."

"That much I agree with."

Her laughter rippled through him, setting off little explosions of joy along the way. He wanted to spend more time laughing with her and less time discussing whether they should get it on. If she'd just loosen up and let things happen, she'd discover how nicely everything would work out.

Scratching behind Gandalf's ears, he turned to her. "Now that he's passed inspection, can I keep him with me tonight if I bed down in the barn?"

"That's one option."

"I'd rather do that than take him to the shelter. I'm sure they're great, but he's been separated from the people he counted on. He's pinned his hopes on me and I don't want to let him down."

"There's another option. I could take him home with me."

"What about your sister's allergies?"

"It should be okay if I confine him to my bathroom and scrub it down after he leaves. Now that I know he doesn't have any parasites and he's neutered, I'm willing to give it a shot."

Grady didn't have to think twice about it. "That's a generous offer, but I'd still rather keep him with me here in the barn. I have a couple of blankets in the truck. Gandalf and I will make out just fine."

"But there's no people food here except maybe a leftover sandwich in the fridge from someone's lunch."

"I have a phone and I know how to use it. I'll order pizza."

She smiled. "What a coincidence. I'm ordering pizza tonight, too."

"From Geppetto's?"

"Is there any other place?"

"Not in my opinion. I found out last time I was here that
they're still in operation. During my Thunder Mountain days
we'd all get together in one of the cabins after Rosie and Herb
had gone to bed and order up food. Pizza, calzones, bread sticks
and enough soda to float a battleship."

"My sister and I used to do that, too, especially if we'd organized a slumber party. We'd meet the delivery guy in the driveway so he wouldn't ring the doorbell."

"We didn't have to worry about that. We'd just direct him
to come around by the back road. I wonder if Rosie and Herb
knew all about it."

"I can't speak for them, but my folks certainly did. They told
us later that they'd lie in bed laughing at the lengths we went
to, as if they'd be upset because we ordered pizza. But doing it
in stealth mode is part of the fun."

"I know. If I'd kept this pizza plan to myself, it could have
been Gandalf's and my stealth pizza move."

"But since you didn't…" She paused as if weighing what she
was about to say. "Want to share a pizza?"

"You want to stick around and eat pizza with Gandalf and
me?" Okay, she had to trust him at least a little if she was willing to hang out alone with him at the barn for a while. He looked
down at the cat in his arms. "What do you say, Gandalf?" He
rubbed the cat under the chin. "Shall we invite the lady to a
gourmet pizza dinner in the barn?"

Gandalf's purr ramped up a notch.

"I think that's a definite yes." He glanced at her. "What do
you like on your pizza?"

Her eyes shone as if ordering a pizza was a really big deal.
"Everything."

Maybe it was a big deal. If so, he was glad he'd brought it

up. "Great. Me, too. You'll have to order it, though. Gandalf's sticking to me like Velcro."

"Okay." She picked up her phone from where she'd left it on the counter. "But unless you really want to sleep on a bedroll in the office tonight, I think we should have the pizza delivered to my house."

"Your…" He stared at her. "Are you sure?"

"Very sure." Reaching out, she stroked the cat and let her hand rest on his arm as she met his gaze. "Come home with me, Grady."

Somehow he got the words out. "I'd like that."

5

AFTER A DAY spent debating whether to risk a brief fling with Grady, Sapphire had rounded the side of the barn to find him cradling a stray cat. He couldn't have chosen a more seductive move. Ironically, the presence of the cat had kept her from throwing herself into his arms and begging him to take her right there in the grass.

So she'd had to table her lust until they'd decided what to do. Grady's protective behavior toward the cat complicated things, but once she'd decided Gandalf could stay in her bathroom, she'd hatched her plan. She'd had no trouble convincing Grady to cooperate, but he'd vetoed the cat carrier.

Consequently, they'd had to leave his truck at the Art Barn so he could hold Gandalf while she drove. The August evening was cool enough that they could leave the windows up and not have to bother with air-conditioning, but she hadn't anticipated that sharing a confined space with Grady would be such an erotic experience. Breathing in all that masculinity turned her into a juicy woman with sex on the brain. She could now testify that pheromones existed.

She was in charge of this operation, though, which meant figuring out how to make Gandalf comfortable once they arrived at her house. Only then would she be able to satisfy her craving for the man holding the cat. She had a decorative basket at home and a plush throw that would make a soft bed. An old plastic storage tote would work as a temporary litter box. To increase the odds that Gandalf would stay in the bathroom without crying, she'd give him some tuna.

When they'd started this journey, the cat had clung to Grady and mewled, but Grady's murmured words and gentle stroking eventually worked. She couldn't hear what he was saying, but the soothing sound of his voice finally convinced Gandalf it was safe to unhook himself from Grady's shirt and curl up in his lap.

Probably a good thing on many levels. She'd been way too focused on Grady's lap ever since they'd left the Art Barn. Now it was blocked from view by a fluffy gray cat. But Gandalf had made little holes in Grady's shirt and probably in his skin, too, although he'd never once complained.

She didn't want to let that go untended. "You probably have some puncture wounds."

"It's okay. He didn't mean to."

"Of course not. But once we get him settled, you'll need to wash any scratches with soap and water. Then I'll give you some tea tree oil to put on them so they won't get infected."

He wrinkled his nose. "Nah. It smells funny."

"I've always kind of liked it."

"Oh, well, then." He chuckled. "Give me a gallon of the stuff."

"In moderation."

"How about you rub it on me so I get just the right amount?"

"How about we drop the subject before I run into a tree?"

He looked over at her. "Conversation getting a little hot for you?"

"Yes." The scent of virile male combined with the thought of rubbing oil on his bare chest had created a persistent throbbing between her damp thighs.

Grinning, he leaned back in his seat. "Good to know."

"We can't get carried away, though."

"I disagree. I intend to get completely carried away."

She swallowed a moan. "I meant not until—"

"I know. Just teasing you. But the good news is that Gandalf's about to doze off."

She glanced at the cat, whose eyes were at half-mast. "I'll go in first and get everything together. Then you can take him straight into the bathroom so he has no chance to bolt."

"Right. Maybe he won't even wake up."

"He'll wake up, probably when I stop the truck. Cats aren't like little kids. They can look sound asleep when they're only dozing. But I'm sure he's exhausted from trying to survive on his own. If I have his new spot all organized and add in a can of tuna, maybe he'll eat that and go back to sleep instead of crying for you."

"I talked to him about the crying thing."

"Oh, did you, now?"

"No, really, I did. He knows what's on the line. He won't bother us."

"Have you been around cats much?"

"Mostly the barn cats when I lived at Thunder Mountain. They were easy, liked everybody."

"Whereas Gandalf seems partial to you. If he isn't happy with the separation, he'll cry."

Grady shook his head. "Nope, not gonna happen. Gandalf and I have an agreement."

"What sort of agreement?"

"That's between us guys."

Damn, but he was adorable. "We're about to find out if you're right. This is my street. Oh, and once you're closed in the bathroom with him, you should take off your shirt."

"Hell, why stop there?"

"Slow down, cowboy. The shirt's to tuck into the basket I'm planning to use for his bed. Your shirt will smell like you and might comfort him so he won't cry."

He winced. "I'll bet it does smell like me, which is not a plus.

I apologize for perfuming your cab with my sweaty body. My plasma torch gives off a lot of heat."

"No problem." If only he knew.

"In fact, I predict Gandalf will take one whiff of that shirt and refuse to set foot in the bed. Don't you have a nice cozy blanket, instead?"

"I'll use a blanket, too, but the shirt on top will make all the difference. Animals don't have the same hang-ups about body odor as people do. They love it." *And when it comes to you, so do I.*

"If you say so, but that brings up another point. The rest of me is pretty ripe, too. I could use a shower before we move on to the next stage."

Over her dead body. "But that would disturb Gandalf."

"Do you have another shower I could use?"

"My sister's bathroom is upstairs, but—"

"Would it be okay if I showered up there? I'll clean up after myself."

"We'll talk about it after we get Gandalf settled, okay?" She didn't plan to talk at all. She'd grab the tea tree oil and a box of condoms out of her cabinet while she was arranging everything. Grady could wash his scratches in the kitchen sink and if she had her way, he'd forget all about that shower he thought he needed.

She pulled into the driveway of the two-story Victorian. "I think it'll be less trouble if I don't park in the garage."

"Me, too." He tipped back his hat and peered out the windshield. "Cute house."

"It works for us. I took the master downstairs and Amethyst has the entire second floor. The landlady let her soundproof one of the bedrooms so she could have a small recording studio."

"Accommodating landlady."

"She's the best, which is one reason we aren't rushing to move." She turned off the engine and hoped Gandalf wouldn't wake up, but those blue eyes popped open immediately. Next thing she knew, he was fastened to Grady's chest again. "Just stay put for now. I'll get everything ready and come back for you."

"We'll be here." Grady wrapped the cat in his arms and started talking to him, although he kept his voice so low Sapphire couldn't discern the words. Maybe he was reminding Gandalf of their agreement.

"Be back as soon as I can." She climbed slowly out of the cab so she wouldn't startle the cat even more. "I'll close my door just in case."

"He's not going anywhere."

She didn't think so, either, but she shut her door anyway. A carrier would have made transportation easier, but it probably would have freaked out the cat. Despite Grady's assurances, she wondered if Gandalf would sit on the other side of the bathroom door and yowl once they closed him away from his hero. That would pretty much cancel out having sex.

She had to laugh as she hurried up the porch steps and across to the door. What if it turned out that a cat threw a monkey wrench into her plans? If that happened, she should probably take it as a warning that she was making a mistake. But if Gandalf didn't interfere, was that the universe blessing the idea of a fun romp with this appealing man?

She quickly arranged everything for Gandalf and was about to go back outside when she remembered the tea tree oil and the condoms. The lamp table beside her four-poster had no drawer. Rather than put the condoms on the table in the open, she shoved them under the bed skirt.

If Gandalf protested being closed in the bathroom, she didn't want a box of condoms in plain view taunting them with what they weren't doing. The tea tree oil, though, could go on top of the table. She planned to have a really good time doctoring Grady's wounds.

The light was fading from the sky as she walked around to the passenger side of her truck. "Okay in there?"

"You bet. Open 'er up."

She opened the door cautiously because she still had visions of Gandalf making a break for it. If she was right about his history, he'd been deceived by humans before and might decide freedom was his best option. But he stayed firmly attached as Grady eased out of the truck.

"Follow me." She led the way to the front porch. She and Amethyst had spent many nights in the white wicker rocking chairs drinking wine. It was during one of those nights that Sapphire had promised her sister that she'd never date an artist again.

This wasn't dating, though. She opened the door and let Grady go in first. Dating implied building something solid. They wouldn't build a damn thing other than memories of great sex.

"Go down the hall and turn right," she said. "That's the master bedroom. The bathroom's connected to it."

"This is a first for me. I've never walked into a woman's bedroom carrying a cat."

"Then we're both breaking new ground. I've never invited a man into my bedroom who was holding a cat."

"I guess you wouldn't, considering the allergy problem. I'll bet your bedroom doesn't usually smell like tuna, either."

"No, but Gandalf is very interested in that aroma."

Grady hoisted the cat a little higher on his shoulder. "I know. I can feel him quivering. Want something yummy, Gandalf?"

The cat meowed.

"Okay, then remember our deal. You get tuna and I get—" He paused to check out the bed. "Four-poster, huh?"

"I decided to buy something that fits the time period of the house."

"Hmm."

"What?"

"Oh, just thinking."

She caught an erotic undertone that shifted her pulse into high gear. "About what?"

"Never mind." He glanced at her. "We can have that discussion a little later. But I do need to ask you about one item we'll need. Do you have—"

"I do."

"Good. I was hoping." He walked into the bathroom with Gandalf. "Go ahead and shut the door. I've got this."

After closing the door with as little noise as possible, she sat on the bed and waited while she tried not to think about what was supposed to happen next. It might or it might not, depending on Gandalf. Because of the uncertainty, she shouldn't count on anything.

She shivered in anticipation anyway. Although the low rumble of Grady's voice was muffled by the door, Gandalf's high-pitched meows came through clearly. A conversation was taking place.

She couldn't help smiling at the idea of this broad-shouldered cowboy communicating earnestly with a homeless cat. She didn't think Gandalf would stay homeless, though. Through her volunteer work with the shelter, she'd seen enough instances of bonding that she expected Grady would take the cat. Perhaps the family would be found, but none of the lost-cat pictures she'd seen taped to light and telephone poles around town had resembled Gandalf.

Negotiations continued on the other side of the bathroom door. Then the strip of light shining under the door went out. More soft murmurs followed, interspersed with cat noises that were a blend of purrs and meows. Finally, all was quiet.

Moments later the door opened and Grady stepped out, shirtless. She took a moment to absorb the lust-inducing sight of his muscled chest with its light dusting of brown hair. Oh, yeah. She'd made the right decision inviting him here.

He must have left his hat in the bathroom, too, because he was no longer wearing it. His hair looked tousled, as if he'd been running his fingers through it. "Gandalf will be fine. He loves the tuna." He seemed relaxed, but a second glance revealed that his eyes had darkened to the color of chocolate.

She picked up the small bottle of tea tree oil and stood. "Now we'll go into the kitchen and wash your puncture wounds."

He eliminated the distance between them. "What if I feel like kissing you first?"

When she placed a hand on his chest to keep him from doing that, the tactile pleasure of soft hair against her palm distracted her from her purpose. But then she noticed the little red dots tattooed on his warm skin by Gandalf. The wounds should be tended to right away.

Cupping her chin, he tilted her head up to meet his smoldering gaze. "The cat's settled in. I've been waiting to do this all day."

"Wait! We both know that once you kiss me, it'll be all over."

"All *over*?" He grabbed her hand and pressed it to his rapidly beating heart. "You insult me, lady. Yeah, I was a three-second wonder when I was seventeen, but I've learned a few things since then."

His heat traveled from her palm to her entire body, leaving her quivering and oh so ready to find out what he'd learned. "I didn't mean it that way."

He brought her hand to his lips and kissed the tips of her fingers. "That's a relief. I was afraid you'd talked to a couple of my old girlfriends. I didn't do right by them but I didn't know it at the time. Now they're married and have kids. I don't think it's appropriate to contact them and say, 'I'm so sorry that I didn't last long enough for you to come.'"

"Yeah, that's a bad idea." The brush of his lips over her fingers left her short of breath. "I doubt their husbands would appreciate it."

"For the record, I've developed a fair amount of stamina."

"I'm sure you have." God, how she wanted him, but she forced herself to be sensible. "Before you prove it to me, let's go in the kitchen and wash your puncture wounds."

"Not necessary. I'll shower in a minute. I just need to kiss you first."

"Humor me. I want to make sure we clean those scratches." Tugging on his hand, she pulled him toward the bedroom doorway. "I thought you were looking forward to having me rub your manly chest with tea tree oil."

"I've changed my mind. Now I have different locations where I want you to rub. After I get cleaned up, I'll point them out."

But he let her coax him into the vintage kitchen. Reconditioned antique appliances and lace curtains always made Sapphire feel as if she'd stepped back in time. Normally, she walked in here and had the urge to sip tea and do needlepoint.

Not tonight. "Stand right there." She let go of his hand. "I'll get soap and a dishcloth."

"I can see you're determined about this."

"I am."

He glanced around. "This house has character. I like it."

"Me, too." She liked it even better with him in it. Dampening a cloth, she squirted it with liquid soap, then walked back to him. "This'll just take a minute."

"Then I get my kiss?"

"Absolutely." She rubbed the cloth over his chest.

"Yikes, that's cold!"

"Sorry! Want me to wait for the water to warm up?"

"No, but give me that." He took the cloth, rubbed it briskly over his chest and tossed it on the counter. "Good enough." He pulled her into his arms.

"But you still have soap on you!"

"Don't care." He lowered his head.

"And we didn't put on the tea tree—" She didn't finish the sentence. His mouth came down on hers with an urgency that made her gasp.

With a low growl, he delved deep with his tongue. Moments later he grasped her bottom to tug her against his stiff cock while he ravished her mouth as if he couldn't get enough. She couldn't get enough of him, either. Holding his head, she kissed him back as frustration gave way to delicious passion.

He lifted his lips from hers for a second and gulped for air. "I could gobble you up." Then he shifted angles and urged her to open wider for the sensual thrust of his tongue.

She'd never been kissed with such energy and power. Lost in a whirlpool of sensation, she clung to him as her heartbeat thundered in her ears and moisture sluiced between her thighs. His grip tightened on her bottom. Without breaking the kiss, he lifted her to the counter, freed her blouse from the waistband of her jeans and began unbuttoning it.

Maybe he was a mind reader as well as a talented kisser, because her breasts ached for the sweet tug of his mouth. Reaching behind her, she unfastened her bra, and in seconds both items lay on the counter. Only then did he end the kiss and step back.

She reveled in his hungry expression as he gazed at her. Cradling a breast in each hand, she brushed her thumbs over the aroused nipples while she watched the fire blaze in his eyes.

"Magnificent," he murmured.

"Touch me."

"Oh, I intend to." Stepping forward, he cupped her hands as his gaze burned into hers. "I imagined doing this in the kitchen at the barn." He slowly drew her hands away. When he replaced them with his own, he closed his eyes and sighed. "Like silk."

Her heart pounded so fast she grew dizzy. "Only warmer."

"Much warmer." He opened his eyes and looked into hers as he began a slow massage. "When I saw your work, I knew..."

Her breath hitched. "Knew what?"

"That you'd be sexy as hell, ready for anything."

"*Oh*, yeah." She let out her breath. She'd been so afraid he'd say something about fate or kismet.

Instead he watched her eyes as he kneaded her breasts. "You're sensitive here."

"Mmm."

"I thought you would be." His breathing roughened. "Lean back."

Bracing her hands behind her, she tilted away from him and propped her head against the cabinet door.

Still holding her gaze, he unfastened her jeans and drew the zipper down. "Lift up." When she did, he deftly peeled her jeans over her hips and shoved them to her knees.

She trembled with need. "I thought this was only going to be a kiss."

"Ah, but I didn't say where I was going to kiss you. A guy would be crazy to limit himself when there's so much to enjoy." His glance traveled from her mouth to her breasts and finally to her moist panties. Then he returned his attention to her mouth and leaned in to brush his lips over hers. "Where should I start?"

She swallowed. "Anywhere you want."

"Good answer." He began fondling her breasts as he kissed his way along her jawline.

Her earrings tinkled as he nuzzled behind her ear and ran his tongue over the tender lobe. When he caught it in his teeth, he pinched her nipples and a tremor rippled through her core. She drew in a quick breath, unable to believe that she was that close to a climax.

Then tension eased as he nipped and nibbled his way along her collarbone, but when he reached her breast and licked the pebbled surface of her nipple, another tremor shook her. Slowly, he drew in the tip. Opening his mouth wider, he took in more as he began rhythmically sucking.

"Grady…" She began to pant. She was close now, so close. Almost…

Sucking harder, he slipped his hand under the elastic of her panties. One thrust of his fingers and she arched off the counter with a sharp cry as her orgasm crashed through her. Struggling to breathe, she begged him to hold her before she fell.

Strong arms came around her and she rested her head against his broad shoulder. "That was some…kiss."

He chuckled. "Needed to give you something to remember me by while I took my shower."

"Please don't shower."

"No, really, I need to."

"You don't." Raising her head, she looked into his eyes. "On the way over, I got turned on just breathing in the raw masculinity of you. Don't shower, Grady. Just take me to bed."

6

GRADY WASN'T ABOUT to argue. After pulling off Sapphire's boots, jeans and panties, he carried her back to the bedroom, which was a trick because his cock felt stiff as a welding torch and he couldn't walk worth a damn. But having her naked in his arms was worth the pain in his crotch.

No woman had ever told him she loved the smell of his sweat. His job left him that way every day and he'd always assumed that he'd better clean up before he climbed into bed with a girlfriend. Apparently, Sapphire didn't care about that. In fact, she actually wanted him to take her without showering off the evidence of his labor. One more reason to assume they were right for each other.

He laid her on the bed and once again his thoughts went to the possibilities of a four-poster. Now that he knew Sapphire had sexual adventure in her soul, he had a feeling she'd like some of his ideas. But as he pulled off his boots and shucked his jeans and briefs, he only cared about the basics for now.

While he'd undressed, she'd tossed aside the lacy throw pillows and pushed the coverlet to the foot of the bed. Watching the process as her breasts moved seductively and her bottom occasionally swiveled in his direction had turned his cock into a heat-seeking missile. He approached the bed with a single goal.

She lay on her side, her head propped on her hand and her gaze focused on his package. She cleared her throat. "Very nice."

"I need to dress it up before it heads to the party."

She opened her other hand to reveal a foil packet resting on her palm. "Will this do?"

That was when he noticed a box on the lamp table that he'd sworn hadn't been there the first time he'd walked into this room. "Where'd the box come from?"

"I hid it under the bed in case Gandalf put up a fuss and we didn't get to do this."

He found that hilarious. He couldn't help grinning. "Are you saying that the unused box sitting there would have depressed you?"

"Wouldn't it have depressed *you*?"

"Come to think of it, yes. Thanks for hiding it. But Gandalf is obviously sound asleep, so I'll take that and make good use of it." As he started to pluck it from her hand, she pulled it away and sat up.

"I have a better idea. Come closer and I'll put it on." She moved to the edge of the bed.

He felt as if he could come just looking at her. "It'll be faster if I do it." And he needed fast.

"It'll be more fun if I do it. Come on over here." She tore the packet open and set it beside her.

He stepped within reach and she grasped his cock the way she might hold a hammer. Matter of fact, he probably could drive nails right now. His chest heaved. "Make it quick."

A slow smile greeted that remark. "What if I want to kiss you first?"

"Sapphire, no. I'm too close. I'll—" *Come.* She took away his power of speech the moment she licked away the drop of moisture trembling on the tip.

That was only her first move. Holding him firmly, she closed her lips over the sensitive head and began a slow slide. His cock touched the back of her throat and he clenched his hands, jaw, even his toes to keep from pouring everything he had into her mouth. By damn, he wasn't going to come until he was buried inside her sweet body.

She tested him. He called on restraint he didn't know he had as she licked and sucked. Oh, yeah, and massaged his tight balls. He regretted bragging about his stamina, although he couldn't imagine a man alive who could easily withstand this. But they'd probably love to try. He loved it, too, despite that the humiliation if he failed would be tough to endure.

About the time he was ready to surrender, she drew back. Cool air wafted over his wet cock and helped him maintain control while she rolled on the condom.

She lay back on the bed. "Now."

Her husky voice hummed in his ears as he climbed onto the mattress and leaned over her. "You're lucky I didn't come."

"You're lucky I didn't make you."

"Oh, so that's how it is?" Braced on his forearms, he settled himself between her thighs, poised at the entrance to paradise.

Her turquoise eyes gleamed with a combination of mischief and desire. "I decided to be nice. I knew how much you wanted this."

"And you don't?" He pushed in a short way and paused while his heart threatened to beat itself right out of his chest. He was about to make love to a woman who fulfilled all his fantasies.

"I might be slightly interested."

"I think you are." He held himself right there, teasing her with the possibilities. Then he leaned down until his lips almost touched hers. "I think you are *very* interested." He gave her an openmouthed kiss with plenty of tongue until she moaned and clutched his hips in an attempt to bring him closer.

Somehow he managed to resist, although every instinct shouted at him to sink into her heat. She was a challenge and he loved a challenge. Taunting each other made sex fun and she was good at that. But so was he.

Slowly, he broke away from the seductive kiss. "What do you want, Sapphire?"

She let go of his hips so she could drag his head down. Then she murmured a very earthy two-word suggestion in his ear.

"I can do that." And he drove in deep. He hadn't expected her to come with one thrust, but she did. Arching her back, she shuddered in the grip of a climax that rolled over his cock. He gritted his teeth against the need to answer with a climax of his own. He wanted to give her one more.

He waited until she'd caught her breath. Then, as she lay soft and pliant beneath him, he began a relaxed, undemanding rhythm.

She looked up at him and smiled. "Now you're showing off."

"Uh-huh." He kept moving.

"I don't need another orgasm."

"But wouldn't it be nice?" He increased the pace.

Her eyes darkened and her body tensed. "I don't believe this."

"Believe it." He gulped for air as he struggled not to tumble over the edge. "You're going to come again."

Her thighs trembled. "You, too."

"Yeah, me, too." He finally slipped the leash on his control, and as he pumped rapidly, he knew his release was just around the corner. Damn, this was good. Her hips rose to meet each stroke. Any second now they'd—

The piercing meow from behind the bathroom door penetrated his passion-soaked brain. He paused midthrust.

"Gandalf." Sapphire's voice was strained.

"Yeah."

"We—" She gasped. "We should stop."

"Hell, no." And he pounded into her until they both came in a glorious rush. The cat's yowls intermingled with their cries, which guaranteed that he'd never forget the moment. But he wouldn't have anyway. A guy didn't forget his first time with his soul mate.

Gandalf continued his serenade as Grady's brain slowly

stopped spinning and his breathing returned to normal. Propped on his forearms, he gazed into Sapphire's flushed face. He wanted to say something tender and significant, but he hesitated.

For one thing, it would lose something with the cat wailing in the background. For another, he'd started to mention his belief that they were meant for each other earlier, when they were in the kitchen. Her decision to invite him home with her had made him think it might be time.

But she'd interrupted him. She'd also looked scared, like she didn't want to hear that sort of thing. He had to admit it was a little soon to get mushy, even if she was the woman he'd dreamed of during the long winter nights in Alaska.

He might be better off not telling her that yet. She probably needed time to catch up before he came out with such dramatic statements. She clearly liked having sex with him, so he'd concentrate on that aspect for the time being.

Smiling, he looked into her eyes. "That was memorable."

"No kidding." She smiled back. "Still breaking new ground."

She had no idea how true that was. Taking a firm grip on the condom, he eased away from her. "I'll go in there and see if I can settle him down."

"He seems to have forgotten your agreement."

"I intend to remind him." He glanced at her. "And I'll also take a quick shower."

She laughed softly. "If you must."

She looked incredible lying there, all rosy and mussed. "Wish you could join me."

"I have a feeling that wouldn't turn out the way you hope. I'll take one upstairs. And order our pizza."

"Oh, yeah. Pizza." He suddenly realized he was ravenous. "Get an extra large, okay?" He started toward the bathroom.

"I will. Be careful he doesn't sneak out."

"No worries." Getting through the bathroom door without letting Gandalf out or losing his hold on the condom took coordination, but luckily, he'd been blessed with a fair amount of it. He blocked the cat with his foot and kept him back while he slipped inside the bathroom and closed the door.

Gandalf rubbed against his leg and purred.

"Yeah, you and I need to have a little talk." Grady disposed of the condom and turned on the shower. "Right after I clean up a bit." He grabbed a washcloth off the towel rack, pulled back the cat-themed curtain of the tub shower and stepped under the spray. It was a little weak but he figured that was because Sapphire was using the one upstairs.

That brought up images of her naked in the shower, which made him think of all the fun things they could do together if they were sharing that experience. He had to stop thinking about that or he'd be hard again, and he had to deal with this cat. That was okay, because Gandalf needed him right now and befriending the cat might have tipped the scales in his favor with Sapphire.

He stuck his head under the water and took a little of her shampoo to lather his hair. She might love his manly scent but he was so over it. As he ducked under the spray again to rinse away the suds, Gandalf meowed.

"Taking a shower here, cat. Can't pet you."

The rustle of the curtain was followed by a thump. When Grady turned around and wiped his eyes, there was Gandalf sitting in the tub staring at him with his blue eyes. The cat seemed oblivious to the water pelting down on him.

"What the hell? Aren't you supposed to hate water?"

Gandalf padded over and began licking Grady's leg. His tongue felt like sandpaper but it tickled, too.

"You are one weird feline, Gandalf. I suppose if I lifted you out, you'd hop right back in. Besides, you're wet now, so you'd make a mess. Can't have that." He quickly used the washcloth while Gandalf continued to lick his leg. By the time Grady turned off the shower, the cat was pretty wet.

Maybe this wasn't all bad. Leaning down, he stroked the washcloth over the cat's long hair, which had darkened to charcoal under the spray. He'd picked out the burrs earlier while Gandalf was eating tuna and now he was able to make some progress on the matted places.

Gandalf stood tolerantly while he was being tended to. He didn't protest when Grady grabbed a towel and bundled him into it. Instead he started to purr.

Grady stepped out of the tub, then sat on the bath mat and gently massaged the cat with the towel. "I can't decide if you're the most maddening animal in the world or the most fascinating." After rubbing the cat until he was damp-dry, he turned him loose. "You finish the job, okay?"

Sure enough, Gandalf began grooming himself.

The towel Grady had used for the cat was covered with hair, so he folded it up and took a different one for himself. As he dried off, he talked to Gandalf. "I thought we had an understanding, buddy. I have something special going with Sapphire and I don't appreciate it when you make noise in the middle of a most excellent roll in the hay."

The cat ignored him.

"You may not be able to relate now that you've lost your family jewels, but for those of us who still have ours, using them is important." He watched Gandalf lick his paw and swipe it over his whiskers. Cute move. "So even if you don't get why I like that activity, I'm asking you to respect my need for it. If you promise not to meow to get my attention, I promise to check on you whenever I'm not having sex with the lady. Okay?"

Gandalf looked up and blinked.

"I'll take that as your word of honor." He wrapped the towel around his hips. "I'm going back out there, and depending on when the pizza's being delivered, I could become intimately involved again, if you take my meaning."

The cat made that funny little noise that was somewhere between a meow and a purr.

"I think you do. Be a good boy." He slipped out the door and closed it securely. When he turned, Sapphire stood there wearing a silky green robe and a smile. "Well, hello there." He took note of the way the material draped and decided she wasn't wearing a bra, which might also mean she wasn't wearing panties, either.

"Hello, yourself." She glanced at the towel around his hips. "Apparently, you took that shower you were so dead set on."

"I did. So when's the pizza supposed to arrive?"

Her smiled widened. "They're swamped. It'll be at least an hour."

"You don't seem very upset by the delay."

"I'm not."

"Were you by chance eavesdropping on my conversation with Gandalf?"

"Oh, I might have heard a reference to timing of the pizza regarding certain other activities."

His cock rose to attention, which couldn't be disguised by a towel. "And how do you feel about that?"

She laughed. "Regardless, I already know how you feel about it."

"That's the thing about guys. We put it all out there." He stepped closer and loosened the tie on her robe. "Girls, not so much. So guys have to learn to read the subtle signs."

"Like what?"

He ran a finger over her cheekbone. "A slight flush on your skin, a widening of your pupils, a catch in your breath."

She shivered. "What else?"

"Puckered nipples, unless it's cold." He brushed his knuckles over the hunter green silk covering her breasts. "Are you cold?"

"No."

"Then judging from what I feel through this material, you're quite possibly aroused. But there's only one way to be sure."

"What's that?"

Parting her robe, he reached between her thighs. His fingers came away wet. He stroked her bottom lip, moistening it with her juices. "Dead giveaway."

She looked up at him with passion-glazed eyes. "And what are you going to do about it?" Her breathy question was barely audible.

"I have a few ideas." As he backed her toward the bed, his towel fell away.

"So I see."

"I'm saving that for later." He cupped her face in both hands and nibbled on her mouth. "I really am hungry and since the pizza won't be here for a while, I'll have to make do with you."

"How you talk." Her voice quavered.

"That's not all I can do with my mouth."

She moaned. "I know."

"Not really." He pushed gently on her shoulders. "But if you'll sit back and relax, I'll be happy to show you."

She sank down to the edge of the mattress and he dropped to his knees on the plush carpet beside the bed. "I don't think you need this anymore." He slipped her robe over her arms and it drifted to the bed to fan around her, making her the focal point of delicious pleasure.

"I love your breasts." Cupping them, he tasted each nipple and rolled it over the flat of his tongue.

She shuddered. "That feels good."

"And this?" He trailed kisses down to her navel and circled it with the tip of his tongue.

She drew in a sharp breath. "That, too."

Coaxing her thighs apart, he blew on her damp curls. "Like that?"

"Mmm."

He scooted lower and flicked his tongue over the sweet spot nesting among those curls. "That?"

She moaned.

"I'll take that as a yes." Slowly, he began his exploration, beginning with her clit. He made love to it with his tongue. He loved the taste of her, loved the way he made her whimper.

Then he grazed that pulsing trigger point with his teeth and finally drew it into his mouth.

Her breathing grew faster with every stage. Sliding his hands under her bottom, he tilted her hips because he needed... Yes, there. She was like velvet and so hot, so drenched with desire. He explored and probed as she clutched his head and made soft mewling sounds.

He knew the exact moment when she surrendered completely. Her knees fell apart and she gave up all pretense of modesty. Throwing open the gates, she invited him to plunder at will. He didn't hesitate.

He took all she had to give—licking and sucking until the flow of her nectar flooded his tongue and her cries filled the room. He pressed on until she came again, her hips bucking and her fingertips digging into his scalp. She called his name. Ah, how he loved that she'd called his name.

"Enough." Panting, she leaned down and kissed the top of his head. "Please stop before I die of pleasure."

He placed kisses along her damp thighs before he rose up and kissed her fully on the mouth. Their lips met in a sensuous dance flavored by her orgasms.

The taste of sex seemed to inspire her, because she closed her hand around his still-rigid cock. She broke away from the erotic kiss. "I can't leave you like this."

"Sure you can."

"I can't. But I don't think I can...reciprocate."

"That's okay. I'll be fine."

"No, it's not fair." Releasing him, she wiggled back up on the bed. "Do me, Grady. I may not have the strength to participate a whole lot, but at least I'll know that I didn't leave you hanging."

He smiled. "Honestly, we don't have to—"

"Yes, we do! I'll feel so guilty if you don't grab a condom and climb aboard." She held out her hand. "Come on, cowboy. You know you want to."

"Nope. I can wait."

"But I'm all warmed up." She put her other hand between her thighs and began to touch herself. "You'll have a good time."

He had only so much willpower. "Yeah, I sure will." He had a condom on in no time and his body hummed with anticipation. "I'll make it quick."

"Take as long as you like." She bent her knees to give him a perfect view of heaven. "Now, come on and make yourself feel good."

He'd defy any man to resist such an offer. Moving over her, he thrust into her orgasm-slicked channel with a groan of pure happiness.

"I told you you'd like it."

"That was never in doubt." He put his weight on his outstretched hands this time so he could watch her breasts quiver each time he shoved home. "I want you to come, too."

"Don't think about that. This is for you. Do whatever makes you feel good."

"I broke that habit a long time ago."

"Then fall back into it." She clutched his butt cheeks. "Show me what you were like at seventeen. Go for the gusto. I want to see you lose it."

Temptation shot arrows of fire through his blood. "Oh, Sapphire."

"I dare you."

No one had dared him in a very long time, especially not a naked woman who was massaging his butt and taunting him to unleash the hedonist he knew he could be. Heart thundering, he withdrew. "Okay. Turn over."

She looked surprised, but she did it.

"Get on your hands and knees."

She did that, too.

He watched her through a red haze of lust. "Lean on your forearms and lift your hips."

"How's that?"

"Good. Move your knees apart. There." Positioning himself

behind her, he dipped his fingers into her entrance. She was drenched.

"Hurry," she murmured. "I think I might come."

That was all he needed to know. One thrust and he was buried to the hilt, his thighs touching hers.

"Go for it." She sounded slightly desperate.

He turned himself loose, driving into her again and again. The slap of his thighs against hers blended with the liquid rhythm of each stroke. Their ragged breathing became moans that turned into urgent cries.

This wasn't about making love. It was about raw, unfettered sex and he reveled in it. She'd given him permission to submerge himself in carnality and he welcomed it with each frenzied thrust of his cock.

He didn't wait for her, because she'd said not to. He came with a roar of triumph as he slammed into her one last time and held himself there as he pulsed within her. Vaguely, he realized she'd come, too, and her spasms milked him until he sank against her, spent and panting.

She dragged in a breath. "Good."

"So...good." He steadied her as he eased them down to the mattress so they could lie spooned together. Eventually, he'd have to move and deal with the condom. Sooner or later the pizza would arrive. But for now he just wanted to hold her. He felt as if he could do that forever.

7

BY SOME MIRACLE, they managed to get out of bed before the pizza arrived, but Sapphire had wondered if they'd make it. Originally, she'd thought that an hour for fun and games was more than enough time, but she hadn't counted on the level of erotic energy she and Grady generated. Their last episode had developed an orgy-like quality that could have gone on for hours.

She'd fully expected Gandalf to interrupt them but he hadn't. Maybe his exhaustion had finally caught up with him and he'd zonked out. That would be great, because in spite of their last sexual episode, she and Grady weren't finished with each other. The air still crackled whenever they exchanged a glance.

But as if by mutual agreement, they'd taken chairs on opposite sides of the kitchen table while they ate pizza and sipped cans of beer she happened to have in the fridge. They'd have to stretch to make contact. Grady's legs were long enough to play footsie under the table but he didn't do that, either.

She hoped the extra-large pizza with everything on it would be enough food. He was a big guy and he'd had an active day plus an even more active night.

"I have ice cream," she said when the pizza was gone.

"Great. I'd love some." He tipped back his head to get the last swallow of his beer.

She longed to go over and kiss the tanned column of his throat. Then she'd move on to his chest, where the little red dots were fading. He must be a fast healer, after all. She wouldn't doubt it. He was a healthy, vital male with a lusty outlook on life. No wonder she craved him.

He set down the empty can and met her gaze. "Or maybe you'd rather have a different kind of dessert." His eyebrows lifted and the corner of his mouth curved just enough to make him look like a rogue, especially when she caught the glitter of desire in his eyes.

Her body tightened in response. Oh, yes, she wanted what he promised with that subtle smile even though it hadn't been that long since the last time. She couldn't remember being this obsessed with a guy. Some restraint might be in order so she wouldn't get carried away. "Let's slow it down a little."

"You sure? Just now you looked quite interested in another round."

"I am."

He scraped back his chair. "Then come with me." He laughed. "Or come first and then come with me. It's all good."

"Yes, it is, but there's something to be said for delayed gratification."

He stood and walked behind her chair. "I'm not a big fan of delayed gratification." Drawing her hair aside, he leaned down and nibbled behind her ear. "I love that you've left these sexy earrings in the whole time. They turn me on."

Closing her eyes, she tilted her head to give him greater access to her sensitized skin. With a murmur of approval, he slid his hand under the collar of her robe to fondle her breast. "Come back to bed," he crooned as he brushed his thumb over her nipple. "Unless you want to do it right here on the table. I tucked a condom in my pocket."

She smiled. "You did not."

"I did." He nuzzled her throat. "I wanted to be ready when you were ready, whenever and wherever that turned out to be."

"Grady...this is insane." But she no longer cared about restraint. He'd thought to tuck a condom in his pocket in case they decided to do it on the kitchen table. And why not, when they both wanted to? Then her phone rang.

Grady's caress moved lower and his voice rumbled in her ear. "Let it go to voice mail."

"It's my mother."

"All the more reason." He reached between her thighs, touching her with knowing fingers. "You're in no position to talk to your mother."

She groaned. "I have to. We scheduled this call. If I don't answer, she'll worry."

"In that case..." He slowly withdrew his hand and kissed her cheek. "I'll check on Gandalf."

"Sorry." Pulling her robe back together, she glanced at him as she rose on wobbly legs.

His fly strained against the pressure of his erect cock, but he smiled as if that was of no consequence. "Unless you plan to kick me out within the next hour, we'll have another shot at it."

"I'm not kicking you out." She wanted him to stay here for the entire week, but she hadn't thought it through very well. Besides her pledge to Amethyst, she'd also promised her mother that she wouldn't date any more artists. Her mom and her sister had taken the brunt of her angst after all four breakups.

"Then I'll catch you later." He left the kitchen.

Her phone had stopped ringing long before she made it to the counter. She took several deep breaths before calling her mother back.

Her mom answered immediately. "Hi, sweetie! I just left you a message."

"I didn't listen to it. Just called you instead." She tucked the phone against her ear while she cinched the belt on her robe. Silly, but she felt the need to do it. "So what have you decided?

The weaving or the sculpture?" A few local artists including her mom were donating finished works for the silent auction.

"The weaving. I've been thinking about Grady Magee."

Sapphire choked and began to cough as she struggled to breathe.

"Honey, are you okay?"

"Fine," she managed to say in a strangled voice. "Swallowed wrong."

"You got that from your father. Scares me to death when he does it. Anyway, Grady's the only other sculptor in the show, and while my work is totally different, I'd like him to have the honor of being the only one."

"I'm sure he'd share the spotlight."

"Probably. He was a nice boy in school, so I'm sure he's become a very nice man."

Oh, yeah. Sapphire swallowed carefully so she wouldn't give a repeat performance.

"To think that kid became a successful artist. I never would have predicted it, but he's a great role model for my students, especially the boys. He came in yesterday, right?"

"He did, and I—"

"I assume you've spent some time with him, then."

"I have, Mom, and that's something I need to talk to you about."

"Please don't tell me he's arrogant. You were sort of quiet when I said he'd probably become a nice man, so maybe he's turned into a jerk and you didn't want to say so. Quick success can do that to a person. If he's arrogant, then I won't ask him to come back and speak to my students in the fall."

Oh, boy. All hope of keeping the situation under control vanished. She'd never dreamed that her mom would see the potential in having a Sheridan High alum who'd made a name for himself speak to her art classes. "He's not a jerk," she said. "He's great and you should definitely ask him."

"Fabulous! I know he visits his foster parents every now

and then, so I could coordinate with his plans. I was surprised when Molly Radcliffe told me he was staying with her and Ben this time. I thought for sure he'd be out at Thunder Mountain."

"When the academy's going, it's crazy busy out there. He didn't want to get in the way."

"Then he could certainly stay here in the fall if he needed a place to crash. I'd love a chance to talk with him. If he's willing, we could set up a visit each semester."

"That would be terrific." Now Sapphire felt greedy for keeping this paragon to herself. Had she really thought they could hide away and have sex all week without the entire town knowing about it? In the privacy of her bedroom, locked in his arms, she'd thought exactly that.

"I've heard via the art grapevine that he's working on some top secret project and shouldn't be disturbed, so I'll wait until the welcome reception to talk with him about it. Of course, I could ask Ben and Molly if I could drop by some evening. I mean, the guy can't be working all day and all night, can he?"

"Mom, he's not at Ben and Molly's." She wondered if Grady had thought of calling them to explain the change of plans. Probably not, since he'd been as preoccupied with Gandalf—and sex—as she had.

"Then where is he?"

"Here."

"You mean *here* as in your house?"

"Yes. A new cat arrived at feeding time tonight and he's not feral. He took to Grady right away and Grady didn't want to leave him at the shelter, so we brought him over here."

"But your sister's allergic!"

"I know, so he's closed up in my bathroom." She found herself talking very fast. "It should be okay if I keep him confined there. I checked him for fleas and mites and tomorrow I'll take him to the shelter vet to make sure there are no issues. After that I may—"

"So the cat's in the bathroom safe and sound."

"Yes, and Grady wants to stay with him until we find out whether he has a home or not."

"So Grady's in your bathroom with the cat?"

"Um, sometimes. Right now he is."

"He'll come out with cat hair on him. You can't let him roam around and sit on the furniture after he's spent time with the cat. Or if you do, you'll have to vacuum that house within an inch of its life."

"Good point. I'll make sure he doesn't spread cat hair around." Maybe she needed to keep him confined to her bedroom, after all.

Her mother was silent for a beat. "Sapphire Jane, what's going on?"

"Grady and I are...involved."

Her mom was silent for a moment. "But he's an artist."

"I know."

"I can't say I'm surprised that you're attracted to him. I've seen him on TV and he's a good-looking guy, exactly your type, or what used to be your type before you swore off artists."

"I said I wouldn't date them anymore. But we're not exactly dating."

Her mother laughed. "Guess not. You skipped right over that part."

"I don't know if I can explain it." Or, more accurately, *how* to explain it. She could tell her mom that she was sleeping with Grady but she didn't want to admit it was only about sex. Saying that to her mom felt weird.

"Honey, you don't have to explain. You're a grown woman free to do what you want in that department. I won't hold you to that statement you made before he showed up and changed your mind."

"He hasn't changed my mind."

"Not yet."

"He won't."

"Whatever you say, sweetie. Anyway, I'd love for you to bring him to dinner tomorrow night."

"I'll ask him and let you know."

"Good."

"Oh, and if we come to dinner, could you please not tell Dad that Grady's staying with me?"

"I won't, but your father's not an idiot. He'll figure it out."

"Yeah, well, I still don't want you to tell him."

"I won't. Good night, honey."

"Night, Mom." She disconnected and stared at the phone. So her mother thought Grady would change her mind about getting involved with an artist. She couldn't allow that to happen. This thing between them was spontaneous and fun. Avoiding any talk of future plans was the only way to keep it that way.

Her mother's brainstorm of inviting Grady to speak at the high school could complicate matters. Oh, well, they could burn that bridge when they got to it. In the meantime, she had some things to discuss with the man of the hour.

She walked into the bedroom and over to the bathroom door, where light shone underneath. Once again cat and man were having a conversation. This close to the door, she could catch most of what Grady was saying. What Gandalf was saying was anybody's guess.

"So good job on staying cool while you're temporarily in lockup, buddy. I'll be back to check on you next time there's a break in the action, okay?"

She had a fair idea what action he was talking about. She knocked lightly on the door. "I hate to interrupt, but can I see you for a minute?"

His light chuckle tickled her nerve endings. "We covered this. A minute is no longer sufficient."

"I'm not talking about having sex."

"Thank God, because doing it is a whole lot better than talking about it. Unless you're referring to phone sex, where you talk and do at the same time. I suppose that could be interesting for a change of pace, but it's not my first choice."

"Then since what I have to say has nothing to do with sex, we could just talk through the bathroom door."

"Nah." Rustling sounds were followed by a plaintive meow. "Sorry, Gandalf, lap time is over. She may think we aren't talking about sex, but when you consider the past twenty-four hours, it's clear that sex underlies everything. Go have a little snooze and I'll be back later." The light went out and Grady slipped through the door. This time he was wearing his hat. "You rang?"

"Take off your clothes."

He grinned. "I like where this is going."

"It's not what you think. My mother pointed out that you'll come out of the bathroom covered in cat hair and I shouldn't let you walk around the house in those clothes."

He unzipped his jeans. "So walking around naked is a better option? I've always liked your mom but now she's a real favorite of mine."

"That's good, because she's invited us both to dinner tomorrow night."

"Oh, yeah? That's great. I'm in." He started pulling off his jeans.

"You wouldn't mind?"

"No, it'll be great to see her again. I only met your dad a couple of times but any guy who can make money with a saxophone has my admiration."

"She already knows we're having sex."

"Oh?" He paused with one leg still stuck in his pants. "Does she have your bedroom bugged?"

"No, I told her."

"Interesting. Is your dad gonna threaten me with a shotgun?"

"Not unless you say something insulting about his jazz trio."

"Wouldn't dream of it." He took off his hat and laid it brim-up on the dresser. "I didn't want to take a chance Gandalf would chew on this. It's old but we've been through a lot together."

She found that endearing, but then, many things about Grady were endearing. Her previous lovers had been charming, too, until one day they weren't.

He stripped off his briefs. "Are we supposed to burn these or what?"

"Would you let me?" Seeing him standing there in all his glory, she was tempted.

"If it's that or give up sex with you, sure. Light 'em up. Just not my hat. I'm very attached to it. But take these." He held them out. "They're dead to me."

"I think tossing them in the washing machine is good enough. Then you'll have something clean to wear in the morning." She tucked his clothes under her arm.

"And not a single thing to wear for the rest of the night. Oh, darn."

She thought about letting him stay that way because he was so pretty to look at. Greek statues had nothing on him. But having no clothes meant he'd be naked in an emergency or when he went in to check on Gandalf. "I have another bathrobe."

"Yeah, no. Not wearing a lady's robe. Thanks, but no thanks."

"It's black and kind of big on me."

"Does it have a sash like yours?"

"Yep. Very simple design. Velour. Not the least bit girlie."

"Pockets?"

"I think so."

"Then I'll take it. I've been thinking we should sit out on your front porch while we have ice cream."

"Really?" She thought he'd forgotten about the dessert she'd offered.

"Really. I live in a barn, literally, and we have no front porch, so naturally, I wish I had one. I'd have fun sitting on yours and watching the world go by, but I'd better not do it wearing just my hat."

She laughed. "We don't have a lot of traffic on this road and the neighbors are usually inside watching TV by now, but yes, sitting naked on the porch might be pushing it."

"And there's a chill in the air."

"That, too." She headed over to her closet, grabbed the robe off its hanger and tossed it to him. "One other thing. What about Ben and Molly?"

He blew out a breath. "Right. I need to call but what should I say?"

"Not what I told my mother, although they may draw the same conclusion no matter what you say."

He shoved his arms into the sleeves of the robe. "I thought about it while I was in there with Gandalf. What if I said that a stray cat brought us together and then we discovered all the things we have in common and want to take the week to explore them?"

"They'll still know it's about sex."

"Absolutely they will." Although the robe didn't begin to cover his chest, the bottom came together just enough to keep him from getting arrested. "But if I don't come right out and announce we're swinging from the chandeliers, we can all save face when I pick up my stuff tomorrow." He hesitated. "I made a leap there. I never asked if you wanted me here for the duration."

"I do." The hint of vulnerability in his brown eyes touched her more deeply than she wanted it to. She brushed a quick kiss over his mouth. "Call them and then go pick your ice-cream flavors while I start a load of laundry."

"There are choices?" He sounded like a kid in a candy store.

"Of course there are," she called over her shoulder as she headed for the laundry room. "I take my ice cream seriously."

"Me, too! See, I'm not lying to Ben and Molly. We do need to explore these things."

Technically, they didn't, she thought as she measured soap and set the dial on the washer. Two people with chemistry, which they had in spades, could have very satisfying sex without ever exploring their ice-cream preferences, or their love of porch sitting or their similar tastes in pizza. Sharing this info might make the connection a little more interesting but it wasn't essential.

At least, that was what she told herself until she walked back into the kitchen and found him with all four ice-cream cartons lined up on the counter. He was studying them with great intensity, which she found adorable. "Did you talk to Ben and Molly?"

He turned with a grin. "I got Ben. He sounded like he wanted to bust out laughing while I stumbled through my explanation. He said to tell you hi."

"He's a good guy." She gestured toward the four cartons. "Find anything you like?"

"I love them all. What are the chances?"

She shrugged. "They're popular flavors."

"Come on. Blueberry cheesecake? I've never known anybody else who loved it enough to buy a whole carton. Or did your sister get that one?"

She wished she could blame that choice on Amethyst, but her sister could take it or leave it. She wasn't even a big fan of ice cream in general. Sapphire was, and blueberry cheesecake had been her favorite for years. "No, I did."

He popped off the lid. "That's my pick, then. There's plenty for both of us, if it's your favorite, too."

She decided there was no harm in admitting they loved the same ice cream. "It is. I'll get us a couple of bowls."

"Why bother? Grab two spoons and we're good."

"You're okay sharing the carton?" She wasn't convinced she was. The symbolism, sort of like a soda with two straws, worried her.

He smiled. "We've already shared something way more intimate than ice cream."

"True." The reminder flooded her with a warm, achy feeling. It didn't make her desperate to have him right now, though.

She could wait. She could also sit with him on the porch and share a carton of ice cream without imagining it as a prelude to a complication. "I'll get the spoons."

8

"I DON'T SPEND enough time outdoors." Grady listened to the crickets chirping in the bushes next to the front porch as he rocked lazily back and forth. "As a kid I was always outside. Porch sitting at Thunder Mountain is an evening tradition, at least when the weather's nice."

"The porch is one of the main reasons Amethyst and I decided to rent this house. We bought the rockers the same day we moved in." She passed him the container of ice cream. "Your turn."

"Thanks. This is delicious. I've been so busy lately that I've scrounged whatever food I could find in the kitchen. I ran out of ice cream weeks ago."

"That can happen when you're involved in your work."

"Yep, and I get to the point where I don't care what I eat. Liam used to stock food and sometimes cook, but summer's his busy rafting schedule, plus now there's Hope."

"Hope for what?"

He laughed. "Sorry. Hope's the woman Liam fell for this summer. I keep forgetting everybody around here doesn't know her." He took another spoonful of ice cream and sent the carton back to her. "She lives in Cody but she came up to Sheridan for Damon and Philomena's wedding in July."

"You mean the wedding where you gave them a ginormous sculpture that has folks driving by their house just to see it?"

"They do?"

"I'm surprised Damon hasn't told you. It's become a tourist attraction for anyone who loves art. It's not like there's a steady stream of cars, although if you get any more famous, that could happen."

Grady winced. "I hadn't thought of that angle. I hope they're not upset."

"More likely they're proud of being your friend."

"Damon's way more than a friend. He— Well, let's just say I wouldn't be where I am today if we hadn't been at Thunder Mountain together. He's the one who encouraged me to pursue a career in welding."

"He is? I didn't know that."

"Yeah." He leaned back in his chair. "I idolized the guy. Still do."

"Then he has even more reason to be proud. You're a big deal."

"I guess so. For the time being anyway." He'd never taken his success for granted and never would.

"I predict you'll have a long career. Your work has a timeless quality."

"Thanks for saying so, but people can lose interest. I've seen it happen to others—artists with a truckload of talent. That's why I'm glad Liam's been investing the money for me. I don't have much ability when it comes to that but he does. He says if I don't buy any mansions or yachts, I should be fine for quite a while."

She laughed. "Do you want a mansion or a yacht?"

"Not much reason to have a yacht in Wyoming."

"A mansion, then?"

"Can't think what I'd do with one. The barn is perfect—living space upstairs and working space downstairs. I just want to keep doing what I love."

"Me, too." She handed him the carton. "I'm done. You can have the rest."

They'd turned the porch light off, so he couldn't see how much was left, but a quick jab with his spoon told him there was quite a bit. "You haven't eaten your share."

"I had enough. You're the ice-cream-deprived person, not me. Enjoy yourself."

"Thank you. Very generous." He tucked into it. Their quiet conversation had been great, but sex had never been far from his mind. Savoring the creamy texture of blueberry cheesecake on his tongue reminded him of other sensuous treats, ones within arm's reach. "I'm enjoying myself quite a bit tonight thanks to you."

"Right back atcha."

"Glad to hear it. That's the really great thing about sex." He paused. "Can I discuss this on your porch or will your neighbors hear me and be shocked?"

"They won't hear you over the sound of their TVs."

"Good to know." He didn't really want to discuss sex. He felt like doing it. Right after he finished this most excellent ice cream.

Sapphire rocked slowly back and forth. "The folks on both sides are avid fans of several shows. They've tried talking to me about them but I've only caught a glimpse of an episode or two."

"Too busy working, right?"

"Exactly. Some nights I stay at the barn and others I'm here sketching and planning out what I'll do the next day. Or reading up on new glazes or a tool that creates unusual effects."

"So you work at the barn at night?"

"Once in a while. Would you like to while you're here?"

"If I need extra time for Rosie's sculpture, you bet. I didn't know how you'd feel about me staying after hours."

"Fine with me. I might keep you company."

"I'd like that. Having you working next to me today was stimulating. And surprisingly, not in a sexual way."

"I know."

He glanced over at her. Soft light came through the curtains over the living room windows, but she had her back to the windows, so her face was in the shadow. "How do you know?"

"Because I watched you submerge yourself in your work today. Your entire attitude changed. I doubt you would have noticed if I'd stripped down and performed the Dance of the Seven Veils."

He nearly spewed ice cream. Instead he managed to swallow it. "I wouldn't go that far."

"I would. I admire that quality and that's another reason you'll make it in this business. You're focused."

"Thank you." He did get into the zone when he worked. If anyone had asked him whether he could stay in that zone while a sexy woman sat at a potter's wheel a few feet away, he would have said no. But he'd proved today that he could. Knowing that she was also absorbed in her project might have had something to do with it.

But they weren't working now and their dessert was nearly gone. He hadn't forgotten that she wore nothing but a silk robe. He wore nothing but the robe she'd loaned him and he'd shoved a condom in the pocket. Having sex out here carried the risk of discovery, and yet she'd said the neighbors were all inside and glued to their TVs.

She continued to rock gently. "So I think we could work together in the barn some night while you're here without worrying that we'd be distracted by sex. Instead we'd inspire each other."

He agreed, but at the moment he was inspired to lift her onto the porch railing and slide his aching cock into her welcoming body. The railing looked sturdy enough. He also had some softened ice cream left in the bottom of the container and he had a great idea for how to use it.

"You're awfully quiet over there, Grady. You okay?"

"I'm super." He licked the spoon and stuck it in his other

pocket. Then he grasped the carton, left his rocker and crouched in front of hers. "But I have a huge favor to ask." He caressed the silk covering her knee.

She laughed. "Why do I get the feeling this has something to do with sex?"

"Because it does." He liked the way silk slid easily away from bare skin. He cupped her bare knee and massaged gently. "I have some ice cream left but it's almost melted. That's an anticlimactic way to finish it off. Licking it from your warm breasts would be a much better ending for this carton of blueberry cheesecake."

"Sounds messy." But her voice trembled.

"Is that a yes or a no?"

"It's a maybe." Her breathing had changed, too.

"You'll be amazed at how neat I can be. I don't want to waste a single drop of my favorite ice cream."

"Was this your plan when you suggested eating our dessert on the porch?"

"Not exactly, but hosing down a porch is an easier cleanup than any place inside the house."

"So some of the ice cream was ultimately going to end up on me?"

"Only if you said yes."

She swallowed. "Okay. Yes."

"Hot damn."

"But we can't get ice cream on these chair cushions. They're half Amethyst's."

"I had a different plan anyway. I thought you could sit on the porch railing."

Her breath caught. "Facing the light from the living room."

"I need to see." He stroked her thigh.

"But a neighbor could come out and…"

"Probably won't happen."

"Probably not." She shivered.

"Are you afraid?"

She shook her head.

"Turned on?"

Her voice was low and sultry. "Yes."

Pulse hammering, he stood and offered his hand. Once he helped her out of the chair, it was a simple matter to boost her up on the railing at a spot where she could reach one of the spindled posts to steady herself.

Then he set the carton on the railing and cupped her cheek. As he leaned in for a kiss, he reached for her sash. He'd been tempted to untie it ever since she'd first appeared in the robe, and he'd fantasized about doing it all during their dinner of pizza and beer. But his plan to get that robe open had gone up in flames with her mother's phone call.

At last he could have the view he'd longed for. One quick tug and the robe hung loosely from her shoulders. Breaking away from the kiss, he stepped back to view his handiwork. Her breasts peeked from the lapels, and with each ragged breath she took, the lapels edged farther apart. He decided to help that process along and swept them aside.

That left her completely covered on the street side but gloriously naked on his side. Her bare feet dangled and her thighs were slightly parted to give him a tantalizing glimpse of his ultimate goal.

If he moved an inch or so, the ambient light from the living room illuminated her smooth skin and luscious curves even more. The mellow glow highlighted the classic beauty of her body and he regretted never taking an art course of any kind. If he had, he'd have her pose so he could sketch her.

As it was, he didn't have a lot of confidence in his drawing ability. He used it to map out plans for sculptures but he had no illusions about the quality of those sketches. Galleries had requested them, even offered him crazy amounts of money, but he'd refused. He was self-taught and he knew his efforts were crude. He didn't want some half-baked representation of his work to circulate.

But just this once he wished that he had the training to re-create what he was seeing in some form, whether it was in charcoal, paint or clay. She might not agree to that. Or maybe she'd already allowed another artist the privilege. In some ways he knew her so well and in others he knew almost nothing.

Given time, he could fix that. He'd thought about the geographical barrier between them and he wouldn't let it be a problem. But first he had to be convinced that she wanted him as much as he wanted her.

Sexually, he knew she did. The evidence was right in front of him. Her chest heaved with each shallow breath and even in this light he could tell the curls between her thighs were damp. She had the same thirst for sexual adventure that he did.

Emotionally, though, he wasn't so sure of her. Something was preventing her from opening up and he couldn't get a handle on it. It was still too soon to talk about deeper feelings, so he'd continue to capitalize on the one emotion that had worked from the beginning—lust.

He dipped his fingers in the carton to coat them with melted ice cream. Although the creamy substance wasn't frigid anymore, she might feel the chill. "Tell me if this is too cold."

She gasped as he began finger painting her breasts.

"Too cold?"

"No. Startling. I've never been painted with ice cream before." She traced the path he'd taken and then sucked on her finger. "But I like it."

Heat surged through him and he considered abandoning the ice cream in favor of snapping on the condom and sliding into her. She was ready. He knew that from the way her body trembled whenever he touched her.

But if he gave up on the ice cream, he'd lose an element that had bonded them together. She might think loving the same flavor wasn't important, but he wasn't so sure. Sometimes a simple thing could be the sentimental link that made all the difference.

So he coated his fingers again and this time he did a more

thorough job of covering her breasts. Licking her clean would take a while but he'd give it his best effort. Her nipples required extra attention because they seemed to collect more stickiness.

Finally, he resorted to sucking on each one for several seconds to make sure he'd removed every last bit of blueberry-cheesecake ice cream. By the time he finished, she was clutching the post with one hand and the railing with the other while she whimpered and moaned.

She was excited, no question. But fooling around with ice cream was different from full-out sex and he didn't know if she'd let him go that far. So he worked his way back to her mouth and kissed her thoroughly with plenty of tongue to gauge her level of arousal. She responded to the kiss with such enthusiasm that he was encouraged.

At last he gave up the pleasure of kissing her so he could broach the possibility of having sex in the great outdoors. He'd meant to be subtle about it.

Instead he blurted out his request in a gravelly voice worthy of a gangster movie. "I want you." He sucked in air. "Right here on the porch, sitting on the railing. Is that okay with you?"

"What if I fall in the bushes?"

"You won't. You'll be anchored to my cock at all times."

"Mmm." Keeping her hold on the post, she ran her free hand down his chest. She paused at the tie holding his robe closed, then yanked it free to reveal his extremely erect penis. Smiling, she lifted her gaze to his. "Got a raincoat in your pocket?"

He pulled out the condom.

Her eyes darkened and she took a firmer grip on the post. Shifting her position slightly, she opened her thighs. "Then you'd better dock that bad boy before you get arrested for flashing the neighbors."

After putting the condom on in record time, he reached inside her robe and grasped her hips. Once he had his bearings, he could have managed the next step blindfolded, but he gave in to temptation. He'd never watched his cock make that journey and tonight he wanted to see his first deep thrust. The sight was way more erotic than he'd imagined. He damn near came.

"Like the view, cowboy?" Her voice had become a husky drawl.

"Love it." He raised his head and registered the flush on her cheeks and the glitter in her eyes. "Best view in the world."

"Hold still and keep watching." Her breasts quivered as her breathing picked up speed. "Allow me to add to your viewing pleasure. Let's start here." She slowly sucked on her finger.

His cock twitched. Guaranteed that whatever she had in mind would challenge him to keep his cool. Mesmerized, he followed the path of her wet finger as she flicked each tight nipple. Then she stroked down her rib cage, over her flat belly and began circling her clit.

He stifled a groan as her hot channel tightened. "Keep that up and I'll come."

"I intend to keep it up. You won't come. I will."

"I wouldn't take bets on that, ma'am." He clenched his jaw but he couldn't make himself look away, even though watching her drove him crazy.

She gasped for air. "Hold on to me. I'm letting go of the post."

"Why?"

"To keep you…from coming." As she continued to touch herself, she slipped her thumb and forefinger around the base of his cock and squeezed.

He gulped at the sensation, which somehow lessened his urge to erupt. Then she loosened her grip and the pressure returned, taunting him with its power. Even though he hadn't moved at all, he was moments away from a climax. So was she. He could tell by her breathing and the faster motion of her finger.

When her first spasm hit, he thought he was a goner, until she squeezed him again, tighter this time. Her soft cry when she came was not much louder than a cricket's chirp. But ah, how her tremors surrounded and stroked every inch he'd buried deep inside her! It pushed the air from his lungs and made him shudder in reaction.

As her body quieted, she dragged in a breath and let go of his cock. "Your turn," she whispered.

Thank God for that. He figured he had about five seconds, tops. By now he couldn't tear his gaze away from the action as he pumped rapidly and his heart kept up a furious beat. The pace made her earrings tinkle like wind chimes. She was so wet, so hot, so...ready for another orgasm?

She drew in a sharp breath as if the sudden twinge had taken her by surprise.

He slowed and looked into her eyes, silently asking the question.

She shook her head. "Don't wait for me. I usually can't come in this position. That's why I..."

"I'm waiting." He didn't know how, but he'd do it and he'd give her a good ride in the process. Clamping down on the orgasm he'd expected to have very soon, he held her gaze and stroked more deliberately. "Maybe you should watch this time."

Her eyes widened.

"Go ahead. I dare you."

Grasping his shoulders, she looked down and her breath hitched.

Although he felt like thrusting fast and hard, he held back and created an easy motion that matched the rhythmic chirp of the crickets. "Like what you see?"

"Yeah."

He smiled at her breathless answer. "You know you're gonna come."

"Uh-huh."

He felt her heat up, felt the climax building, his and hers. Sex didn't always have to be wild and urgent. It could be like this—slow and rich, like warm syrup. There. Her fingers dug into his shoulders and she shuddered. Once more, maybe twice and she'd let go.

It only took once. When she came, her undulating channel and her muted wail of joy triggered his release. His breath hissed out between his teeth as he plunged deep, surrendering at last to wave upon wave of pleasure.

As he drifted in the aftermath of great sex, the creak of a door hinge penetrated his languid state.

"Dennis!" a woman called. "What are you doing out there?"

Grady put his mouth next to Sapphire's ear. "Stay very still."

She nodded.

"Thought I heard something," the guy named Dennis called back. "Don't want those skunks setting up house under the porch again. Think I'll look around."

From the corner of his eye, Grady saw the beam of a flashlight sweep the neighbor's yard. If Dennis decided to aim it in their direction, he'd discover two people locked together in an obviously sexual embrace. It was the risk they'd taken, after all.

"Sapphire and Amethyst's porch light is out," Dennis called to his wife. "Wonder if they know."

"You could go tell them, but the commercial's almost over. You'll miss the next part."

"I'll tell them tomorrow. Don't see anything out here." He mounted the porch steps. The door hinge creaked again.

Sapphire started to giggle.

Grady wasn't sure how loud those giggles would get and so he disengaged himself from her, tossed the condom in the bushes and hustled them toward the front door.

Sure enough, her giggles got louder. "Did you just throw the condom in the bushes?"

"Shh. I'll get it in the morning."

"Okay. Sure." She was still laughing as they stumbled into the living room, both of their robes hanging half on and half off their bodies. "That was hysterical."

He grinned. "Glad you had fun."

"I had a blast. That position's always been a tricky one for orgasms."

"You weren't doing it with me."

"True." She gazed at him, a smile playing over her well-kissed mouth. "I think I hear your cat."

He had, too, and was trying to ignore the meowing. But in Gandalf's shoes, he wouldn't like being closed in a small space, either. "The tuna worked pretty well. Any left?"

"I only gave him half the can. He shouldn't have a steady diet of the stuff, but I can give him the other half to get him through the night."

"And us."

"Yep." She stifled a yawn.

"I saw that."

"Sorry. I didn't sleep well last night."

"Me, either. What do you say we feed the cat and turn in?"

"To sleep?"

He laughed. "Knowing this could damage my reputation as a stud, I'll admit that one more climax and I'll be done for the night."

"Your reputation is safe with me."

"Thanks." *But is my heart?* He wouldn't ask the question now, but soon. He was afraid she'd already stolen it when he wasn't looking.

9

SAPPHIRE DIDN'T NORMALLY sleep naked, but she did that night because a nightgown seemed silly when it would come off once Grady returned. He'd taken the rest of the tuna into the bathroom and was in there giving Gandalf his instructions, namely that the cat was to stay quiet the rest of the night. When he switched off the bathroom light and walked into the darkened bedroom, she was aroused in a lazy, relaxed way she'd never felt with other men.

The whisper of his footsteps on the carpet signaled her body to flush and moisten. The sound of his breathing caused her nipples to grow taut. The snap of latex sent a message to her core and the sweet ache returned. She was ready.

"Once more," he murmured as he climbed into bed and gathered her into his arms.

"Once more," she echoed, and opened her thighs.

"Nothing fancy." He entered her with one firm thrust.

She sighed with pleasure. "I don't need fancy."

"We'll call it sleepy sex."

"Sleepy sex. I love it."

Leaning down, he kissed her gently. "I hope you do." And he began to move.

She knew him now—the friction of his cock, the rhythm of

his strokes, the press of his fingers as he lifted her hips to drive deeper. Her body knew him, too, and her response came quickly. Wrapping her arms around his strong back, she arched upward with a moan as her orgasm flowed over her.

He pushed home once more and shuddered in her arms. "So good," he said, gasping for breath. "So damn good."

"Yeah." She hugged him close and smiled in the darkness. Sleepy sex. She was a fan.

He'd thought to bring in the wastebasket from the bathroom so he didn't have to leave the bed to dispose of the condom. That preplanning also made her smile. As she nestled against his muscled body and drifted off to sleep, she felt more content than she had in months, maybe years.

Sometime during the night she woke up still enclosed in his arms, her back against his warm chest and her bottom nudged against his currently inactive package. She lay there staring into the darkness, her contentment replaced with anxiety. What the hell was she doing inviting him to spend the week with her? Was she insane?

One night, considering the situation with Gandalf, was understandable. That would be resolved tomorrow, though. Gandalf was a temporary visitor and she'd never intended for the cat to occupy her bathroom for a week. He deserved more freedom than that.

Once the shelter vet gave him a clean bill of health, the Art Barn was a logical alternative for him until they knew whether he had a family in the area. He'd be fine in the office at night, especially if he was allowed to roam the entire barn during the day. He'd make friends with the artists. At the end of the week Grady could decide if he wanted to take Gandalf home to Cody.

That all made perfect sense, unlike asking Grady to leave Ben and Molly's guest room and move in with her. If that wasn't an invitation to begin a relationship, she didn't know what was. Great sex and a shared love of blueberry-cheesecake ice cream had addled her brain. It wasn't the first time that kind of thing had happened, but she liked to think she'd learned from her mistakes. Apparently not.

"What's up?" Grady's drowsy voice rumbled in her ear.

"Nothing. Go back to sleep."

"Can't. You're all tense."

"Sorry." She took a deep breath and started through one of her relaxation techniques.

"Is it a project? Sometimes I can't sleep if I'm thinking about a design."

Why did he have to be so considerate? It tempted her to think of him as an exception to the rule, but they were only a couple of days into this. Fatal flaws took weeks or months to show themselves.

She sighed. "It's not a project." *It's you.* But how could she admit all her misgivings after the fact? That was plain mean on a personal level. She also had an obligation to the shelter and her upcoming event. Causing problems with the star of the show wasn't a great way to proceed.

Besides, he'd done nothing to deserve that kind of rejection. *Yet.* Past experience told her that he would disillusion her sooner or later, and she'd rather skip that part, thank you very much. But if she said any of that now, she'd sound paranoid.

Gently, he urged her to turn toward him. "I've wanted to ask you this but I've put it off."

"Don't ask me." Panic constricted her chest. "Let's just go back to sleep."

"You're trembling like a leaf. What are you afraid of?"

"You!" She hadn't meant to say it but he'd pushed her.

"Me? I'm the biggest pussycat you'll ever meet!"

"Not you, exactly. Artists in general."

"Good grief." He chuckled. "We're the least scary group in the world. We make love, not war. You should know. You're one of us."

"Oh, Grady." She cradled his face, scruffy with the beard he'd shave off in the morning, probably with her razor. "Artists can make war, too, only they make war on the spirit. I've learned that the hard way, and I—"

"Hang on, Sapphire. Who are we talking about? If someone's been crushing your artistic spirit, I want names and locations. I'm a welder. I have muscle mass."

She smiled at that. She wanted him to be her defender, her knight in shining armor, but others had claimed that position and shown themselves to be unworthy. She'd lost the ability to believe in knights and flashing swords.

Drawing in a breath, she took stock. She'd started the conversation and she couldn't leave it dangling. Besides, they were supposed to go to dinner at her parents' house and all sorts of personal info could pop up during that encounter. "I have a weakness for creative guys."

He caught her hands and nibbled on her fingers. "My good luck."

"The first one was Gregory. I fell madly in love with him when we were in high school. He turned out to be gay."

"Sapphire, I'm so sorry, but obviously, I don't have that issue."

"Then there was Jeremy, who seemed to mean well and was insanely talented but *so* undependable. He couldn't remember appointments, my birthday or when the rent was due. He was more child than man. Living with him was exhausting and I ended up caretaking instead of doing my work. He cried when I broke up with him and I felt awful, but he wasn't an adult."

"You don't need someone like that."

"I figured that out and moved on to Edgar, also a talented artist. Neat and focused. But ultimately, so jealous of my talent that he started undermining me and came damn near to destroying my confidence."

"Dear God." Grady stroked her hair. "That's criminal. Where is he now? I'd be happy to rearrange his face for you."

"I don't know and I wouldn't tell you if I did. I don't want you arrested for assaulting someone who's not worth it."

His voice was low and dangerous. "I could be in and out without leaving a trace. Thunder Mountain boys know things."

"I still wouldn't tell you where he is." But it worried her that he cared that much. She didn't want him to become invested.

"I could ask Rosie. She knows every blessed thing that goes on in this town."

"Don't ask her. I decided long ago to let sleeping dogs lie."

He combed her hair away from her face. "Is that it, then? Your collection of slimy artists?"

"One more. Cal. Women loved him. I loved him. I didn't figure out until months into the relationship that he was sleeping with every attractive woman who gave him a second glance. When I confronted him, he claimed that such behavior fueled his creativity. He said artists couldn't be held to the same conventional standard as other people."

"That's bullshit."

She sighed. "I know, but Cal was the final straw."

He didn't say anything for a while. When he finally spoke, his tone was wary. "So what's this all about, then?"

"This?"

"You, me, getting naked. *This*."

"We're attracted to each other."

"Yeah, and?"

"At first I decided not to give in to that attraction, but…"

"But you did." He reached over and switched on the bedside lamp. "Even though Cal was the final straw." He turned back to her, a question in his brown eyes. "Does that mean you're reevaluating?"

Her stomach hurt. She couldn't lie to him, but because he'd asked the question, he probably wouldn't like the answer.

His expression closed down. "You're not reevaluating."

"No." She swallowed. "I just—"

"Wanted some good sex." He turned away and swung his legs over the edge of the bed.

"Didn't you?"

"You know I did. But I didn't realize my days were numbered." He stood and pulled on the robe.

"Grady, we don't even live in the same town."

He pulled the robe across his chest as best he could and tied the sash with an angry jerk of his wrist. "And that's an issue we'd have to deal with. Maybe we're not destined to have more than a few nights of wild sex. But it never occurred to me that you'd already decided that's all we'd have. Now I know." He started for the door.

"Where are you going?"

"To eat ice cream. Double-chocolate fudge brownie is my second favorite." He left the room.

Flopping back on the pillow, she stared at the ceiling. She'd certainly made a mess of that, hadn't she? She could have kept her big mouth shut and they'd still be cuddled in this bed.

But now she knew something more about him, too. While she'd ruled out getting seriously involved, he hadn't. He'd thought that was a possibility, even if it might be a remote one. He hadn't seen their geographic distance as being an insurmountable barrier. If they'd continued to get along this week, they would have had this confrontation eventually.

The freezer door opened and then the silverware drawer rattled. He must have the ice cream and a spoon. By now it was too cold to sit out on the porch. The scrape of a chair told her he'd stayed at the kitchen table. She didn't like to think of him in there brooding.

She climbed out of bed and put on her robe. She'd wounded him, and even though that had never been her goal, she needed to say she was sorry.

He glanced up when she walked into the kitchen. "Hey."

"Hey, yourself." She couldn't read his expression, which was probably his intent. She got a spoon out of the drawer and sat across from him. "Can I have a bite?"

"You bet. Your ice cream." He shoved the carton across the table.

"Thanks." She took a spoonful and pushed it back over.

He sent it sailing back. "You keep it for a while. I ate too fast. Brain freeze."

She probably shouldn't laugh at a time like this, but it was funny.

"I know, right?" He rubbed his bristly chin. "I've been eating ice cream by myself since I was two. You'd think I'd have the hang of it by now."

"Maybe you wanted to freeze your brain for a while."

"Maybe."

"Grady, I'm really sorry if I misled you. I didn't mean to." She did her best not to stare at him but he was extremely stare-worthy, with his tousled hair, roguish beard and the swath of muscled chest the robe couldn't cover.

"See, the way you're looking at me right now is part of the problem. That look gets me hot."

"Sorry." She dropped her gaze from the hunk across the table to the hunks of chocolate in the ice cream.

"But the thing is, I like getting hot when there's a chance I can do something about it."

She glanced up. "Oh?"

"Could be that brain freeze helps a person think better, because I've been doing some of that." He blew out a breath. "I have to take some responsibility for the situation. You gave me no reason to think you wanted more than sex from me. Just the opposite. I could tell you wanted to avoid anything mushy."

"Which sounds pretty coldhearted, like all that interests me is your package and I don't care about you as a person."

"I know that's not true." He smiled. "And it's okay to be enamored of my cock, just like it's okay for you to look at me as if you need it right this minute."

Heat spiraled down between her thighs and she was ready again.

Resting his corded arms on the table, he leaned forward, a

gleam in his brown eyes. "Do you need it right this minute, Sapphire?"

Her heart pounded loud enough that he could probably hear the staccato beat. She nodded.

"As it happens, I'm prepared for that contingency." He pulled a condom out of his pocket and pushed away from the table. "Come on over here, sweet lady. Let's try that position again, the one where you think it's difficult for you to come."

Trembling with need, she left her chair and walked around the table. There was nothing atmospheric or subtle this time. The overhead light was on, leaving nothing to the imagination.

Hooking a finger in her sash, he pulled it open. "You're shaking."

"Uh-huh."

"Scared?"

"No."

"Good, because you never have to be afraid of me." Spanning her waist with both hands, he hoisted her to the edge of the table. "I'll never hurt you."

"I know."

"No, you don't. But that's okay. I'll make a believer of you." He moved between her spread thighs. "To start with, I'm not going to kiss you, because I'd give you whisker burn."

She smoothed a hand over his beard. "I don't care."

"I do. Now grab on to my shoulders, because I'm coming in." Holding her gaze, he slid slowly forward. "You're very wet."

"Mmm." She couldn't talk. She was too busy absorbing this moment when he filled her and locked himself in tight. His eyes had darkened to the color of rich chocolate.

"That'll make it even easier. We're gonna tilt back a little." Holding her hips, he leaned toward her. "Wrap your legs around me. Perfect. Now hang on." He began to thrust, easily at first, then faster and faster yet.

The intense friction made her gasp and within seconds it made her come. Her cries echoed off the hard surfaces as he kept pumping at that same rapid speed. She came again, and this time so did he. Bellowing at the top of his lungs, he closed his eyes and drove in tight. The strong pulse of his cock blended with the ripples of her climax to create the most dramatic orgasm she'd ever had.

Slowly, he opened his eyes and grinned. "Now, that's what I call a good time."

Unexpected tears pricked her eyelids. "Thank you."

"You're welcome. You got something in your eyes? They're watering."

She sniffed. "Must be dust. I'm fine. But I wasn't thanking you for the sex, which was amazing. I was thanking you because you've forgiven me."

"Nothing to forgive. I was missing some critical info and made a wrong assumption. Now I get it and we're good."

She wasn't sure what that meant but she wasn't going to ask him to clarify. "We should go back to bed." She glanced at the kitchen clock. "It's past three."

"And I just heard Gandalf. I probably woke him up when I yelled."

She smiled. "I liked it when you yelled. Very manly."

"Except now we have a crying cat." He eased away from her and disposed of the condom in the kitchen trash. "I'd better go in there and settle him down." He tied his robe and had started out of the kitchen when he turned back. "I didn't put away the—"

"Never mind. I'll do it. Go see your cat."

"Meet you in bed."

"Okay." After he left, she picked up the ice-cream carton. He'd loved her so fast and so well that the ice cream hadn't had time to melt much. She put the lid back on and tucked it in the freezer.

She'd never known a man like Grady. When he was upset, he didn't shout or bang around or sulk. Instead he ate ice cream and thought about things. He'd promised never to hurt her. He'd also vowed that eventually she'd believe in him.

They were beautiful words and she'd certainly heard beautiful words before. Creative men were usually good with them. Was she wrong to think Grady was different? Probably. She'd been wrong before. But for now, the storm had passed. He appeared willing to enjoy what they had for the time they had it. That made her happy.

10

GRADY SLEPT LIKE the dead until Sapphire's alarm went off at six. She reached over and shut it off. Then she lay very still, breathing lightly. He was about to find out if she was a morning person.

He hoped so, and not because he had the woody of the century. If he and Sapphire expected to get showered and out the door with Gandalf in tow before seven, they'd have to move it, and soon.

His interest in her attitude toward mornings went beyond whether she enjoyed sex at sunrise. He loved mornings. If she didn't and they worked through all the other crap she'd thrown at him last night, they'd still have that minor issue of different body clocks.

His last girlfriend had hated mornings with a passion. It hadn't been the only reason they'd broken up, but it had been a factor. He was already half in love with Sapphire, though, and a body-clock misalignment wouldn't change that. Nothing would change that after she'd taken the initiative to come into the kitchen and smooth things over.

They'd been well and truly smoothed. He'd accept part of the blame for the blow to his ego. He'd sensed something had her spooked and now he knew what it was. Her past experience had taught her not to trust any man who created things for a living.

He even understood her attitude. That didn't mean he believed that she was only in it for the sex. Maybe she was now, but she wouldn't be for long if he had anything to say about it.

"Grady?" Her voice was thick with sleep.

"What?"

"We should get up."

"I know." Maybe *not* a morning person. Oh, well.

"But I have a problem."

"You don't want to get up?"

"That's not the problem. I woke up from a dream of having sex with you and it left me sort of...achy. I was wondering if—"

"Say no more." He reached for the box of condoms. "I've got you covered." He didn't linger over the niceties. This morning his beard would scrape the rust off a tailpipe. But his cock was easily as hard as one when he sank into her slick channel.

She hadn't been kidding. That must have been some dream. A few quick strokes and she orgasmed, which allowed him to do the same. Breathing hard, he pushed the damp hair back from her face. "There you go."

"Thanks." She smiled up at him. "Good morning."

"And so it is." He kissed her lightly without making contact with his beard. "I'm using your razor, if that's okay."

"Go ahead. Take whatever you need. I'll go upstairs to shower and meet you in the kitchen. I have some yogurt in the fridge, so help yourself. We'll get coffee at the barn."

"What about tuna?"

"I have a couple more cans in the pantry. Can opener is on the counter. He'll get dry food later at the barn."

"Got it." They each left the bed without any more conversation. She didn't put on a robe and neither did he.

She grabbed some undies from the dresser and clothes from the closet before hurrying upstairs. Because he was a guy, he watched her running around the room naked and was so glad they'd had a quickie before starting the day.

Once she left, he tossed the robes over a chair and pulled up the covers on the bed. No sense making it when they'd be rolling around in it again tonight. For a little while last night, that had been in doubt, but a woman didn't wake up and ask for sex if she intended to send a guy packing. At least, this one wouldn't.

In the kitchen, he located the tuna, opened a can and found a bowl like the one she'd used for the first batch. When she'd first explained her problem with artists as partners and he'd gone off to the kitchen to lick his wounds and eat ice cream, he'd considered setting up sleeping quarters in the barn. What a stupid move that would have been.

His younger self would have done something like that to make a point. Thank God he'd reconsidered as he'd spooned in the ice cream and given himself brain freeze. He wasn't like those guys who'd treated her so rotten, but going off to sulk every night in the Art Barn might convince her that he was exactly like them.

When she'd walked into the kitchen and grabbed a spoon, that gesture had helped get his head on straight, too. She liked him. She craved his body. Maybe she'd lumped him in with those other schmucks, but he could fix that. At least, he could if he didn't create a rift between them by reacting like an asshole.

Then he'd caught her looking at him as if she'd gone a week without candy and his dick was made of caramel. Only an idiot would turn away from that. He wasn't always as smart as he should be, but he'd figured that out real quick.

She wanted him, but she didn't trust him or herself. Given her history, that wasn't surprising. He had a week to show her that he wasn't cut from the same cloth, that he wasn't gay, juvenile, a jealous bastard or a cheating one. A week wasn't much time, but it was what he had.

Gandalf was overjoyed to see him. The cat seemed more excited about Grady's presence than the tuna, which was touching. So Grady stroked him and encouraged him to eat. Once he'd buried his nose in the bowl, Grady turned on the shower and hopped in.

A thump a few seconds later told him Gandalf was showering with him yet again. He turned to look at the cat. "That's unnatural. You're not supposed to do that."

Gandalf regarded him steadily.

"No, really. Cats don't like water. Didn't you get the memo?"

Ignoring the shower pelting down on him, Gandalf walked over and started licking Grady's leg.

Laughing, Grady finished his shower quickly. Once again he had to towel off the cat and himself. He piled the towels in a corner because everything would have to be washed. While he tackled his beard with Sapphire's pink razor, Gandalf hopped up on the sink, sat down and started purring.

"I'm getting kinda attached to you, cat." He met Gandalf's blue-eyed gaze in the mirror. "Liam's moving out as soon as he renovates that house and marries Hope. I could use some company. What do you say?"

Gandalf made the half-purr, half-meow noise that was definitely a response to the question.

"I'll consider that a yes. But first I have to make sure I'm not taking you away from some family who loves you. If we can't locate anybody in a week, you can hit the road with me, buddy. Sound good?"

The cat's sharp meow made him grin. "Hey, I'm excited about the idea, too. It's a deal." He finished up with the razor. It wasn't the closest shave he'd ever had, but at least he no longer looked like a vagrant. "Stay put for a bit, okay? I'll be back to get you." He left, closing the cat in. Gandalf heartily protested. "I know. I promise you won't have to stay there all day."

Not long afterward, dressed and fueled up with raspberry yogurt, he came back to the bathroom and scooped the cat into his arms. They were even slightly ahead of schedule, so he'd had time to go out front and retrieve the condom he'd thrown in the bushes.

Sapphire had loaned him a blue buffalo-plaid shirt that was way too big to have been hers. But Gandalf had spent the night lying on his shirt, and wearing it would spread hair all over the house. This one likely had belonged to one of the scumbags she'd told him about. He wore it, but he'd change at his first opportunity. He didn't want her associating him with that bunch.

Gandalf began to shake when Grady climbed into the passenger seat of Sapphire's purple truck. "He's scared."

"I'm not surprised." Sapphire started the engine. "He doesn't know what's going to happen to him." She looked over at Gandalf. "It'll be okay, kitty. You're safe with us."

Grady liked the way she'd said that—*safe with us*—like they were Team Gandalf. In a way they were. They'd worked together on this deal, although she had the resources and he'd simply been the support staff. "Do you have a plan for this guy?"

"A potential plan." She backed the truck out of the drive. "See what you think. We'll close him in the office and give him some dry food while we take care of the ferals. Then we'll take him over to the shelter for a quick vet check. Assuming he's fine, I'll contact the co-op members to see if they're okay with him staying at the barn while we put the word out and see if he belongs anywhere."

"Think they'll be okay with that?"

"I'm sure they will since we've talked about having a barn cat eventually, but I want to ask first."

"And if no one shows up to claim him?" He suddenly realized she might assume Gandalf would become a permanent fixture at the Art Barn. He wouldn't blame her if she wanted to keep him. He was a great cat.

She glanced at him with a smile in her eyes. "You get first dibs."

"Thanks." He blew out a breath. "Selfishly, I hope no one

claims him." He stroked Gandalf's soft coat. Thanks to a couple of showers, it was looking pretty good.

"I doubt they will. I think you have yourself a cat."

"Then I need to get him some stuff today. A brush, for one thing. And his own food and water dish. And a litter box and bed. I guess if he's going to stay in the barn this week, he'll be there by himself at night." Grady scratched behind the cat's ears and murmured whatever soothing things came into his head. He wasn't crazy about leaving the cat alone in the barn all through the night but he also wanted to be with Sapphire. He finally came up with a compromise. "How about if I work on Rosie's sculpture for a while tonight?"

"Do you want to cancel going over to my mom and dad's for dinner?"

"I forgot about that. No, I want to go. I could come here afterward, though."

She gave him a knowing look. "I'm sure Gandalf would be appreciative."

"I'll lose some time today buying his stuff and picking up my clothes from Ben and Molly's, so working tonight could make that up. Which reminds me, do you think he'll be all right while I run those errands?"

Her lips twitched as if she wanted to laugh. "Grady, he'll be *fine*. If you're like this with a cat, Lord help you if you have a kid."

"Am I being overprotective?"

"Just a little. It's cute, actually."

"Ugh." He scowled at the cat. "Gandalf, you're gonna have to man up, because I won't be coddling you anymore, buddy. I can't have the lady calling me *cute*. I'm looking for descriptions like *hot*, *ripped* and *sexy as hell*."

She lost it. As her laughter spilled out, he got a kick out of her pink cheeks and sparkling eyes. Her outfit sparkled today, too. Her blouse and skirt were dotted with sequins and her long earrings glittered with multicolored crystals that drew his attention to her graceful neck.

Good thing he had an armful of cat or he'd be tempted to lean over and kiss her there. "Damn, but you're beautiful, Sapphire."

Her breath caught. "Thank you." She looked over at him and for a brief moment soft yearning filled her eyes.

She wants to believe I mean it. That I'm not some selfish bastard who says things like that and then acts like a jerk.

Then her expression changed and a teasing light replaced the glow that had been there. She returned her attention to the road. "You're not so bad yourself."

He could guess what was coming next.

"I'd go so far as to say you're hot, ripped and sexy as hell."

"You're welcome to come up with your own words. Those were just suggestions to start you off."

"All right." She drummed her fingers on the steering wheel. "Ogle-worthy and lickable eye candy."

"Not bad."

"An orgasmic fantasy, a walking wet dream, a—"

"That'll do. You're making Gandalf uncomfortable."

"He understands English?"

"No, but he's sitting on my lap."

"Oh." She smirked. "I see."

"Fortunately, you can't see, because the cat's hiding the evidence." As they approached the Art Barn, he noticed a tan pickup parked beside his truck. "So who's here?"

"That belongs to George Reavis. He's our wood-carver. He didn't make it over yesterday because he and his wife took a quick trip to see the grandkids. Now that George is here, we should have the whole contingent today." She opened her door. "You coming in?"

"Go ahead. Gandalf and I will be along shortly, after decompression happens."

She looked contrite. "Sorry."

"Hey, don't ever be sorry that you got a rise out of me. You're a lusty lady and I treasure that. I plan to treasure it even more tonight."

"Good."

"It will be. Now head on in and start on the food bowls."

"Okay." Bending down, she dipped her head under the brim of his hat and kissed him lightly on the mouth. Then she drew back and smiled. "See you in a minute."

He would have pulled her close for a more satisfying kiss but couldn't risk letting go of the cat. He settled for a mild protest. "You can do better than that."

"I didn't want to make things worse."

"A little bit of tongue never hurt anybody."

"You're a scoundrel, Grady Magee." Pushing his hat up and cupping the back of his head, she angled her mouth over his and thrust her tongue inside.

Then she proceeded to kiss the living daylights out of him. It was all he could do to stay calm and hold on to Gandalf without squeezing the poor animal.

After sweetly torturing him for a good long while, she finally lifted her mouth away. "Did you like that better?"

"Much." He dragged in air.

"How's your lap?"

"Painful, but I'm not gonna mention it."

Leaning back, she gazed at him. "Better not. Hang on. You're wearing my lipstick." She grabbed her purse from behind her seat, then dug out a tissue and wiped his mouth. After settling his hat where it belonged, she peeked in the rearview mirror and wiped her mouth, too. "That needs a do-over."

By the time she'd reapplied her lipstick, he'd recovered enough to leave the truck. "Crisis is over. I can walk in with you now."

"Then I'll get your door." She came around to the passenger side and helped him out.

Happily, Gandalf didn't sink his claws into the plaid shirt

when Grady stepped down to the pavement. Maybe the cat recognized the place and wasn't too worried about going inside.

"So give me some background on George," Grady said as they neared the building. "I'm trying to keep everybody straight."

"He's retired military, about sixty, has a bushy white beard, a great laugh and a little potbelly."

"You just described Santa Claus."

"He used to have a gig as Santa but now he only dresses up for our holiday events at the barn. I've known him for about five years. We did craft shows together and that's when we came up with the idea for the co-op."

"His carving's really nice. I was thinking of getting something for my mom, maybe the heron. She loves waterbirds."

"I'm sure he'd be honored." She held the door open for him. "We're still ahead of schedule. Let's close Gandalf in the office with a bowl of dry food and go say hello to George before we feed the ferals. I know he's eager to meet you."

"Sounds great."

Moments later Gandalf was munching away and didn't even look up when Grady and Sapphire slipped out, closing the office door behind them.

"He might just be happy to be out of the bathroom," Grady said as they walked down the barn aisle to George's spot.

"I hear the *trip-trap* of feet!" boomed a voice from the last stall on the left, right across from Grady's.

"I'm bringing you a visitor," Sapphire called back.

A Santa look-alike appeared in the aisle holding a knife and a piece of wood. He even wore the frameless half-glasses Santa favored. "I'm gonna take a wild guess that this is Grady Magee."

"In the flesh." Grady stepped forward and offered his hand. "I admire your work."

"And I yours." He transferred the knife to his shirt pocket and shook Grady's hand. "Thanks for coming up to our event! I'm a huge fan. So's my wife, Eloise. We have one of your smaller pieces in our living room."

"That's great to hear. Thank you." Grady smiled. "I've been thinking about your heron for my mother. She'd love it."

"Good eye, son. That heron was a bitch to carve, but I'm mighty proud of it. I took a peek at what you're working on. Wolves, right?"

"It's for Rosie, his foster mom," Sapphire said. "It's a surprise, so we're all sworn to secrecy."

"I won't tell. Rosie and Herb are good people. A credit to the community."

"I'll go along with that." Grady rolled his shoulders. The stupid shirt had begun to itch. It hadn't before, so he thought it might be all in his head, but he wanted it off. "Listen, I need to run a quick errand, so I'll leave you two and be back in a little while. Great meeting you, George. And if you'd set that heron aside for me, I'd be obliged."

"I'll put a sold sign on it right now. See you soon. I look forward to sharing the workspace with you."

"Same here."

Sapphire glanced at him. "I'll walk you out."

"No need." He gave her a quick smile. "I'll be back before you know it." It was just a dumb shirt, but it was bugging the hell out of him. He moved swiftly toward the front door.

Sapphire kept up. "You're acting twitchy. What's up?"

"I have to pick up my stuff from Ben and Molly's sometime, so I might as well do it now. Then that part will be taken care of. And I can return this shirt to you."

She followed him out the door. "No rush on that."

"Yeah, there is. Whose was it?"

"Does it matter?"

"Just morbid curiosity."

"Jeremy's."

When he reached his truck, he turned to face her. "Jeremy was the immature slob, right?"

"Right."

"And you dumped him, so the shirt means nothing." Or so he tried to tell himself.

She took a deep breath. "That's not quite true."

Oh, God. She still loved him.

"There's a reason I kept the shirt, which he forgot that he left at my place. So typical."

"What reason?" He braced himself for a sob story about how Jeremy was bad for her but she couldn't forget him and she slept in his shirt every night except this last one when they'd boinked each other senseless.

"I keep it to remind myself never to get involved with someone like him again."

He was somewhat relieved but still not in a happy place. "So now I'm wearing this negative reminder."

"It really was the only thing in the house that would fit you! I worried about offering it but thought it would only be temporary. I wasn't ever going to tell you where it had come from."

"Have you kept anything else? From the other guys?"

She hesitated.

"Never mind. It's none of my business."

"Yeah, it is, now that I loaned you the shirt. I just— Nobody knows I've kept reminders, not even Amethyst. It's my own silly way of trying to stay on track. I didn't keep anything from Gregory. He was trying to deny he was gay, poor guy. That was biology, not a character flaw. I started keeping reminders when Jeremy left his shirt."

"And the next guy?"

"Edgar was a wine snob and made fun of people who didn't drink the best, like me, for example. He left a bottle of wine worth about two hundred bucks. I've never opened it but I keep it so I can remember what arrogance looks like."

"What about the cheater?"

"I kept the sentimental card he sent with his Valentine's Day roses. The woman who works at the floral shop is a friend from high school. We went out for drinks one night and after a few too many she told me he'd sent the same message and bouquet to three girlfriends that day."

The shirt itched even worse now. "Then you need this back." He took off his hat and laid it on the fender of his truck. After undoing a couple of buttons, he pulled it over his head and gave it to her. The morning breeze was chilly but he'd never been so glad to get rid of a piece of clothing in his life.

"Grady, I apologize for the shirt."

He shrugged. "Like you said, I needed something and this was what you had." He gazed at her. "Sounds like you've put a lot of effort into deciding what you don't want."

"I suppose."

"Have you put any thought into what you do want?"

She seemed taken aback by the question.

"It's another way to approach the problem." Grabbing her by the shoulders, he gave her a quick kiss. Then he put on his hat and unlocked his truck. When he drove away, she was standing in the same spot staring after him, exactly as she'd done three weeks ago.

He might be tempting fate to make a prediction, but she'd confided some important information in the past twelve hours. He might be ahead of where he'd been three weeks ago.

11

SAPPHIRE HAD PLENTY to think about as she maneuvered through her day. Fortunately, George was in charge of handling any customers who came in, which left her free to go with Grady to the shelter for Gandalf's vet check. The cat got a perfect bill of health and the shelter set their pet alert program in motion. If anyone in the general area had reported losing a gray long-haired male, the shelter would hear about it.

She'd texted all the co-op members and they were fine with having Gandalf as a guest for the next week. She'd warned them that he likely wouldn't be permanent. But a barn cat was still a good idea and she hoped eventually Fred would be socialized enough to take on the job.

Grady had fetched his things and was dressed in a faded blue Western shirt instead of the buffalo-plaid one that had caused so much trouble. She'd known that loaning it to him was a mistake. She hadn't wanted to be reminded of Jeremy when she looked at Grady any more than he'd wanted to serve as a reminder.

He had a sixth sense about things. She'd counted on him wearing it for a couple of hours until he'd picked up his clothes. Turned out a couple of hours had been a long enough time to create a problem.

Then again, that tense conversation might have been necessary. He'd made an excellent point. In her determination not to repeat the same pattern, she'd focused only on the negatives she was avoiding. She hadn't thought at all about the positives she was seeking.

That was tricky because her previous lovers had possessed good qualities, too, ones that had attracted her in the first place. She'd conveniently pushed away thoughts about those because, hey, when a girl broke up with someone, she wanted to think of him as totally evil, right?

Creativity was the real bugaboo for her, the one that set off warning bells. Jeremy had been creative but irresponsible. Edgar had been creative but arrogant. Cal had been creative but fickle. The one trait they had in common, the behavior that drew her like a bee to pollen, was their ability to enrich the world with their art.

Maybe she hadn't focused on what she wanted because she knew subconsciously that she still craved a man with that magical gift, required it, in fact, before he was interesting to her. In her experience, imagination had always been linked to a fatal flaw. She hadn't discovered Grady's, but she had to believe he had one. It just hadn't shown itself yet.

Whatever her personal misgivings might be about him, the co-op members obviously loved having him around. Inspiration hummed through the building. Usually, the artists wandered around chatting with each other and generally wasting time, but today there had been none of that. At the end of the day when they gathered in the office for a last cup of coffee and the cookies Arlene had brought, everyone thanked Grady for energizing them with his work ethic.

Grady shrugged and looked mildly embarrassed by the praise. "Just trying to set a good example for the cat."

"I believe it," George said. "Gandalf kept an eagle eye on you all afternoon from the top of that cat tree."

"Yeah, that was a great purchase." Sapphire had been a little startled when Grady had gone for cat-care essentials and had come back with a six-foot multitiered playground for Gandalf in addition to the smaller items.

Occupying a far corner of Grady's work area, it allowed Gandalf to observe his hero without being anywhere near the torch. He was wary of the instrument but clearly wanted to keep Grady in sight. The carpeted structure let him do that.

"Now's a good time to vote on how we handle having a cat here at night," Sapphire said. "We can give him the run of the place or close him in the office."

"I vote we give him the run of the place." George grabbed another cookie. "We all store our supplies when we go home, so there's not much he could get into and I'll bet he'd rather be free than cooped up."

"I feel the same." Arlene reached down and petted Gandalf, who'd followed everyone into the office. "He's a good cat. Let him roam." She glanced around. "Everybody agree?" They all did.

"That's settled, then. " Sapphire drained her coffee cup. "I need to load up the food dishes for the ferals. Any questions about the event? We're only three days away, so now's the time to talk about anything we've forgotten."

"Now that I think about it," Grady said, "we should close Gandalf in the office during the event. He might be okay with the crowd, but I don't want to take a chance he'd get spooked and run off."

"Good call," George said. "For one thing, we'll have little kids here. We don't know how he'd react to them."

"Then we'll make sure he's tucked away before we open the doors. Anything else?" When nobody spoke, she gave a quick little nod. "Okay, then. See you all tomorrow."

Everyone left but Grady. She glanced at him, not quite sure where they stood. They'd had very few moments alone today and he hadn't used any of those moments to talk about this morning's incident. "Want to help me feed?"

"I do." Laying his hat on the counter, he moved in close and rested his hands on her shoulders. "But I desperately need a kiss." He massaged her shoulders gently. "Think that could be arranged?"

"Absolutely." Her pulse quickened as it always did the minute he put those talented hands on her. So he was ready to continue what they'd started. Hallelujah. She wound her arms around his neck. "But the cats are out there waiting and we're due at my parents' in an hour."

"And I need a shower and a change of clothes, so I'll make it quick." His mouth hovered over hers. "Semiquick." He touched down and lightly tasted her lips. Then with a low moan, he gripped her shoulders and delved deep. The erotic movement of his tongue told her what he really wanted.

So did she. Tunneling her fingers through his hair, she whimpered and tried to wiggle closer, but he held her fast, keeping their bodies apart.

Gasping, he lifted his head. "If I let myself settle against your hot body, guaranteed we'll do more than kiss and we don't have time."

"Are you saying you brought—"

"I told you I'd always be prepared." He pressed kisses at the corners of her mouth. "Which means I have a condom in my pocket, but we're not gonna use it."

She gulped for air. "No, we're not."

"No matter how much my cock aches for you."

"I ache for you, too."

"That helps." His chuckle sounded strained. "Sort of. No, it doesn't. God, how I want to—" A sharp, demanding meow stopped him in midsentence.

They both glanced down.

Gandalf sat primly, front paws together and fluffy tail wrapped around his feet. He stared up at them with his sky blue eyes, blinked once and uttered the same quick meow.

"Oh, boy." Sapphire couldn't help laughing. "I don't know if you got that, but the message is clear to me."

"He's hungry?"

"I doubt it. Last time I checked, he had dry food in his dish. I'm guessing he wants you to quit fooling around with me and pay attention to him."

"Really?"

"Really. They get jealous, too, you know." She'd meant it as kind of a joke, but his expression told her he hadn't taken it that way. Whoops.

"Sapphire, I wasn't jealous." Then he blew out a breath. "No, that's a damn lie. I didn't like thinking you'd kept an old boy-friend's shirt. If I'm being totally honest, I still don't like it, even though it's supposed to be there as a warning. It's like *he's* there, and worse yet, he's one of the reasons you're afraid to get close to me."

She swallowed. "Yes, he is."

"That's not fair, you know, to judge me based on what an-other guy—"

"Three other guys."

"I don't care if it was twenty." His gaze intensified. "I'm me, an individual, yet you've lumped me in with them and I don't like it."

"I don't blame you."

Gandalf meowed again, but this time more plaintively.

With a heavy sigh, Grady rubbed the back of his neck. "You know what? We need to feed those cats."

"I do, but you don't have to. I'll give you my house key. You can go back and take your time cleaning up."

"Think we need a breather?"

"Maybe."

"First I'll give Gandalf a nice brushing. Then I'll take you up on that offer. Come on, cat. I left your brush in your tree house." He started out of the kitchen and Gandalf trotted after him, tail in the air like a victory flag.

"I'll leave my key on the desk in the office."

He kept walking. "Thanks," he called over his shoulder. "See you soon."

Although she felt icky and disoriented by the exchange, she forced herself to get out the bowls, fill them quickly and layer them into the basket. She pulled her keys from her purse on the kitchen counter, then unhooked the one for the front door and laid it on the desk as she went through the office.

Fred was there with the other cats when she set out the bowls. After last night's episode, he didn't want to show up late. Apparently, he hadn't appreciated waiting for his food and was determined to claim a bowl before another cat edged him out again.

All eleven looked healthy. She always eyeballed each one during feeding time to make sure some issue hadn't cropped up, but they moved well and ate with enthusiasm. She hadn't fed them alone since Grady had arrived two nights ago. Funny how quickly she'd become used to having him there. The sound of his truck leaving the parking lot added to her funky mood.

Although they hadn't exactly fought, the spontaneous joy they'd first enjoyed might be gone temporarily—or maybe for good. He could always decide she wasn't worth the angst and back off completely but he probably wouldn't. The sex was too good. In spite of everything, she couldn't wait to be alone with him again and she knew he felt the same way.

Seeing her folks' reaction to him would be interesting. Her dad tended to like everyone, but her mom was pickier. Gregory had been the only boyfriend of hers she'd warmed to. When he'd finally accepted that he was gay, she'd been as supportive as his own folks had been. But her mom had never quite accepted any of the three guys who'd come along after Gregory.

Sapphire had become so absorbed in her thoughts that she hadn't noticed that the cats had begun to leave. It seemed nobody craved attention tonight. By the time she became aware, they were all headed back for the woods...all except Fred. He'd finished all the food in his bowl and he crouched there staring at her.

"Hey, Fred," she said softly. "How's it going?" Then she used a technique one of the shelter volunteers had taught her. She blinked. That was supposed to indicate friendly intentions. "You're a handsome boy, Freddie." She blinked again.

The cat blinked back.

She gave a slight gasp. "Oh, Fred, it makes me very happy that we exchanged blinks." She tried it again but an owl hooted nearby.

Fred tensed. Then he turned and bounded back to the shelter of the woods.

"That's okay, Freddie. You need to protect yourself against owls. Just not against me." Feeling triumphant, she collected the bowls and hurried into the barn. In the midst of washing them, she heard a cat purring. Sure enough, Gandalf had heard her come in and had decided to join her.

"I hate to tell you this, cat, but Grady's not with me." She finished cleaning the bowls and dried her hands. "But he plans to come back to see you later tonight." Crouching down, she held out her hand.

Gandalf came over and gave her a good sniff before bumping his head against her hand in an obvious bid to be petted.

She obliged him. "Any port in a storm, huh, Gandalf? Listen, kitty, I'd love to stay here and love on you, but I have places to go and people to see." After one last scratch, she stood.

The cat meowed in protest.

At least, that was what it sounded like to her. "Yeah, well, that's life, kiddo. Sometimes you're rolling in clover and sometimes you're wallowing in muck. Considering the fact that you've captured Grady's heart, I'd put you in the clover category." She picked up her purse and headed to the door. Gandalf followed her, so she exited quickly so he wouldn't dash out.

On the drive to her house she glanced at the dashboard clock. Running late. Locating her phone in her purse, she pulled it out and called her mom. "Hey, Grady and I are about fifteen minutes behind schedule."

Her mom laughed. "So he said when he called."

"He called you?"

"Not long ago. Must have found our number somewhere in your house. He said you were out feeding the cats and would need a little time to get cleaned up before you two came over. Is that code for having a quickie?"

"Mom!"

"Whether it is or not, I appreciate his call. He sounds nice on the phone."

"He is nice, but that doesn't change the fact that he's an artist."

"Has it occurred to you that your father and I are both artists?"

"I, um— Well, sure you are, but—"

"In case you haven't noticed, we've managed to stumble through twenty-nine years of marriage without killing each other. If artists are incapable of having a decent relationship, how do you explain that?"

The conversation was giving her a headache. "You're both obviously exceptions to the rule. I just pulled into the driveway, so I need to go. See you soon!"

"Don't rush, dear. I remember when your father and I started dating and we couldn't get enough of—"

"Bye, Mom." She so didn't want to hear whatever her mother had been about to confide. That topic hadn't been discussed when she'd dated Jeremy, Edgar or Cal. Why now? Had Grady won her over with a single phone call?

When she walked into the house, Grady was sitting there in the robe she'd loaned him. "I thought you'd be dressed."

"I bought us a little time for makeup sex."

"Makeup sex?" She put her purse on the table by the door. "We didn't have a fight."

He stood and came toward her. "No, but I said some things I shouldn't have. You have a right to handle your life however you want and I was out of line to suggest any different."

"And you have a right to be jealous and upset because you ended up wearing an old boyfriend's shirt this morning. I don't blame you in the least. That can't be pleasant, especially for someone with your level of testosterone."

Stopping in his tracks, he stared at her. "My *what*?"

"Testosterone level. You're extremely virile. That's part of what makes your sculptures so exciting. Virile men are usually territorial like wolves."

"Wolves? Hey, I don't—"

"Last night we talked about my other lovers, but it was fairly abstract. This morning you had to wear the garment, or the skin, in a way, of someone who had encroached on what you temporarily claim as yours. Naturally, you got a little snarly."

"Oh, my God." He grinned at her. "You're too much."

"I happen to think I'm on target!"

"I happen to think you're adorable." He gathered her close. "We used to have ten minutes for this but after that testosterone speech we only have about eight. I might have to do it with most of your clothes on."

Although he was exciting the hell out of her, she pretended that she didn't need what he was offering. "Grady, this isn't necessary. We should just get ready and go."

"It is necessary." He edged her over to the sofa. "We can accomplish this right here."

"You're making it sound like a chore to be completed."

"Believe me, it's no chore." He guided her down to the sofa and urged her back on the cushions. "I've decided I like the wolf analogy you came up with, after all. Since I was subjected to wearing the skin of my rival, I need to reassert my dominance." He pushed up her skirt and pulled down her panties.

"This position is awkward." But her heart was beating like a snare drum.

"No, it's not." He worked one of the leg openings of her panties over her foot. "That does it." He stroked her and slid a finger into her. "I think you might be more interested in this makeup sex than you're letting on."

"My mother wanted to know if you called because we were going to have a quickie."

A condom appeared, no doubt tucked in the pocket of his borrowed robe. "Smart woman, your mother." He rolled it on and moved between her trembling thighs. "The alpha wolf is taking control. Just go with it." And he drove into her with all the authority of the leader of the pack.

She responded with a moan of ecstasy. She'd known from the moment she'd walked in to find him wearing the black robe that barely covered his magnificent physique that this would be the final outcome. Whether he called it makeup sex or alpha sex didn't matter.

Nothing mattered but the firm thrust of his cock and the orgasm he would soon coax from her quivering body. Bracing herself against the cushions, she rose to meet him. In this, the primitive language of male and female, they understood each other. Their communication was exquisitely timed to the rhythm of his strokes and the undulation of her hips.

His voice was thick with passion. "I love how this feels."

"I love how you feel." She gasped. "Moving inside me. Ah, like that. Like *that*." She tipped over the edge, falling into a whirlpool of color and light.

He followed soon after with a deep groan of satisfaction. As he shuddered in her arms, his happiness became hers and in that brief moment life was perfect.

THEY TOOK SHOWERS in different bathrooms or they would never have made it to her parents' house. Arriving at her childhood home after having explosive sex with the man who walked in with her was a surreal experience made even more so when her mother clearly was in the know.

She gave Sapphire a big hug. "You're looking so happy."

"I'm a happy person."

"But tonight you're especially so." She turned to Grady with a wide smile. "How generous of you to be a part of the Art Barn's fund-raiser." She held out her hand. "You're a credit to your alma mater, even though I never had you in class. Why was that?"

He took her hand in both of his. "Because I was young and stupid, Mrs. Ferguson."

"Please call me Jane. You're not a kid anymore and I can tell you're older and wiser."

"I sure hope so, ma'am."

Sapphire had expected her mother to be friendly. After all, she wanted Grady to talk to her classes sometime this fall. But the level of welcome was even greater than she'd counted on.

Her mom had put on her favorite dress, a purple caftan embroidered in gold that complemented her salt-and-pepper hair. She wore it with lots of gold jewelry and she was tall, almost as tall as Sapphire's father, so the outfit made her look like a queen.

Her bangles jingled and sparkled as she gestured toward Sapphire's dad, a lanky, balding man who liked wearing black turtlenecks and faded jeans. "You remember Stan, don't you? His band played for several of the school dances."

"I sure do remember." Grady shook his hand. "Good to see you again, sir. Sapphire tells me you still have a jazz band."

"Yep, and we're busier than ever. It's great to see you again, too. Impressive what you've accomplished, son, and I want to personally thank you for driving up for the silent auction. People really appreciate it and I know Sapphire was turning cartwheels when you agreed."

"Happy to do it."

Her dad had always been a jolly sort, so his effusive greeting wasn't a surprise. He entertained for a living and everyone he met was a new friend. Maybe her mom's reaction wasn't so shocking, either. She admired talented people, especially when they were focused. She'd probably heard from a couple of the co-op members by now and no doubt they'd raved about him.

Conversation flowed easily during dinner and by the end of the meal she had no doubt that both her parents liked Grady very much. He'd readily agreed to talk to her mother's classes in the fall and possibly again in the spring.

They were at the door saying their goodbyes when the discussion turned to her mother's entry in the silent auction. Grady wanted to see the weaving she planned to donate, so she took him back to her studio for a quick look.

After they left, her dad chuckled. "Your guy was a hit, Sapphie." He was the only person in the world who called her that, but a nickname from her dad was an expression of love and affection, so she treasured it.

"He's not really mine, Dad."

"Maybe not yet, but I can tell he wants to be. I recognize that look. He thinks you hung the moon. Which of course you did, so that makes him smarter than the other schmucks you brought home."

"You didn't like any of them, either? I know Mom didn't, but you like everybody."

"I like everybody until they prove they're dumb as a box of rocks. Anybody who doesn't appreciate your value falls into that category. I've only spent one evening with Grady and there's a lot I don't know about the guy. But I've already learned the most important thing about him. He thinks you're fantastic." He looked into her eyes. "It's important, Sapphie."

She'd never received romantic advice from her dad before. She had a feeling this might be the one and only time she would. "I'll remember that."

12

"THEY LIKE YOU." Sapphire started her truck and backed out of her parents' driveway.

"I like them, too. They're great." If Jane and Stan were in charge, they'd make sure he had a prominent place in their daughter's life. But they weren't in charge and he wouldn't wish them to be. If she didn't make her own decisions, she wouldn't be the same independent woman he admired.

"Are you still planning to work tonight?"

"Yep. If I don't, I'll be worried about rushing the sculpture and I'd like to take it to her tomorrow night." He glanced at her classic profile illuminated by the dashboard lights. She was so beautiful it made his heart hurt. "Want to come with me?"

She hesitated. "Do Rosie and Herb know anything about... us?"

"I doubt it. I haven't talked to them since I got here. I didn't want to take a chance that I'd slip and mention the sculpture."

"Or me?"

"I didn't consciously decide not to tell them about you, but if Rosie thought I had a girlfriend, even a temporary one, she'd be here in a shot."

"How come?"

He laughed. "She has this old-fashioned idea that each of her boys needs to find a good woman and live happily-ever-after. She's more set on that than my own mother. I guess it's because Rosie's had a great marriage and my mom had to make her way through a couple of losers."

"Hmm."

"What?"

"So what will Rosie think if you show up with me in tow?"

"She'll pick up on the fact that I think you're pretty special. I'm sure your folks did."

"They did, which makes my point. Let's not complicate this any further. I don't think it's a good idea for me to go out to Thunder Mountain with you."

Her answer disappointed him more than he wanted to admit. "Don't you want to see Rosie's reaction to the sculpture?"

"Yeah, but—"

"Then come with me. It'll be fine."

She sighed. "If I thought she couldn't read you like a book, I might consider it, but I don't want to get her hopes up. When you get back, you can tell me all about it."

"All right." Maybe he shouldn't have said anything about Rosie's dream of seeing all her foster boys settled. No, he was glad he'd said it. Taking her out there without mentioning it would have been unfair.

But he'd wanted her to be on hand when Rosie caught sight of the wolf sculpture, and yeah, that was selfish. He'd hoped Rosie's reaction would make Sapphire like him a little more. He was no different from a ten-year-old doing tricks on the monkey bars to impress a pretty girl.

"I'm sorry, Grady. I just don't think it's a good idea."

"Probably not."

"I had to let my mom know about us since you're staying in my house instead of at Ben and Molly's, where she'd planned to contact you. But going to see Rosie would open up a whole new can of worms."

"I hate to say it but you're right. The last time I brought a girl out there, it was senior prom. Taking you to meet Rosie and Herb would be seen as a significant move." No point in kidding himself. He'd wanted to raise the stakes but Sapphire hadn't let him.

"My dad's band played for that prom."

"Yeah, they did. I wonder if we appreciated what a great band we had. Probably not."

"You might not have then, but you do when you look back on it." She smiled. "I'll bet my mom's hoping you'll tell her students that you regret not taking her class when you were at SHS."

"Don't worry. I will."

"Thanks for agreeing to do it. I know she's thrilled."

He was glad to do it for Jane, but he had ulterior motives. Keeping the connection with Jane meant keeping the connection with Sapphire. "I was flattered. I never thought of myself as a role model before."

"I'm sure that's one of the reasons they like you. You're modest."

He'd had enough of that kind of talk. He didn't want her thinking of him as some effing choirboy. "About my art, always. About my sexual attributes, on the other hand..." He reached over and stroked her thigh.

"Stop that before I run us into a ditch."

"Or you could drive into a ditch on purpose and we could climb into the bed of your truck."

"Don't tell me you brought a condom with you for the trip to my folks' house?"

He pulled it out of his pocket and tossed it on the dash. "But sadly, we're not going to use it to have sex in the back of your truck. Never fear, though, I'll have it handy when I finish up for the night." He scooped it up and shoved it back in his pocket.

"I believe you." Her laughter had a tremor of excitement in it.

Well, good. At least he still had that going for him. "Are you going to work tonight, too?"

"I thought about it, but I'm pretty well caught up. Instead I'll stay home and clean."

He winced. "Cat hair."

"It's been on my mind. Might as well take care of it."

"That's just wrong. My cat, my cat hair. I'll do it."

"I appreciate the offer but you said you needed to work on Rosie's sculpture so you won't feel as if you rushed it."

"True. Maybe when I get back."

"Seriously?" She glanced at him. "With a hot condom in your pocket?"

"Maybe not. How about tomorrow?"

"We'll be up early to feed the cats, both the ferals and Gandalf. Tomorrow night you'll be going out to Rosie's. Think of it this way. If I clean the bathroom and wash all the towels, we can shower together in the morning."

"That's a powerful argument, lady. But I still hate to stick you with the job. I'll find a way to make it up to you when I get back tonight."

"I'm sure you will." She pulled into her driveway, turned off the engine and took something out of her purse. "Here's a spare key."

"Was this—"

"Don't read anything into it."

"Okay." But he already had. He'd bet money this key had belonged to the cheater. He wouldn't care except her old boyfriends had left a toxic legacy. Anything associated with them was a reminder of the mess he faced because of their bad behavior.

He hopped out of the truck in time to go around and hoist her down. Drawing her close, he gazed into her starlit face. "I'm not going to kiss you, because if I do, I won't leave."

"And I want you to leave, cowboy." She gave him a playful little push. "Get the hell out of here. We both have work to do."

Backing away, he touched the brim of his hat. "See you soon."

THAT HAD BEEN his sincere intention. But it was after three in the morning when he picked up his phone to check the time. His string of obscenities woke Gandalf, who'd been sleeping peacefully on his cat tree.

"Sorry, cat." He walked over and ran his hand over the soft fur. "I just blew it." The sculpture was nearly finished. A couple more hours should do the trick, but he'd promised Sapphire he'd be back to make sweet love to her as a thank-you for cleaning up the cat hair. She'd probably fallen asleep cursing his worthless ass.

He considered staying to complete the sculpture since he wouldn't make any points showing up now. But that didn't feel right. He'd go back, use the cheater's key and climb into bed as quietly as possible so he wouldn't wake her. It was the least he could do.

Driving through the silent streets, he was torn between guilt and elation. Rosie's sculpture looked good. Parts of it had been a challenge but he'd met those challenges tonight and he was proud of the result. In the process, he'd forgotten all about Sapphire.

How could he do that? He'd counted on his hormones to keep him aware that he had a sexy woman waiting for him. He'd never wanted any woman as much as he wanted her, so if thoughts of her hadn't penetrated his single-minded absorption in his work, nothing would.

What if she was right, and he had a fatal flaw like all the other guys? He might not be disorganized and immature. He certainly didn't have a superiority complex and he couldn't imagine cheating on her. But he'd allowed his work to blot out all thoughts of his promise to return to her tonight.

Worse yet, he'd probably do it again, either with her or the next girlfriend. His concentration on his art had been an issue more than once with the women he'd dated. He'd considered himself so much better than the jerks she'd been with, but had any of them been capable of forgetting her completely?

He couldn't even claim she'd been on the fringes of his mind. He hadn't thought of her once as he'd labored over the sculpture into the wee hours. She likely wouldn't be comforted to know he hadn't thought of Rosie, either.

Using his devotion to his foster mother was tempting, but it wasn't the reason he'd kept working. His foster mother had inspired the original concept, but after he'd fully involved himself in the process, the piece had become an end in itself. He loved his work and he wondered for the first time if that precluded him loving anything or anyone else.

The house was dark. By the time he'd put away his tools and started the drive back here, the clock on his dash had shown him that four o'clock wasn't far away. Her alarm was set for six. He'd mucked up whatever chance he'd had to convince her he was the right guy for her.

Because he wasn't. A woman like Sapphire deserved better than being stood up when she'd spent the evening cleaning cat hair out of her bathroom. He thought of the pile of towels he'd left and the fur in the bathtub drain. He'd never mentioned Gandalf's love of showers.

He parked behind her purple truck and remembered the moment when he'd held her close and made that asinine comment about not kissing her because he'd never leave if he did. She'd sent him on his way and encouraged him to get his work done. She'd trusted him to keep his part of the bargain.

The cheater's key slid smoothly into the lock and he let himself into the quiet house and locked the door behind him. The place smelled of soap and lemon oil. As his eyes adjusted to the darkness, he saw the black robe lying over the arm of the sofa. He picked it up and sniffed. She'd washed that, too, and left it for him.

He felt lower than a snake's belly. Deciding to undress in the living room because that would make less noise, he carefully took off his clothes, folded them and laid them on the sofa. Then he put on the robe she'd readied for him. His incurable optimism prompted him to transfer the condom from his jeans to the robe.

Maybe he should bed down on the sofa and not disturb her. But that seemed wrong, as if he wanted to distance himself from her. If he had any decency, he would distance himself and let her find a nice guy who didn't have a creative bone in his body.

But whatever happened between them, he'd never want her to think that he didn't want her. He might not deserve her. In fact, he was pretty damn certain on that point. But that didn't mean he didn't crave her with every fiber of his being, selfish bastard that he was.

Luckily, he knew the bedroom layout by now and even in the dark he could find the bed. She'd always favored the right side, so he felt confident in taking off the robe and sliding in on the left. But she must have switched positions, because he bumped up against her warm body and she immediately came awake.

"Grady?"

"Shh. Go back to sleep. I'll climb in on the other side."

"No." She grabbed for him and caught hold of his arm. "I took this side so I'd know when you got in. Let me scoot over. Are you okay?"

His breath stalled. He'd pictured her angry, not worried. He slipped under the covers and gathered her close. "I'm fine. I got involved in the sculpture and lost track of time. I'm so, so sorry."

"I told myself that was what happened." She snuggled against him. "I've seen how you focus. But I have a good imagination, so I dreamed up all sorts of tragic scenarios. I'm glad none of those were true."

He was stunned. "You're not upset with me?"

"How could I be? You were lost in your work. It happens." She wrapped her arms around him and promptly fell asleep.

Holding her close, he stared into the darkness. He'd found a woman who understood his preoccupation with his work, which was a certified miracle. He'd been prepared to exit her life because that was the decent thing to do when he couldn't be the man she needed.

But she'd just accepted the single worst thing about him without so much as a whimper or a whine. He couldn't have predicted that in a million years. He'd known she was special, but he hadn't known how special. She wasn't going to get rid of him easily.

HE SLEPT THROUGH her alarm. She must have showered and dressed upstairs, because the first noise he heard was the sound of her truck starting up. *Shitfire.* Leaping out of bed, he was about to race after her when it occurred to him he was naked. The neighbors hadn't caught him having sex with her on the front porch, but they'd likely notice if he ran down her driveway with his junk jiggling.

Rushing into the freshly cleaned bathroom, he found the note she'd taped to the mirror. *Morning, Sleeping Beauty. Take your time. I'll feed Gandalf. We'll see you when you get there.*

Nothing else. No smiley face, no *Love, Sapphire*. No signature at all. But then, it wasn't like he wouldn't know who'd written it. She wouldn't want to put anything in writing that could be misinterpreted as mushy.

She didn't sound mad, though. Considering he'd stumbled in at four in the morning and had slept straight through the alarm and her preparations to leave, she had a right to be mildly irritated, at least.

Instead she was acting like a person who understood what happened when the work took hold and wouldn't let go, as if she'd been in that same place. That was exciting to think about. Ever since the day three weeks ago when he'd come over to the Art Barn with Cade, he'd known he and Sapphire had a sexual connection. What a bonus if she got him.

With no Gandalf to join him in the shower, he made it out of the house in no time. On the way to the Art Barn he detoured past the bakery and bought a couple dozen assorted doughnuts.

Then he picked up a fast-food egg sandwich and coffee from the drive-through and ate on the way.

He was feeling reasonably human by the time he parked in front of the barn. Only three other vehicles were there, so the whole group hadn't arrived yet. Sapphire, George and Arlene were in residence. He'd identified Arlene and George as Sapphire's core supporters of the program.

He grabbed the box of doughnuts and walked through the front door. Then he paused and listened to the sound of artists at work—Arlene singing under her breath as she painted, George sanding a piece of wood in preparation for carving, Sapphire's wheel humming. He enjoyed the energy of this place. Working alone had its value, but this had been a nice change.

George stuck his head out. "Hey, Grady. Whatcha got?"

"Something for the coffee break. Pretend you never saw it."

"Gotcha." He went back to work.

Grady set the treats on the desk in the office and was in the process of getting a cup of coffee to take back to his stall when Gandalf rubbed up against his leg. "Hey, buddy!" He put down his mug and picked up the cat. He got a kick out of knowing Gandalf had heard or smelled him and had come to say hello.

The cat purred like there was no tomorrow as Grady scratched under his chin. "Looks like you survived staying alone for a little while. Wasn't long, though. Tonight you'll have to hang out by yourself for a good twelve hours. But at least you have a whole barn to explore. Gotta be more interesting than staying in a bathroom."

Gandalf closed his eyes and stretched his neck in ecstasy. Whatever trauma he'd suffered while he was on his own seemed forgotten. The shelter vet had mentioned that he'd need a cat carrier for the long drive to Cody, but Grady hated the idea of sticking him in an enclosed space. He'd look for one with mesh sides so Gandalf could see him.

"Hey, I need to get to work, buddy." After one last scratch, he put the cat down and picked up his mug of coffee. Gandalf trotted at his heels on the way to his space.

Arlene leaned around her easel and waved. He smiled and gave her a thumbs-up. Sapphire was intent on her wheel as red clay responded to her touch, rising to form a vase that resembled the hourglass shape of a woman. He paused for a bare second, not wanting to interrupt. Besides, the sight of her molding that clay got him hot.

He hadn't felt her hands on his naked body since yesterday morning, and that was his own damned fault. Moving on, he glanced over at George's workbench and exchanged a quick salute with the wood-carver. The heron Grady coveted had a big red *sold* sign hanging around its neck.

Gandalf leaped to the top of his cat tree and curled up as if he'd lived in the barn for years instead of hours. Grady chuckled at the cat's smug expression as he stared down from his perch. Finally, though, he couldn't put off the moment any longer. It was time to take a look at the wolves in the light of day. Something that he thought was genius at three in the morning might have turned to crap by the time he'd had some sleep.

Setting his hat brim-side-up on a nearby shelf, he took a deep breath and turned toward the sculpture. His heart beat faster. It was good, really good. Thank God for that, because if it hadn't been, he wouldn't have had time to fix it. He had a little more to do, but not much. He could finish this morning and then start organizing what he'd need for the cougar.

He grabbed his welding gloves and his goggles, intent on those few touches—an ear that wasn't quite what he wanted and a tail that needed adjustment. Minor tweaks.

"Before you start…"

He glanced up.

Sapphire stood just outside his area wiping clay from her hands with a damp cloth. "Uh-oh. You've already started. I can see that from the look in your eyes. It's okay. We can talk later." She turned to leave.

"No, wait. Don't go away." He set down the goggles and gloves. "You deserve an apology…" He paused to lower his voice. They weren't exactly alone. "I was supposed to help you with the cats this morning." *And make love to you last night and again this morning in the shower.*

"No worries." She smiled. "Fred came over and sniffed me."

"You're kidding!" And he'd missed it.

"He's definitely changing his ways. Last night I blinked at him and he blinked back, and this morning—"

"Hold on. What's blinking have to do with it?"

"I learned that from a shelter volunteer. If a cat blinks at you, it's a sign they're willing to be friends. The human can start it off and see if the cat responds. It's a good way to find out how socialized they are."

"I'll be damned. Never heard that before."

"Anyway, it's possible that you were right. Fred might have noticed your interaction with Gandalf and maybe it triggered a distant memory of human interaction. But that's not what I came over to talk about."

"I'm glad to hear about Fred, though. I know you like him." He needed to hold her more than he needed to breathe. This definitely wasn't the time. He had hours to wait for that privilege.

"The important part is coaxing him to like me. I think he's getting there."

"Good." He was miles ahead of that tuxedo cat. He'd shot way past the liking stage and was fairly sure he'd entered love territory.

"I came over to ask if I can go out to Thunder Mountain with you."

He couldn't have been more surprised if she'd pulled out castanets and launched into a flamenco dance routine. "Well, sure, but… I thought you had reservations."

"I did. I do. But then I came in this morning and saw your wolves." She held his gaze. "They're magnificent."

"Thank you." Her sincere praise affected him enough that he had to clear his throat. "Glad you like them."

"I love them and she will, too. The moment she first sees them will be very special. I can't bear to miss it."

"Great." He sucked in a breath. "That's great." Now *he* felt like pulling out castanets and launching into a flamenco dance routine. Or better yet, he wanted to pick her up and whirl her around like guys did in the movies. But too much enthusiasm might freak her out and telegraph their situation to the others. He settled for a smile. "I'll text Rosie and tell her to set an extra place for dinner."

"You're not going to say who it's for?"

"You tell me. Which way would you rather play it?"

"Tell her I'll be with you. I don't want a little surprise of me showing up to take anything away from the big surprise of the wolves."

"Okay." This was shaping up to be a fantastic night.

"Can I bring anything?"

"I would say a bottle of Baileys because she loves that with coffee, but apparently, she's still working on a case of it three of the guys got her last summer. You don't have to bring anything."

"But I've never been out there. I don't like arriving empty-handed."

"Then how about a bottle of wine? That always works."

"What kind?"

"Anything. Just some decent brand. They're not picky."

She brightened. "I know!" Then she looked uncertain. "But maybe that's not such a good idea."

"What?"

"I have this bottle of two-hundred-dollar wine I've never opened…"

"Hell, yes. Bring it."

"That wouldn't bother you?"

"Not a bit. Terrific idea." And maybe before he left, he'd talk her into giving away the shirt and burning the Valentine's Day card. Progress was being made.

13

SAPPHIRE FOUND OUT that Grady's truck had a CD player, so she brought one of Amethyst's albums for the trip out to the ranch. Her sister tended to sing upbeat tunes and Sapphire figured they'd need a distraction since they'd both be nervous and excited.

The wolf sculpture lay in the back wrapped in a tarp, secured with rope and cushioned by a thick piece of carpet. Fortunately, the bundle sat low in the truck bed, virtually out of sight unless someone leaned over the side to peer in. They'd arrive after sunset, so the gathering darkness should keep Rosie and Herb from noticing anything.

"Your sister has an awesome voice," Grady said after Amethyst's first number. "Thanks for bringing the CD. I feel like a Mexican jumping bean but the music helps."

"I listen to her albums whenever I need to get out of my own head."

"She just goes by Amethyst?"

"Yeah. It's a great name. Stands on its own. She's a local talent now but I predict she'll get her big break."

"With a voice like that, she should."

They talked about her sister's career during the next song, but then they lapsed into silence. Amethyst's music usually had that effect on people. They wanted to shut up and listen to the lyrics, most of which her sister wrote. Some of the tunes were love songs and a couple of times Sapphire caught Grady glancing over at her.

She wasn't an idiot. She knew he was falling for her, and if she allowed herself to, she'd fall for him. He'd be easy to love, this broad-shouldered cowboy with the drive and talent to make beautiful art and an earthy sensuality that turned sex into an adventure. He was exactly her type, and that was the problem.

If he lived in town, she could get to know him better and watch for that relationship-wrecker trait to show up. Or not. But he didn't live here and a week wasn't enough time to uncover all facets of his personality.

She'd learned he could get lost in his work, which could be seen as a negative, although she didn't consider it one. He was mildly possessive, but she couldn't blame him for objecting to the shirt. He was okay with her bringing Edgar's wine. She'd debated whether to retrieve the bottle afterward, but maybe she didn't need these reminders so much anymore. Taking it back with them would be kind of dorky.

The sun had dropped below the Bighorn Mountains by the time they drove up to the one-story ranch house. Grady turned off the engine. "This is it, the place that I called home for two years."

"I can see why you loved it." Sapphire took in the long front porch lined with Adirondack chairs painted in the academy colors of brown and green. The porch was empty but she pictured it filled with kids drinking soda and soaking up the ambiance.

"You can't see the meadow or the cabins from here." He rolled down the window. "But you can hear the kids." Music and laughter drifted on the evening breeze. "Man, that brings back memories." He inhaled deeply. "They must be burning logs in the fire pit. Probably toasting marshmallows."

She smiled. "Sure you wouldn't rather go down there and eat burned marshmallows with the kids?"

"Nope. I can also smell Rosie's meat loaf. It's good to be home." He paused. "That might sound strange when I only lived here two years, but we moved a lot when I was a kid. Mom would get a raise and we'd pack up and go to a nicer rental. I never lived in the house she and my stepdad own, so this is the one constant from my early years."

"And a comforting one, I'll bet."

"Yep." He gazed at the barn a short distance away. A couple of slender kids walked out and closed the double doors, then slid a beam across to secure them. "They've finished their evening chores. I miss having horses around. I used to ride every chance I got."

"Could you have them on your property?"

"I could, but I'll monitor how things go with the cat first. As you discovered, I can disappear into my work and animals need a routine."

"I think you could figure that out."

"Probably." He glanced at her. "By the way, Cade will be eating with us. Lexi's conducting a riding clinic down in Casper."

"Catch me up on that situation. Are they engaged or not?"

"Not yet. Cade wants to get married but she's reluctant until he proves that he's domesticated and won't expect her to handle what used to be considered women's work. That's why he was buying art three weeks ago."

"Fascinating." Sapphire grinned. "Too bad Lexi won't be here. Back in high school she treated him like a god."

"Yeah. She's over that." He reached for his door handle.

"Wait. Before we go in, what's the plan?"

"Oh, right. I got caught up in nostalgia and forgot to tell you. Cade and I worked it out on the phone this afternoon. His cabin's a short walk from here. After we say hi to everyone, he'll suggest going up there to show me how it looks. Instead we'll unload the sculpture."

"What about me?"

"You can go with us or stay and talk to Rosie and Herb."

"I'm going with you, cowboy. If I stay with Rosie, she's liable to ask some pointed questions."

"She might, but she means well."

"Of course she does. She loves you and wants the best for you. I just don't want to be asked about my intentions."

"Then you can say you're dying to see how the artwork looks in Cade's cabin."

"I actually am now that I know he bought it to prove he's domesticated."

"He'd probably take us up there for real after dinner if you want. I just thought you might want to head back to your house."

In the soft twilight she turned to gaze at him. She couldn't see his face very well but she could feel his heat. "Now that you mention it, I'm not that curious to see the inside of Cade's cabin."

He smiled. "Me, either."

They were halfway to the porch steps when Rosie came out the door followed by Herb. Short, plump and blond, she looked fairly harmless, but Sapphire had heard things over the years. You didn't want to get on Rosie's bad side and the quickest way to do that was by hurting someone Rosie loved.

"I thought I heard your truck, Grady Magee!" Rosie hurried down the steps. "But then you didn't come in, so I had to find out what was keeping you!"

"We got to talking."

"That's nice." Rosie smiled as if she liked hearing that. "Now come here and give me a hug, you rascal!"

As he leaned down and gathered her into his arms, Sapphire knew she was already in trouble. Rosie likely had put her own spin on Grady's "We got to talking" comment and had concluded they cared about each other. She wasn't wrong. Watching Grady hug his foster mom warmed Sapphire's heart and tightened her throat. She'd failed to maintain an emotional distance from this man.

Grady moved on to embrace Herb, a wiry guy with thinning

hair, and Rosie turned her attention to Sapphire. "I'm so glad you could join us tonight!" She took Sapphire's hands in hers. "Thanks for coaxing our boy to come up for your fund-raiser."

"Yeah, thanks." Cade came down the steps grinning all the way. "It's always a treat to see your ugly mug, Magee." He exchanged a bro hug with Grady.

"And I'm so happy about this event, Sapphire." Herb came over and shook her hand. "I really admire what you're doing. I became a large-animal vet because the overpopulation of dogs and cats broke my heart. Had to work in a different area."

"Needless to say, Herb and I will be there Saturday night," Rosie said. "We're putting Cade in charge of the kids."

Cade laughed. "Yeah, we're going to do drugs and rent porn. It'll be epic." He clapped Grady on the shoulder. "Hey, I was just thinking you haven't seen how the artwork looks in the cabin."

"Sure haven't, but I'd love to."

Sapphire picked up her cue. "I wouldn't mind checking that out since I was the one who sold it to you."

"We could make a quick trip up there right now." Cade turned to Rosie and Herb. "Unless dinner's ready."

"The meat loaf needs another fifteen minutes," Rosie said. "If you want to take Grady and Sapphire up to see your cabin, go ahead."

"Then I will. Come on, guys. We'll take a secret route to avoid running into any teenagers along the way."

Sapphire lifted the wine bottle she held. "Before we leave, let me give you this, Rosie. But if you've already opened something to serve with dinner, no problem."

Rosie looked at the bottle. "I haven't opened anything yet and red goes great with meat loaf. I've never tasted this one, so thanks! We'll try something new tonight." She and Herb walked back into the house.

Cade watched them go inside. "Give them a few minutes. Let them get involved in setting the table and opening the wine." He glanced over at Sapphire. "I could be mistaken, but that looked like a bottle I decided was out of my league."

"It was a gift, I could never find the right time to open it but tonight seemed like the perfect situation."

"That's very cool. And even cooler that you didn't tell them it was expensive stuff. Now, let's get the masterpiece out of the Torch Man's pickup."

Sapphire laughed but Grady rolled his eyes.

Cade moved closer to Sapphire and lowered his voice, but not by much. "I think he secretly likes us to call him that but he pretends not to. It got started at the wedding and you know how these things go."

"Which is forever." Grady lowered the tailgate, climbed in and began untying the ropes. "When it comes to running something into the ground, nobody does it better than the Thunder Mountain guys."

"Not *guys*." Cade looked pained. "Thunder Mountain *Brotherhood*."

"I remember that from high school." Sapphire had thought it was touching that the foster boys had come up with a way to reclaim a sense of family. "It was you, Damon and… Who was the third one?"

"Finn. He's a brewer up in Seattle now. It used to be just the three of us, but we've expanded the name to include everybody. Torch Man here keeps forgetting."

"Torch Man is ready to take this thing out of the truck whenever you finish working your jaw, Gallagher."

"Excuse me, sweet lady. Time to use my impressive muscles." Cade rounded the back of the truck. "Where're we going with it?"

"I thought you had a spot picked out."

"I sort of do." He vaulted into the truck. "Tell me the dimensions again."

"Five feet, seven and three-quarters inches long, three feet, two and a quarter inches high."

"Okay." Cade hopped down and began pacing along the front of the house.

Sapphire didn't think it belonged in front of the house at all, but this wasn't her decision.

"Here." Cade gestured toward a spot beside the porch steps.

Grady shook his head. "We can't put it there."

"Why not? It'll show up real good."

"Rosie likes her little flower bed."

"Then maybe at the far end of the house. Or how about on the porch?"

Grady blew out a breath. "Definitely not on the porch."

"The far end?"

Sapphire finally couldn't keep her suggestion to herself any longer, and besides, they were running out of time. "Under that pine tree in the side yard," she said. "It would be perfect there."

Both men looked at her. Then they turned in unison toward the side yard.

"She's right," Cade said.

"Yeah, she is." Grady resettled his Stetson. "It'll be more natural instead of sticking it somewhere out front. Thanks, Sapphire. Listen, while we get it off the truck, would you walk over and scope out the most level spot?"

She gazed up at him. "Wouldn't you rather back the truck over there so you don't have to carry it so far?"

Grady glanced at Cade and they both started laughing.

"Yeah," Grady said, wiping his eyes. "That would be the intelligent way to do it. Cade, why don't you and Sapphire find the spot while I back the truck over?"

"Of course, there's the chance Rosie will hear the truck," Sapphire said.

"She might." Cade scratched the back of his neck. "Hell, we need to get this done without giving ourselves a hernia. Let's risk it."

In moments she and Cade had found the spot and Grady backed right up to it. Then he and Cade used the carpet to pull the wrapped sculpture partway out. With much grunting and groaning, they lowered it to the ground.

"Heavy sonofabitch," Cade muttered.

"That's the idea." Grady was breathing hard, which could be a combination of effort and excitement. "That way it'll stay put. Let's—"

"What in God's name is going on out here?" Rosie walked around the truck with Herb right behind her. "Are you fixing to bury a dead body under my pine tree, Grady Magee?"

"If he is, then rigor mortis has already set in," Herb said.

Rosie eyed Cade. "I thought you were taking them up to your cabin."

Cade went over and put an arm around her. "That was what you call a subterfuge. We're trying to do something special here, so how about you and Dad go back inside and we'll call you when we're ready?"

She turned to Herb. "Are you in on this?"

"I know nothing about it, Rosie. I'm as clueless as you are."

She continued to stand in the circle of Cade's arm while she stared hard at Grady, who had laid his hand on the wrapped sculpture. Suddenly she covered her eyes and began to cry. "It's my sculpture! That's what it is! Oh, my God."

Cade sent a pleading glance Herb's way and he took his sobbing wife in his arms.

"I won't look," she wailed as she buried her wet face against Herb's shoulder.

"I won't, either." Herb bowed his head. "Finish up with what you have to do and tell us when."

Sapphire hurried over to pull the tarp away while Grady and Cade lifted the sculpture. She bundled it in her arms and went closer to watch as the two men wrestled with the base until Grady was satisfied with the angle.

"That's good," he murmured.

Cade stepped a couple of feet away. "Wow," he said quietly.

Glancing over his shoulder at Sapphire, he mouthed the word again.

She nodded. Her heart pounded as she wondered what Rosie would say. She'd bet Grady's heart was beating as fast as hers.

His hand trembled as he picked off some fibers left by the tarp. Moving away so he wouldn't block Rosie and Herb's view, he took a deep breath. "You can look."

Herb raised his head and Rosie turned in his arms. They both gasped and Rosie began to cry again. But this time she rushed into Grady's arms. "It's b-beautiful!" She hugged him tight and he hugged her back. "A mama wolf with her pups! How did you know that's what I'd want?"

His voice was thick. "Good guess."

"Oh, Grady." She gazed up at him, tears streaking her face. "I'm sorry if I spoiled your wonderful surprise."

He smiled. "You didn't."

Sapphire had to work hard to keep from crying herself. Grady had nailed it. Instinctively, she knew that of all the sculptures he'd created, some immense and worth untold amounts of money, this relatively modest one he'd made for Rosie was the most important piece he'd ever done.

She wanted to hug him, too, but that wasn't appropriate. She could congratulate him later, when they were alone. For now, she could watch with a full heart as Herb joined Grady and Rosie's embrace. Rosie had to examine every inch of the sculpture while she raved about the cleverness of each part and the beauty of the whole. Herb contributed his share of praise and kept patting Grady on the back.

Finally, Cade walked up and pulled Grady into a bear hug. "Incredible job, Torch Man. You impress me, big guy."

"We'll need a spotlight," Rosie said. "A low one." She turned to Sapphire. "Would you consider helping us set that up? You must have lots of experience with lighting artwork."

"I'd love to. We might have to wait until after Saturday, though."

"That's fine! I just want to be able to see it at night, but I can wait until next week. The beam needs to be positioned so it shows the wolves to the best advantage. I love that little one with his paw over his nose! That's so adorable. How do you think of such things, Grady?"

"I didn't." Grady smiled at Sapphire. "It was Sapphire's idea."

Rosie looked over at her. "You got to watch him make this, didn't you?"

"I sure did. It was inspiring."

"I can imagine." Her attention went back to the sculpture. "I could look at it forever. I hate to go in."

"But the meat loaf's not getting any younger," Herb said.

Rosie sighed. "That's true. If we don't take it out of the oven pretty soon, it'll be all dried up. Let's go eat. Later we can come back out with a flashlight and look at my wolves some more."

Everyone followed Rosie back to the kitchen. Sapphire discovered that was where they ate unless they had a crowd. They all helped get the food on the table and Grady opened Sapphire's wine. To her surprise, he held out the cork.

"Want this?" His brown eyes relayed a challenge.

She shook her head. "You can toss it."

"Maybe we should save it," Rosie said. "After all, this is a red-letter day."

"Then take it with my blessing." Sapphire's gaze met Grady's. She knew that look by now. He wanted to kiss her. And that was just for starters. This kitchen was cozy and welcoming, but she could hardly wait to leave it.

14

"THAT WAS A real high, giving the sculpture to Rosie and having you there with me." Grady had pleaded exhaustion in order to get out the door with Sapphire rather than stay for a game of poker and more viewings of Rosie's wolves. Technically, he should have been worn-out, considering how little sleep he'd had recently. Instead he was strung tight as a hunter's bow.

They were finally on the road and he fought the urge to pull onto a side road and make love to Sapphire. But the cab didn't have enough room to do it right and the bed of his truck was a mess. She'd worn a skirt with bright red hibiscus flowers on it and a red blouse, neither of which should be scrunched up in the cab or subjected to the grime in the back.

"I'm so glad I asked to be there."

Her musical voice stroked his already sensitized nerves. He wanted to hear that voice urging him on as he thrust into her. He passed narrow dirt roads that he'd used as teenage make-out spots. Back then he'd outfitted the bed of his truck with a self-inflating air mattress that he could deploy at a moment's notice.

"Rosie loved those wolves, Grady."

"I do believe she did." Part of his desire for sex was a response to everyone's admiration of his work. He needed to let off steam and dispel the nervous energy that successfully completing and delivering a project created in him. He liked having sex at moments like this, but sometimes that hadn't been an option, so he'd made substitutions—downing a couple of six packs, maybe taking a nude swim in an icy lake or going on a midnight run through the pines.

Tonight he had the option with a terrific woman who might actually understand the untamed emotions pumping through him. He also had a condom since he'd made it a practice to carry one at all times this week. All he lacked was a viable horizontal surface. Hell, he'd settle for a vertical surface but his truck needed a wash, so he wasn't going to take her up against the fender.

He was approaching the last secluded dirt road he knew about when he remembered the blanket he'd rolled up and tucked behind his seat. He'd found it on sale at least a year ago. It was more a plush throw than a blanket and for some reason the leopard spots had appealed to him.

After buying it, he'd tucked it behind his seat and forgotten about it. Why would he remember? He'd had no girlfriend in the past year and no emergencies where he'd been stranded in icy winter conditions. But he had an emergency now. He turned off on the dirt road.

"Grady?"

"There's something I have to do."

"If you need to answer nature's call, go right ahead. I won't look."

"I want to answer a different call from nature, more a call of the wild." He searched for a break in the trees. There. A clearing he remembered from the old days. With luck, it would still have some grassy spots. He pulled off the road.

"Is this about sex?"

"Yes, ma'am. I just remembered I have a blanket behind my seat. It's not very big but it'll protect you from the cold ground." He switched off the engine and glanced at her in the darkness. "Unless you don't want to."

"I want to." Lust added a dark, rich flavor to her words.

He let out a breath. "Thank God. Let me scout around and find a place for the blanket." He laid his hat on the dash and shut off the dome light. He'd learned early in his make-out career that nothing ruined the mood faster than the harsh brilliance of a dome light coming on when he opened the door. He'd never expected to use that information again, but here he was. "I'll come back for you."

"All right." Her voice was breathy.

Unsnapping his seat belt, he leaned over and cupped the back of her head. "I'm going crazy from wanting you. I'm a danger on the road." He captured her mouth and kissed her hard. Then he released her, climbed out and grabbed the blanket.

After letting his eyes adjust to the darkness, he scanned the clearing. His teenage instincts came back to him and he made his way to one of the few grassy areas. Spreading the throw over the ground reawakened that seventeen-year-old he used to be and his arousal strained against his fly.

He ignored the pain as he returned to the truck, opened the door and discovered that Sapphire had been busy in his absence. She wore nothing but a smile.

She held out her arms. "I thought I'd help things along."

"Oh, lady, what you do to me." He scooped her up and nudged the door closed with his shoulder.

"I have a fair idea."

"I'm about to give you all the information you need on that topic." He managed to lay her on the blanket without dropping her. Then he took off his shirt, rolled it up and bent down to tuck it under her head.

She caught his face in both hands. "Kiss me."

With a groan, he fell to his knees. The first contact with her warm lips snapped his control and he couldn't seem to stop kissing her. His hungry mouth sought the hollow of her throat, the curve of her shoulder, the fullness of her breasts.

He nipped and suckled his way down, then dipped his tongue

in her navel, which made her squeal. He liked the sound so much that he did it again.

"I'm sensitive there!"

"Good." Sliding his hand between her thighs, he began an assault on her belly button with his tongue while his fingers kneaded the moist recesses that would soon welcome his cock. The more he explored, the wetter she became. She lifted her hips with a husky moan, inviting him deeper.

Women had wanted him before, but not like this. Sapphire's response was instantaneous, a rush of heat and desire that humbled him with her generosity. He recognized that she couldn't help wanting him just as he couldn't help wanting her, but he still considered her response a precious gift.

Learning what would make her come was such a joy. His tongue licking the tender crevice of her navel made her gasp and giggle, but it was the steady stroke of his fingers that teased an orgasm from her shuddering body. She called his name as she arched upward.

"I'm here." Sliding his fingers free, he eased between her thighs and covered her pulsing center with his mouth.

She said his name again, this time on a sigh of pleasure. Savoring her juices, he settled in and took her up again until she was gasping and thrashing against the blanket. When she came a second time, he nuzzled and licked until her tremors subsided.

Now. Pushing to his feet, he pulled the condom from his pocket, unzipped his fly and put it on. The moon peeked through the trees to give him a glimpse of her lying sprawled on the blanket in reckless abandon.

Her hair fanned out in disarray and her breasts quivered with each ragged breath. The moonlight caught the sheen of passion on her silken thighs. She'd given herself without hesitation, like some wild thing he'd met in the woods. He rejoiced in her total surrender, even if it was only for tonight.

As he knelt beside her, she reached for his hand and laced her fingers through his. He had just enough light to see the gleam in her eyes and her knowing smile. Realization hit him with the force of a lightning strike.

She got it. She understood his urge to celebrate with raw, uncivilized sex in the woods because she knew how rarely an artist's creation turned out exactly right. His world shifted. He'd never shared that depth of understanding with anyone.

Taking her other hand, he slid his fingers through hers and pressed their joined hands against the blanket as he moved between her thighs. His body blocked the moonlight, but it didn't matter whether he could see her eyes. Slowly pushing his cock into her warmth, he felt a connection that took his breath away.

Maybe this wouldn't be the hard-driving, no-holds-barred experience he'd anticipated, after all. He loved her with long, sure strokes. Each time he locked his body against hers, he paused a moment to breathe, to treasure the beauty of being so intimately joined with Sapphire, the woman of his dreams.

Her nipples brushed his chest with each deliberate thrust and her fingertips pressed into the backs of his hands. He didn't want this to end but his climax edged closer. Giving in to the demands of his cock, he gradually increased the pace.

Ah, that was good, too. The sweet friction seemed more intense than before. She moaned and tightened around him, sending shock waves through his entire body. He pumped faster. Every sensual pleasure was amplified—the earthy smell of sex, the liquid sound of each stroke, the satin touch of her thighs as she raised her hips and wrapped her legs around his waist.

They were in shadow, but if he closed his eyes, he saw color everywhere—the red of desire, the blue of trust, the yellow of creativity, the green of hope and the entire rainbow that was love. The first ripple of her climax rolled over his cock and he bore down. Panting, he rode the crest of her orgasm and claimed his own. Their cries mingled in the cool night air.

Later, after he'd carried her back to the truck and helped her dress, they smiled and kissed, but no significant words were spoken. He didn't plan to say them now. He knew what he knew and she had to be aware they'd crossed a line.

He'd see how things went for the next two days. He was scheduled to leave for Cody on Sunday. If he hadn't found a time before then to make his case, then he'd make it on Sunday. He wasn't leaving town until he'd said what was in his heart.

NOW SHE'D GONE and done it. She'd fallen in love with him. But she couldn't tell him so or he'd say it back to her. Then they'd have a problem because she didn't know what to do about this love situation.

Lucky for her, conversation wasn't necessary for the rest of the night. When they were both naked, they managed to communicate quite well without saying a word. They made love again after they reached her house, and making love was the only way to describe it. They were now incapable of just having sex. Then they slept like a couple of hibernating bears until her alarm went off.

They fooled around in the shower before leaving the house and she managed to enjoy the heck out of that without blurting out something stupid. She sensed he was waiting for her to say it because she was the one with hang-ups about artists. She was counting on their busy schedule to keep her from making a huge mistake. Once those three little words were out, there was no taking them back.

She suggested they drive separately to the Art Barn because she had lots of errands today. That was very true, but she also needed some privacy so she could think. That didn't work out quite as smoothly as she'd imagined, because they left together and the lack of traffic at that hour meant his truck stayed in her rearview mirror the whole way.

At every light, he was right behind her, and when he caught her looking in the mirror, he smiled. That smile jacked up her pulse every damn time. But just because she'd fallen in love with him, didn't mean she had to do anything about it.

If she hadn't gone out to Thunder Mountain Ranch with him, she might have avoided the love part. That fateful decision was totally on her because she'd been all set to stay home until she'd looked at those wolves. She didn't regret being there when he'd presented the sculpture to Rosie, though.

She didn't regret anything. Their moment of clarity in the woods would be a cherished memory forever. Two people seldom communicated on that level, and because of that, she might always love Grady Magee.

That didn't mean she was ready to take a chance on him as a life partner, not with her track record. For all she knew, his glaring faults were obvious but she was too blinded by love, artistic bonding and great sex to see them. Once he left and took his powerful charisma with him, she might realize how wrong they were for each other.

She doubted that he was viewing it that way, though. For that matter, he might be blind to her faults, too. The world was full of miserable people who leaped into commitment in the heat of the moment and then had to figure out how to extricate themselves from bad situations.

This week observing Grady making a sculpture for his beloved foster mother was bound to make him seem like a hero. No wonder she'd fallen for him after last night's emotional episode. No wonder she'd had the lovemaking experience of her life afterward.

So her private thinking time had brought her around to that hot topic and she arrived at the Art Barn feeling restless and aroused. She might as well have had him sitting in the passenger seat of her truck. At least then she could have glanced over to admire how his faded jeans hugged his thighs.

George's tan truck was in the parking lot, which was a good thing. She'd be less tempted to steal a kiss or ten from Grady. She shut off the engine, grabbed her purse and hopped down.

Grady pulled in next to her and got out. She waited for him and tried hard not to look besotted as she watched him approach.

From the way he was staring at her, she almost expected him to kiss her before they walked in.

But he surprised her. "Before I forget, your left taillight is out."

"It is?" She'd thought he'd been intent on her mouth and he'd been focused on her truck's taillight.

"Yeah, and I want credit for not kissing you out here in broad daylight."

She gazed at him. "Admirable."

"Better not push it, though. I'm weakening."

So was she. "Let's go in."

He nodded and fell into step beside her. "Unless you think I'll spook Fred, I'd like to help with the ferals this morning so I can see the progress you've made."

"I'd like you to see it, too. It's possible he'll revert back to the way he was, but let's find out what happens if you're there."

"Sounds good. I'll need to feed Gandalf and pay attention to him, so just holler when you're ready."

"I will." Because her mind was a traitor to the cause, she immediately remembered how she'd hollered last night during that episode in the woods. So had he. They'd probably frightened the wildlife.

After they got inside, George poked his head out from his workspace. "Hope you don't mind, Grady, but I fed your cat. He's back here hanging out with me."

Grady laughed. "I'm sure he gave you the pitiful face."

"Yeah, he did. I didn't think you'd mind if I put some food in his bowl. Oops, here he comes. Guess he loves you best, after all. Fickle cat."

"If you had tuna, you'd be golden," Grady said as Gandalf trotted toward them, tail in the air.

"Go ahead and love on him." Sapphire watched as the cat loped up and marveled at the transformation. With his coat brushed and his manner confident, he looked like a whole different animal. "I'll fill the bowls."

"Okay." Grady crouched down and started talking to Gandalf while giving him a full-body massage.

Sapphire forced herself to turn away and go about her business. Creative men were her weakness. Being kind to animals added a whole new layer to their appeal. If she wanted to blame anyone for the fiasco of falling in love with Grady, she could probably start with the cat.

She filled the bowls with dry food and called for Grady. He appeared in the kitchen doorway with Gandalf riding on his shoulder. "He wants to go, but I've told him he can't."

"Better not. No telling what would happen. We don't know if he was accepted by the colony. I'd advise keeping him inside until you leave for Cody." She was proud of the matter-of-fact way she said that, as if his departure was just another event that would take place in the course of this weekend.

Grady gave her a long look, though, as if trying to decipher her comment. "Good advice," he said at last. He set Gandalf on the floor. "Stay here, buddy. I'll be back in a little bit."

"You'll have to watch him as we go out." She was amused by Grady's assumption the cat would obey a command. "He might try to slip through the door. You're leaving with food. He might want to know what that's all about."

"I'll watch him." Grady picked up two sets of stacked bowls. Sure enough, Gandalf followed him as he walked to the front door. "I said *stay*."

The cat gazed up at him, tail twitching.

"I mean it, Gandalf."

George came down the aisle toward them. "I'll hold him while you go out there. I agree with Sapphire. He's gonna want to follow you and he shouldn't be out there. He wasn't born to be wild." When he scooped up the cat, Gandalf wiggled in his arms. "Better go before he scratches me."

"Thanks, George." Sapphire opened the door and they both made it out before Gandalf got loose.

"He could learn to stay." Grady paused to glance back at the closed door. "He just hasn't been trained."

"I suppose if you worked on it long enough. I've seen trained house cats, but they're not like dogs, who will do anything to please you."

"It would have been a whole lot easier if I'd stayed inside with him."

"It would, but I'm glad you wanted to come out here. You're the only one who knows how much I've wanted to domesticate Fred. I'm hoping he's there waiting for us."

"Really?"

"We'll see in a second." They rounded the corner of the barn and, sure enough, Fred sat with the others, his attention fixed on the spot where he knew she'd appear. Her heart melted. "There he is."

"I'll be damned. He doesn't seem like the same cat."

"I know. I really think you and Gandalf had an effect on him."

"Gandalf will be happy to hear that."

That made her smile. She studied at him. "You're so—"

"In love with you." He turned his head and met her gaze.

Her heart hammered and she felt slightly dizzy. "Grady…"

"I swore I wouldn't say it before you did. You don't have to respond at all. It'd be better if you didn't. My timing sucks. But the words have been lodged in my throat for hours. I was ready to choke on them. So they're out there. Now let's get these cats fed." He broke eye contact and set his bowls on the ground.

She did the same and they both dropped to their knees to watch the cats. Or rather, Grady did that while she looked at Grady. His throat moved in a slow swallow and a muscle tightened in his jaw. He'd nicked himself while hurrying to shave after their sexy time in the shower. She wanted to lean over and kiss that spot but she didn't dare.

Instead she forced herself to turn away and stare at the cats lined up in front of them, although her thoughts were still on the Stetson-wearing man beside her. *So in love with you.* She contemplated what would happen if she admitted to loving him back. He'd expect that to change things, to pave the way for them to be together.

If anything, it was exactly the opposite. Loving him meant she was in that addled state that allowed people to screw up their lives. She wasn't thinking straight, and oh, by the way, neither was he.

In the three weeks since they'd met and fallen in lust, he'd built an elaborate fantasy involving her. Yes, they had a great time together and her artist's soul communed with his. That was nice, but it didn't guarantee happiness. Some issue was lurking in the background waiting to zap them with a dose of cold, hard reality. She just didn't know what it was.

The cats finished their meal and began grooming themselves, except for Fred, who sat and gazed at Sapphire. Snow White came over for a scratch and Sapphire gave her attention while continuing to watch Fred. When Snow White wandered away, Sapphire blinked at Fred. He blinked back. Slowly, she extended her hand in his direction.

He looked at her outstretched hand. Then he stood. His body tense and poised for flight, he gradually inched toward her.

She held her breath. Tail twitching, he edged close enough to sniff her hand. She stayed as still as possible, although her hand shook from the effort of keeping it in that position. Then, to her astonishment, he rubbed his head against her curved fingers.

Her gasp of surprise startled him and he dashed away. Halfway to the woods he paused and looked back. A second more and he was gone, disappearing into the shadows.

With a sigh, she glanced over at Grady. "I scared him."

His smile was tinged with sadness. "It happens."

"But I'll get there."

He nodded. "You will, and that gives me hope."

She gazed at him in confusion.

"I think I know why you're so attached to Fred."

"Oh?"

"He's a lot like you."

15

GRADY WISHED HE'D kept his mouth shut. His ill-timed declaration of love affected his interaction with Sapphire for the rest of the day. She was wary and skittish whenever their paths crossed. Just like Fred.

Oh, she loved him, too. He didn't doubt that for a minute. But now he was paying for the actions of those other guys who'd professed undying love and later kicked her in the chops. She believed he might be capable of the same thing.

The day would have been more awkward if they hadn't both been busy getting ready for the fund-raiser. In checking his materials for the cougar, he noticed he was missing a couple of things. He ended up calling around town to find them and eventually driving to a junkyard outside town. He made it back just in time for his scheduled TV interview, which would be part of the nightly news to ramp up attendance.

Sapphire's efficiency was something to behold as she made sure everything on her list was accomplished by either her or one of the other co-op members. Rented tables and chairs were picked up, mini lights were hung throughout the barn, and every stall was dusted and swept.

A velvet rope strung down the middle of the barn aisle was designed to facilitate traffic flow, and the same style of rope cordoned off each stall so that visitors would keep a respectful distance from the artists at work. Sapphire and Arlene painted a large banner to hang across the front entrance.

Grady found out from George that Rangeland Roasters, a local coffee shop, had volunteered to set up a cart outside next to the entrance. Scruffy's had agreed to operate a cash bar on the other side and offer happy-hour munchies. All profits from food and beverage sales would go to the shelter. Stan Ferguson's jazz trio was playing free of charge.

"She's thought of everything." George folded his arms and glanced around. "This event wouldn't have happened without her. Hell, the co-op wouldn't have happened without her. I wouldn't have become friends with you, either, come to think of it. Gonna miss working across the aisle from you when this is over."

"I'll miss you, too. This has been a great experience." Now that he had so little time left here, he wasn't ready for it to end, and not only because of Sapphire. He'd enjoyed the camaraderie of artists working under the same roof.

But his studio at home was better suited to his needs, and living in the same town as Liam and his mom was important. They'd been through a lot together. Rosie and Herb meant a great deal to him, but his mom and Liam anchored his world.

"I hope you'll pay us a visit now and then," George said. "If this fund-raiser does as well as we hope, Sapphire might decide to organize another one next year. I'm sure she'd love to have you be a part of it." He peered down the aisle where she was adjusting the velvet rope. "Isn't that right, Sapphire?"

She glanced up and tucked her mane of auburn hair behind her ear. "What's that?"

"If we do another fund-raiser next year, we should invite Grady to be a part of it."

"Of course." Her answer was cheerful but her body stiffened.

Grady wondered if she'd figured on his making friends who

would want to see him again. He'd become an honorary member of the co-op, whether she wanted him to be or not.

"But remember," she continued, "he's getting more famous by the day. That adds responsibilities to an artist's schedule, so he might not be able to spare the time."

George turned his all-knowing Santa smile on Grady. "You won't get too highfalutin for us, will you, son?"

"Sure won't." He looked over at Sapphire. "If you have another event like this, you'd damn well better invite me or I'll have to crash the party."

"Duly noted."

"There you go." George chuckled. "I knew you'd developed a good opinion of this outfit. Well, we'd better quit jawing and get back to work before Sapphire cracks her whip." He winked at Grady and retreated into his area.

"And I might, too." She made one last adjustment to the rope. "I have high hopes for this, both for raising money and for giving us exposure prior to the holidays. It's not too early for people to start thinking about Christmas presents." She called out to George. "Should you put on the suit tomorrow night?"

George came back into the aisle. "Too obvious. And it's only August."

"You're right. Forget the suit, but could we make up some cute signs with a subtle Christmas motif to put in each work area to remind people that original art makes a great gift?"

George nodded. "I'd go along with that."

"I'll talk to Arlene." She started to leave.

"Wait a sec," George said. "Are we all having dinner at Scruffy's tonight? We talked about it a couple of weeks ago."

"We did, and I completely forgot. Do you want to?" She directed the question to George and didn't look directly at Grady.

"I think it would be good for all of us to have some drinks and loosen up. We've been working pretty hard lately."

"You're right."

Grady could almost see the wheels turning. Loosening up

in a social setting was probably the last thing she wanted to do. Chances were excellent that everyone would figure out he was in love with her. And vice versa.

But George was pushing for it. "Eloise asked this morning if it was still on. It's been a while since I danced with my wife."

"Then we should do it. I'll see who else is free." Sapphire started to leave again.

"FYI, I'm free," Grady called after her because he couldn't resist.

"That's the spirit." George clapped him on the shoulder. "Work hard, party harder. That's my motto."

She turned back to gaze at them. "Well, okay, then. That's four of us confirmed. I'll check with the others."

He watched her walk away.

"So have you told her yet?"

Grady glanced at George. "Told her what?"

"That you're in love with her."

He hesitated and decided there was no point in trying to fool George. "Yep."

"She's gun-shy. Dated some real losers."

"So I've heard."

George squeezed his arm. "She's got a winner in you."

"Thanks for that, but how can you tell I'm not like the rest of them? You've only known me a few days."

"Number one, I've lived a lot more years than you and Sapphire and I've become a pretty good judge of character. Number two, and this might sound a little out there, but I see honesty in your work. Some artists are technically amazing but their work isn't honest. I trust someone who does honest work. Does that make any sense?"

"It does, and I can't think of higher praise than that." Grady's throat tightened. "Thank you."

"You're most welcome. Her work is honest, too, which is why you two get along so well. But she's young and she's been burned. Give her time."

He blew out a breath. "I will."

"She might need a lot of it."

"I know, and there's no guarantee she'll ever come around."

"Life doesn't come with guarantees, son. Only possibilities."

POSSIBILITIES WHIRLED IN Grady's mind as he grabbed a chair beside Sapphire's at Scruffy's. The group had pushed two tables together and, in the scramble for seats, Grady made sure he was in the right place at the right time so he could spend the evening next to her.

They'd driven from the Art Barn in separate vehicles and would have to drive back to her house that way, too. It wasn't his favorite way to do things, especially tonight, when he wanted to stick close. So he'd be damned if he'd sit at the opposite end of the table from her.

Pitchers of beer were ordered and everyone filled their mugs, including Sapphire. Grady was glad to see that. She could have decided not to risk getting too happy, all things considered. But she'd worked hard and deserved to let go a little. Talk was lively around the table and many toasts were made.

The food was slow in coming but more pitchers of beer arrived. Grady had grabbed a fast-food lunch that hadn't been very filling, so he didn't take any more beer when the pitcher went around. He wanted to be fully functioning so he could dance with Sapphire. The band was playing a slow number he liked, so he decided to ask her.

"Okay." She gave him a bright smile, maybe a little too bright.

He led her out to the floor and drew her into his arms.

She nestled against him and gazed into his eyes. "Grady, I'm drunk."

"Already?"

She nodded.

"But we just got here a little while ago." He pulled her in a little tighter because she didn't seem very steady on her feet.

"I forgot to eat today."

"Uh-oh. How much beer have you had?"

"Not sure."

He stopped dancing and guided her to the edge of the dance floor. "What do you want to do?"

"Go home."

"I'll take you. But you need food." He tried to remember what was in her refrigerator. "Do you have eggs?"

"Yes."

"Bread?"

"Yes."

"That'll work." Scrambled eggs and toast usually helped soak up the booze. Sliding an arm around her waist, he walked her back to the table. "Sapphire's not feeling good. I'm going to drive her home."

Amid a chorus of "Feel better soon" comments, he grabbed her purse and maneuvered her out the door.

The sight of the parking lot must have reminded her that she'd driven here. "My truck."

"No worries. We'll pick it up tomorrow."

She nodded. "Thanks."

"Welcome." He got her over to his truck and lifted her into the passenger seat. He had to buckle the seat belt for her.

"I'm an idiot," she murmured.

"No, you just got distracted by all you had to do and forgot to eat." He squeezed her shoulder before closing the door and going around to the driver's side. When he climbed in, she'd leaned her head back and closed her eyes. "Are you okay? Do you feel sick to your stomach?"

"No." She sighed. "Just embarrassed."

"There's nothing to be embarrassed about. These things happen. I'll take you home and make you some food." He shoved the key in the ignition.

"I love you, Grady."

He looked over at her. She hadn't moved and her eyes were still closed. He wanted to bang his head against the steering wheel. She'd said it, but only because she was plastered. "I know." He started the engine and left the parking lot.

On the drive back he watched the road for bumps and potholes. If she was embarrassed about being drunk, she'd be mortified if she barfed in his truck. He managed to get her home and into the house without incident. Then he left her on the couch while he rummaged around in the kitchen.

He used up all the eggs she had because he was pretty damned hungry himself. He toasted several slices of bread, too. Then he found herbal tea in the cupboard and made some of that.

When it was all ready, he went into the living room. At first he thought she was asleep. He stood there a moment wondering if he should wake her.

As he debated, she opened her eyes. "It smells wonderful."

"Think you're up to eating something?"

"Yes." Taking a deep breath, she sat up.

He held out his hand. "Then dinner is served."

She smiled and put her hand in his. "You're the best. I owe you one."

"No, you don't." He pulled her up and into his arms. "You took in my cat, which was a major pain in the ass. Bringing you home and fixing you dinner doesn't come close to paying that bill." He gave her a quick kiss but didn't linger. She needed food more than kisses. "Let's eat."

"Let's do." She looked much steadier as she walked into the kitchen and sat down. "Aw. You made tea."

"I'm handy that way." He took the seat across from her so he had a better view and could judge how she was doing. "I'd advise you to eat slowly."

"I will." She picked up her fork. "You sound experienced in this matter."

"Let's just say the guys I worked with in Alaska enjoyed their booze, especially during those long winter nights."

"I'll bet." She took a bite of her eggs, chewed and swallowed. "Good job on these. Not too dry and not too runny."

"Rosie taught me. She required every boy to take a turn in the kitchen, either helping her cook or helping her clean up afterward. She said our future wives would appreciate it."

"I'm sure they will." She kept her eyes on her plate as she ate more of the eggs.

Maybe he shouldn't have mentioned that, but Rosie's comment came back to him often when he messed around in the kitchen. He tucked into his eggs. They were excellent, if he did say so himself.

She finished off her eggs at a leisurely pace. "I'm feeling much better." She munched on a piece of toast. "Fixing this was a really good idea and the tea is perfect."

"Thanks." He had a feeling she had more to say.

"Maybe it's a good thing that I drank too much beer and had to come home."

"Maybe it was." He wished she was leading up to a seduction but nothing about her voice or her body language suggested that.

"We need to talk."

Bingo. He sighed. "I suppose so."

Pushing her plate away, she folded her arms on the table and stared at him. "This morning you said you're in love with me."

"Which I am. Head over heels." Saying it made his heart beat faster.

Her breath hitched but she kept her arms calmly folded. "A little while ago I said that I love you."

"I won't hold you to that. You were—"

"You can hold me to that."

For one glorious moment he was the happiest guy in the world.

"But people in love aren't rational. They do stupid things like make promises they'll never keep."

The bubble burst. "Sometimes." He regarded her steadily. "Other times they know exactly what they're promising and are faithful to those promises."

"How do I know you would be?"

"You don't. You'd have to take it on faith."

"And if I can't do that?"

He shrugged. "We have a problem. Which I know we do. You're afraid to trust me and get slam-dunked again. I don't blame you."

She studied him over the rim of her teacup. Then she drained the contents. "What if I did take it on faith that you'll be loyal and true forever? What then?"

"We're getting ahead of ourselves."

"Not really. I have a feeling you've mapped this out the same way you make a sketch before you create a sculpture."

She really did know him, which was both thrilling and terrifying. "Ultimately, I'd want you to move down to Cody. There's more than enough room for you to share my studio on the ground level of the barn and Liam will be vacating the top floor within a month or so."

"I was right. You have thought this through."

"Of course I have. I'm in love with you."

"So you'd expect me to relocate?"

"It makes the most sense."

She flushed. "To you, maybe, but what about Amethyst and my folks? What about the co-op?"

"I've considered all that." He could see she wanted to argue the point and he held up a hand. "Honestly, I have. But the co-op needs you more than you need the co-op." He leaned forward. "Sapphire, your pottery is dynamite. I've made some valuable connections in the art world and you're welcome to them. Let George run the co-op. He'd do a fine job."

"So I'm supposed to leave my family—"

"I don't suggest that lightly, but you and Amethyst won't live together forever. As for your folks, maybe you do need to be in the same town. If so, we'd have to figure that out. Maybe we can come up with a decent compromise. But after having Liam and me in foster care for two years, my mother needs to keep us close. The truth is, we need that, too."

Her gaze softened. "I can understand why."

"Sapphire, I'm asking you to give us a chance."

"You're asking a whole lot more than that. You want me to leave my family and the co-op I've created. You're asking me to move in with you after we've only known each other for a few days. Talk about a leap of faith, especially considering—"

"Damn it, I know! You've had some rotten experiences! How I wish I could somehow wipe the slate clean and start fresh."

"You can't."

"I'm becoming increasingly aware of that." He looked at her. "Am I beating my head against a stone wall?" He thought of George's comment that changing her mind could take quite a while. For the first time he wondered if he had the patience.

Heartbreak shimmered in her turquoise eyes. "I do love you."

"And that's the toughest part of this! I know you do, and yet—"

"Because I love you, I'm telling you to give up on me. Don't stick around waiting to see if I'll change my mind. I won't leave you dangling like that. I can't make that leap of faith you're asking for. Let me go, Grady."

His heart stalled. "You really mean that."

"I do. We're done."

Despair howled within him, but he managed to sit there as if his world hadn't suddenly imploded. "Then I should probably take my stuff and move into the Art Barn for the night."

"You could, but then I'd be stranded here."

"Oh."

"Stay here tonight, Grady. It'll be okay."

Of course it wasn't. He agreed that sleeping on her couch was stupid, and once he was in her bed, they made love. And made love again. Each time it was like a dagger through his heart, but he couldn't lie next to her without taking her in his arms.

The next morning they moved through their routine like zombies. He packed up all his stuff because he knew he couldn't spend another night like this. After the fund-raiser he and Gandalf would hit the road.

16

SAPPHIRE HAD ALREADY ranked Saturday as one of the most
miserable days of her life and it wasn't over yet. By the end of
the night it could earn the top spot. She hoped the only people
who knew that were Grady and her mother.

Her mom had come looking for her while her dad was setting
up his sound equipment and had found her in the kitchen crying. She'd convinced her mother that Grady wasn't at fault. If
she hadn't, there would have been an ugly scene. Grady didn't
deserve that just because he thought falling in love was the
endgame.

Besides, the fund-raiser was off to a great start and much
of the credit was his. The crowd had filled the parking lot long
before the artists were scheduled to start. When she'd realized
they might pack themselves into the barn and violate the fire
code, she'd asked Herb to stand at the entrance and monitor the
number of visitors going in.

Belatedly, she'd figured out that she shouldn't be one of the
performing artists. As the person in charge of this event, she
should be free to roam and make sure everything went smoothly.
Fortunately, the director of the shelter offered to do that and
Rosie said she'd help, too.

Ten minutes before showtime, Sapphire went inside and

stopped at each work area to give hugs and encouragement. For some it was the first time they'd worked in front of an audience. She saved Grady for last.

He wore his work gloves and his goggles hung around his neck. A sketch of the cougar was tacked on the wall and the recycled metal pieces lay on the floor in a precise order. His steady gaze told her he was focused on the work and ready to begin, but he hadn't put up the velvet rope blocking access to his space.

She stepped inside but didn't move within touching distance. "Thank you for doing this."

His expression didn't change. "My pleasure."

"I guess you know there's a mob of people out there. I think the majority came to see you."

His chest heaved, the first sign of any emotion. "I'll do my best to give them a good show."

"I know you will. Good luck." She turned to go.

"Sapphire." His voice was edged with strain.

Heart pounding, she faced him.

"You know I'm planning to leave for Cody when this is over, right?"

"I figured that when you packed up this morning." Her voice quavered and she hated that. She forced herself to smile. "Especially when you took your toothbrush."

"I can stay an extra day if you need me to." Hope flickered in his brown eyes. "You'll have some massive cleanup. I'd be glad to help with it."

So tempting. But it would only prolong the pain. "Thank you for offering, but we can handle it. You and Gandalf have a long drive ahead of you."

His expression closed down again. "We do."

"Just don't leave without saying goodbye."

"Wouldn't dream of it."

"Okay." Taking a deep breath, she rounded the wall to her work area. A moment later his torch hissed to life.

The next few hours passed in a blur. She had her share of people come by to say hello and many stayed for several minutes to watch her progress on a large salad bowl. She'd lived in Sheridan all her life and had made a lot of friends.

But the evening belonged to Grady. He was more of a crowd-pleaser than she'd imagined he'd be. Because of his intense focus, she'd expected him to weld the piece without interacting with his audience, but instead he paused to answer questions in an easy, relaxed manner that noticeably charmed the onlookers.

She could talk and work at the same time, too, but it took far more concentration than when she could simply create without interruption. She assumed it cost Grady, too, and he was planning to drive to Cody afterward. Maybe she should ask him to stay, after all.

The results of the silent auction dramatically capped the proceedings. All the pieces brought a respectable price, but a wealthy couple from Jackson Hole paid a small fortune for Grady's cougar. Apparently, word had spread that far. The shelter would be funded for months on the basis of that single sale.

The director was ecstatic, and despite Grady's protests, she hugged his sweat-soaked body. He grinned and made jokes for the benefit of the television crew that had appeared for the final part of the event, but Sapphire saw the exhaustion in his eyes. She'd steal a moment and suggest he stay until morning. If that was in her bed, so be it. She didn't want him risking his neck on the road.

Gradually, the crowd dispersed and George started organizing the cleanup crew. "You're excused, Grady," he said. "You, too, Sapphire. You both look like you've been rode hard and put away wet. Go get some rest."

Grady started packing his tools. "Thanks, George, but I'm heading out."

George blinked. "Tonight?"

"Yeah." Grady smiled at him. "Tons of work at home. Might as well get back to it."

George glanced over at Sapphire. "See if you can talk him out of that plan, okay?"

"I will."

"You're probably the only one who can convince him not to do something foolish." He turned to Grady. "For what it's worth, son, don't be an idiot."

Grady laughed. "Too late."

Shaking his head, George walked away.

"He's right," Sapphire said. "Don't leave."

He lifted his head, his gaze sharp. "Do you mean you don't want me to leave now or you don't want me to leave at all?"

Her breath caught.

"I see from your expression that this is a temporary request, not a permanent one. In that case, I'd prefer to go now." He went back to putting everything away.

"But you're exhausted."

"I've been exhausted before." He closed up a box. "Matter of fact, exhaustion can be a cleansing experience. Clears the mind."

"Meaning what?" Maybe he'd realized that he wasn't ready to make a commitment, either.

He stopped packing and looked at her. "I want you in my life. I believe we'd have a great time together. Not perfect, but pretty damned wonderful. You told me not to hang around and wait for you, so I won't do that. But Liam is moving out of the loft of our barn in October. I'm gonna hope like hell that you decide to move in."

Her pulse raced. "Grady, I already said—"

"I know exactly what you said. It's etched in my brain. You're giving up because you don't trust either of us to get this right. I, on the other hand, trust both of us. If you change your mind, you know where to find me."

"No, I don't. Not that I'll drive down there, but—"

"Just stop anywhere and ask. They'll give you directions."

His expression softened. "You really should go home and get some rest, like George said. You look wiped."

She lifted her chin, "I'll go home when I decide to go home."

"Independent woman." He sighed. "Damn, I promised myself I wouldn't do this." Abruptly pulling her into his arms, he kissed her. His lips came down hard on hers as if he needed to vent his frustration, but eventually, his mouth gentled and then he slowly released her. "Please get out of here. It'll be tough enough to go as it is, but we both know I have to."

She dragged in air. "You don't have to go tonight."

"Yes, I do." A tender light glowed in his eyes. "The sooner I leave, the sooner you'll start to miss me. Now take off."

"All right." She turned and walked away because that was the smart thing to do. Yes, she might be crying right now, and yes, she'd miss him like crazy for a while, but she'd get over it at some point. Once she did, she'd be proud of herself for dodging a bullet.

A MONTH AND a half later she was still telling herself that and waiting for the persistent ache in her heart to go away. The progress with Fred helped. Everyone had agreed to put his food dish inside the barn door so he'd become used to eating apart from the others.

He wouldn't let anyone pet him, but he was willing to stroke his face against an outstretched hand. Project Fred seemed to be working. He might become a barn cat yet. After Gandalf's departure, they all agreed they needed one.

She'd just finished the feeding routine one weekday morning and was washing the bowls when someone rapped on the front door of the Art Barn. It wasn't officially open yet, but she never wanted to pass up a chance to sell some art. She dried her hands and went to see who'd shown up at seven thirty in the morning.

Rosie stood on the other side of the door. "Have you finished with the kitties?" She glanced around as if expecting cats to be prowling around the parking lot.

"Yes, but how did you know I would be here doing that?"

"Grady told me. Do you have a few minutes?"

"Sure, sure! Come in!" Grady had told her? When? She ushered Rosie into the office and offered her a chair and coffee. She politely declined the coffee but took the chair. It was the only one other than the desk chair, so Sapphire leaned against the desk rather than sitting behind it.

"You probably wonder what on earth I'm doing here." Rosie settled into the chair.

"You're always welcome, but yes, I'm curious."

"Herb and I drove down to visit Liam and Grady last weekend."

Sapphire's pulse leaped. She'd had no word from him, but then, he hadn't said he'd communicate with her.

"I wanted to see the little house Hope and Liam are moving into and I took Grady an apple pie. He loves my apple pies, and I wanted to do something nice for him after he made those wolves for me."

"The sculpture! I was supposed to help you with the lighting. Do you still need me to?" That couldn't be the reason for this early morning visit. A phone call would have been sufficient.

"Damon and Phil rigged up something, although it might need tweaking."

"Let me know if you need me to come out."

Rosie met her gaze. "I was hesitant to ask you because I thought you and Grady had a big fight."

"A fight? No, not at all."

"He said the same thing. I hope you don't mind, but I talked him into explaining the issues."

Sapphire took a shaky breath. Rosie was in matchmaking mode. "He told me you wanted to see your boys settled, but I'm afraid that in this case—"

"Would you be willing to hear me out?"

What could she say? "Of course."

"If I understand this correctly, you don't think a few days

together gave you enough information to risk throwing in your lot with Grady."

"That's right." She steeled herself for an argument.

"Good for you."

She stared at Rosie. "Excuse me?"

"Sure, there are times when a few days are enough, but after your experiences with bad boyfriends, you'd have to be crazy to follow Grady down to Cody after such a short acquaintance. He was naive to think you would."

She sighed in relief. "Thank you! I expected a lecture about not trusting in the power of love."

"Not my style." Rosie leaned forward. "But I was a mother to that boy for two years and I've been a part of his life ever since. I have a strong feeling you two belong together, so I'm here to give you the information you need so you can put your faith in Grady Magee."

GRADY HAD TOLD himself not to pin his hopes on Rosie's visit with Sapphire. Rosie could make him do nearly anything in the world, but that didn't mean she'd have the same effect on Sapphire. The plan made sense, though. Rosie had proposed giving Sapphire a crash course in all things Grady.

When he thought of the pranks he'd pulled during his time at the ranch, he hoped she'd leave out those episodes. Her goal was getting Sapphire down to Cody, so she'd likely emphasize his good side. But if she made him sound too angelic, that would seem suspicious, too. He'd have to trust her to get the right mix. Her text after the visit was cryptic. Talked to Sapphire. We'll see.

He texted a quick thank-you. Then he got to work because it was the only thing he'd found that would block out the intense yearning he'd dealt with since leaving Sheridan. Watching Liam feather his love nest with Hope certainly hadn't helped, although he was happy for them. The little house located a short walk from the barn was in the last stages of renovation and was in good enough shape for Liam and Hope to move in. The wedding was set for November.

Working like a demon had put Grady ahead of schedule, so he could make a wedding present for Hope and Liam. He didn't have to cover it every night now that Liam had moved out, which was helpful. The piece was a challenge because it was unlike anything he'd attempted.

No wildlife was involved. Instead he'd created a river raft to represent Liam, but rather than being filled with people, the raft was loaded with books. Hope was an author and this was how Grady saw their partnership—Liam as the raft keeping Hope's dream afloat.

He was deep into it one afternoon when he heard someone pull up outside. So did Gandalf, who'd been asleep on top of his cat tree. He lifted his head and stared in the direction of the front door.

The cat's presence was bittersweet. Grady loved having him around, but he also served as a reminder of Sapphire. Gandalf was probably sick of hearing Sapphire's name come up constantly in their daily conversations.

"I sincerely doubt it's her," Grady said to the cat, "so don't get your hopes up, okay? Unless it's her, we're not opening the door. We don't let random folks come barging in when we're working. You should know that by now."

Gandalf's answering meow was sharp and to the point. He clearly wanted Grady to investigate. He was a social cat and loved visitors a lot more than Grady did.

"Oh, all right." He shut down the torch and took off his gloves and goggles. "I'll check to see who's out there, but if it's tourists, they don't get a tour. I'm finally getting those books sitting in the raft to look right."

He glanced out the window and nearly had a heart attack. Sapphire's purple truck sat in front of the barn. If this worked out, he might need to make Rosie another sculpture.

Breathing was an effort as he unlocked the double doors,

stepped outside and closed the doors behind him to keep Gandalf from running out. Then he raked his fingers through his damp hair and shivered as the cool air hit his sweaty body. She'd claimed to like him covered in sweat.

She climbed out of the truck and he gobbled up the sight of her like a man dying of starvation. Sunlight gleamed in her wild auburn hair, which was caught back on one side with an elaborate clip. She'd worn the embroidered jeans he liked, but he'd never seen the colorful patchwork jacket. He remembered the earrings, though, the ones that dangled to her shoulders. As always, she knocked him out.

But instead of going to her, he hooked his thumbs in his belt loops and waited for her to come to him. She'd driven down here, which was a good sign, but he didn't know what that meant. Maybe she'd been in the area and had decided to stop by. Maybe she'd found something he'd left at her house and was here to return it.

She shut the door of the truck and walked toward him without anything in her hands—no purse, no package, no gift. Just her.

He drew in a breath. "Hey, Sapphire."

"Hey, Grady." She stopped several feet away. "How's Gandalf?"

"Good."

"Glad to hear it." She paused before continuing. "I guess you know Rosie came to see me."

"Her idea."

"But you approved it?"

"Absolutely." He looked into her eyes and tried to read her emotions. Couldn't do it.

"She really loves you."

"I really love her."

"She told me quite a bit about you."

"Mostly good, I hope."

"Mostly, but I heard about the firecrackers in the bathhouse and the spiked Christmas punch."

At least she hadn't made him out to be perfect. "I see."

"But I also heard about the puppy you rescued from a snow-drift and the time you slept in the barn to watch over a horse with colic. I heard about your loyalty to your brothers—Liam, of course, but all the foster brothers, too. She told me that you took on three guys at once because they called the Thunder Mountain boys losers."

"Almost got my ass kicked, too. Then Liam came along."

She nodded. "That's the other thing Rosie explained—the special bond between you and Liam. I respect that."

"Because you have a sister." Maybe she was here to tell him she wouldn't leave Sheridan for the same reason he didn't want to leave Cody.

"I do, and we're close, but…it's not the same, Grady. I get that now."

He held his breath, afraid to hope.

She stepped closer. "After the fund-raiser you issued me an invitation." She swallowed. "Is it still open?"

His heart beat so fast he prayed he wouldn't keel over. "It is."

"Then I'd like to accept."

"Thank God." He closed the distance in two strides and swept her into his arms. "Thank God, Sapphire." He looked into her turquoise eyes. "I've been dying down here."

She threaded her hands through his hair. "I've been dying up there. But I needed…"

He smiled. "A character reference?"

"Was that wrong of me?"

"No." He'd start kissing her any second, but for now, he was content to hold her and look into her eyes. "Rosie said you were smart to be cautious after what you'd been through. I thought you should instinctively know I was different."

"My heart did. But my head wasn't convinced."

"And now?"

"You've got all of me, Grady. Body and soul."

A surge of joy made him tremble. "I think this calls for a celebration."

"Champagne?"

"I was thinking of something more basic. Something more naked."

"But you've been welding. I don't want to interfere with—"

"It can wait." For the first time in three years, he abandoned his work without hesitation. It would be there after he'd made mind-blowing love to Sapphire, and miracle of miracles, so would she.

Epilogue

THE TWO-STORY HOUSE engulfed in flames was supposed to be vacant, but the Jackson Hole firefighters were well trained and none of them took that as gospel. Battling intense heat and smoke, they conducted a room-to-room search on the first floor and found nobody. The stairs were impassible, so Jake Ramsey went up a ladder to a second-floor window.

He ripped off the screen, broke the glass and climbed in. The first two rooms yielded nothing. One more to go and then he'd get the hell out of there. The floor could give way any second. In the third room, he found a kid curled up in a ragged sleeping bag. *Shit.*

The kid was unconscious but still breathing. Looked like a boy, judging from the haircut. Dragging him out of the sleeping bag, Jake hoisted him over his shoulder and returned to the window. He had to set him down while he broke out more of the glass.

He slung him over his shoulder again and started down. The kid was a lightweight, thank God. At the bottom a couple of guys took him and headed for the ambulance. Jake stared at the blazing house. The boy could have started it by leaving something turned on downstairs. Critters could have chewed on some wires in the attic.

Didn't really matter. What did matter was that no kid that age should be sleeping alone in an empty house. But it might have been the best option the boy could come up with. Jake knew all about that. He'd been that kid. If somebody hadn't caught him and turned him over to Child Protective Services, he never would have ended up at Thunder Mountain Ranch.

Later that night he stopped by the hospital to check on the kid. Sure enough, the terrified thirteen-year-old lived with an alcoholic, abusive father. According to the nurse on duty, the boy had told his dad that he was the most popular boy in the eighth grade. Since his friends supposedly kept begging him to spend the night, he'd had to rotate among the houses to keep everyone happy, which explained why he couldn't sleep at home. CPS had been called in.

A couple weeks later Chief Stanton summoned Jake into the office. "I know you've been worried about that kid you hauled out of the fire. Thought you'd be happy to know he's been placed in a real nice foster home."

Jake smiled in relief. "That's great news."

"Yeah, it is. I know the couple that took him and they're very nurturing. The boy should have a good Christmas for a change."

"I'm glad."

"Me, too. Could've been a whole lot worse ending for that kid. He's lucky."

Jake blew out a breath. "Yeah."

"Speaking of Christmas, you've worked every single one since you started. How'd you like to have it off this year?"

"I'd love it. How many days can you give me?"

"The twenty-third through the twenty-sixth is all I can spare, but that should at least give you enough time to head over to Sheridan."

"You bet it would. Thanks, Chief. This makes my day."

"You gotta work Thanksgiving, though."

"That's fine. No worries." He left the office whistling. He hadn't spent Christmas at Thunder Mountain in years, but he had great memories of the big tree, the great food and the holiday joy spread by his foster parents.

Then there was Amethyst Ferguson. She might have a gig somewhere else during the holidays, but he hoped not. His memories of Amethyst were more recent than his memories of Thunder Mountain. And a lot hotter.

He'd known she was performing in Jackson this past August, but he hadn't been able to catch a show until the last one. Afterward he'd sent a note backstage and she'd agreed to meet him for a drink for old times' sake. They'd had some epic make-out sessions in the back of his truck when they were in high school but he'd never had the nerve to go all the way.

They'd joked about the missed opportunity over drinks, jokes that had gradually taken on a seductive tone. She'd invited him up to her room at the resort so they could take advantage of this new opportunity. They'd taken advantage of it several times.

While they'd both had fun, they'd parted with the clear understanding that they'd shared a one-night stand. He'd been fine with that. His work was in Jackson and she was based in Sheridan. If her travels brought her back to Jackson, she'd let him know. Easy come, easy go.

Except that had been two months ago and he couldn't get her out of his mind. He'd ordered her albums and played them constantly. He remembered her scent, her voice, her touch and the delicious taste of her body.

He wasn't expecting a happily-ever-after. She didn't seem like the type. But if she happened to be in town, maybe they could give each other the gift of pleasure for the holidays. Sounded like a perfect Christmas present to him.

* * * * *

Come On Over

Debbi Rawlins

Debbi Rawlins grew up in the country and loved Westerns in movies and books. Her first crush was on a cowboy—okay, he was an actor in the role of a cowboy, but she was only eleven, so it counts. It was in Houston, Texas, where she first started writing for Harlequin, and now she has her own ranch...of sorts. Instead of horses, she has four dogs, four cats, a trio of goats and free-range cattle on a few acres in gorgeous rural Utah.

Books by Debbi Rawlins

Made in Montana

Barefoot Blue Jean Night
Own the Night
On a Snowy Christmas Night
You're Still the One
No One Needs to Know
From This Moment On
Alone with You
Need You Now
Behind Closed Doors
Anywhere with You

All backlist available in ebook format.

Visit the Author Profile page at millsandboon.com.au for more titles.

Dear Reader,

I've been living in a small rural town for almost a decade now and I must say it's been quite a learning experience. Often it's been fun, certainly surprising. And, admittedly, I do a fair bit of eye-rolling. Best thing about living here, though? It's been great inspiration for the fictional town of Blackfoot Falls in my Made in Montana series.

Yes, I've shamelessly eavesdropped while getting my hair cut, grabbing lunch at the local diner or waiting in line at the post office. With so many of the ranches passed down from one generation to the next, there always seems to be an interesting story or piece of gossip surrounding the families who first settled here a hundred and fifty years ago. It got me wondering about the legal aspect of passing down land and livestock. Are things made nice and tidy via a will? Or is an assumption enough? Or maybe a handshake?

In *Come On Over*, the Eager Beaver Ranch arose from my latest "what if" game. You'll meet Trent and Shelby, two characters who were a pleasure for me to write, especially since they did all the heavy lifting...

Thanks so much for visiting me and the folks of Blackfoot Falls!

Debbi Rawlins

1

THE EAGER BEAVER was cursed. Trent Kimball had always been a skeptic, but right now, trying to get this damned old tractor to run, he was tempted to rethink his position.

His dad had moved the whole family off the ranch when Trent was sixteen, swearing by the words of Trent's great-granddad that anyone who tried to make something of the place was doomed to failure.

Three years later Trent's older brother had tried to give it a go but after seven years, he'd gone belly up. When Colby had blamed it on the curse, Trent had given him a load of crap about superstition and other nonsense.

In truth, if his bottom-feeding, soul-sucking ex-wife hadn't damn near cleaned him out, Trent wouldn't be here trying to whip the ranch into shape. But cursed? Nah, when it came right down to it, he wasn't about to jinx his future when he'd barely gotten started. Eight months was nothing when it came to building a new life.

Using a clean rag to wipe the sweat off his forehead, he squinted at the gap in the east corral where a pair of rails had come loose and fallen during the night. He'd get to that later today. The job he was on right now was far more urgent. He stared at the tractor engine. If he didn't get it running soon, he was gonna be in a world of hurt. Alfalfa wasn't cheap. He needed to be ready to plant come spring. And after building the stable his bank account was dwindling fast. He jerked the wrench. And caught the edge of his thumb.

He let loose a string of cussing everyone in Blackfoot Falls, sixteen miles away, must've heard. Mutt didn't even raise his head. The mangy hound stayed put, a huge lump of black fur curled up under the shade of a cottonwood. Damn lazy dog.

Violet, his unwelcome neighbor, didn't miss her chance to mock him and she sure as hell didn't hold back. The unseasonably warm fall breeze carried the sound of her cackling straight to him. He turned to the wiry old woman sitting on the porch of her double-wide parked near the faded barn. As usual she was smoking an oversize pipe and having a fine time in her dilapidated oak rocker.

One of these days she'd end up on her butt. Twice he'd offered to fix the chair for her. *Twice.* But as she so bluntly put it…his carpentry skills sucked. Much as he hated to admit it, she had a point.

Though he was getting better. He'd done a meticulous job of finishing the inside of the stable himself, making sure it was hazard-free, before he'd brought Solomon and Jax, a pair of quarter horses he'd purchased a couple of years back.

Still, the laughter coming off the porch was frying his nerves to a crisp. Here he'd cleaned her gutters, repaired the stairs by her front door and built her a handrail. But had she thanked him?

Okay, so he'd done those things when Violet was off to town so she wouldn't give him any lip. And yes, the woman was a burr in his boot, but he didn't want her hurt. Just quiet. And minding her own business.

"I know you have an air conditioner and a TV inside, Violet Merriweather," he said, taking off his hat then resettling it on his head. "Why the hell are you sitting out here in the heat watching me?"

"You're funnier than any of them reality shows." She might've grinned, hard to tell with the pipe hiding half her craggy features. "Anyhow, I'm all caught up on *Duck Dynasty*."

Trent sighed. If he had any sense he would've run her off the property when he'd first returned to Montana. The old woman had a knack for making him feel like a complete loser, and that was the last thing he needed right now. But she had no kids, no family since her brother had passed away some years back, and she'd watched him and Colby grow up. Over the years, Violet had become a fixture at the ranch. But they'd both been nicer then.

Somewhere in her mid-eighties, she was still spry and wiry, and had plenty of opinions she was more than willing to share. For all he knew, being cantankerous was the secret to staying young.

A stiff crosswind out of the west brought the aroma of baked beans and cornbread. Had to be coming from Violet's stove. Their closest neighbor lived three miles away. Another whiff and Trent's stomach growled loud enough for Mutt to lift his head. Or maybe it was the smell that roused the dog's attention. His eyes looked mighty hopeful.

"You think that's coming from our kitchen?" Trent snorted. "Dream on."

Mutt let out a huff.

"You know as well as I do she won't share." Which was a shame. Anything beyond frying eggs and bacon tested his kitchen skills. He'd offered to pay Violet to cook for him, but she'd turned him down flat. "Don't look at me like that," he told Mutt who'd let out a whine. "You eat better than I do."

The dog had shown up the day Trent arrived. Halfway down the gravel driveway, he'd noticed Mutt trotting behind the U-Haul he had towed all the way from Texas. Most of the stuff he cared about probably could've fit in the back of his truck. But he'd jam-packed the small rental with a few chairs, an end table, his favorite couch, the king-size bed he and Dana had shared and a few other things he didn't particularly want, but damned if he'd let her have them. He'd been too angry to see anything but red.

Two days after the race that'd had him and everyone else in the racing world questioning his ability as a horse trainer, she'd walked into their bedroom with an empty suitcase and handed it to him. Told him she wanted a divorce. Just like that. How had he not seen that side of her before? They'd married too young, still in the giddy stage of love and lust when they'd eloped without a word to anyone. And in the three years they were together, he'd seen her angry, hurt, pouty, even spiteful at times, but to kick a man when he was already down?

Clearly he'd underestimated Dana's need to have a wealthy, successful husband. She'd given up on him before the dust had even settled. Her lack of confidence in his ability to train more winning horses, making the big bucks she'd never had trouble spending, had taken a chunk of his heart. That last race, that one missed call, couldn't have been the only straw. But he'd had no idea it would be the last.

As for their divorce settlement, he figured giving her the big house and fancy sports car he'd paid for with his bonus money was more than enough. Hell, he'd never wanted the big colonial anyway. Or the car for that matter.

Mutt turned toward the driveway. The dog was smart, probably half border collie, and at least five years old. Poor guy was on the homely side, with one brown eye and the other a spooky gold. It had taken two baths before Trent was able to tell Mutt's chest was gray.

When he let out a long, low growl, Trent shaded his eyes and peered toward the road. He didn't get many visitors, and certainly none driving black luxury sedans.

"It's okay, boy." Trent bent to stroke the dog's side, but kept his gaze on the car as it turned down the long driveway. He glanced at Violet. "You expecting anyone?"

"What do you think?" she muttered, her frown aimed at the slowly approaching vehicle.

Right, silly question. "Sit," he told Mutt, and the dog promptly obeyed. "Stay." As the car neared the barn, Trent tugged down the rim of his hat to block the afternoon sun and started walking.

The tinted windows wouldn't let him see the driver but he noticed the Colorado plates. Whoever it was had to be lost. Not many people came out this far. After idling for a bit, the engine was cut. Trent stood near the hood on the passenger side, dusting off the front of his jeans while he waited for the driver's door to open.

A few seconds later a woman stepped out. The breeze whipped long strands of honey-blond hair across her face, preventing Trent from getting a good look at her. With a delicate hand she swept the hair out of her eyes.

She blinked at him, then smiled. "Hello."

"Afternoon," he said, touching the brim of his hat. She was pretty. Real pretty. High cheekbones. Full mouth. "Can I help you?"

"I hope so." She glanced at the small brick house. "I think this is the Eager Beaver ranch? The sign on the post is really faded."

"Yeah, um…" Trying not to grimace, he rubbed the back of his neck. Only the word Beaver was left on the wooden sign. He'd kinda thought it was funny. Until now. "I've been meaning to get around to that."

"Oh?" Her brows rose. She blinked again, looking confused as she scanned the rundown barn, sheds and chicken coop. When she lifted a hand and smiled, he saw Violet leaning forward. "I'm sorry," the woman said. "Please excuse my bad manners. I'm Shelby." She came around the hood, one hand extended, the other busy trying to keep from being blinded by the breeze tangling her hair. "Shelby Foster."

"Trent—" His fingers grazed hers. He yanked his hand back just in time. Grease and dirt streaked his palm. "Sorry, I've been working on the tractor."

She smelled good, sweet. Not perfumy, but more like the first clean whiff of spring. And her eyes, they were green. Like fresh-cut hay. When she narrowed them he realized he was staring like a jackass.

"Okay," she said. "I'm not sure I understand. If this is the Eager Beaver, you must be—" Her worried gaze darted to the equipment shed, then back to the house. "So, are you the—caretaker?"

"If I were, I'd be doing a mighty sorry job of it," he said with a laugh.

"Whew." Shelby grinned. "That's what I was thinking."

"Wait a minute—" His indignation only lasted a second. But then he got so distracted by her long slender legs, he forgot what he was about to say. "Who are you again?"

"Shelby Foster."

"No. I mean why are you here?"

"Well…" With a tentative smile she glanced at the porch that needed repairing. "I'm the new owner."

He pushed up the brim of his hat as if that would improve his hearing. "Come again?"

"Okay, not *new*. Actually it's been a year. But this is the first time I've come to see the place for myself."

Trent studied her face, the overly bright smile, the uncertainty in her eyes as her gaze swept toward the barn. It didn't seem as if she was joking and somehow he didn't think she was crazy.

"Who put you up to this?" he asked, closely watching her reaction. "Was it Colby?"

Her puzzled frown seemed genuine. "Put me up to what?"

"I know you're not the owner because I am."

Shelby raised her eyebrows. "You can't be."

"Yes, ma'am, I can." He removed his Stetson and shoved a hand through his hair, damp from sweat and starting to curl at his nape. He jammed the hat back on. "This ranch has been in my family for four generations."

"I don't understand," she said, a flicker of panic in her eyes. "How is that possible?"

Trent sure hoped she wasn't a victim of one of those auction scams. Buy property sight-unseen for cheap, then find out the paperwork is fake. The car, the clothes screamed success. She didn't look like someone who'd be that foolish. "There are a whole bunch of ranches around Blackfoot Falls. Maybe you got confused?"

"Any of them named the Eager Beaver?"

At her insulting tone of voice, any sympathy he'd felt for her dimmed. He liked the name, dammit. "Let's back up here. What makes you think you own the place?"

"I have the deed."

"The what?"

"The deed...it's a legal document—"

"I know what a deed is," he said, cutting her off. Hell, did she think he was some hayseed? Which brought to mind... "You don't look like a rancher or an outdoor kind of gal." He'd started his inspection with her fine leather boots, probably perfect for a night in the city but not out here. Her designer jeans could go either way, he supposed. But her clingy blue top? And those full pink lips...

He finally met her eyes. An icy chill darkened them and dared him to say another word. Or take another look.

Trent just smiled. She was safe from him. He was done with women, but looking was an entirely different matter. From his kitchen window, he loved watching the sun dip behind the Rockies. Didn't mean he planned on climbing them.

Lifting her chin, she said, "Now that we've established I'm the owner, who are you?"

"We what?" And here he'd worried she might be the victim of a con. Jesus. She really did think he was a country bumpkin. "You have a deed? I'd like to see it."

Her confidence faltered. Or maybe swiping her tongue across her lips was supposed to distract him. It almost worked. "I don't have it with me," she said, taking a deep breath that made her chest rise. "It's with my things, which will be arriving next week."

"Your things?" He stared at her, and she nodded. "No. No way. You call whoever's hauling your stuff and—" From his peripheral vision, he noticed Violet edging closer. He didn't need her sticking her nose in this. "Let's go in the house," he told Shelby in a more reasonable tone. "We can get something cold to drink. Figure this thing out."

She moistened her lips again, her expression cautious as she inspected his stained brown T-shirt, worn jeans and dusty boots.

"I'm not gonna bite," he said when she didn't move.

"Fine." With a toss of her hair, she picked her way through the gravel to the porch steps, having some trouble with those skinny, impractical boot heels.

He followed behind, torn between checking out her shapely rear end and keeping an eye on Violet. It would be just like her to stir up trouble, for sheer sport if nothing else. When he saw the old busybody closing the distance between them, he whistled for Mutt to run interference. At best, Trent had a fifty-fifty shot the dog would listen.

Shelby stopped at the screen door and turned to him.

"Go on inside. It's not locked."

She glanced past him, then entered the house.

He caught the screen and smiled when he saw that Mutt was doing his job. Violet stood near the barn, spewing curses and trying to evade the dog's long eager tongue. She liked the mooch well enough, even slipped him treats, but she couldn't stand him licking her.

"Come on, boy." Trent waited for the dog to bound up the steps and charge inside.

Yanking off his hat, he walked into the living room. Looking terrified, Shelby stood frozen, against the far wall where Mutt had cornered her. Jesus, he hadn't considered…

"Come," Trent commanded, but Mutt ignored him.

SHELBY FIGURED IF the dog was going to bite her, he'd have already done so. She tucked her purse under her arm, and crouched to pet the big shaggy fur ball that had to be over sixty pounds. She loved dogs but couldn't for the life of her identify his breed.

"Well, aren't you a cutie pie trying to look all ferocious." She found his sweet spot—a patch low behind his ear—and lightly raked it with her nails until his big eyes rolled back in contentment. "He has mud on his paws," she said, eyeing the dusty wood floor. "If you care."

She immediately regretted being snide. Trent ignored it, but she knew he'd heard. It wasn't like her to be rude. But she was tired, hungry and not completely enamored of the run-down Eager Beaver ranch. Stupid name, anyway. She'd look into changing it first thing.

And then there was Trent, whoever he was…besides tall and hot. Though being good-looking didn't work in his favor. Not with her. She'd had it with men. And their expectations. And… well, just about everything.

"How many times have I told you to use the doormat?" Trent said to the dog, then ducked out and returned with a faded towel. "He get any mud on you?"

She shook her head, then looked up. Trent's eyes were an unusual gray. She hadn't been able to tell earlier, but she'd noticed the strong jaw shadowed from a couple days' growth of beard. With his dark wavy hair, tanned skin and long, lean body, he was the perfect image of the untamed cowboy conquering the rugged West. If a woman had a fanciful imagination, which she did not. Anyway, she was from Colorado and knew better. Not all cowboys were equal. But all men were.

No, that wasn't fair. She looked at her left hand, where her engagement ring used to be. She was still raw from Donald's betrayal. From the proof that while he wanted to marry her, he didn't know her at all. In time the sting would fade. She had to believe that if she wanted to start fresh, prove to herself she could be successful on her own terms.

"Come here, boy." Trent crouched beside her and gave the dog's collar a light tug until his front paws were on the towel.

Huddling between Trent and a console table felt too intimate so she stood. "What's his name?"

"Mutt. Actually, it's Ugly Mutt. Sometimes I call him Ugly. But mostly just Mutt."

She stared down at him, ready and waiting to disappoint him when he looked for her reaction to his baiting. But he never looked up, simply concentrated on cleaning the dog's paws while her gaze followed the play of corded muscle along his forearms.

"You're kidding, right?" she said finally.

"About?"

"His name. You don't really call him Ugly."

"Sure I do." He gave the dog an affectionate pat. "Look at him."

"That's awful." How could he treat the poor animal that way? "*You're* awful."

Trent smiled. "You know he doesn't understand, right?"

Her gaze caught on the laugh lines fanning out at the corner of his eye. Then slid to his muscled bicep straining the sleeve of the T-shirt. When she finally noticed that he was giving her a funny look, she realized she'd stopped listening.

She cleared her throat and surveyed the room. "We need to straighten out this mess."

Trent glanced over his shoulder and frowned at the magazines and newspapers littering the coffee table. A pair of boots, one turned on its side, butted up to the burgundy recliner. "Which mess are we talking about?"

"The Eager Beaver," she said, as it slowly dawned on her that the place was furnished with chairs, a high-quality leather sofa, a flat-screen TV, rugs… Trent wasn't simply squatting or passing through. "And how quickly you can clear off my property."

He wasn't taking her one bit seriously. With a lifted brow he slid his gaze down her body. "You suddenly found that deed somewhere?"

"No. I explained where it is. But you seem so sure of yourself, I'm assuming you have one."

That wiped the smirk off his face. "I do. Not here. My folks have it in their bank safe-deposit box."

"In Blackfoot Falls? Shouldn't take you long to get it."

"They live in Dillon, four hours from here."

"Oh, how convenient."

"Says the woman who claims her papers are in transit." He pushed to his feet, bringing him a good five inches taller than her even with her three-inch heels. "What kind of—" He cut himself off, clamped his mouth shut.

They were standing too close to each other. Boxed in by the wall, table and Trent, she could feel his body heat and a hint of his breath on her cheek. Oddly, he smelled good, sort of woodsy, even though she knew he'd been working outside in the sun.

When he wouldn't move, she slipped around him. "You were saying?" she said, sneaking a peek in the bright yellow kitchen, surprised to see an open laptop sitting on a table.

"Nothing."

"Please." She turned to find him meticulously wiping his hands with the towel. "By all means, finish what you were about to say."

He looked up, his gaze narrowing.

Okay, that might've come out a bit haughty.

With his sights locked on her, he said, "I was wondering what kind of idiot packs important legal papers with their belongings instead of keeping the documents locked up or with them."

Heat surged up her neck and into her face. Someone who'd left in a hurry. Someone who'd been foolish enough to overstay where she hadn't belonged in the first place.

"I deserved that," Shelby said quietly. "I'm sorry."

His gaze lowered before he looked away. "We'll get this straightened out, but I'm warning you, it won't be the outcome you want."

She bit her lip. He seemed awfully sure, she thought, again

taking in the furniture, most of it quite nice. The truth was, she didn't really have the deed in her possession, only her grandfather's will. Of course she'd call the attorney who'd drawn the will up. Something she would've already done if she hadn't been in such a rush to get away from her ex-fiancé and his family.

"You should try The Boarding House Inn in town. Better hurry, though, it's getting late and there isn't another inn for miles."

Shelby studied his expressionless face. Naturally he was trying to get rid of her. "Hmm, I could ask around about you."

"Good idea. Most folks know me, or at least they know my family. They'll confirm what I've told you."

Her mouth went dry. Her heart sank. This wasn't looking good at all. Maybe he was bluffing.

"Hey, how about that cold drink I promised? I've got orange juice, water, beer…"

Annoyed that he must've noticed her difficulty swallowing, she shook her head. "How far is it to town?"

"Sixteen miles."

"And you don't care if I inquire about you," she said, watching him closely.

"Nope. Ask anyone."

A knock at the door had them both turning their heads.

Through the screen she saw it was the older woman who'd been sitting in the rocker. She was holding a covered dish.

Trent looked at it and groaned. "Really, Violet?"

Shelby didn't know why he sounded grumpy. It smelled like cornbread and something else, maybe molasses. Whatever it was, the aroma was divine.

The woman glared at him. "You gonna let me in?" She was tiny, not even five feet, her voice surprisingly rough.

When Trent didn't respond, Shelby looked at him. Why the hesitancy? The woman was obviously his neighbor…

Unless…

Shelby hurried to open the door. "Of course, this is perfect timing," she said, then glanced at Trent, who sighed with disgust. She smiled sweetly. "You did say I could ask anyone."

2

ANYONE BUT VIOLET.

Damn, no telling what the old busybody would say. She'd stir the pot just to see what bubbled over. She did it to him all the time.

Shelby held the door open wide.

Trent didn't try to hide his irritation. "I see you're making yourself right at home."

"Thank you, dear," Violet said, smiling at Shelby as she crossed the threshold.

He didn't miss the shrewd gleam in the troublemaker's eye. Shaking his head, he caught the door when Shelby let it go and kept it open. "Violet, I know you're not one for visiting. Don't let us keep you."

"Don't mind him." Violet passed the foil-covered dish to Shelby. "Nobody does."

"As a matter of fact, this young lady isn't staying, either." He swatted at the fly he'd let in. "She needs to get to Blackfoot Falls before The Boarding House Inn is full."

Shelby shook her head and smiled at Violet. "I'm Shelby."

"Shelby, huh?" Violet completely ignored him. Which was what he generally preferred, just not at the moment. "What a pretty name. I'm Violet Merriweather."

"Nice to meet you, Ms. Merriweather." Shelby sniffed the dish she held. "Is this cornbread?"

"Homemade. Along with my own baked-beans recipe. It won me a blue ribbon at the 1989 county fair. I use a couple shots of bourbon. And, honey, I'd be pleased if you call me Violet."

Trent would call her a cab and gladly pay the fare all the way to California if he thought that would get rid of her. She hadn't been inside the house even once since he'd moved back. As far as he knew, anyway. Probably came in to snoop when he went to town for supplies.

"For pity's sake, Trent Kimball," Violet said, wildly waving a hand around. "Must you let in all these damn flies?"

"They were invited. You weren't."

When Shelby stared at him as if he had the manners of a baboon, he let the screen door slam. But only because the flies were getting out of hand. Good. Let Ms. I've-got-the-deed know what ranch life was like. Full of flies, hard work and no time for this kind of bullshit.

"I've been here eight months now, and this woman has never offered me so much as a crumb," he said, gesturing to Violet. "She's nosy and is up to no good. Plain and simple."

Shelby blinked. "I thought you said your family's been here for generations?"

Trent sighed. He needed a beer, or preferably a whole bottle of tequila.

"Ah. I see..." Violet said, her face lighting up as she gave Shelby a head-to-toe inspection. "You must be the wife."

"Wife?" Shelby darted him a stunned look. "His? God, no."

Trent clenched his jaw. He wasn't so much insulted by Shelby's reaction as he was pissed at Violet for bringing up his failed marriage. Which she was dying to know more about. She could be a pain in his ass but this was the first time she'd made it personal.

Signaling for Mutt to follow, Trent headed for the kitchen. It didn't matter that he glimpsed a trace of regret in the old woman's pale eyes. If remorse got her out of his house quicker, then good, otherwise he didn't give a shit.

After he'd filled Mutt's food bowl and the dog was wolfing down his supper, Trent grabbed a beer out of the fridge. The two women could stand out there yakking for the rest of the afternoon for all he cared. Let Violet do her worst. Hell, Shelby could bunk with her in the double-wide.

He twisted off the bottle cap, threw it at the trash can and missed. Maybe Violet's comment was innocent. She hadn't actually said anything about him being divorced. Not that he kept it a secret. He just didn't like talking about it. Especially when some things about Shelby reminded him of his ex. The way she dressed, for instance. Designer jeans and high-heel boots around here? And those soft slim hands, she couldn't use them for much. So what the hell did she want with a ranch, anyway?

A nagging thought finally took hold. Violet hadn't put him in a sour mood. Well, no more than normal. Shelby's horrified reaction at being mistaken for his wife had done it. Which made no sense. He didn't know the woman and only wanted to get rid of her. Sure, she was attractive but he honestly wasn't interested.

The horde of flies he'd let in weren't helping his mood. Jesus, they were everywhere. He swatted at the persistent little bastard buzzing near his ear. And missed. He had a mind to set out Violet's beans and cornbread. That should keep them busy for a while.

Dammit, that one fly seemed determined to drive Trent crazy. It dive-bombed his ear again. He stayed completely still for a few seconds, waiting, waiting for the perfect moment, then spun around and slapped…

Shelby. Right in the face.

He stared at her and she stared back, eyes wide, lips parted. He looked at his hand again. What the hell…

When he looked back at Shelby, she'd hardly moved. Or blinked. It was some kind of miracle that she hadn't dropped the casserole dish.

He went to take it from her and she reared back.

"Jesus, I didn't mean to... I was going for a fly...then you were...you were in the living room... I didn't hear you. I swear I would never..." He nodded at the dish that was starting to sag. "Maybe I should just take that from you?"

He moved slowly, wishing she'd stop staring at him like he was the devil himself. Thankfully, she let him have the dish with no fuss.

Her head tilted a smidge as she blinked. "You slapped me."

"No, I was— There was this fly," he said, wondering why, the one time in his life when he'd needed a fly, it had vanished into thin air. "I'm truly sorry. Let me see," he said, reaching for her.

She moved back again, lifting a tentative hand to her face.

"It wasn't on purpose." Trent couldn't see any kind of mark or discoloration but that didn't make him feel much better. He'd never hit a woman in his life, and he hoped to never do it again. Even by accident. "Why'd you sneak up on me?"

"I did no such thing."

"Sorry, I didn't mean... Please, let me have a look..."

"I'll live." She slowly flexed her jaw. "For your information I was bringing in the food, not sneaking up on you."

"What happened?" Violet rushed in with a concerned frown.

"I hit Shelby."

"It was an accident," she said, giving him an exasperated look.

"Well, I expect it had to be," Violet muttered. "Trent can be a stubborn jackass just like his great-grandpa, but he wouldn't strike a woman. Where did he get ya?"

"Really, it's nothing." Shelby turned her head, away from their prying eyes. "I could use something cold to drink."

He saw her eyeing his beer and he grabbed another one from the fridge. "What about you, Violet?"

"Wouldn't mind some whiskey if you got it."

No surprise there. He opened Shelby's beer and as he passed it to her, he snuck a look at her jaw. He doubted it would bruise, it hadn't been that hard. But that wasn't the point. Shit. He got out the Jack Daniel's from an upper cabinet, wondering if he could convince Shelby to use some ice on her face.

Violet took the bottle from him, then helped herself to a glass sitting on the draining rack.

He watched Shelby take an impressive gulp of beer. "How about—"

"No," she said, her voice firm. "Thank you."

"You don't even know what I was gonna say."

"No ice. I'm fine."

Trent hid a sigh by drinking his own beer. He hated when women did that. Pretended they could read your mind. He hated it even more when they were right. Well, screw that. "Not ice. I have a thick T-bone in the fridge."

Shelby let out a short laugh. "You're not serious."

He wasn't but she didn't need to know that.

"I'm not putting a slab of raw meat on my jaw."

"It's supposed to work for black eyes."

"That's a foolish, archaic old wives' tale."

"Good. Because I've changed my mind. I'm frying that steak for my supper."

Violet threw back a healthy shot of whiskey and poured another. "Is it big enough for all of us?"

"No." It wasn't enough that she was guzzling down his whiskey? She wanted his steak, too? He noticed Shelby checking out the silly daisy wallpaper he hadn't had time to get rid of yet.

"Yep," Violet muttered. "You're just like your great-grandpa. Cut from the same ornery mold."

Trent looked at her. "What was that crack earlier? I'm not stubborn, and neither was Gramps."

Violet snorted. "Like hell." She nodded at Shelby. "So was yours. I reckon that's why you two are here in this mess."

"Excuse me?" Shelby stared at her. "How could you know my grandfather?"

"Can't say I ever met *him*, but I knew your great-granddaddy.

You said your last name is Foster. Harold Foster was your great granddad, wasn't he?" Violet said, and Shelby nodded. "Harold was a kind, mild-mannered man most of the time."

"Wait. Hold on. What mess?" Trent asked, knowing in his gut he wouldn't like the answer. "Because I was doing just fine before…" He glanced at Shelby, saw her absently probing her jaw, felt a stab of guilt and closed his mouth.

"While you were in the kitchen swatting at flies, this young lady told me why she's here," Violet said, "and I've got a fair notion as to what might've happened."

Shelby's green eyes brightened. "You think I really do own the Eager Beaver?"

"Look here, Violet, you can't just make up stories because you're bored," Trent warned. "I swear to God, if you stir up trouble, I'm gonna sic Mutt on you."

Shelby inhaled sharply. "You wouldn't."

He ignored her, determined not to let Violet off the hook even if Mutt would just lick her to death. "This woman has driven all the way from Colorado and—"

"How do you know where I'm from? I didn't tell you."

"License plates."

"Oh."

He wished she'd quit wetting her lips and distracting him. "How's the jaw?"

"Don't change the subject."

"Well, excuse the hell out of me for being concerned." Trent started to take a pull of beer but pointed the bottle at Violet instead. "Tell her how long my family's owned this ranch. You ought to know. I remember you had that old brown trailer when I was a kid living here with my folks. You'd just gotten the double-wide when I visited Colby six years ago. Now, go on and tell Shelby that this property rightfully belongs to the Kimballs. Please."

Violet ignored him. As usual.

Shelby looked like all the air had left her lungs. If she hadn't been set on taking his last chance away from him, he would've felt sorry for her.

He turned back to Violet, who was watching the byplay as if she'd have to testify in court. "You have no intention of straightening this out, do you? Makes sense, since it would be the first nice thing you've done since I came back home. I don't even know why I let you stick around. I should've given you the boot."

Shelby gasped.

He looked at her. "What?"

"Could you be any ruder?"

"Sweetheart, you have no idea." Trent tossed back more beer, and then wiped the back of his hand across his mouth. "You got a problem with my etiquette, there's the door."

"Huh." Shelby sniffed with disdain. "I'm surprised you know such a big word."

"What?" He snorted. "You mean a Neanderthal like me?"

"Now you're just showing off."

Violet's rusty cackle reminded them she was still there.

Shelby blushed and took a dainty sip.

He probably should've offered her a glass. "You gonna tell her, Violet? Instead of letting her get her hopes up." He did a quick once-over of Shelby, from the top of her tawny hair all the way down to her city boots. "Not that she'd last more than twenty minutes out here."

"Honey," she said, her chin lifting, "*you* have no idea."

Trent met her feisty green eyes. She had grit, he'd give her that, but with those dainty manicured hands and soft skin, she'd chosen the wrong zip code.

"Well, ain't you two a pair?" Violet muttered, sounding more troubled than amused. "It's like watching Harold and Edgar all over again. This isn't good. Not good at all."

They exchanged frowns, then both turned their attention to Violet.

Edgar was Trent's great-grandfather, though he'd died when

Trent was eleven, so his memory of him might be a little fuzzy. "So, out with it," he said. "Say what you want to say."

"Pigheaded and impatient. You're just like him," she said, her fondness for Edgar obvious in the small smile tugging at her weathered mouth. She nodded at Shelby. "Harold was another one. You couldn't find a pair of mules more ornery than those two boys. Both of them twelve years my senior and acting like kids. Fighting all the time, mostly over nothing at all. Makes a body wonder how they ever became friends much less business partners."

He watched Violet pour more whiskey, then he glanced at Shelby. From the dread on her face, he figured she was thinking along the same lines as him. Hell, he sure hoped his folks had an honest-to-goodness deed in their possession or this could get sticky.

"Business partners," Shelby repeated. "What kind of business?"

"Well, the Eager Beaver, of course."

Trent muttered a quiet curse.

Sighing, Shelby rubbed her left temple.

Mutt stood at the kitchen door and barked. After Trent let him out, he saw Shelby frowning at the unsightly grooves on the doorframe, remnants from Mutt's habit of scratching to go outside. The job required the wood to be sanded before he could paint. It was on his to-do list along with a hundred other chores.

He had a feeling he was going to need another beer. The fridge door squeaked when he opened it. Just like the other dingy white appliances, the poor old Frigidaire was on its last leg. "Obviously the partnership didn't work out," he said, and nodded at Shelby's nearly empty bottle.

She shook her head. Her resigned expression should've made him feel better. It was clear Edgar had stayed and worked the ranch. Had Harold given up his share and moved to Colorado?

Violet wasn't looking smug as expected, but kind of glum, so he let her be and waited until she was ready to continue.

It was Shelby who finally broke the silence. "I'm not sure what any of this means. Are you saying my great-grandfather sold out to Edgar?"

Violet shrugged her narrow shoulders. "Can't say one way or the other."

Okay, Trent wasn't sticking around for any more of her tap dancing when the truth was plain as day. The tractor wasn't going to fix itself and he was losing daylight. It wouldn't kill him to let Shelby stay in the spare room for a night... Yeah, it could. Next thing he knew, she'd be moving her stuff in and taking over the house.

His gaze caught on the rise and fall of her breasts and he had to remind himself he wasn't interested. Not in her, not in any woman. Now, he wasn't opposed to some recreational sex once in a while. But with Shelby? As his granddad used to say, Trent had as much chance as a one-legged man in a kicking contest.

"Some folks need to argue about everything. It's just their way. Those two even fought over naming the ranch," Violet continued. "Edgar claimed he saw a beaver over at Twin Creek reservoir, and Harold swore up and down it was a marmot. They finally flipped a coin."

"As fascinating as all this is," Trent said, grabbing the whiskey and returning it to the cabinet. "I have work to do."

Violet didn't protest being cut off, which was peculiar in itself. Then her faraway gaze drifted to the window over the sink, as if she'd slipped into her own little world. "Always arguing like those two did, no one ever paid them any mind...but that Saturday-night poker game at Len's they had a terrible falling out. Both of them with full-blown cases of booze blind, they said things they couldn't take back." She shook her head, the sadness in her face giving the room a chill. "Stupid old mules. A day later, Harold up and left."

He glanced at Shelby. Hugging herself, her expression sympathetic, she stared at Violet.

When Shelby turned to look at him, he avoided her eyes and took a swig of beer.

"What the hell did you do with my whiskey?" Violet had returned to the present with her usual cantankerous disposition, and Trent couldn't say he was sorry. At least it helped prove to Shelby that Violet was a nightmare.

"*Your* whiskey?" He put his empty beer bottle in the sink. "The tea party is over, ladies. I'm going back to work."

"Don't let us stop you." Violet pulled her pipe out of her pocket.

"On, no. Not in here, you don't. Put that away."

Violet huffed in annoyance.

Shelby cleared her throat. "So, I guess we're back to where we started."

Not from where he stood. Although she claimed to have a deed. And he didn't peg her for a liar. Obviously there was more to the story. "I'd be happy to give you directions to The Boarding House Inn. It's on Main Street. You can't miss it."

"Actually, I'll be staying here until one of us can prove ownership."

"Are you kidding me?"

"It's the only fair thing to do."

Violet chuckled. "Attagirl."

Mutt barked from outside the door.

"You can let him in on your way out," Trent said to Violet, who gave him the familiar glare, basically telling him to kiss her ass. He grinned. "Thanks for the beans and cornbread."

3

SHELBY WATCHED THE interplay between Trent and Violet. Any other time it might have amused her. Neither of them would admit it, but they liked being neighbors. They liked each other. Had it been that way with her great-grandfather and Edgar? Had their friendship been based on harmless banter and a genuine concern for each other...until it hadn't?

What had caused the final showdown, she wondered. Violet knew the answer, of that Shelby was quite certain. Just as she was convinced the older woman would never reveal it. Shelby didn't consider herself the romantic sort, but she couldn't help wondering if Violet had been the source of the trouble between the two men. Although she would've been fairly young.

Violet still had the pipe in her hand as she walked toward the door. "I reckon I'll go on home and leave you two to figure out sleeping arrangements."

Shelby and Trent looked at each other at the same time. Annoyingly, she felt a blush spread across her cheeks. She was quick to refocus her attention. Which happened to land on his left hand, his ring finger to be exact, and the pale mark that could easily be from a wedding band he'd once worn.

Violet had mistaken Shelby for his wife. Not ex-wife, and he hadn't corrected her so they were probably separated. Interesting that Violet didn't know the woman. Not that it made a difference to Shelby. He could have five wives for all she cared. Though she doubted he'd find that many women willing to put up with him.

He took her empty bottle and rinsed it out along with his. As he stood at the sink she got her first good look at his behind. His very nice behind. He was tall and muscular without being too husky, a body type she'd always appreciated. Okay, so he had a few decent assets.

A loud bark made her jump.

Just as the dog came bounding in, she caught Violet's mischievous grin. The woman had paused at the screen door and watched her ogle Trent.

Shelby did the only thing she could do. She smiled back. "Thank you for the food. I'll be sure to return your dish," she said. "Or maybe you'd like to join us for dinner?"

Trent turned, his eyes narrowed. "Excuse me, but this is still my house."

"Half," Shelby said. "Half your house. I think we can agree on that for the time being. Don't you?"

"Hell no."

Violet let out a howl of laughter as the screen slammed behind her. Shelby could see how her cackle might get on a person's nerves after a while. She bent to pet the dog's head and as the sound faded, watched Trent drop the rinsed bottles into a plastic milk crate, purposely ignoring her.

"I'll get my things from the car," she told him, not surprised when he didn't answer. "I hope there's a spare room."

"Nope."

"This is a three-bedroom house. You can't be sleeping in all three rooms."

"Yes, I could, but as it happens, I use one for storage." He paused. "And the third as my office."

She glanced at the laptop sitting on the table, then raised her brows at him. "I bet there's enough space for me to sleep."

"I have private stuff in there. I can't give just anyone access."

"Hmm, well, I suppose I'll have to take the couch."

"I watch TV late. Sometimes till three in the morning."

"No wonder you don't have time to keep the place up," she said, sweeping a gaze over the cracked linoleum floor and chipped Formica countertops, before returning to Trent.

His eyes had turned a steely gray. It made him look a bit dangerous, and she suppressed a shiver. "See, that's the beauty of owning my own place. I don't have to answer to anyone. And you know what else? The couch is mine."

She drew in a deep breath, refusing to look away. If she hadn't met the *other* Trent, the more affable man who'd teased Violet, the man who had seemed genuinely stricken over accidentally hitting her, Shelby would've left by now. She'd be too afraid to be in the house alone with him. Also, knowing Violet was next door helped.

No, she couldn't afford to lose ground now. What was that saying about possession accounting for nine-tenths of the law? "I'd like to see the storage room. And your office. Maybe we can move things around. I don't need much space." *For now.* Luckily, she'd noticed the perfect spot to make her jewelry.

He snorted a laugh. "Lady, you are something else. You wanna stick around, feel free to sleep in your car."

"I thought about it," she said, pleased that she'd surprised him. "But since neither of us can actually prove ownership, I don't think I should be inconvenienced."

Trent stared back, shaking his head. "You're willing to stay in a house, alone, with a strange man. I could be a serial killer, a bank robber, an ex-con—"

"With a whole town willing to vouch for you? I don't think so." She smiled. "Shall I poke around on my own, or do you want to show me the rest of the house?"

He folded his muscular arms across his chest. "Look me in the eye and tell me you honestly don't believe this dispute is going to turn out in my favor."

She blinked, once, then met his steady gaze. A jitter in her tummy prevented her from speaking right away. This last week had taught her several important lessons. Not the least of which was to stop being a pushover, stop compromising her individuality in order to be liked and to belong.

Shelby understood his anger. It appeared his ancestors had stayed, hers had not. Trent was right. When the dust settled, it was very likely she'd have no claim at all. But in the meantime, in case there was the slimmest possibility she was entitled to even a fraction of the place, she'd stay right here. Where she had the best chance of proving she could stand on her own two feet. Enjoy the creative freedom to design jewelry she loved without having her work belittled.

"We have no way of knowing what happened to Harold and Edgar's partnership, or how it affected the ownership of the Eager Beaver," she said calmly, very aware that she'd skirted the question.

Unless she was mistaken, Trent was seriously considering calling her on it. He studied her for a long excruciating moment, then brushed past her without a word.

She followed him out of the kitchen and to the hall. She took a quick peek down both sides. Only one bathroom. That sucked.

"This is my bedroom," he said, motioning to his left, his lips a thin straight line. "The one at the other end is yours."

The door was open. No furniture in her line of sight. Just ugly brown carpet. "Okay. What about—"

"We'll split the house in half. You stay on your side and I stay on mine. As soon as I get my hands on the deed, you're outta here. Agreed?"

"Well, no…" She poked her head into the no-frills bathroom. There was a shower-tub combo, a toilet, sink, no counter space to speak of, blue wallpaper from the eighties. But everything looked clean. "How are we supposed to divide the bathroom?"

"We're not. It's on my side. Feel free to use the john in the barn."

She turned back to him. "You're not serious."

"If the toilet gives you any trouble, shake the handle a few times. The shower is mostly used to get off the grime before coming in the house, so it's not enclosed. But don't worry. No one's gonna look."

Shelby stared into his smug face, while holding on to her temper by a thread. So this was how he wanted to play it. Clearly he'd forgotten a not so small detail. "All right, so I guess the kitchen is mine."

"Part of it."

"No, it's definitely on my side—"

He shouldered past her as if she were speaking to the wall.

"Where are you going?"

"Stay right there," he said as he put one booted foot in front of the other and paced off the room.

Diagonally.

"No," she said. "Stop. That's not how dividing works."

"You'll have the same square footage as me."

She tried to picture the kitchen. Exasperated, she couldn't remember it clearly, but she was pretty sure the sink, stove and fridge were not in her corner. Assuming she'd put up with this nonsense.

Yeah, when pigs fly.

"You're being a child," she told him.

He ignored her, disappeared into the kitchen, then reappeared holding up a roll of blue duct tape. "Just so you're clear on your areas."

"You're insane," she said, and caught a glimmer of a smile as he ran a long strip of tape across the hardwood floor. Of course that's what he wanted her to think so she'd get in her car and drive as far away as possible. "I'm surprised the tape can stick to all that dust."

He paused and gave the floor a thoughtful inspection. "To show you what a good guy I am, I'll loan you a broom so you can sweep your side." He frowned. "I almost forgot," he said and walked past her, back into the hall.

She found him standing just inside the door to her assigned room. Staring at a very nice unmade sleigh-style daybed that had been pushed against the beige wall. Blinds covered the lone window. "So, was this your storage room or your office?" she asked sweetly.

Trent's mouth curved in a slight smile. "Give me a few minutes and I'll get that out of your way."

The daybed? The mattress looked brand-new. And comfortable. She cursed her big mouth. "It's fine where it is. I wouldn't want to inconvenience you."

"No trouble."

Shelby watched him approach the bed. The brown carpet was looking less and less appealing. "Um, Trent..."

He cocked a brow.

Okay, humbling herself wouldn't kill her, but sleeping on the stained carpet might. "I would appreciate you leaving the bed." She cleared her throat. "Please."

Even as he made a show of mulling it over, humor glinted in his eyes. "You seem like a modern, independent woman. Just so you won't feel beholden, I'll rent it to you."

She sighed. "How much?"

"Hmm...let's see." Rubbing his jaw, he studied the bed. "Fifty bucks a night sound about right?"

"Fifty?" She paused to dial down her growing temper. Two could play this game. "Sounds high to me," she said, gingerly probing the spot where he'd clipped her. It didn't hurt in the least, but he didn't know that. "I guess I don't have much choice, though. I'm afraid the floor may be too hard."

Trent studied her, his expression that of a man who knew he'd been bested. "It's yours. On the house," he said walking past her. "Find your own sheets."

"Thank you," she called after him, and grinned when he cursed under his breath.

"YOU LIKE HER, don't you?" Trent shook his head at Mutt, who stood at the door whining to go after Shelby. "You're a damn traitor, that's what you are. Next time you want a treat, you'd better hope she packed some for you. She certainly has enough luggage," he muttered, watching her from the window as she pulled another suitcase out of her trunk, this one even bigger than the monstrosity she'd already carried to her room.

Mutt moved closer and barked at him.

"What? You just had your supper. And quit slobbering all over the linoleum. You want your new girlfriend to think you're uncouth?"

Trent wiped down the stained porcelain for the third time before he realized what he was doing. Hell, he didn't have to pretend to clean the kitchen sink just so he could keep an eye on her. Mutt didn't know the difference.

Anyway, this was still his house. His window. His damn driveway. He could look at anything he damned well pleased. He tossed the sponge aside, dried his hands and pushed his fingers through his hair.

The dog panted loudly, his long pink tongue hanging out of his mouth as he stared up at Trent.

"Forget it, buddy. I'm not going to help her. Why should I? She's lucky I don't call the sheriff and have her locked up for trespassing." In spite of himself, he looked outside again and watched her set a big cardboard box on the ground. "Hell, how deep is that trunk?"

Man, she had a lot of stuff. This was her third trip into the house. Each time she'd been loaded down with bags, pillows and whatnot. Hadn't she said her belongings were gonna be delivered next week? How much crap did she have? He shouldn't be surprised. Not after being married for three years.

She picked up the box, struggling to get a hold on it. She wasn't all that short, maybe five-six, but her arms couldn't make it all the way around. Stopping midway from her car to the walk, she set the box down. Or more like dropped it.

Mutt whimpered and ran back to the door, tail high and swishing back and forth.

"All right." Trent grabbed his hat off the peg behind the door and pointed at the dog. "You owe me."

By the time he made it to the porch, she was dragging the box up the front walk. She must've heard the screen's squeaky hinges because she looked up. "I assume I have a grace period to cross your side of the house until I finish unloading?"

Without a word he walked over, hefted the box and carried it to the porch, then left it there while he grabbed the suitcase. The suckers weighed a friggin' ton. Obviously she wasn't kidding about moving in.

"I didn't ask for your help," she said, a bit snippy when he crowded her off the stone walkway.

"You're welcome." He dropped the suitcase next to the box. "Anything else?"

"I'll get it." She started to turn and paused. "And thank you."

Trent watched her open the back door and lean across the seat. Gave him a real nice view of her butt. Naturally Violet was watching them from her porch. He wondered why she hadn't invited Shelby to stay with her. Just to fill her ears with a bunch of crap about him. Maybe create her own little reality show right here at the Eager Beaver.

He returned his attention to Shelby. Yep, a damn nice butt. Now if she knew how to cook, he might consider putting up with her for a week or so. Looked as though she planned to put down roots for longer than that. Damned if she didn't haul out another box the size of Wyoming. As with the other one, she could barely get her arms around the thing.

Sighing, Trent left the porch, taking the steps two at a time. "I've got it," he said.

The way she was bent over he could see right down her blouse. He forced himself to look away but not before he glimpsed the swell of her breasts plumping over a plain white bra. He didn't know why but he expected something snazzier.

Red or black, maybe some lace. Though he was more interested in her...

"Did you hear me?" She straightened with a hand on her hip.

"Huh?" He met her accusing eyes. "Yeah, I heard you," he said and hoisted the heavy box.

"I said, I can manage."

"I'm not trying to be nice. You throw your back out and God knows when I'll ever get rid of you."

"Charming to a fault."

Sunlight shined directly on her face, and he was relieved there was no visible mark from his hand. She caught him staring and turned away to get another smaller bag from the backseat. The fact that striking her had been an accident wasn't making it any easier to ignore. She didn't seem to want to be fussed over. Earlier, though, in his old bedroom, when she'd touched her jaw, he had a feeling she might've been playing him. Didn't matter. Guilt nudged him either way.

Instead of leaving the box with the others, he set it just inside. He wasn't about to make the mistake of propping the door open and letting more flies in. By the time he moved everything off the porch, Shelby had joined him, carrying an overnight bag and a sack of groceries.

Puzzled, Trent grabbed the suitcase and smaller box, then led the way down the hall. This woman wasn't easy to peg. How she dressed, taking a chance on a place sight-unseen, out in the boonies no less. While she'd brought her own pillow, it seemed she'd been willing to sleep on the floor until her bed was delivered. Maybe she'd robbed a bank and was on the run.

He passed the room he actually was using for storage, and stopped at the one that had been his as a teenager. Holes from his old rodeo posters were still visible on the beige walls. The carpet didn't look too bad, though he imagined the dark color had a lot to do with that.

The wood blinds were slanted up to keep out the morning sun.

He'd completely forgotten about the pop-up trundle underneath the bare mattress, which fortunately, looked brand-new. If he remembered correctly the bed had occupied the second guest room back in Texas.

"If you don't like sleeping on a twin I can set up the trundle and push them together," he said.

"A twin is fine."

It took him a few seconds to remember he wasn't supposed to be making this easy on her. He set the suitcase near the closet and the box beside it. The contents clanged. Pots maybe? His gaze slid back to her sack of groceries.

"Is that it?"

Shelby frowned, puckering her lips in a way that made him forget what they were talking about. She turned to peek into the small closet and his eyes drew to her nice round backside.

He'd never understood why a woman would spend so much for designer jeans. He did now. Shelby turned to face him. Her eyebrows rose expectantly.

"Violet tell you this place is cursed?"

Shelby laughed. "No, she didn't."

"I'm not saying I believe it, but lots of folks do."

"Ah. I'll keep that in mind."

"I don't have to scare you off," he said, irritated by the amusement in her voice. "We both know you don't have a claim."

"If I thought that I would've left by now." She paused. "If you're so sure of yourself, why haven't you kicked me out?"

"Despite your low opinion of me, my mama raised me to be a gentleman." He couldn't say why her faint smile riled him. "If you've got any questions, I'll be outside."

"Aren't you worried I'll rob you blind?"

"Sorry, sweetheart—" Trent snorted a laugh "—someone else beat you to it."

4

THIRTY MINUTES LATER Shelby had hung some clothes and sorted her toiletries. The bathroom was small, typical of older homes, and sharing it with a virtual stranger wouldn't be easy. But it was better than having to trudge out to use the one in the barn. She really hoped he'd been teasing about that.

So she divided her makeup and personal hygiene stuff into two groups of must-have and optional, then packed them in smaller bags to take to the bathroom—wherever that turned out to be—with her as needed.

Fortunately she'd remembered to pack a couple of towels and her pillow but she'd forgotten about sheets. What was left of her jewelry-making supplies, though, those she'd kept close. It would've been so much easier to let the movers bring the boxes along with her furniture since it was doubtful she'd be setting up shop soon. She was low on just about everything she needed to make the silver and brass pieces that would bring in some good money. And she knew for sure she had to replace the old soldering iron. But after that awful scene with Donald, she'd been too hurt and angry to think straight.

She sighed, not eager to ask Trent for sheets. Maybe she could lay a towel on the mattress and bring in the emergency blanket she kept in her trunk just in case she was ever stranded in foul weather. Along with it she kept a first-aid kit, a flashlight, batteries, bottles of water and power bars. Someone who was that careful should never have ended up in this mess. She wasn't normally impulsive; she was cautious, prepared for anything.

Except, of course, a broken engagement.

And a run-down ranch.

And no job.

Hopefully she wasn't starting a new trend, she thought, glancing around the small room. What the hell…there was a roof, walls; it was dusty but clean, and she hadn't had to pull out her credit card, so the situation wasn't completely awful.

Thinking back on the wedding gown she'd found just last week, she sighed. It had been love at first sight, and not because Mrs. Williamson would've disapproved of the retro style. Regardless of her ex-boss and erstwhile future mother-in-law's insistence, Shelby had never done anything to deliberately spite the woman. Shelby really did like trendy shoes and modern art, and a few other things Mrs. Williamson found vulgar. They simply had different tastes.

And Donald, well, he…

Shelby swallowed hard, trying to clear the lump in her throat.

Donald should've been on her side. Silly her, she'd misjudged his silence for support when she'd mentioned dusting off her old equipment and stretching her creative boundaries. But she could see the truth now. He'd assumed she'd be too busy designing pricy pieces for his parents' pretentious stores and inhabiting the role of Mrs. Donald Williamson to be bothered with her "tacky hobby." Well, screw him.

Sinking to the edge of the daybed, she traded her boots for well-worn sneakers and thought about making the dreaded call to her mom. Though not today. For one thing, it was the middle of the night in Germany where she was living with her new husband. But mostly, Shelby wasn't ready to listen to her mom go on and on about how Donald was a successful attorney, wealthy, handsome and a good provider. How Shelby would never have to work another day in her life. In one minute, Gloria Halstead could send feminism back a century.

Of course she'd call her father, too, but he had his hands full with his teenage stepchildren. He'd barely blink at the news. Just give her a verbal pat on the head and promise she'd find the *right one* soon. Which was completely fine with her. Shelby preferred his laidback approach to life. With her mom there was always so much drama.

She picked up her bag of groceries and wondered how serious Trent was over the whole dividing the house thing. Maybe he just needed to cool off. In the meantime, she could keep her perishables in the foam cooler she'd bought along the way. She went outside to fetch it from her car and saw Trent fiddling with something on the tractor. His T-shirt, damp with sweat, strained against his muscular frame. When he leaned across the engine, the worn denim of his jeans hugged his butt. Without his hat, his dark wavy hair gleamed in the late afternoon sun.

A tingle of awareness did something funny to her stomach. It wasn't difficult to ignore the unwanted reaction. Sure he was attractive, but annoying. And hadn't she just gotten rid of a pompous, annoying man?

Thinking of Donald again made her ache. Though not nearly enough considering they'd been dating for three whole years and engaged for ten months of that. This wasn't the first time she'd worried about not being more upset. Was it shock? When it wore off was she in for a heart-crushing plunge? After all, the wedding was planned for spring. They'd already decided on everything. She should feel devastated, not relieved. Or concerned over her faulty judgment in accepting his proposal.

Mutt spotted her first. He lifted his head from his shady nook in the grass, then came running toward her, tail wagging. Violet was nowhere in sight.

Trent's gaze followed the dog. His mood didn't seem to have improved. Whether because of the tractor or his comment about someone else robbing him blind, she didn't know. She figured he'd been referring to his wife, or ex-wife.

"Am I allowed to use the fridge?" she asked, shading her eyes to look at him. "I forgot."

"That's why I used tape. The stove, fridge and sink are all on my side." He eyed her sneakers, then her messy ponytail before turning back to the engine.

"Basically that means I have no access to water in the house."

"That would be correct."

God, she hoped he wasn't serious about the ridiculous setup. But then, what did she expect? She was a stranger, an intruder invading his space without warning... She bit her lip. See? Her judgment was completely messed up.

If it weren't for Violet living right on the property, Shelby would never have made the impulsive decision to stay. By the same token, it was Violet who had given her hope that Shelby's grandfather's bequest was valid. And if she ever needed a time for that to be true, it was now. She'd never felt so lost, not when her parents had divorced or when she'd changed high schools in the middle of junior year and immediately become the girl with the ugly glasses.

"Wait," he said, when she turned back toward the house. "I'm pissed off at this engine. I didn't mean to take it out on you."

"I don't blame you for being upset." She wasn't fibbing, though she'd also decided that being nice to him could benefit her restricted living conditions. "I appear out of the blue, disrupt your life. If the situation were reversed I'd be upset."

"Yeah, well..." He rubbed a hand down his face and rolled his neck, grimacing with the effort. "I've been doing some thinking. Obviously you didn't show up here on a whim. You believe you have a stake in the place, and from what Violet said, you just might," he said, squinting at her. Then yanked up the hem of his shirt and blotted the sweat from his eyes.

She stared at his bare belly, tanned and ridged with muscle. How did a cowboy get a six-pack like that?

"Don't get too excited."

With a soft gasp, she snapped her gaze up to his face. He hadn't caught her gawking. He was still wiping his face.

"Our great-grandpas might've been partners at some point, but it seems the Kimballs ended up sticking around and making something of the place."

Could've fooled her. The barn, even the sheds looked horribly run-down. With the exception of the large, freshly painted structure closest to the corral. "Is that the stable?"

"Yep."

"Do you have horses?"

"Why? You want those, too?"

Shelby bristled. Here she'd thought they were moving toward détente. Still, no point in antagonizing him. She forced a smile. "Just making conversation."

"I have two quarter horses. One is a racehorse. That's what I do—I train them."

"Oh." Now it made sense that the stable was in such great condition. Beside it was parked a very nice horse trailer that probably cost a chunk. "So you're not really a rancher or farmer."

"Nope."

"I thought I saw some chickens."

He studied her a moment. "I have a milk cow, too. But the horses are my main focus."

"May I see them?"

"I'm sure you will," he said, resigned. "Just not right now."

"Okay." She looked up at the sky, then toward the Rockies. "It's pretty around here." She smiled, and ignored the suspicion in his narrowed eyes. "Peaceful," she added, wondering if now was the time to ask again about using the fridge.

She had a better idea. "Well, sorry I bothered you. I came out to get something from my car." She popped open the trunk and lifted the cooler, then balanced it against her hip while she closed the trunk.

She slowly carried it down the walkway to the front door, fairly sure he was watching her. Halfway there he said, "Wait."

Bingo.

Him offering the fridge instead of her asking again would be better in the long run. Let him lord his generosity over her, she didn't care. She got her cocky grin in check before turning to him.

"While you're out here, I might as well show you to your bathroom," he said, nodding toward the barn, a little smile betraying his amusement.

She could only stare at him.

What a prick.

WHILE HE WAS still working outside, Shelby hurriedly took a shower. In the house. Afterward, she pulled on a pair of old khaki shorts and a comfy T-shirt, then wiped down everything, until the place was exactly as she'd found it, which was clean. Like the kitchen. It seemed he only had a thing against sweeping.

She hung her damp towel over the rod in her closet and considered her next move. The refrigerator was old and didn't have an icemaker. Something she'd discovered when she'd tried to swipe some fresh ice for the cooler. She hadn't dared touch the two trays. The jerk probably knew exactly how many cubes were in there. She supposed she could bargain with him, offer a trade of some sort. Maybe do the sweeping and mopping?

Trent had shown her the barn bathroom just as he'd promised. And she honestly couldn't tell if he meant to carry out his edict, threat, whatever it was. But the so-called bathroom was horrible. The toilet was semi-enclosed by two walls and stacked hay bales. And the shower was a joke. Anyone walking ten feet into the barn had a clear view of it. No way could he think she'd use the stupid thing. Probably wanted to see how long it would take before she begged.

He'd really had her going with all that talk about how it was

possible she had a claim. Which made him showing her the outdoor pit of a bathroom seem cruel. It certainly set her on edge.

Once she'd calmed down and realized that was likely his
game plan, she decided on her strategy. It wouldn't be light for
much longer, but he was still cussing at the tractor when she
walked to her car.

Mutt trotted over to her and Trent looked up. She opened her
trunk, then glanced around, scoping out the floodlight under
the eave of the barn, the pair on either side of the stable door.

"The bulb's burned out," Trent said, gesturing to the barn.
"I'll get around to changing it sooner or later."

"No problem." She pulled the flashlight from her emergency
kit, as well as extra batteries. Well, it was more of a spotlight,
which was perfect, though she doubted she'd need it for long.

"I have a twelve-foot ladder if you want to change the bulb,"
he said and swung up into the tractor seat.

"Maybe I will." She smiled, closed the trunk. "But not today."

His eyes narrowed at her, but his curiosity was forgotten
the second the engine started. "Yes!" He sunk back in his seat
and stared up at the sky. "Thank you. Thank you. Thank you."

Shelby smiled. She couldn't have cared less about his tractor victory except that his improved mood might extend to her.

"Have you been working on it long?"

"A couple days." He gunned the engine, then turned to her.
His gaze lingered on her bare legs, then swept to her T-shirt.
The instant he met her eyes, the flicker of interest died, and his
expression changed. "How about that, sweetheart? You might've
brought me some luck."

The phony endearment grated on her ears. Letting it go was
the smart thing to do. She suspected he'd meant to irritate her.
Maybe not. Some guys were still Neanderthals. But for some
reason she doubted Trent was one of them.

You can catch more flies with honey, she reminded herself.
She forced a smile that she suspected came out all wrong. "Since

it appears we'll be roommates for a while, I think we should be completely honest with each other."

"Come again?"

"Honest about—"

He angled toward her and ran a hand through his dark hair. "No, the first part."

Instead of fixating on the bunching bicep straining his sleeve she rolled her eyes. "Housemates, if you want to be technical, but not the point. You should know that I don't appreciate being called sweetheart."

His mouth curved in a lazy arrogant smile. "Good to know," he said and jumped down. "Now, you mind moving out of my way so I can finish up...sweetheart."

Shelby pressed her lips together. Why hadn't she seen that coming? No sense trying to reason with a mule. She told herself she'd be the bigger person and not respond in kind.

He motioned to her car. "Park closer to the stable." He picked up a toolbox and looked at her again. "By the way, we aren't roommates or housemates, whatever. Out of the goodness of my heart, you're my guest."

"You deprive all your guests of bathroom and kitchen privileges?"

"Only the unwanted ones," he said over his shoulder, already returning his attention to the tractor. "Which reminds me, later we'll go over your chores. Hope you're an early riser. Lots of work to be done on a ranch."

His back to her, she gave him a one-finger salute. And hoped Violet hadn't seen it from a window.

As Shelby rounded the front of her car, she noticed that he'd fixed the corral railings. Holding in a grin, she paused at the driver's door. "They're crooked."

"What?" He turned and frowned at her, before following her gaze.

"The rails." She tilted her head to the side. "They're slanting to the left."

"Like hell." He glanced back at her, then grudgingly mir-rored her head angle to study his handiwork.

"I guess it doesn't matter." Afraid she couldn't keep a straight face, she opened the door. Yes, she was messing with him. The bastard deserved it.

"Which one?"

"Both," she said and slid into the leather bucket seat, grin-ning behind the tinted windows.

TRENT SMELLED THE beans and cornbread the second he en-tered the house. And something else that made his stomach growl. Ham, maybe? He didn't have any in the fridge or freezer. Shelby had to have brought it with her, or maybe the suddenly helpful Violet had made another delivery while he was water-ing the horses.

Earlier he'd made a tactical error. The microwave sat on a cart on Shelby's side of the kitchen. Had he thought quickly, he would've rolled it over to his side before he'd duct-taped the place. He used the microwave more than he did the stove or oven.

He ducked his head into the kitchen. Shelby wasn't there and no food had been left out. He checked the fridge and found only the beans and cornbread, so he took out leftover roasted chicken legs to go with it. Not that he had any idea how to heat up everything without the microwave.

He'd washed up some in the barn but he still needed a shower. The bathroom door was open, and the one to Shelby's room closed. Much as it irritated him, he returned to the kitchen and heaped a portion of the food onto a pie tin and stuck it in the oven at a low heat. He briefly considered cheating. All he had to do was keep the microwave from dinging, but if she caught him that would screw up everything.

They would have to renegotiate and he had no intention of making this easy on her. Not only was she trying to take his home away from him—the only home he had left—she was also killing him parading around in those shorts. She had great legs, and he figured she knew it. He'd finally managed to curb errant thoughts of sex during the day, and given himself free reign during showers and bedtime. In a matter of minutes she'd screwed that up for him.

Thinking about the expression on her face when she saw the barn bathroom made him feel better. Wouldn't have surprised him if she'd gotten in her car and left then and there. Damn, he wished she would have. It wasn't in his nature to be ugly like that, Violet notwithstanding.

But Shelby had recovered quickly. And he expected that she'd already snuck in a bathroom visit or two while he was outside. That didn't bother him. She'd be forced to go to the barn sooner or later, and just one time would do it. If the sorry condition of the toilet didn't, the feral cat that lived part-time in the barn would probably scare some sense into her. The woman didn't belong here. And Trent was just helping her see that.

The sooner she left, the happier he'd be. Working alone, his schedule was ruthless. Having to think about *her* was already costing him. So every time his inner voice said he'd never force a lady to use the barn bathroom, he shut it down. This was just another woman trying to take what was his. No warning. No nothing. He couldn't deal with another loss. Not now. Maybe never.

He took a faster shower than usual. Partly so his supper wouldn't burn, but mostly out of self-preservation. The moment his soapy hand had touched his cock, his thoughts had gone straight to Shelby. Instead of indulging, he'd turned the water on cold. And cursed her until all the soap ran off his body. It was a sorry day when a man couldn't even shower in peace.

Her bedroom door was still closed when he settled on the couch with his food and turned on the TV. He'd almost finished eating and was considering seconds when he heard her door open.

He knew she was moving around just behind him but he

stayed focused on the television. If she was going outside she'd have to leave via the kitchen.

"Excuse me," she said. "Would you mind flipping on the porch light? It's on your side of the house."

"No problem." Holding back a grin, he rose with his plate in hand. "I put the stable lights on for—"

Shelby was naked.

Almost.

All she wore was a blue towel. It wrapped around her breasts, tucked in at the side and ended high on her thighs. Another towel was draped over her arm and she held a bar of soap in one hand, a flashlight in the other. On her feet she wore bright yellow flip-flops.

"It seems I forgot to pack my robe," she said, glancing down at herself. "I hope you don't mind. I'm just running out to the barn."

Trent couldn't find his voice. He couldn't look away. Trying to swallow didn't help. His mouth was too dry. "You were wrong," he finally muttered. "They weren't crooked." He flipped the light switch then walked past her, looking straight ahead, as if he had on blinders. "Go ahead, use the front door if you want."

"What wasn't crooked?"

Jesus, why had she followed him into the kitchen? "The rails." He set his plate and fork in the sink, and for the life of him, couldn't recall where he kept the dish detergent. "I used a level."

"Oh. False alarm. Sorry." She smelled good, standing somewhere behind him. Not that he was about to look. "Oops!"

He turned his head.

She was rearranging the towel. "Almost lost the sucker," she said, pulling the terrycloth snugger.

Her breasts swelled and plumped over the top with each small tug of the towel. He could barely drag his gaze away.

Talk about playing dirty. She was baiting him. And it was

working. All the blood and oxygen had rushed south leaving his brain to fend for itself.

Man, he didn't want to fold this early in the game.

He caught himself staring again and forced his attention back to the sink.

"Okay, well," she said, "thanks."

"Sure." He heard the kitchen door open and close, and he slowly lifted his head for a clear shot of her out the window.

Only he couldn't see her. What did she do, turn the wrong way? How could she miss the barn?

The hinges squeaked as the door opened. He barely had a second to lower his chin.

"I need to take some clothes. Or I'll have to come back in a wet towel," she said with a soft laugh as she crossed the kitchen.

It took all of a second for him to imagine her wearing nothing but a wet towel plastered to her body. His heart pounding like a Derby winner at the finish line, he ordered himself not to watch her exit, then gave up and looked. She was taking her sweet time, making a show of staying on her side of the duct tape.

The woman's legs were world class, no argument from him. And if he'd had the slightest doubt she was toying with him, it was gone. Guess it was time to prove he was made of stronger stuff than being a dope for a half-naked woman.

He turned to face her, leaned back against the counter and glanced at Mutt, who was curled up by the door. "Hey, boy." The dog looked up. Trent nodded at Shelby. "Fetch the towel."

She froze. Her eyes widened at Mutt, who had no clue what the command meant.

Trent smiled and watched her take off to her room as if she had the hounds of Baskerville on her heels.

5

SHELBY HEARD A noise and briefly opened one eye. It was still dark out so she buried her face in the pillow.

The pounding persisted.

She burrowed deeper, grabbing the scratchy blanket at her waist and pulling it over her head.

Someone was knocking, she realized, the exact moment the door opened.

"Shelby? It's five thirty. Rise and shine."

She peeled back the blanket and squinted at Trent, who'd poked his head in.

"You awake?" he asked.

"What?" She was still groggy. "Get out of my room."

"This is the second time I've knocked. Don't you go back to sleep."

The fog cleared. She felt around for something to throw and discovered her exposed butt. Tugging down the blanket, she scrambled into a sitting position. "Get out, or I swear I'll scream."

"That's okay. Everyone's already up," he said. "Come on. This is a ranch. We have hungry animals to feed."

Catching his smirk before he closed the door, she slid her head under the pillow. Who was he fooling? A ranch, her ass.

Which reminded her… She knew she was wearing panties but wanted to be sure.

Groaning, she rolled off the bed and padded to the door. No lock. That's right. She'd checked last night. Dammit. She'd have to do something about that.

The sleepiness had worn off, thanks to her hospitable host, and she glanced around for her jeans and T-shirt. After grabbing the bag with her toothbrush and other toiletries, she stepped out of her room and stopped dead in front of the bathroom.

She muttered a curse, then headed for the kitchen, resenting the smell of coffee the whole way. How could she have forgotten to bring her single-cup brewer with her? She'd have to mooch some from Violet.

Trent was leaning against the counter with a steaming mug in his hand and a smug expression on his face. "You're welcome to a cup, this being your first day," he said as she continued to the door without a word. "Not a morning person, huh? You're living on a ranch now, sweetheart. Better get used to this."

She let the door slam behind her, not bothering to flip him off. If she gave in to every urge, she'd dislocate her finger. Too late she realized she should've brought her flashlight. It was that dark. And not a single light was on in Violet's trailer. Made Shelby wonder how much earlier than usual Trent had gotten up just to tick her off.

With only one cow, two horses and some chickens, how long did it take to feed the animals? She'd bet he normally didn't get out of bed until after seven. A pebble poked through her thin rubber flip-flops. She brought her foot up and hopped on the other the last yard to the barn.

She found the string to the bare bulb and a dim light showed her to the sink. It wasn't in very good shape. Until she'd wiped it down yesterday, the chipped bowl looked as if it hadn't been cleaned in years. And now mud was caked to the sides. Again. From Trent of course.

Today she was going into town. She didn't care how many

chores he threw at her. She needed several jugs of water, a large bowl to use for things like brushing her teeth in her room, and maybe she'd pick up a set of sheets— she could always use spares, even after her stuff arrived. He thought if he made life difficult he'd send her running. The hell with him. She'd show him she was tougher than that. He wanted to show her rustic? Maybe she'd go really old school and keep a chamber pot in her bedroom.

Ew.

Nope. No way.

The thought alone creeped her out.

She saw something small and furry scurry across the hay-scattered ground and willed herself to ignore it. She got busy with her toothbrush and wondered what would happen if they discovered they each owned half, or even part, of the Eager Beaver.

She shuddered at the thought.

God, that name really had to go.

While she wasn't holding her breath about her chances, it was possible that she'd inherited part of the ranch. Which would send Trent through the roof. He'd do everything he could to make her life miserable.

So much for the quiet peaceful place she'd envisioned.

Last night, traipsing around in the towel, she'd thought she had him for a few minutes. Subtle, he was not. He'd been ogling her since she'd stepped out of the car.

If she was honest, and she needed to be, she'd done some ogling herself. But that wasn't the point. For the first time in her life, she'd used her sexuality to try and get her way. She'd lost. Okay, fine. But doing that wasn't *her*. She felt nothing but shame for stooping so low.

They needed to have a talk. Admittedly, the situation was sudden and awkward. But now that he'd had some time to get used to her, maybe he'd be willing to listen and have a serious, adult discussion. And rip off the silly tape and give her full access to the house.

While rinsing out her mouth she thought she heard something. She turned off the water, quit swishing and listened.

Clucking.

There were chickens. A whole flock. Right behind her. Near her feet. Everywhere. Pecking at the ground between frenzied squawking and wing flapping.

Shelby shrieked when one pecked her bare toe. It didn't hurt. Just scared the crap out of her.

"Hungry this morning, aren't you?" Trent pretended to ignore her, smiling at the chickens as he scattered feed on the ground around her. "I know it's late. But don't blame Shelby."

So much for having an adult discussion.

"You're pathetic," she said, stepping over the noisy hens, and trying to get away. "No wonder you're divorced."

His head came up. Their eyes met.

He looked stunned. As stunned as Shelby herself felt. She didn't know if he was divorced, but she never should have said that. It wasn't like her to be so mean.

"Hell, you're probably right." He shrugged, as if her words hadn't fazed him, and threw a final handful of feed. But he couldn't hide the hurt in his expression.

She watched him walk out of the barn, shame taking a bite out of her. Just because he was being an ass didn't mean she had to be one. Unless he cut off her access to coffee. Then all bets were off.

By MIDMORNING TRENT had finished his barn chores and was almost done with the tractor when he heard the kitchen door slam. He watched Shelby walk to her car and get behind the wheel. She hadn't mentioned where she was off to, and he wasn't about to ask.

He wasn't sorry he woke her up so god-awful early. A lot earlier than he'd risen since he'd moved here. Getting her up at dawn was only right. Thanks to her, he'd tossed and turned most of the night. Jacking off normally relaxed him. But he hadn't been able to do it without thinking of all that silky skin of hers. Or how her habit of nibbling at her lower lip made her look sweet and vulnerable. He couldn't afford to think of her in that light. Or he'd feel as if he was throwing her out, putting her on the street. It wasn't his fault that she'd have to find some other accommodations.

He didn't know what she did for a living but whatever it was she obviously was doing okay. She could afford that nice car. As for him, this ranch meant everything. He'd put a lot of money and sweat into building the stable and making the place suitable for training. For all the bellyaching he'd done about trying to whip the Eager Beaver back into shape, he was proud of what he'd accomplished. He wasn't about to let his hard work and dreams go down the drain.

He had a good shot at restoring his reputation and returning to doing what he loved best. Even winning some serious money in the bargain. Solomon had already won two races, and placed in a third. If the gelding could win just a few more decent purses, Trent would not only have enough wins to remind owners he was still in the game, he'd also have the resources for more improvements to the ranch. Might even be able to hire some help so he could concentrate solely on training.

He watched her taillights disappear from view, then turned back to the tractor. All he had to do now was change the oil and he was in business. The engine might've taken a while but he was becoming a better mechanic as well as a decent carpenter.

"Why the hell'd you feed my chickens?" Violet seldom left her porch, but she came up right behind him.

Trent sighed, wondering what he'd done to deserve Violet.

"The noise wasn't bad enough to wake everyone for a mile but you had to use half my scratch, too? That should've lasted them four more days."

He knew she had some in reserve because he'd fixed her feed

bin the last time she'd left to do her monthly shopping. "I'll pick up an extra sack next time I go to town."

She squinted up at him from under the same brown battered hat she'd owned since he was a kid. "You never feed them. Must've had something to do with tormenting that poor girl."

"Poor girl? I sure didn't hear you offering her a place to sleep. I know you got a second bedroom in that trailer."

"Don't be a jackass." She turned toward the road but even the dust had already settled. "Is she coming back or did she leave for good?"

"Her clothes are still here." He only knew because she hadn't taken the suitcase with her.

"You find out what made her show up out of the blue like that?"

"No." Trent hesitated. "You?"

She shook her head. "Haven't talked to her at all today."

"Come on, Violet, give it to me straight. Do you think she has a claim?"

"Hard to say."

He didn't like the sound of that. There was no mischief in the woman's face or voice, so he had to believe this mix-up wasn't as cut and dried as he'd expected it to be.

"Have you talked to your pa yet?"

He shook his head. "They're visiting my sister and her family in Wyoming," he said, and rubbed at his tired eyes. "I should call though. Even if they can't get their hands on the paperwork they might know something."

Violet was staring at him, her leathery skin wrinkling around her pinched mouth. "You look like crap."

"Thanks."

"You get any sleep?"

"Not much."

She chuckled. "Nope, I don't imagine you did."

He took off his hat and slapped it against his thigh, sending up a cloud of dust just as Violet pulled her pipe out of her pocket. She glared at him.

Trent laughed. "I didn't do it on purpose. Are you ever gonna cut me some slack?" he asked, and caught the beginning of a small smile as she turned toward her double-wide.

"I got a pot of stew simmering. Should be ready in an hour if you're hungry."

Okay, now she was scaring him. He watched her climb the steps and disappear into the trailer without giving him another glance. Violet being nice to him had to mean something was about to blow up in his face.

Since he never kept his cell on him while he was working, he went inside and found it in the charger. His parents disliked cell phones, only used a prepaid one in case of an emergency when they traveled. So he called his sister's landline.

His mother answered.

"Hey, Mom."

"Trent? Is anything wrong?"

"No. Everything's fine." Yeah, he knew he didn't call them often enough. "How are you and Dad?"

"We're good. Happy to see the grandkids. I swear your nephew has grown a foot since Christmas."

"I bet. Emily and Ron are all right?"

"Yes." She paused. "Trent Edgar Kimball, you better not be lying to me. Something is wrong. I can feel it."

"No, Mom, nothing. I promise." It bothered him to picture her face, flushed with worry. Course she fretted about everything while letting his father make the big decisions. Which hadn't always worked out so well for them. "I have a question about the Eager Beaver, that's all. I was wondering if you had the deed in your safe deposit box at the bank."

"Well, huh. I'm not sure. Hold on. Let me ask your dad." There was talking and laughter in the background, then her muffled voice, "Bob, it's Trent. He wants to know if we have the deed to the Eager Beaver."

The long silence that followed made him edgy. He walked to the window and peered between the blinds. Not that he expected Shelby home this soon. She'd probably just arrived in town. Assuming that's where she was headed.

"Trent?"

"I'm here, Mom."

"Your father doesn't remember what kind of paperwork we have. He's assuming it's a deed since there was never a mortgage on the place. Your grandfather paid off any debts long before he passed it down to your dad. I know for certain we have nothing on the lease agreement with Violet. That was a handshake deal. Why are you asking?"

"What lease agreement?"

"Oh, honey, I'm not sure. It's from years ago. Hold on. Your father is talking to me at the same time. What is it, Bob?"

Trent heard his dad's voice but nothing he could make out. It would be simpler if he got on the phone and explained himself, but he wouldn't. He liked to pretend he had a head for business, which couldn't be further from the truth. So he always seemed to find a middleman he could blame for any "miscommunications." Trent loved his dad but he'd never wanted to follow in his footsteps. Whatever the man's faults, though, his parents seemed to have a happy marriage and that was good enough in Trent's book. Hell, he'd failed at keeping his own marriage intact.

"Trent? Your dad says the deal was between Violet and your great-grandfather. She can stay on the land as long as she wants in exchange for paying the taxes. As far as checking on the deed, I can go to the bank next Wednesday. We should be home the night before."

"Nobody told me about Violet," he muttered, thinking about all those times she'd pissed him off and he'd threatened to give her the boot. She'd never said a word about her lease deal. Course she knew he wasn't serious. They just liked to rile each other. But still…

"She's been there forever. No one really thought anything

of it. Why are you asking about the deed?" She let out a soft gasp then lowered her voice. "You're not in financial trouble, are you, honey?"

"No, Mom. Nothing like that. Does the name Harold Foster ring a bell? Don't ask Dad," he added quickly. The last thing he needed was everyone making a big issue out of this. Or his dad blowing smoke. "I'm just curious."

"Foster. Sounds familiar. Sure you don't want me to ask?"

"Actually, I'd prefer you don't bring it up at all."

"All right." She knew not to ask why. Sometimes the Eager Beaver could be a touchy issue between Trent and his dad, who liked to go on and on about the curse. "I'll call you next Wednesday after I go to the bank."

"Thanks. Say hey to everyone for me."

"I will. Can I tell them we'll see you for Thanksgiving?"

"Wouldn't miss it." He hung up, still confused, and a little angry.

The deal with Violet… He could see how it was one of those things everyone just accepted and never spoke of. Especially since the ranch had been abandoned twice, each time for a few years. It was probably a good thing Violet had been around to deter vandalism or squatting. What bothered him was the feeling he had that Violet knew more than she was letting on. Even after denying it to his face less than an hour ago.

THE PEOPLE IN Blackfoot Falls seemed friendly. And, naturally, curious. But not nearly as curious as Shelby had expected. She hoped that meant a lot of tourists passed through. If so, that would be excellent for her. She might be able to find a shop owner willing to sell her jewelry on consignment. Though she was getting a bit ahead of herself. So far all she'd done was cruise down Main Street to get her bearings, then parked and walked two blocks to Abe's Variety Store.

Not too many folks were out. She'd noticed the parking lot at the Food Mart was crowded, probably because it was Saturday. Though she suspected weekends in a ranching community meant something different than they did for city people.

Most everyone smiled or nodded to her. A couple of young women stared, but that was it. Folks must've pegged her for a tourist or visiting relative. The town was small enough that a stranger would stick out.

She stopped outside the variety store and scanned the bulletin board. There was a flyer for the county fair, another announcing Halloween happenings for the kiddies. Also, ads for sale items, but no upcoming festivals. That was a bummer. Her jewelry would sell well at a festival. Although she hadn't actually tried to sell any of her pieces since college.

After she'd started working as a designer for the Williamsons, she'd given the items she made on the side as gifts. God forbid her *tacky* private pieces be associated with the snooty Williamson Jewelers in any way. No, they'd practically owned her. Too bad it had taken her so long to see that.

A bell above the door jingled as she stepped inside the store. The older man behind the counter looked up. One of the women he was talking to turned and gave her the once-over. Shelby just smiled and went in search of sheets. Although, judging by the size of the store and the type of merchandise she could see on the front shelves, she wasn't expecting much.

"Anything I can help you with, young lady?" The man from behind the counter approached just as she found a package of sheets.

"Hi. I don't suppose you have any colors besides white?" Or with a decent thread count, she thought, but kept that to herself.

"Not in stock, no. But I can order any color and size you want." He frowned at her over the glasses resting on his bulbous nose. "I figured you were staying at the Sundance, but then you wouldn't be needing sheets."

"The Sundance?"

"It's part dude ranch. Owned by the McAllister family," he said, waiting expectantly for her to fill in the blanks.

"I'm staying at the Eager Beaver."

"Okay." He nodded. "The Kimballs' place. You must be a friend of Trent's."

Her heart sank. "Um, not exactly," she said and realized too late she should've gone with his assumption.

"You can't be related to Violet. I don't believe she has any family."

The Kimballs' place kept echoing in her brain. "By the way, I'm Shelby," she said and gave him a bright smile.

"I'm Abe, like it says out front." He scratched his balding head.

"Have you lived here long, Abe?" She kept her tone casual and picked up a plastic-wrapped pillowcase.

"All my life."

"Then you must know the Kimballs pretty well."

"Oh, yeah, I went to school with Trent's pa. Bob and I used to go hunting together. Now, how is it you're related to the family?"

"Actually, my last name is Foster." She looked for a sign of recognition in his face and found none. "My great-grandfather and Trent's were partners at the Eager Beaver."

He reared back with a look of surprise. "When was that?"

"Well, way, way before your time, of course."

Her subtle compliment registered, and she caught his blush before he turned away. "Louise, Sadie, come over here a minute, would ya?"

It took all of three seconds for the two women to sidle up to him and check her out.

"This here is Sadie." He gestured to the fifty-something brunette with a warm smile. "She owns the Watering Hole."

"And I'm also running for mayor." She stuck her hand out. "And you are?"

"Good grief, woman, do you always have to jump the gun?" Abe gave a snort of disgust, sounding much like Trent with Violet.

"Shelby." She grinned and shook Sadie's hand.

"I'm Louise," the other woman chimed in. "Part owner of the fabric store down the block. So, you're staying out at the Kimballs' ranch."

Shelby held in a sigh. Yes, it was clear the women were eavesdropping, but it was the *Kimballs' ranch* reference that got to her. Again.

"Do you two even wanna know why I asked you over here?" Abe looked from one to the other.

"Foster doesn't ring a bell with me, either," Louise said.

Sadie was frowning and shaking her head.

Abe threw up his hands and walked away.

For the next two hours, Shelby explored the town and heard "oh, the Kimballs' ranch" so many times she wanted to scream.

Sadly, she was starting to like the name Eager Beaver.

6

TRENT WAS IN the stable when he heard the car pull up. Shelby had been gone most of the day, and he'd wondered if she'd driven all the way to Kalispell. He waited until the car door opened and closed before he strolled outside.

She grabbed an armful of packages from the backseat and immediately dropped one. He didn't make it to her in time to pick it up. She scooped it up herself. Standing back, he watched her redistribute her haul and close the door with her hip.

"Need help?"

"No, thank you." She gave him a small polite smile, then started toward the kitchen door.

If she was still pissed at him over the stunt he'd pulled this morning, he couldn't tell. She didn't seem to be in a particularly bad mood but more resigned. Asking around town about the Eager Beaver had probably dashed her hopes.

Feeling like he was on shaky ground himself, he understood completely. After hanging up with his mom, he'd called Colby. His brother hadn't heard anything about Foster, or the deal with Violet, either. But that didn't make Trent feel any less like a damn fool, and he'd wasted half the day because of it.

And here he had so much to do. Yet he'd been working in fits and starts, preoccupied with memories of the times he and

Violet had bickered over one thing or another. A couple of those instances had ended with him threatening to kick her off the ranch. Anyway, she always gave as good as she got. But how smug she must've felt inside. To give her credit, she'd never shown it. He had a feeling she knew he had a soft spot for her, but that was a fact he would never, ever acknowledge.

So far, he hadn't said a word to her about the conversation with his mom. He wasn't sure why since she might be able to put his fears to rest. His fear that Shelby had a legitimate claim. That he would have to buy her out or divvy up the place with her. Yeah, he still had some money, but he wanted it to go toward horses and training expenses. He couldn't afford to start over again.

The more he thought about the situation, the weirder it seemed. Violet loved a good argument and she liked poking at him but she'd never been outright mean. If she knew something that would settle the dispute with Shelby, he figured she'd speak up.

Maybe she was keeping quiet to protect him.

The thought made his stomach turn.

He glanced at the double-wide. Violet, who sat on her porch every afternoon, rain or shine, was nowhere to be seen. Beyond the trailer clouds were gathering over the foothills. In another hour or so it would be dark. He decided to finish cleaning his saddle tomorrow and tossed aside the rag and went inside.

Shelby's door was closed and he could hear her moving around in her room. After finding out how deep the Kimball roots went, maybe she was packing. The thought cheered him. He held nothing against the woman, but the sooner he got her and her tempting backside out of here the better.

He'd skipped lunch and still wasn't hungry. But with his improved mood he figured he'd heat the leftover beans and cornbread, maybe broil the T-bone after he took a shower. The steak was big enough to share with Shelby. After all, he wouldn't want to send her off hungry.

Thirty minutes later he'd finished showering and was checking the food in the oven when Shelby entered the kitchen. She was wearing old faded jeans and a snug white T-shirt that came to just above her waist and exposed a narrow strip of skin. They didn't seem like traveling clothes.

Not that he was capable of being all that logical. It wasn't only the unexpected peek that had his heart accelerating. Wearing this getup she was giving him a real good look at her shape. Small waist, nice curvy hips, not too thin. To his mind, the perfect woman's body. What he couldn't figure out was how his mouth could water and go dry at the same time.

"Be careful," she said, just as his thumb made contact with the blistering hot casserole dish.

"Son of a—" He jerked his hand away and burned the back of his knuckle on the oven rack.

Trent managed to bite off a pithy four-letter word. His damn thumb felt like it was on fire.

Slowly shaking her head, Shelby stared at his hand. "Ever heard of an oven mitt?"

"Your concern is touching."

"I'd have a look," she said, glancing at the blue tape on the linoleum. "But you're too far over. I'd have to cross into enemy territory."

"Very funny." He couldn't remember if he was supposed to use cold water or not. "For your information, I was heating this up for the two of us. And I was even gonna throw in the T-bone."

Shelby's gaze slid to the steak on the counter. "You're going to let a minor burn stop you?"

Sighing, Trent used the toe of his boot to kick the oven door shut. His thumb was pretty red, so were his knuckles. It wouldn't be fun wearing work gloves tomorrow.

"Seriously, you should run cold water over that hand then apply some Neosporin. If you don't have any, I've got a first-aid kit in my car."

"Worried you won't get dinner?"

"I am," she said with a smile, but he could see that she was genuinely concerned.

Maybe he needed to take it more seriously. While she frowned at his thumb, he studied her face. She had a cute nose. A weird thing for him to notice. Crazy long lashes. Could be fake but he didn't think so since she wore minimal makeup.

She did that thing with her bottom lip again. "You might want to wrap some gauze around it overnight."

"You some kind of burn expert?"

Holding her hand up, she showed him a mean scar on her inner wrist. "I have a couple more. Which you won't see."

That sent his mind scrambling to dark erotic places. "Arsonist?"

Shelby grinned. "I make jewelry. Sometimes I use a torch."

Trent turned on the faucet and let the cold water ease the sting. "A torch, huh? What kind of jewelry?"

"Do you still want the oven on?"

He figured he'd stay away from the broiler and fry the steak. "Off, please," he said, finally noticing the small bag in her hand. Last night she'd carried it out to the barn with her.

Neither of them mentioned her crossing the tape to get to the oven. He had to admit, the whole dividing-the-house-in-half thing seemed silly now. Not that he'd give voice to the admission. If he pulled the tape up, he wondered if the issue could die a natural death?

"Should I take the food out?" she asked.

"Mind checking it first? I forget if I got that far."

She grabbed the dishtowel hanging from a cabinet door and used it as a potholder. "I think it'll be fine left in the oven. You'll be eating soon, right?"

"About ten minutes. Will you be ready?"

She closed the oven door and straightened. Then glanced at the large round wall clock, taking a long time to make up her mind. "Sure."

He turned off the water and she tossed him the dishtowel.

"Ten minutes," she confirmed and headed for the door.

"Where are you going?"

Pushing the screen open, she gave him a wry smile. She started to step outside when an eerie howl pierced the air.

Shelby froze. "What was that?"

"A coyote. Didn't I warn you about them?" His thumb began to throb. Probably punishing him for teasing her. "They mostly stay in the foothills and on the ridges."

"Mostly?"

More frantic howling and yapping exploded. The noise he'd long grown accustomed to and unconsciously dismissed had her taking a step back. She jerked her hands away and let the screen slam.

"I know it sounds bad," he said. "Some people think it's a feeding frenzy. But it's just the pack communicating with each other."

"Saying what? Dinner's about to walk out the kitchen door?"

Trent grinned. "They're not even close by. Coyotes stay away from people. I promise, they're more afraid of you than you are of them."

"I doubt that." She moved forward a few inches. "Remember, a lot of people in town know I'm staying here. You don't want to have to explain my sudden disappearance."

"Hell, that's nothing. All I'd have to say is you tucked tail and ran back to the city. They'd get it." He laughed at her eye-roll and reached for the heavy wood door to shut out the noise.

"Wait." She put a hand on his arm, then drew back. "I need to go to the barn."

He sighed. "No, you don't."

"Are you kidding? I've had to go for five minutes."

"No, I meant..." He shook his head. They were close. Too close. Her scent did something unsettling to him. "No more boundaries. Use any room you want," he said, reaching again for the door.

"No. You said they won't hurt me." She cleared her throat.

"I'm fine," she said, despite the fact that she'd gone pale. "The barn is fine." She lifted her chin and pushed the screen open.

"Come on, Shelby." He caught her wrist and tugged her around to face him. "Are you going to make me say it?" She blinked, then stared into his eyes. "Fine," he said. "Dividing the house, all this duct tape, I was being a dumb ass, okay? I've admitted it."

Another loud howl.

She jumped.

He drew her closer. Just so he could shut the door, he told himself. Not because she smelled so damn good it was driving him crazy. Or because her bright green eyes hit him square in the gut.

"I'm not going to go running back to Denver," she whispered. "Sorry, but I'm not." She let out a shaky breath. "I can't."

"Okay." He brushed the hair away from her cheek, reluctant to lower his hand. Damn, she was soft. "I was only teasing."

"No, you weren't," she murmured, a tiny smile twitching at the corners of her lush lips.

He shrugged a shoulder. "Half and half."

Her gaze flickered to his mouth. "I understand your position. I do. If I were you, I'd probably be furious."

"Probably?"

With a short exasperated sigh, she met his eyes. "An attorney contacted me. Explained that I'd inherited the Eager Beaver. I didn't get too excited at first but—I mean, what would you have done?"

"I know I wouldn't have packed up and moved everything before I even saw the place."

Her shoulders sagged. "This is so unlike me. It's insane, right?" She sidestepped him.

And boy did he want to kick himself. He hadn't meant to chase her off, though it was for the best. No use him getting soft now. Like wondering if she'd left Denver because she'd lost her job or suffered a nasty divorce.

He turned and watched her leave the kitchen. "What about dinner?"

"Bathroom first," she called back.

"Got it." He looked at his thumb. The sucker was red and throbbing.

After getting out the frying pan and setting it on the stove to heat, he went to get a cube of ice. The list of chores he'd stuck to the fridge was still there. He wondered if Shelby had seen it. He yanked the paper down and dropped it in the wastebasket under the sink.

She wasn't off the hook. Plenty of work around the place and she'd have to do her share. Though not necessarily the unpleasant things he'd initially had planned for her. Like milk Daisy. That cow had to be the moodiest animal he'd ever run across. More trouble than she was worth. He didn't even like milk all that much. Violet used most of it. He knew it made more sense to get rid of Daisy, but he didn't want to see her butchered. Not that he'd ever admit it. Especially not around here in cattle country. He'd get shit from Blackfoot Falls to Twin Creeks.

The ice was beginning to help. With his good hand, he unwrapped and seasoned the steak, then carefully set the T-bone in the frying pan. He didn't need another burn. At least the knuckles weren't so bad.

Behind him, Shelby noisily cleared her throat. She was holding up a tube of Neosporin. "I brought some gauze, too. I can wrap your thumb for you." She shrugged. "If you want..."

She hadn't changed her clothes, hadn't even brushed her hair, and yet she looked even better than a few minutes ago. No explaining why. Her shy smile faded. She lowered the tube.

"Yes," he said, stepping forward. "I'd appreciate it."

Shelby waited for him to extend his hand, then she inspected the burns. "I don't think your knuckles need wrapping," she said, after applying the antibiotic. "But your thumb, definitely. Does it sting?"

"Um...not too bad," he lied and saw she was trying not to

smile. He tried to hold back a wince while she gently spread the white ointment.

To distract himself, he focused on her necklace. Jewelry wasn't something he usually noticed. But the purple pendant hanging from a silver chain was interesting. Gold flecks and veins caught the light and seemed to shift with her movement. "Did you make that?"

"What?" She looked up and touched the necklace. "Ah, yes. A long time ago."

"Nice."

With a brief smile, she unrolled a piece of gauze. For some reason, it seemed as if she didn't believe him.

"That's not a stone, is it?"

She shook her head.

"So, that's the sort of style you make?"

"Not since college." Her obvious reluctance to talk about her work baffled him.

"You might make great jewelry but your salesmanship needs work."

Shelby looked up again and laughed. "I'm not trying to sell you anything."

"You should be. My sister would go nuts over something like that. If I get her another scarf and wallet for Christmas, she'll disown me."

"Gee, I can't imagine why." She paid close attention while she wrapped the gauze then used a small pair of scissors to snip the excess.

"I'm serious. You're really talented."

She finished off the dressing with tape. "There you go," she said, purposely ignoring his comment. "Maybe between this and the ice your thumb won't swell and you'll heal quickly."

"Thanks," Trent murmured, appreciative but irritated. "What, you think I'm a country bumpkin with no taste?"

Her green eyes widened. "Of course not. It's just— Well, this isn't exactly fine jewelry."

"Nope. It's not. Believe me, I've bought my share of the expensive crap. Just ask my ex-wife." Trent hadn't meant to throw in the sarcastic remark, and he quickly moved on. "This is different, and it's really nice. Better than nice."

Shelby blinked and glanced down at the pendant. "Thank you," she said in a small quiet voice. "That means a lot."

Weirdly, he believed she was being truthful. His praise had meant something to her. And that gave him the uncomfortable feeling someone had done a number on Shelby's confidence. Even more weird, it pissed him off.

Keep your distance, Kimball. She isn't your friend.

"I plan on going back to working with turquoise and silver and maybe fire art like this while I'm here." Excitement had crept into her voice. "Hopefully I haven't lost my touch."

"Good. I need to score points with my sister. I give Emily something like that for Christmas, she'll keep me in chocolate-chip cookies for a year."

Shelby laughed.

He gestured to the pendant. "You mind?"

For a second she looked startled. "Sure," she said, lifting it off her shirt. "Or I can take it off."

"No need. I just want a quickie."

She coughed, or laughed. Maybe both.

Trent sighed. "I meant a quick look—"

"It's okay. I know."

The chain put the pendant at collarbone level. He carefully took it from her and angled it to the left, then right.

"How did you do this?" he asked, more impressed each time the light caught on another deep rich color.

"Trade secret."

He glanced up.

She was smiling. "I'll show you some time. It's pretty cool."

Trent couldn't drag his gaze away from her perfect pink lips, how they parted slightly. How she might be thinking along the same lines as him. But even one kiss could be trouble.

Shelby took a deep breath that made her chest rise. He released the pendant, but she stayed right where she was. Close. Close enough that all he had to do was lean in a few inches...

She didn't move. Stayed completely still when he brushed his lips across hers. And then she lifted herself on tiptoes a little, just enough to increase the pressure of the light kiss.

Taking his cue, Trent pressed his mouth more firmly against hers. Her lips were soft and yielding, her breath warm and sweet, slipping out in a tiny, tempting puff. She surprised him by putting a tentative hand on his chest and leaning slightly into him. Her shy initiative was enough to take a nip out of his self-control.

Tongues became involved, and he put a hand on her waist. His fingers met with the silky skin below the hem of her T-shirt. It took all of his willpower not to slide his palm up higher.

Her hand slipped up to his shoulder. Fingernails lightly scraped the side of his neck then pushed into his hair. His racing heart jumped gears. He wrapped an arm around her, pulling her against his aroused body.

She tensed. "The steak needs to be turned over," she said, ducking her head. "Or it'll burn."

The meat was sizzling like crazy and he hadn't heard it. He let her go and watched her flip the T-bone. As soon as his body calmed down he mentally kicked himself. Kissing her was not keeping his distance. Neither was staring at her ass while she bent over to check the food in the oven.

What a goddamn fool he was. One hundred percent certified prime idiot.

He walked to the cabinet under the sink, fished out the list of chores from the wastebasket and stuck the paper back under the fridge magnet.

"After supper we'll go over your share of the chores," he said without looking at her. "Better set your alarm, sweetheart. You'll have to get up early."

7

SHELBY WAS OUT of bed and dressed before the alarm went off at six. It wasn't a hardship since she'd been awake for a while. Embarrassed over last night's misstep, she hadn't slept well.

God. She'd actually kissed Trent. More proof that she was insane. Not at all herself.

While technically *he'd* kissed her, she sure hadn't objected. Or resisted. In fact, she'd fully participated. No matter how she tried to spin things, that was the truth.

Pausing with her hand on the doorknob, she listened to him moving around, then heard the quiet sound of kitchen noises. She really hoped she was right. If he was in the kitchen, she could make a dash to the bathroom without running into him. She wasn't quite up to that yet.

Trent probably wasn't, either. After the kiss his mood had changed. He'd been plain grumpy. She got it. She did. When she was scared, she did a lot of things that she wouldn't do normally. Like kiss him. And think about what he'd look like without those worn jeans.

Him calling her sweetheart pretty much told her that he'd also realized the kiss had been a mistake.

Looking back, it might've been wiser for her to have taken the bait and made herself scarce. Instead they'd gone ahead and eaten dinner together, mostly in uncomfortable silence and very quickly. Then when she'd tried to escape to her room, he'd insisted on going over her list of chores. Today she would learn how to milk a cow. Lucky her.

She made it to the bathroom without seeing him. Hurriedly finished her business, and then let the aroma of coffee lead her to the kitchen and the inevitable.

He was standing at the sink, steaming mug in hand, peering out the window. A faded navy blue T-shirt stretched across his broad shoulders.

"Good morning," she said, after taking a second to admire how his jeans hugged his butt. Dammit. Before he turned, her gaze skittered to the coffeepot. Beside it was a yellow floral cup she hoped was meant for her.

"Help yourself, if you drink coffee." He gave her frayed jeans a brief look. "Otherwise there's tea in the pantry. Milk in the fridge."

"Thanks."

The sugar was sitting out. Organic sugar, according to the bag. She didn't know why that surprised her. No reason Trent wouldn't be as health conscious as the next person.

She poured her coffee, skipped all the other stuff. Her first sip improved her disposition, as had Trent's neutral tone of voice. She was totally okay with them pretending the kiss had never happened. She only hoped he hadn't gotten the wrong idea. Because she wasn't needy and certainly would never barter herself in order to stay on the ranch. But he didn't know her, and no telling how he'd interpreted her actions. All she could really do was make sure it never happened again.

"How's the thumb?"

"Not bad." He'd stared down at it. "I should probably take off the gauze."

"Your work gloves might irritate the burn."

He snorted a laugh. "Too bad. A ranch doesn't run itself. I'd have to be half dead to take a day off, and then I'd still have to feed and water the animals."

Knowing that was added strictly for her benefit, she tried not to roll her eyes.

"I'll be in the barn," he said as he topped off his mug. "Come when you're ready."

"Are we feeding the chickens first?"

"No." He took a hasty sip. "Violet will take care of them. I'm going to show you how to milk Daisy."

"You named the cow? How adorable."

He sighed with disgust. "No, I did not name the cow," he said. "My six-year-old niece decided to call her Daisy and—it just sorta stuck." He pulled the door open. "I wouldn't mention it to people around here. They'll laugh you out of town."

Shelby pressed her lips together and nodded, not trusting herself to speak. Under all his bluster, Trent was a softie. He was very lucky she wouldn't tattle on him.

After several more gulps, she refilled her mug and headed to the barn with it. In the far back Trent had set out a pair of buckets near a weird-looking wooden contraption. She heard a pitiful bleating sound coming from behind the stacked bales in the corner and walked over to investigate.

Shelby gasped with delight. "Oh, my God, you didn't tell me you had a calf."

"Don't get attached. She's being picked up this afternoon."

"Why?"

"Because I sold her, that's why. We have too damn many females around here as it is," he muttered.

"Oh, sweetie, are you gonna miss your mama?" Shelby moved a bit closer to the narrow stall. "Is that mean man separating you from her?"

Several yards away, Trent grunted. "Yeah, you'd do a great job running a ranch."

The little one seemed curious at first. Then let out a frightened *mawww* and backed away. Shelby wondered what type of treat would be safe to give her. Either she'd ask Violet or look it up online. She wouldn't ask Trent. Leaving the calf in peace, she went over to where the "mean man" was waiting for her. "Who told you that's what I wanted to do?"

He looked up from positioning one of the buckets and frowned. "What else would you do with the Eager Beaver?"

"I want a place that's peaceful and quiet and inspiring where I can work."

"Making jewelry?"

"Yes."

"Can't you do that anywhere? You were working in Denver, right?"

"Have you ever lived in a city?"

"Just outside of Dallas. Close enough to count."

"On a ranch?"

He nodded slowly.

"Go into the city much?"

"Hell no," he said, his voice trailing off when he must've realized he'd helped make her point.

For good measure she said, "Then you should get it." She turned away when he'd stared too long and hard at her. There was something about him that made her feel vulnerable. As if with a look he could unearth her deepest secrets. "Anyway, you have to admit, the Eager Beaver isn't much of a ranch."

"Hey, hold on there—"

"Come on, Trent. You have a cow, some chickens, a dog and a couple of horses. Not exactly a ranching empire."

"Not just horses... I have American quarter horses," he said, looking insulted. "Two of them. And Solomon has already won two races."

She stared back. "Why is it okay to name horses and not cows?"

His gaze narrowed. "You're kidding, right?"

"No. Enlighten me."

"It's different."

"Obviously." She truly didn't understand. "But what makes it different?"

"You're trying to get out of milking Dai—the cow," he said, jabbing a finger at her. "Won't happen."

He was wrong but she didn't bother correcting him. Instead she watched him scoop some grain into one of the buckets and then set it in front of the wooden thing that looked like some sort of torture device.

A moment later he led Daisy out from somewhere in the back of the barn. "You'll want to put her in this head catch while you milk her."

"Won't that hurt her?"

"Of course not. Watch."

Daisy had no problem with the setup. She dove into the grain with relish.

Trent turned the second bucket over closer to her hind end before bringing out a medium-size pail from a cabinet. "I'll show you what to do, then you try it."

She watched him as he sat on the overturned bucket, strategically placed the steel pail, grabbed a teat and started squeezing. Milk streamed into the pail. It looked simple enough but Shelby was willing to admit she was nervous. What if she hurt Daisy?

"Can you see what I'm doing?"

Shelby nodded.

"Ready to give it a try?"

"I think so," she said in a stupidly girly voice.

Trent rose and stepped back. "Better hurry before she finishes her grain."

Taking a deep breath, Shelby sat on the bucket.

"Now, squeeze the top of the teat, then close the rest of your fingers down on it one at a time and tug gently."

She did exactly what he told her to do. And nothing happened.

"Don't worry. It takes some practice. Keep trying."

Her next attempt produced a few drops. She looked up to see Trent grinning. "I can't do it with you watching."

"I want to make sure she doesn't kick you."

Shelby half whined, half whimpered.

"Here," he said, laughing. "I'll help you." She started to get to her feet, but he said, "No, stay right there."

After some jockeying for a suitable position, Trent crouched behind her. She turned to see what he was doing and the stubble on his chin grazed her cheek. He needed a shave, yet he smelled good.

"Stay facing Daisy," he said quietly, and put his arms around Shelby so that her back was pressed to his chest. "Give me your hands."

Her heart took a giant leap. "Is this really necessary?"

"Put out your hands."

She did as he asked, unclear as to his intentions. Was he trying to scare her off? Show her the kiss hadn't affected him in the least? More likely, he hadn't given it a second thought.

His palms were tough and calloused but less so than she'd expected. He guided her to the top of the teat, and then closed his large hands over her much smaller ones. "This is the amount of pressure you want to use," he said. "Can you feel what I mean?"

Oh, she felt something, all right. Tingling. Excitement. His body heat. His lips against her hair. She was wrong of course, about that part, and wrong to feel the sudden longing to repeat last night's kiss.

She really was losing it.

"Shelby?" He leaned back slightly. "You okay?"

"Fine." For heaven's sake, she'd been lounging against him as if he was a chair. Straightening, she cleared her throat. "I had a leg cramp."

"Need to walk it out?"

"No. Let's finish this."

He said nothing, but she felt the vibration of his silent laughter, reminding her how irritating he could be.

She tried to relax and let him guide her hands but it just wasn't happening. "You know what," she said, struggling to her feet, not caring if she knocked him over. "I think I'll do better without you helping. No offense."

Trent's little smirk was deliberate, or she'd eat her new Gucci purse. "You sure about that?"

"No." She smiled. Let him guess if she meant on both counts. "But I'm willing to try. I bet you have more important things to do."

He folded his arms across his chest, his boots planted a couple of feet apart. The stance seemed to narrow his waist and broaden his shoulders. He probably knew it and stood like that on purpose.

"I said, go."

"In a minute. I just want to watch you get started."

Shelby huffed. "Well, make yourself useful and get me a second pail so I won't have to get up."

His eyebrows rose. "While I appreciate your optimism, I doubt that'll be a problem." He dropped his arms to his sides. "Look, if she doesn't give you much milk, don't worry about it. Milking takes practice and Daisy can be prickly. And do not try to milk her from the back."

"Got it."

His hesitation was beginning to unnerve her.

Finally, he made a move to leave. "I'll be in the kitchen or the stable." He rubbed his arms as he turned to go. "It's kind of chilly this morning."

While he'd barely looked at her, something made her glance down at her T-shirt. And see her tightened nipples straining against the stretchy fabric.

TRENT HAD JUST put on a second pot of coffee and was debating rescuing Shelby when he heard the screen door open. He didn't blame her for giving up early. Daisy could be stubborn as all get-out. But he'd give Shelby some grief, anyway. He turned just as she set two full pails of milk on the kitchen counter.

"I wasn't sure if I should keep going. Daisy finished her grain and was getting antsy so I stopped."

Once he got past the shock he nodded. "Violet helped you."

"Excuse me." She frowned, looking insulted. "I haven't seen Violet since the day I arrived. Like you said, it wasn't hard. Daisy just needed a pep talk."

He eyed the pails. Okay, she deserved to be a little smug. "Glad it was easy. That's your chore from now on."

Some of the smugness slipped. But she nodded. "So, do you have pitchers? I assume this goes in the fridge?"

"Keep what you want and give the rest to Violet." He thought a moment. Yeah, he really needed for Violet to bend her ear. "I'll take it to her later."

Shelby grinned. "Afraid she'll tell me all your secrets?"

"If you think I'd let that old busybody know anything about me, you're out of your mind."

"Oh, that's probably true," she said, sighing. Then she studied Trent, her eyes even more green with the sunlight flooding in through the window. "You like her."

"Who?"

"You do," Shelby said matter-of-factly. "And she likes you. It's nice."

He frowned at the slight wistfulness in her voice. "Not that nice. Wait until you've been around a while," he said, and refilled his mug. "Now, what's that smile for?"

She walked over to him, and he got a bit itchy until he saw she only wanted coffee. "Good to know you haven't packed my bags and loaded my car."

He shouldn't have felt disappointed. What had he expected? Another kiss? Right, as if the first one hadn't been a dumb mistake. Damn, he wished he could forget how sweet she'd tasted. Forget the softness and warmth of her body pressed against him. Two nights in a row now, he hadn't slept for thinking about her.

"Look, when I said wait till you've been around awhile, I meant until your belongings are delivered. We should know who owns the Eager Beaver by then." Was it his imagination or was she struggling to keep a straight face? "As soon as you redirect the movers, you can hit the road. Better yet, leave me a forwarding address. I'd be happy to take care of it for you."

"Maybe I should just call the moving company now."

"Excellent idea."

"Dream on." She tore off a paper towel and wiped a spill on the counter. "Trash? Under the sink, right?" She opened the lower cabinet and frowned. "You have a leak."

"Gee, what was your first clue?" Maybe he should kiss her again. Just to shut her up. "I know there's a problem. Why do you think I put a bowl under there?"

"This might sound silly, but you could...oh, I don't know—" she moved a shoulder, tilted her head to the side "—maybe fix it instead?"

Trent ground his molars together. "It's gonna take some time. I'm not a plumber."

She dropped to a crouch and moved the wastebasket to the side. "It looks fairly straightforward. Shouldn't take much."

"Be my guest."

After poking around she asked, "You have a wrench?" When he didn't respond, she looked up. "Just bring me your toolbox."

He was more than happy to call her bluff. By the time he returned with three different size wrenches—with the toolbox sitting outside the kitchen door just in case—he wasn't surprised that she'd disappeared.

The cabinet door had been left open, the wastebasket set aside. The half-filled bowl hadn't been moved. He thought for a moment, trying to decide if he should go ahead and tackle the job since he had the tools out. If he screwed up, his neighbor four miles down would bail him out. For a kid, Jimmy was fairly handy with this sort of thing and he owed Trent big time for helping him move cattle. Actually, the guy wasn't that young, maybe twenty-five, six years younger than Trent. But somehow Jimmy managed to make him feel old.

"Oh, good." Shelby walked in wearing a different T-shirt, with a faded green towel draped over her arm. Her bed-tousled hair was now pulled into a ponytail. He'd liked it better before.

"I figured you'd skipped out," he said.

"I told you I'd fix it."

"Yep, you did. Here you go." He passed her the wrenches and couldn't help noticing that the new shirt was tighter, stained and sported a few small holes.

She laid the wrenches on the linoleum, then spread the towel next to it.

"Would you like a pillow, too?"

"Oh God." She rolled her eyes as she lowered herself to the floor. "You're going to be one of those guys, aren't you?"

"What?"

"Get all macho and then pissy over a woman showing you up."

"Hell no. I want it fixed. And someone else doing the work is right up my alley." He folded his arms across his chest. "Assuming that someone knows what they're doing."

"Yeah?" She smiled. "Watch and learn…sweetheart."

The worn T-shirt was a size too small for her. And distracting as hell. But he wasn't comfortable leaving yet.

Something unpleasant had just occurred to him. Three months ago he'd installed the garbage disposal himself after watching a DIY video online. So far so good, but knowing she'd be tinkering under there was making him nervous.

"Tell you what, Shelby, I'll take care of the leak this afternoon." He watched her lie back, then do a little shimmy as she tried to get in a suitable position. "Before dinner."

"That's okay. I'm here."

He was probably worried for nothing. If it was going to come loose it would've done so already. His gaze lingered on her hips as he waited for the next little wiggle.

"I thought you had chores to do," she muttered, her voice muffled from partway inside the cabinet.

"Right after I finish my coffee." Where was his mug, anyway? He turned and saw it on the counter near the stove. After replacing the cold brew he resumed his post.

"Wow, this pipe is old." With her arms stretched back, the shirt's worn fabric cupped her breasts. "And stubborn."

He refrained from commenting, too busy watching her and thinking things he shouldn't be thinking.

A thud cut him off. Metal clanged against metal.

"Shelby?" He dropped to his haunches, sloshing coffee everywhere, including her jeans.

"What?"

"You okay?"

"Fine. I told you, it's this old pipe…" She muttered a curse. "Why are you still here?"

This was his house and he'd leave when he was darned good and ready. She shifted, giving him a glimpse of smooth toned belly just below her navel. His splashed coffee had gotten her T-shirt. A wet spot had spread across her hardened left nipple.

Trent shot to his feet. "I'll be outside. Watch out for the disposal. I put it in myself."

8

By MIDAFTERNOON SHELBY was disappointed that she hadn't seen Trent. Having fixed the leak, she'd wanted to gloat. Nothing too obnoxious. Just a smug nod of her head would be fun. Or a perfectly intoned "well, yeah." She'd even decided she might not be above a plain "duh."

Although, the reason he'd made himself scarce was most likely to avoid her. So, no, she'd keep her mouth shut. Her trip to town had confirmed her worst fear about the Eager Beaver. Her inheritance was worthless. Of all the stupid times to have acted impulsively. Returning to Denver wasn't an option.

Her gaze automatically went to her cell where it sat charging on the nightstand. She hadn't checked it once this morning. She'd lost count of Donald's texts and voice mails. It wasn't as if she would never speak to him again. She just wasn't ready yet. In truth, there was little left to say. But she'd return his calls at some point. If only to make certain he understood it was over between them.

She sat on the edge of her bed and sighed at the grime she'd had little luck removing from under her fingernails. Between living out here and making her own jewelry, no more manicures for her. She wouldn't miss them. Just like she hadn't missed her luxurious studio at Williamson Jewelers.

Oh, she'd gotten used to having her mini-fridge stocked with mineral water, diet sodas and fruit juices. Anything she or a client consumed was replaced overnight. It wasn't something she'd miss, though, not like daily lunch delivery and having her dry cleaning picked up in the morning and hung behind her door that same afternoon, if she wanted. Mrs. Williamson had made it clear from the beginning that Shelby's sole focus was to be on her exclusive designs and the super-rich customers who paid outrageous prices for them.

One week Shelby had been a struggling college student about to graduate and hoping to get a job in marketing. The next thing she knew she'd been swept into the posh and glamorous world of Tad and Anastasia Williamson. They'd been nice, if a bit too reserved, though not in their effusive praise of her work. Their job offer had come with a salary so huge Shelby had been speechless. Something they'd mistaken for hesitancy and tacked on more money.

Eight months later she'd met their son Donald, a prominent Denver attorney. She couldn't say it was love at first sight, but with his good looks and smooth moves, her head had turned plenty. At heart, Donald wasn't a bad person. It simply had never occurred to him that the world truly did not revolve around the Williamsons. His class-conscious mother was mostly at fault. But Donald was a bright guy. It was past time he figured it out.

For Shelby the dream had begun five years ago. But she had never belonged in that world. Turned out her large salary hadn't gone far at all. With the Williamsons, it was all about image, and that had cost Shelby plenty, both emotionally and financially. She really should've woken up long before last week.

She stared at the box containing her supplies. Tempted as she was to unpack them, the timing was wrong. She needed a large, well-lit, ventilated space to work. Trent would have heart failure if she took over the living room. She doubted fixing the sink had earned her that much grace.

Since she'd finished some light housekeeping, she changed

from her old work T-shirt to a more flattering turquoise cotton knit. Next she planned on making dinner, glad she wasn't a messy cook. She hoped that was still true. It had been a while...

She went to the fridge and took out the hamburger she'd bought in town yesterday. Trent's meager assortment of spices and herbs was pitiful but she'd make do. She found a mixing bowl and baking pan, and everything else she needed to put together a decent meatloaf.

If Trent had plans for dinner, that was okay. But he'd shared his steak with her so she figured it was her turn. The view of the Rockies from the kitchen window was really amazing.

The late afternoon sun had sunk behind the peaks, leaving behind clouds that looked like wisps of pink cotton candy. She thought about running to get her phone so she could take a picture but got distracted.

Shelby wasn't sure how she'd missed him at first. Trent was in the corral working with a reddish-brown horse, his focus completely centered on the beautiful animal. Anyone half blind could see that Trent was in his element. For him, the rest of the world seemed to have disappeared. Spellbound, she could barely drag her gaze away. But if she worked quickly...

While waiting for the oven to preheat, she peeled and cut up potatoes, then put them in a pot to boil. Once the meatloaf was in the oven, she calculated how much time she had before she needed to turn the stove off, then walked outside. If she was intruding, she'd know right away. One good thing about Trent, she thought wryly, he didn't hold back.

She'd been leaning against the corral for almost five minutes before he even noticed her. His fleeting frown told her nothing. He tugged down the brim of his hat and led the horse toward her. Her racing heart made sense when she flashed back to the excitement of her first pony ride. A time when things had still been okay between her parents. She must've been about nine.

"Am I interrupting?" she asked, her gaze glued to the muscled horse. "If so I'll leave."

"For good?"

Okay, she'd laid the welcome mat out for that. "What's his name?"

"Solomon." Trent stroked the horse's neck. "This is Shelby," he told the animal. "How do you greet a lady?"

Solomon went down on his front legs and bowed.

Surprised and delighted, Shelby giggled like a silly schoolgirl. "What kind is he?"

Trent's smile vanished in a second. "A quarter horse," he said, clearly insulted.

"Ah, right. You mentioned that before. Sorry."

"Damn straight. Everybody knows the American quarter horse is the best all-purpose breed in the world," he said with a brief self-mocking smile. "They're used for rodeos, barrel-racing, steer roping, pleasure rides, ranch work. As for racing? They can turn more quickly and accelerate faster than any other horse." He gave Solomon a fond smile. "You've won a couple races yourself, haven't you, buddy?"

The horse moved his head in a vague nod.

Shelby let out a short laugh. "He's amazing. May I pet him?"

"Sure." Trent brought the horse closer.

"He's smaller than I expected."

"Don't let that fool you. Quarter horses generally are more compact. But they're powerful sprinters, agile and well-balanced. That's partly what makes them so versatile."

"You're so handsome." With a tentative hand, she stroked the side of Solomon's neck just as she'd seen Trent do.

"No need to be afraid. He likes you. See how his ears are pricked forward. If he didn't like you touching him you'd know it."

"Kind of like his owner." She realized that hadn't come out right when Trent raised a brow at her. "No, not— I meant the part about him not holding back."

With a little smile betraying his amusement, he lifted his hat and resettled it on his head. "You take care of that leak?"

"All done."

His expression said it all. He hadn't expected that outcome.

Shelby grinned. "Don't look so surprised. I'm very resourceful."

"I don't doubt it. But I figured you would've come out gloating."

"Oh, I thought about it. I even practiced what I was going to say while I did some tidying up."

His gaze narrowed. "You cleaned, too?"

She stopped petting Solomon and held up both hands. "I didn't touch any of your personal stuff."

"I wasn't worried about that. Can you cook?"

"Depends. What's it worth to you?"

"Are you serious? I'm already giving you bathroom and kitchen privileges."

"Well, aren't you just a knight in shining armor?"

Solomon snorted.

"Yes, I know, handsome. But we'll just ignore him," Shelby said, and went back to stroking his neck.

This time Trent snorted. "You'll never turn him against me."

He sounded so serious she had to laugh. "It just so happens I made dinner." The reminder had her checking her watch.

"Real food? Not chef's salad or quiche or anything like that."

"Oh, no." Shelby tried her best to look disappointed. "You don't like quiche?"

He cleared his throat. "It's okay."

"Good." She gave him a bright smile. "Dinner will be ready in thirty minutes. See you later, handsome." She gave the horse an extra pat, then hurried toward the house before she burst out laughing.

"Do I HAVE time for a shower?" Trent entered by the back door twenty-five minutes later. "Or is that gonna ruin the quiche?"

By the time Shelby looked up from the salad she was toss-

ing, he was sniffing the air, his brows drawn together in a suspicious frown. "No, go ahead," she told him.

"What's that smell?"

"Meatloaf."

He hung his hat on a wall peg, a faint smile curving his mouth
as he walked out of the kitchen.

Shelby grinned, too, but didn't let him see. Figuring she had
a spare ten minutes she decided to make gravy for the mashed
potatoes. It had been her favorite comfort food as a kid, and
even in college, mostly because it was a cheap dish. But it'd
been years since she'd indulged. Thanksgiving dinner with the
Williamsons was always a gourmet affair—no mashed potatoes and gravy.

Deciding to go all out, fat and calories be damned, she pulled
out butter along with the other necessary ingredients.

She repeated the earlier ritual of searching cabinets and drawers, this time for a whisk and the right size pot. Before she actually started on the gravy, her cell buzzed.

Dread slithered down her spine. Her good mood fizzled. It
was probably Donald again. She owed him another conversation,
she knew that. Something made her grab the phone instead of
letting it go to voice mail. She frowned at the caller ID. Wasn't
it kind of late in Germany?

"Hi, Mom, is everything okay?"

"You tell me."

Shelby briefly closed her eyes and rubbed her temple. *Wait
for it. Any second now...*

On cue, her mother let out a long-suffering sigh. "What on
earth is wrong with you, Shelby Ann?"

She knew, Shelby thought, but how? Her mother had never
called her at work, only on her cell. And very seldom. "Nothing's wrong. I'm terrific. Never felt better."

"Not according to Donald."

She pulled a chair away from the table and sat down. "Donald?" she murmured, the smell of meatloaf making her stomach turn. "You called him?"

"No, of course not. How would I know his number? Donald called me."

That made even less sense. They hadn't met yet. "What did he want?" she asked calmly.

"How could you be so stupid?"

Shelby flinched, though it wasn't the first time she'd been called that by her mom. It shouldn't still hurt. "Do you even want to know why I broke the engagement?"

"Do you honestly think you can do better?" Gloria's voice had risen. "He's an attorney. He's rich. His family is rich. He'll inherit everything one day. Don't you understand how lucky you were to find a man like him? A man who wants to marry you and not just keep you on the side?"

"Oh, Mom, please." Shelby let out a sigh that sounded depressingly like her mother's.

"Lord knows I tried my best with you, Shelby. I did. With no help from your worthless father, I might add. But you—"

"Mom, stop. Just stop."

Silence lasted only seconds. "Where are you?"

"Montana." The word slipped out before Shelby had a chance to think. No one needed to know where she was.

"Montana? Why? What could you possibly expect to—" Gloria paused, then huffed out a breath. "It doesn't matter. Donald hasn't given up on you. It's not too late. He wants you back."

"Tough."

"What did you say?"

"I am not going back to Denver or Donald or my job. There will be no wedding. I don't know how to say it any simpler." Knots of tension cramped her shoulders. A small insistent headache had begun to throb near her temple. "And you need to stay out of it. Are we clear?"

"What happened, baby?" Now came the cloyingly sweet conciliatory tone her mom had decided made her sound maternal.

"Did he have a small fling? Men stray from time to time. It's a fact of life. Certainly not a reason to cancel the wedding."

"I have to go. We'll talk again soon."

"But, honey—"

"Goodbye, Mom."

For the first time in her life, Shelby hung up on her mother.

She dropped the phone on the table, then dropped her chin to her chest, waiting for guilt to set in. She felt pretty good, actually. Her shoulders and head not so much. Her eyes were moist but no tears had fallen. That was progress.

God, she was almost twenty-eight. A grown woman who'd supported herself since she was eighteen. How could she still let Gloria get to her? Shelby had already predicted her mom's reaction. Nothing new there. She hadn't even met Donald yet she was rallying to his side.

Okay, that part was hard to take.

Shelby breathed in deeply, trying to dislodge the lump blocking her air passage.

Well, so much for dinner. Everything but the gravy was made. At least Trent could eat. Her stomach couldn't take any food. Still, she would never recommend the *Gloria diet*.

She pushed to her feet, anxious for the safety of her room. The meal was warm enough. If not, Trent was a big boy. He could figure it out.

The gravy ingredients were scattered on the counter. The thought of putting everything away made her want to weep. But she couldn't just leave it. Exhausted suddenly, she took a step and, from the corner of her eye, caught a glimpse of Trent.

Wearing a clean T-shirt, his hair damp, he stood in the doorway. For how long was anyone's guess. Judging by his expression, he'd heard plenty.

TRENT WAS AT a loss. The second he'd figured out she was on her cell he should've made himself scarce.

"Hey, good timing. Dinner's ready." Shelby forced a quick

smile, then couldn't turn away fast enough. "I have this stupid headache or I would've made gravy. Should I leave out the stuff for you, or put everything away?"

"Leave it."

She cleared her throat. "So, the salad is done. I made a simple dressing. It's in the fridge. Don't feel obligated—it won't hurt my feelings if you don't like Italian," she said with her back to him while washing and drying her hands. "Please, go ahead and eat. I'll have something later after I get rid of this headache."

He didn't know Shelby well, but it was obvious she was uncomfortable. The smart thing for him to do was pretend he'd forgotten something outside. Let her have her privacy until she could escape to her room.

But he knew a little of what she might be going through, and he'd feel like shit if he just did the easy thing.

"Shelby?"

"Huh?" If she continued drying her hands she wouldn't have any skin left.

"I overheard part of your conversation. I'm sorry for that."

She turned slowly to face him. "What did you hear?" No tears, but her eyes were misty, more sad than embarrassed.

If he made her cry he'd kick himself into next month. "I know you were engaged and now you're not."

She smiled a little. "Is that a stab at diplomacy?"

Trent sighed, wishing he'd just walked on outside. "Look, you know I'm divorced, and no, it doesn't make me an expert on breakups. But I wanted to say that it might feel like the end of the world right now, but it gets easier if not better. And take it easy on yourself. Respect the grieving period, but remember there's still life on the other side." He shrugged. "Whatever happens, trust your instincts. That's how animals survive. We could learn a lot from them." Something he needed to get through his thick skull, himself.

Shelby nodded, but was giving him the oddest look. Probably hadn't expected him to be so talkative. That made two of them.

"Ending the engagement was for the best. It was scary at first, but a huge relief, too. I'm good with my decision," she said. "I honestly am okay. It's just—" Her voice cracked and she looked away. "I need to lie down for a bit. It's this headache—"

Head down, she started for the door to the living room. He stepped aside to let her pass, and was surprised when she stopped to put a hand on his arm.

"Thank you," she said softly.

"No problem." He hadn't really done anything. So he'd fessed up to overhearing her phone conversation. As for the advice, normally he was the last person he'd listen to. But he knew something about the pain of lost love.

"I mean it. Thanks." She leaned in and kissed his cheek.

His arms came up around her. Not planned. It was the worst possible thing he could do. So he tried to mitigate the situation by patting her back.

Shelby looped her arms around his neck and gave him a light squeeze. Her soft breasts pressing against his chest had his body responding before he could order himself to heel. Luckily she retreated before discovering the flag had been raised.

He plowed a hand through his damp hair, hoping to keep her attention directed above his chest. "I don't mind waiting to eat."

"No, please, don't wait." She smiled, but it wasn't her usual. The woman could light the whole house without electricity when she wanted.

"Hey, listen," he said as she turned. "Tomorrow we should set up a place where you can work on your jewelry."

She blinked. "That might be premature," she said cautiously. "Don't you think?"

"No, not necessarily." He understood what she was getting at, and he hoped he wasn't being a first-class sucker. "How about we make a deal? Right now. No matter what happens with the Eager Beaver, no matter who holds the winning ticket, the other person has a grace period, two or three months before they have to clear out—whatever you think is fair. What do you say?"

She studied him a moment. "You don't have to be nice to me."

Trent laughed.

"I meant extra nice because of what you heard back there." She made a vague gesture. "I'm really fine."

"I believe you. Do we have a deal?"

She bit at her lip which made him want to forget the whole thing. "How about three months?"

"Three months," he agreed.

Reluctantly he accepted the hand she'd extended, knowing full well this agreement came with a catch. This woman was going to have him tied up in a hundred knots. More like a thousand if they lasted the entire three months. Knowing what he did now, he couldn't touch her again. No matter how tempting.

She might think everything was okay, but based on his own experience, the shock might not have worn off yet. He seriously doubted she knew how she felt and he wasn't about to get caught in the middle of anything.

9

"GET YOUR LAZY ass out of the way." Trent waited for the dog to move. Mutt barely lifted his head then settled in a more comfortable position in the loose hay. "Why aren't you bothering Shelby? I thought she was your new best friend."

Mutt continued to ignore him.

Trent leaned the pitchfork against the barn wall and yanked off his hat. The temperature was too warm for September. Course in a matter of weeks he'd be looking over his shoulder for the first sign of snow and griping about that.

Since making the deal with Shelby two days ago, everything seemed to irritate him. He knew the cause. And it wasn't the fourteen-hour days he'd been working. The look-but-don't-touch vow he'd made to himself seemed to be hanging over his head like a rain cloud ready to burst. It didn't make any sense because nothing had changed since day one. He was through with women. Not with sex, just emotional involvement.

The part where you laid your heart on the line never knowing when it would get trampled. Uncomplicated sex was the way to go.

Someday soon he'd dip his bucket in the well again. But it wouldn't be anywhere close to home. And not with a woman who had any expectations beyond a satisfying few hours in bed. Or a woman who was on the rebound. That could get sticky.

Another thing irking him was Violet's radio silence. She had practically pulled a disappearing act. She hadn't been sitting on her porch or coming out to collect eggs and making wise-cracks. It had gotten so bad that he'd worried she was sick and knocked on her door two days ago. She'd about taken his head off for disturbing her television program.

While he was relieved her health appeared okay, he couldn't help worrying that she was either up to no good or knew something about the Eager Beaver she wasn't anxious to reveal. By the time the horses were fed, the idea of checking on her again wouldn't let him be. Something was on that old lady's mind, and dammit, he didn't need any more surprises.

Leaving Mutt to soak up the sun, Trent headed over to the double-wide. Expecting to hear himself being called every name in the book, he knocked. Violet swung the door open and said, "'Bout time you came by. What if I'd had a heart attack or something?"

She moved back to let him in. A very rare experience that made him even more nervous. He shook his head as he passed her into the living room. The trailer had all the standard conveniences, along with a big plasma TV, and was neat as a pin.

"Now you know I won't worry about that," he said. "Seeing as how you've told me yourself you don't have a heart."

She gave him a wicked look. "For the next five minutes you are to keep your mouth shut, you hear me?"

"What are you talking about? Jesus, it smells like smoke in here. Don't you ever open any windows?"

"Okay, you're just eating up your minutes, and if you keep it up, you're not gonna hear something that you ought."

"Fine," he said, his heart beating fast, and not from second-hand smoke. Dammit. She did know something. But if she knew the Eager Beaver was his, she would have said already. On the other hand, when had Violet done anything the easy way.

"You gotta swear on your great-granddaddy's grave that what I'm about to tell you is just between us. That means you don't call your momma or tell your friends or your...houseguest. You can talk to me, but that's it."

"Okay, now I'm worried. Did you fall and hit your head?"

"Shush, I'm telling you something. Swear now. Right now, that you won't say a word 'bout this to anyone."

"Okay, okay. I swear."

"The Eager Beaver is yours. And in two weeks, I'll have what I need to prove it."

The double-wide seemed to sway. "What? How? Why in two weeks?"

Violet glared at him. "Because that's how long it'll take me to get the paperwork."

Trent didn't like this, didn't like it one bit. "You mean the deed?"

"I ain't saying no more about it." Violet got that stubborn glint in her eye that always meant trouble. "Now, get out of here. My shows are coming on."

TWO HOURS AND two phone calls later, Trent still couldn't make heads or tails out of the situation. His mom had barely set foot in the door after returning from her trip when he'd called to see if she'd been to the bank yet. She must've sensed his panic because she checked their safe deposit box and got back to him in thirty minutes. Turned out Violet was a trustee of some kind. Legally. According to a handwritten document that had been notarized. That was all his mother could find. What in the hell had his great-granddad been thinking? If Trent didn't end up with an ulcer before this mess got straightened out it would be a damn miracle.

It was Mutt that pulled him out of his swirling thoughts. The dog raised his head, ears perked.

Seconds later Trent heard an engine and stuck his head out of the barn. It was his neighbor. Jimmy parked his four-wheeler behind Shelby's car and then circled the sedan, checking out the chrome wheels.

"You got some fancy company?" he asked when he saw Trent.

"Not exactly." Of all the times for Jimmy to come by. Instead of being the happiest man in Salina County that his home still belonged to him, Trent had been doing some thinking. Having thoughts he shouldn't be bothered with. Like how Shelby was gonna take the news, and how they'd just gotten to a real civil place but that was tricky, too. And now, Jimmy.

"What's going on?" he asked, as much to himself as to his company.

"Dad and Cal are busy sorting and weighing calves." Jimmy gave the car a final once-over before joining Trent outside the barn. "Any chance you can help me with weaning vaccinations?"

Trent eyed the younger man. He was a tall husky guy, much like his brother Cal, only Jimmy wasn't sure he wanted to stick around and be a rancher. He had a long list of chores he hated, all of them relating to cattle, something which he and Trent had in common.

"You can't do that by yourself?" Trent said, figuring there was more to Jimmy's request. "You wouldn't be doing some branding now, would you?"

Jimmy's wry grin confirmed Trent's suspicion.

"Nope. No way." Trent peeled off a glove. "You know how much I hate branding."

"Well, me, too."

"Yeah, too bad. Talk your dad into breeding horses."

"Come on, Kimball. We'll hit the Watering Hole afterward. All the beer you can drink on me."

"Nope." Trent bent over to pick up Mutt's water bowl. He liked Jimmy, and he even felt for the guy. Growing up on a ranch in a place as isolated as Blackfoot Falls with limited skills, his options were few. He could end up staying on the family ranch for the rest of his life.

"Holy shit. Who is that?"

Trent didn't have to turn around to know who Jimmy meant. "Keep your mouth open like that and you'll be coughing up flies for a week."

Jimmy finally closed his mouth but he didn't move, just kept staring. "Come on, who is she?"

Trent turned, curious whether Shelby could see them. She was standing on the porch wearing her normal work clothes— tight faded jeans, ripped in several places and a white T-shirt. This one wasn't as snug as some of the others. But it didn't hide anything, either.

"That's Shelby," he said, still not sure if she'd seen them. "Quit staring like a jackass."

"Is she yours?"

"Jesus." Trent laughed, shook his head. "You have about as much chance with her as you have of getting me to help you brand calves."

Jimmy patted down his curly blond hair. It had a tendency to stick out. Like now. "Call her over. Introduce us."

"You're barking up the wrong tree, kid."

Shelby shaded her eyes and searched the cloudless sky. Hoping to spot a hawk, he imagined. She loved watching them wheel and soar. Occasionally she'd catch sight of an eagle, and get as excited as a five-year-old on Christmas morning. She stepped off the porch and went straight for the double-wide.

Seeing her got Mutt up and moving. Tail wagging, he chased after her. She stopped to pet him, noticed them standing in the shadow of the barn, and waved.

Jimmy responded with a raised hand and a flushed face. "Don't just stand there. Ask her to come over here," he grumbled.

Trent had been hoping she wouldn't, but it was better than her knocking on Violet's door. He let out a breath when she walked toward them.

"Hello," she said, smiling at Jimmy and then glancing at Trent. "I hope I'm not interrupting."

"Nah, I came to do some arm-twisting," Jimmy said, all teeth.

Shelby grinned. "Is it working?"

"Not with the rotten mood he's in."

"Oh, I thought it was just me."

Holding in a curse, Trent looked at Mutt's water bowl and remembered he was supposed to fill it. "Shelby, this is Jimmy," Trent said, gesturing. "Jimmy... Shelby. I'm going back to work."

"Wait." Shelby caught his arm as he turned. "Where's the circuit breaker?"

"You blew a fuse?"

"I'm sure I just tripped it."

"I'll take care of it," Trent muttered, annoyed that he'd caught a whiff of her. She had no business smelling this good while she was making her jewelry. Her scent was the equivalent of an earworm. It would stick with him for the rest of the day. Shit. How was he going to hold it together when he'd have to smell her, see her, every day for three months.

"Um, you should probably show me where the box is located."

He cleared his throat. "So, you trip fuses a lot?"

She ducked her head. "I wouldn't say a lot..."

"Shoot, I'll show her where it is," Jimmy said with a sly grin for Trent. "I know you're busy."

"If you still want help with the vaccinations I'll have time later. Tomorrow I'm leaving at first light and I'll be gone all day." He felt Shelby's eyes on him. Probably because he hadn't mentioned he was going anywhere. Not that he needed her permission.

Jimmy sighed. "Still a no on the branding, huh?"

In answer, Trent grabbed the pitchfork he'd left against the wall and with the bowl, headed toward the back of the barn. A second before he was out of earshot, he heard Jimmy ask, "So, have you been to the Watering Hole yet?"

SHELBY WISHED SHE knew what was bothering Trent. She'd narrowed the list to two possibilities, neither of which she wanted to bring up. Though if he regretted agreeing to a grace period, she needed to know pretty quick.

The movers had phoned to make a delivery appointment. Thankfully the call had gone to voice mail while she was showering. She still hadn't made up her mind. Did she let them bring her belongings? Or tell them to store everything?

Storage would be the obvious choice if Blackfoot Falls had an adequate facility that allowed her access. The hardware store owner kept four containers in his storage barn available to rent. She'd checked, but they were all taken.

Getting her hands on the deed to the Eager Beaver wasn't an issue. At least in terms of taking possession of her things. She already knew all she had packed away was her grandfather's will.

Since it was getting late, she poured herself a cup of decaf, then glanced out the kitchen window. No Trent. No Violet. Not even Mutt was in sight. As far as she knew, Jimmy had left as soon as she'd gone back to work.

In spite of herself, she wondered where Trent was going in the morning. He hadn't said, though he had no reason to tell her anything about his schedule, or his life. Especially if the point of leaving tomorrow was to get away from her.

Three evenings ago, after the call from her mom, he'd wowed her with his compassion and insight. The next day? Boom. He'd become a completely different person.

He hadn't been rude, not even all that grumpy. The change was more subtle than that. He'd seemed almost...detached. A couple of times he'd mentioned fall was a busy season, and while she didn't doubt it, she recognized it was also an excuse not to engage with her.

"Hey…" The man in question strolled into the kitchen, surprising her since she'd assumed he was outside.

She saw his gaze zero in on the coffeemaker. "It's decaf."

He made a wry face.

"Columbian decaf. It's good." Oh, damn, the coffeemaker was his, and she was tying it up. She set down her mug. "I'll make a fresh pot."

"No, that's okay."

She was already opening the upper cabinet where he kept the mugs, coffee and sugar.

"I shouldn't stay up late, anyway." He lightly touched the small of her back as he reached around her to grab a mug.

The contact startled her, made her clumsy. "Right." She almost knocked over her coffee trying to slip out of his way. "You're leaving early."

"I can wait, head out around nine-thirty," he said, concentrating on his mug. "If you thought you might wanna go with—" He shook his head, frowned. "I'm saying this backward."

She didn't care. She'd heard the important part. What a relief he wasn't upset with her… "Go where?"

"Have you thought about renting a booth at the county fair?" He turned to face her and must've noticed she was confused. "To sell your jewelry."

"Huh. The fair?"

"I know you want to set up an online business but you mentioned festivals are a good place for the style you make. So, why not at a fair?"

"I don't know. I've never been… I thought a county fair would be about livestock and baking contests."

Smiling, he nodded. "It is. But there are also crafts on display and for sale. Afraid I can't be more specific." One corner of his mouth lifted a bit higher than the other. "It's been a long time since I've gone to one, myself."

She had to stop staring and concentrate on what he was saying. The sudden knowledge that she'd been starved for that smile unnerved her. Gathering her wits, she thought for a moment. A flutter of excitement flickered in her tummy.

"Yes, I want to do it." Her mind raced, collecting and cataloguing, as she started to pace. "I don't have too many pieces ready but I can— Wait. When is the fair? I can't remember. How long does it run?"

Trent was leaning against the counter, mug in hand, watching her with a curiously warm smile. Nothing like the slightly lopsided grin from a minute ago. His eyes had darkened so much they might've been brown instead of gray.

He straightened and sobered. "I should've said before getting your hopes up. It starts in a week, runs for three days but they might not have any booths left. Rent is cheap and people tend to snap 'em up. But I have a string or two I can pull."

She nodded, digesting the information and thinking back to her trip to town. The fair had been the main topic of conversation. "Only if it's not too much trouble." She kept her expression blank, not wanting any hint of disappointment to show. "Really. No big deal if it doesn't work out."

"It'll be big to me. You're really excited."

"I am," she admitted, and grabbed her mug, mostly to have something to do with her hands. "It would take a lot of preparation, so if it doesn't fly, no harm, no foul. Okay?"

"Tomorrow I'm going to see a guy about a horse he wants trained and then go have a look at a colt I'm thinking of buying. If you're interested in going with me, we can stop in town on the way back and see about signing you up for a booth."

"Tell me what time and I'll be ready."

"How does nine sound?"

"I can be ready earlier."

"No, nine is fine. It gives me plenty of time to feed the stock and hitch the trailer. I'll even buy you breakfast."

Shelby let out a squeak of joy that sounded entirely too obnoxious and loud.

Trent reared back, frowning and chuckling at once. "What was that?"

"Eating out. Someone else cooking. I'm totally in." She paused, hoping she hadn't given him the impression she resented making meals. It was only fair, after all. "Can I ask you something?"

He didn't look too keen on it. "Go ahead."

"When I broke off my engagement, it wasn't on a whim or because I didn't get my way or—"

"None of my business," he said, cutting her short and shaking his head. "I haven't given it a thought."

"I know, it's just that you haven't been yourself and since you're divorced and that might be a touchy subject..." She watched him dump the rest of his coffee in the sink and rinse the mug. Dammit, she hadn't meant to chase him away. Why had she even... "I thought you were angry with me."

"I'm not angry," he said, pausing to look her in the eyes. Then walked out of the kitchen.

She'd give anything if she could take back what she'd said. She'd never been this clumsy and awkward around anyone. So why Trent?

THE MORNINGS WERE cold enough for Trent to wear a jacket when he fed the horses at sunrise. Hard to believe when the daytime temperatures had been hovering well above normal. Since they'd be gone until late afternoon, he'd suggested to Shelby that she dress in layers. Not like she was going bobsledding.

He glanced at her, bundled up in a puffy down coat, sitting on the passenger side of his truck. "Didn't you say you lived in Denver most of your life?"

"All of it. Until a week ago." She turned to look at him. "Why?"

She'd wrapped a blue scarf around her neck and over her head and ears so that all he could see were her eyes and nose.

He chuckled. "I can adjust the heater."

"No, thanks. I'm very comfy." She pulled off one mitten and picked up her to-go mug of coffee. She'd prepared one for each of them and filled a thermos, even though he'd assured her they were only driving a hundred miles, give or take.

"I don't get it," he said. "I know for a fact Denver gets downright frigid at times."

"Yes, it does."

"It's still September, Shelby." He divided his attention between her and the road. "Look at you."

"What?" She glanced down. "I need an adjustment period between seasons," she said with a defensive lift of her chin.

"Okay. I meant no offense."

"I know." She sighed. "This coat and the mittens came out of the emergency kit I keep in my trunk. I wasn't thinking clearly when I left," she murmured and stared out the window.

He was more than happy to drop the subject. He didn't want to hear about her departure, or her engagement, or whether she was second-guessing herself. It was difficult enough thinking about his own situation. Now that he knew the ranch was his—according to Violet, at least— he'd been hard-pressed to think of anything else. The whole reason Shelby was coming along this morning was to get a booth at the fair. He didn't know what kind of money she expected to make selling her jewelry, but he figured either she'd earn enough to help her move on or she'd find out Blackfoot Falls wasn't a good place to set up shop.

Trent sure didn't want to regret bringing her along. The other day he'd learned too much about her, then said too much. Neither of them needed to forge a bond. It would make everything harder in the long run.

He was weirdly grateful they'd already agreed to the three-month grace period. Even so, he knew the news that she didn't own the ranch would crush her. He understood about last chances and chasing dreams.

Dammit, thoughts like those were exactly what he was supposed to avoid. If they were going to live together for three whole months, he had to stop thinking about her life and her dreams, and put all his energy into his own.

So what did he go and do? Put himself in a truck with her for a long drive. He'd like to think his offer was inspired by his good nature and had nothing to do with Jimmy chatting her up yesterday. The kid was too young for her. And even if he wasn't, Trent didn't care what she did.

"Oh, shoot." Her gaze was fixed on the dashboard clock. "I forgot to call the movers." She pulled off the other mitten and fumbled inside her coat pocket. "They called yesterday for a delivery appointment."

"How much stuff do you have?"

"Not a lot. My apartment was small."

He told himself to keep his mouth shut. Shelby was a grown woman. Let her figure out what to do. He checked the Exiss in the rearview mirror, mostly out of habit. The trailer was empty and it might well be returning empty. Deciding to bring it had been a tough call. He hoped it didn't make him seem too eager about buying the colt. Though this wasn't Dallas. He knew the Landers family and they'd ask a fair price.

Glancing over at Shelby, he saw the cell in her hand. She was staring at it and giving her lower lip a workout.

None of my business, he reminded himself and went back to concentrating on the road ahead.

A few silent minutes passed.

"The spare bedroom," he said wanting to kick himself. "And the equipment shed behind the barn. They both have extra room. The shed is solid, waterproof and airtight."

She blinked at him, then frowned slightly. "How far away is Kalispell?"

"A little less than an hour from Blackfoot Falls. Tack on another twenty minutes from the Eager Beaver."

She thumbed the small keyboard on her phone. A few minutes later she shook her head. "I still can't get online."

"Service will be spotty for the next couple of hours. You should be able to make a call, though."

"I need to know what I'm going to tell them first."

Okay, so she didn't like the spare-room-and-shed idea. Good. Made things simpler.

"What about when we stop for breakfast? Can I get online then?"

"Probably not. The place I have in mind is ten minutes out. There's a diner and a gas station, that's it."

"Well, that's just crazy," she muttered. "How can anyplace not have decent internet in this day and age? Have people not heard of satellites?"

Trent grinned. "You're not in Kansas anymore, darlin'."

She raised her brows at him. "Darlin'?"

"At least I didn't call you sweetheart."

She let out a disgusted sigh. But he saw the small smile before she looked down at her phone. He thought she'd found a local cell tower, but she didn't call until they'd parked in front of the roadside diner. Instead of heading in, she told him she'd be along in a minute and wandered off to a private spot.

So she didn't want him to hear her conversation. Fine. As he'd told himself a hundred times, none of his business.

Let her have her secrets.

After all, Trent had one hell of a doozy of his own.

10

AS THE TRUCK bounced along the rough, pitted road Shelby stared at the ranch they were approaching. It looked like a small village. There were far more buildings than she could account for with her limited knowledge of ranching.

She was about to ask Trent what they were all for when he turned onto a paved driveway and drove under the elaborate wrought-iron archway announcing the Castle Ranch. Elm trees turning gold and red lined the seemingly endless driveway. The terrain was hillier than at the Eager Beaver and well-maintained.

"Wow, it's pretty out here." She twisted around to watch a pair of beautiful white horses galloping, the epitome of grace and beauty. "Is this all one ranch?"

"Yep."

She saw the main house. Who could miss the gorgeous, sprawling Tudor-style home with all the natural stone and glass? The sloping manicured lawn that surrounded it was impossibly green.

On the far right stood a long white structure that had to be the bunkhouse. Two men standing in front talking turned and lifted their hands in friendly waves, which Shelby returned.

The large rust-colored barns were easy to identify, all three of them. A few other scattered buildings were probably sheds, although five times the size by her definition.

"I think you're wrong about this being all one ranch," she said, pointing to a cluster of four small houses each with its own yard and beds of faded flowers.

Trent glanced at them with a faint smile. "The married hired hands live in those."

"Are you serious?" She stared at him, then got distracted by their surroundings again. "They have their own gas station?"

He laughed. "A place this size runs a lot of equipment. Those two gas pumps are more necessity than convenience."

"Huh." Closer to the house was an impressive building in both size and appearance. "What's that?"

"The stable," he said, frowning at her as if she'd committed blasphemy by needing to ask.

"Right." She noticed what had to be a racetrack but refrained from commenting.

A tall distinguished-looking man with white hair walked out of the stable and motioned for Trent to park under a large cottonwood tree.

Trent eased the truck into the spot and cut the engine. "Is this how you expected the Eager Beaver to look?"

"Oh, sure." She scanned the front of the house. The stone work was awesome, and so was the aggregate circular drive sweeping around hundreds of yellow mums. The whole place was really something. "I didn't even know ranches like this existed outside of the movies."

"You should see some of the spreads in Texas." He grabbed his black Stetson from the backseat and put it on. "Ready?"

She nodded. "Don't worry. I won't ask any more stupid questions."

"Ask anything you want," he said, grinning as he got out of the truck.

She did a quick check in the visor mirror. She'd gotten rid of the scarf, mittens and her coat before going into the diner but her hair was still flat so she poufed it out some.

Her door opened. Trent stood there holding it for her. "You look great," he said with a trace of amusement.

Accepting the hand he offered, she slid off the seat and touched ground. "So do you," she said and winked.

His low sexy chuckle did a number on her nervous system. As if being confined to the truck's cab for two hours, sitting close enough to notice the spot he'd missed shaving and admiring his firm, chiseled jaw hadn't already left her a tad weak in the knees.

They headed toward the man who stood outside the stable, cleaning his sunglasses while waiting for them. He wore perfectly creased black jeans and a crisp long-sleeve blue shirt. Shelby didn't really know boots but she'd be willing to bet his cost as much as her entire shoe collection, which was nothing to sneeze at.

"Mr. Calhoun." Trent approached with his hand extended.

"Trent Kimball." The man folded his white handkerchief slowly and slipped it into his pocket, then put on his aviator-style sunglasses, adjusting them carefully. Finally, he shook Trent's hand. "Call me Hank. We're all friends here." He smiled at Shelby. "And who's this?"

"Shel—"

"Shelby Foster," she said, not meaning to cut Trent off, and automatically offered Mr. Calhoun her hand.

"A pleasure to make your acquaintance." He picked up her hand and kissed the back.

Startled, she pressed her lips together and forced a smile. He was older, from a different generation, and was just being polite…

Like hell. While working for the Williamsons, she'd dealt with a wide range of wealthy clients, up to and including the obscenely rich. She'd found most of them to be pleasant and reasonable. But there had been a few, rude, arrogant men like

Hank Calhoun. Though she'd never before experienced such a strong and instant dislike for someone.

Maybe she'd rushed to judgment. But she doubted it. His posturing was too obvious. First, he'd made no move to greet Trent, then left him standing with his hand out while the jerk wiped his glasses?

And then kissing her hand? Calhoun knew better. All she'd offered was a handshake.

Ew. Now she needed a shower.

But this was Trent's show so she kept a smile in place, calmly withdrew her hand.

"Quite a spread you have here," Trent said, glancing around. "You raise cattle, too, don't you?"

Glad for the change of subject, she breathed out a sigh of relief that neither man appeared to have noticed her reaction.

"My sons handle that side of the business," Calhoun said with a dismissive wave. "I have a much greater interest in horses. Arabians in particular."

Trent gave him an odd look, frowned for a moment, then said, "Mind showing me inside your stable?" His gaze followed the high pitch of the roof. "I'm already green with envy."

Calhoun laughed. "Sure, I'll give you a tour. A little later, though." Trent didn't seem pleased. "Have you folks eaten yet? I have a terrific cook. Ruth will whip up anything you want."

"No, thanks." Trent patted his flat belly, drawing Shelby's attention. "We stopped on the way."

Her gaze lingered on his narrow waist and hips. Today he wore a blue chambray shirt tucked into his jeans. They weren't very worn but still fit him nice and snug.

"Shelby?" Trent touched her arm.

She blinked.

Both men were looking at her.

Her mind had been wiped clean. She couldn't come up with a blessed thing to say.

"Would you like something to drink?" Trent asked, a gleam of amusement in his gray eyes.

"I'm good. Thanks. Would you excuse me a moment?" She took a step back. "Don't wait. I'll catch up," she said, then turned and walked to the truck as quickly as she could manage without tripping, keeping her head down and taking deep breaths.

She'd been staring at Trent's fly.

Of course he'd noticed. And in case he'd chalked it up to his imagination, she'd just provided confirmation by stalking off like a two-year-old. Her cheeks had to be flaming every shade of red.

She climbed into the truck and slid down in the seat. There had to be good internet here. She couldn't see Hank Calhoun tolerating spotty service. Reaching for her coat, which was on the backseat, she pulled her cell from the pocket. A quick glance assured her the men had continued their discussion and showed no interest in her. She focused on her cell. Busy morning. Texts from Donald and the movers. A voice mail from her mom. And one from Mrs. Williamson, Donald's mother. That was a first. And it presented a tricky problem. The woman had been Shelby's employer for five years. It could be a business call.

After all, Shelby had left without much notice, something that would haunt her conscience for a long time. Although she had tried to tough out a week, just to tie up loose ends if nothing else. But Donald had refused to leave her alone. And if Mrs. Williamson could've killed her with a look, Shelby would be dead by now. The hostile work environment hadn't inspired creativity so instead of finishing the week Shelby had left the next day.

She scrolled through texts—the movers needed to hear from her ASAP. So did Donald. She felt badly about not setting up a delivery appointment last night so she called the movers before listening to messages. And was sent straight to voice mail. Okay with her since she was still iffy about what to tell them.

Bracing herself for Mrs. Williamson's message, Shelby hit

Speaker and let her gaze wander toward Trent and Hank standing at the fence surrounding the racetrack. The men were too
far away to make out Trent's expression. But she recognized
his body language. Arms folded, shoulders back, jaw angled
up. He looked pissed.

Hank gestured with his hands, clearly talking about the horse
and rider running around the track. She would've never guessed
he could be so animated.

Her cell beeped signaling the end of the voice mail. She
hadn't heard a word of it. Quickly she replayed the message
while opening the truck door. Mrs. Williamson's sickeningly
sweet tone was a complete surprise, and enough to make Shelby
nauseous. The woman usually reserved the syrupy voice for
rich clients. Shelby listened a bit, then disconnected. Pleading
on behalf of her grown son...for God's sake. But then the over-
bearing woman had become a big part of the problem between
Shelby and Donald. Everything had to be his mother's way,
and Donald didn't seem to care. He just took the easy path to
keep the peace. But so had Shelby. Until she'd realized Donald
would never be on her side. He'd never appreciate her need to
be her own person. His mother would always rule.

Because Shelby didn't want to be rude, she would eventually
return Mrs. Williamson's call. But for now she slipped the phone
into her jeans pocket, more interested in Trent and whether he
needed reinforcements. As she got closer, she saw Hank hold
up a stopwatch just as the horse, the rider crouched forward in
jockey position, ran past them.

"Look at that." He motioned to someone inside the fence. The
young man was bent forward, hands on his thighs, squinting at
the horse's legs, but he waved an acknowledgement. "Tell me
that isn't a damn fine-looking animal," Hank said and clapped
Trent on the back.

"No argument from me," Trent said, unsmiling.

"People have underestimated Arabians. The racing world
started to wake up in the nineties, but the breed still has too few

tracks available to them. But you wait. In the next five years, these beauties will win higher purses than any quarter horse could dream of."

Shelby stood on Trent's left, not sure if he'd seen her yet. She brushed her arm against his.

He turned and gave her a smile. "Everything okay?" he asked quietly.

"Service is great here," she said, holding up the phone. "So yay."

Hank glanced at her, then swung his attention back to the track. "You'll appreciate this next stallion. I bought Thor a few months ago. He's four years old and he's already won his first race. With the right trainer, I think he could be a real money maker. I got him for a steal. The idiots who owned him had no idea what they were doing."

Shelby reminded herself that horseracing, ranching and horse trading, or whatever they called it, were businesses. A difficult concept to grasp when the commodity was a gorgeous gray horse with an impressive mane that looked like silk. But obviously Hank had brokered a good deal. She shouldn't dislike him more than she already did because of it. Yet she did.

The silver-gray stallion pranced onto the track as if the whole world were watching. He flicked his tail, arched his neck slightly. With his gleaming coat, Thor was really that breathtaking.

"He's beautiful," she whispered, unable to tear her gaze away. "Isn't he?"

Trent heaved a sigh.

She felt his breath on her face. Felt the heat from his body, startled to discover that she was leaning into him. And with a fair amount of her weight. She immediately straightened.

He slid an arm around her and lightly squeezed her left shoulder. "Yes, he is."

"What was that?" Hank asked her, then proved he'd heard

by adding, "The lady has excellent taste. Watch him, Kimball. You'll be impressed."

Trent kept his eyes on the horse, his hand on her shoulder. She could still feel his tension and wished she understood what was wrong.

For the next twenty minutes they watched Thor beat his last recorded time. Then Hank showed them another horse, a bay mare, who apparently needed a lot of training. Hank continued to communicate with hand signals, though sometimes using his cell to give curt orders to the men running the horses. The whole time Trent remained silent.

Finally, he spoke. "You have a nice setup here, Hank. Some impressive horses. Glad I got to see it. But at this point, there's no sense wasting any more of each other's time."

As he turned to Trent, the other man's mouth tightened. "You don't want the job?"

"Like I told you, I don't work with Thoroughbreds or Arabians. I've got nothing against them. But I only train quarter horses."

Hank removed his sunglasses and narrowed his dark eyes. "I know for a fact you trained a winning Thoroughbred for Tucker Lawson."

"Hell, that was over seven years ago, and I only did it as a favor."

Hank studied him with a critical eye. "After what happened in Texas, I figured you wouldn't be so picky."

Trent stared at the man until Hank looked away. "Guess you thought wrong."

"Is it the money?" Hank asked, taking a hundred-and-eighty degree swing with a kiss-ass tone that seemed to irritate Trent even more. "Look, whatever they were paying you in Texas, I'll double."

"Nice meeting you, Mr. Calhoun. I wish you well." Trent extended his hand.

Hank ignored it. "All right," he said, sounding petulant again.

"You can take Thor and Aces to your place. I've never allowed any of my horses to be trained anywhere but Castle Ranch. This is a damn big concession for me."

"I'm sure another trainer will appreciate it." Trent shook his head. "Look, I'm not trying to play hard to get or squeeze you for more money." He shrugged. "I'm really not interested."

"I'll go six-figures as well as winning bonus," Calhoun said with a smug lift of his chin. "How's that?"

Trent didn't even blink. He turned, gave her a tired smile and steered them toward the truck.

"No one else will offer you a better deal," Calhoun called out, then added something completely undignified.

"Someone needs to tell him he's too old to be a sore loser," Shelby muttered.

Trent stopped on the passenger side and opened the door for her. "Think I'm a fool for turning down all that money?"

"No." She looked up at him. "I think you'd be nuts to work for an egomaniac who has more money than brains. For God's sake, he didn't have enough sense to be tactful."

He waited until she'd slid onto the seat. And then he leaned in and kissed her.

His lips were warm and firm, patient. She had a feeling he'd intended to keep it light. But when she strained up to meet him partway, he became more insistent, the increasing pressure of his mouth matching her eager reaction. At the first touch of his tongue she parted her lips.

He slid inside, then cupped her jaw with his slightly calloused hand while his tongue made a thorough sweep. Good thing she was already sitting down. It was as if he'd found a magic switch. Her whole body jolted to life. She put a hand on his arm and the swell of his bicep under her palm sent a tingling sensation skipping down her spine.

Trent pulled back, his breathing ragged. "Let's get out of here before Calhoun turns a hose on us."

She laughed, stopped abruptly. "God, he probably would do

something like that, wouldn't he?" When she saw Trent staring at her mouth and making no move to plant himself behind the wheel, she said, "Well, get in already."

"Yes, ma'am," he said, and stole another quick kiss before climbing into the truck.

TRENT'S CARELESS DISREGARD for his promise to stay away from Shelby hit him hard. So did Shelby's reaction. The kiss had been a give and take, and, damn it, he wanted more. He seriously considered pulling the truck to the side of the road to finish what he'd started back at Castle Ranch. So much for being noble.

Even now, when he was focused on driving, the taste of her was still strong in his mouth. The feel of her soft skin still plagued his memory. He didn't know if he could trust his own word. Telling himself to stay away from her and believing he could do it had been a whole lot easier when she wasn't within reach.

"Are you having second thoughts?" she asked, breaking the tension-filled silence.

"About?"

"Calhoun's offer."

He shook his head. "I'd never work for someone so controlling. Hell, I've trained Thoroughbreds and Arabians, and I'd do it again. They're good horses. But he'd led me to believe he had quarter horses which he obviously doesn't, and that pissed me off."

"I'm glad you won't work for him. Not that you need my approval."

He thought about his ex-wife and how she would've been fawning all over the man. As Trent had eventually discovered, a guy's net worth was what impressed Dana. Power came a close second. Everything had been just fine between them when he'd been pulling in big bonuses. She would've called him three kinds of stupid for turning down Calhoun's money.

Shelby wasn't like that. But then he barely knew her. He and

Dana had been married for a couple of years before he'd seen that side of her. Maybe he just hadn't been paying attention.

Anyway, he had no business comparing the two women. Man, he used to hate it when his dad had compared him to his older brother.

Naturally, Trent always ended up with the short end of the stick. Colby was nearly a carbon copy of their dad. Though he tended to stay with a job or project a good while longer. But ultimately, when things got rough, he'd quit just like their old man and move on to something else.

Trent was the exact opposite, and while he hadn't actually been called an overachiever, he knew that's what his dad believed. Maybe Trent's successes made him feel uncomfortable with his own failures.

He glanced at Shelby and caught her watching him. Probably curious about what had happened in Texas, but she didn't ask. She smiled before looking away.

"I have another quick stop to have a look at that colt. It'll take forty minutes, tops. After that, we'll head to Blackfoot Falls and see about getting you a fair booth. You still game?"

Her eyes flashed with excitement. "Totally."

Three months.

Hell, he'd never make it.

11

SINCE THE MAYOR'S office was closed, they tried Abe's Variety next. Posters were up all over town about the fair. It seemed to be a bigger deal than Trent remembered. He'd last been to the fair when he'd visited Colby and his family, the year before his brother had given up on the Eager Beaver.

After the usual few minutes of jawing about nothing, Abe sent them to the Watering Hole. According to him, Sadie, the owner of the bar, had been helping the mayor's secretary with organizing this year's event. Made for some interesting speculation since Sadie was running for mayor in the November election, against Clarence Leland who'd remained in office, unopposed, for twelve years.

Trent imagined the situation gave everyone a lot to talk about. In fact, showing up with Shelby was likely to add a lot more spice to the gossip stew. Some things just never changed no matter how many years he'd been away.

Sadie had opened for business five minutes earlier, and she stood with her hands on her hips, facing the door when they walked into the bar.

Trent laughed. Shelby stared up at him with a puzzled frown. He knew right away Abe had already called Sadie with a heads-up, and Shelby would understand soon enough.

"The fair is next weekend," Sadie said. "Three weeks later than usual because Mayor Leland, in all his finite wisdom—as in thimble-size—decided we should team up with Cooper County this year. And now you think you can waltz your sweet-talking self in here and flatter me into renting you a booth this late in the game?"

"Yep." Trent grinned. "In a nutshell."

"Well, you're right." Sadie laughed, then swatted him away when he tried to kiss her cheek. She went behind the bar and pulled out a form from a manila folder wedged in next to the cash register. "Fill this out and give me forty bucks."

Trent automatically reached into his pocket at the same time Shelby opened her purse.

"Now, this should be interesting." Sadie leaned forward, resting her forearms on the bar, her face full of mischief and amusement.

He caught Shelby's warning look and lifted both hands in surrender. "Just a reflex." He glanced at Sadie. "This is Shelby."

The older woman nodded. "We met the other day at Abe's store."

"Just forty dollars...really?" Shelby glanced at the form as she passed her the money. "The county must get a percentage of sales, then."

"Nope. We try to keep it simple. We don't have many outside vendors come in. Mostly it's local folks and we like giving them the chance to make a little extra money."

Shelby looked disappointed.

"What are you planning on selling?" Sadie asked.

"Jewelry. Nothing very expensive. I make the pieces myself."

"You should do okay," Sadie said. "No one else will have jewelry for sale. And Christmas will be here before you know it."

"She'll do better than okay," Trent said, completely convinced. "Wait till you see her jewelry. It's really something."

Sadie gave him a soft, knowing smile. Shelby was staring

at him with a wary expression. What had he said that justified that look? He was just being honest.

Behind him the door opened. A young cowboy Trent didn't recognize stuck his head inside as if looking for someone.

Sadie straightened. "You'll have to fill the form out right now and not mention this to anyone," she said in a hushed voice. "You missed the deadline by two weeks."

"I don't want you getting in trouble over this."

"Nah, she won't. Sadie's gonna be our next mayor," Trent said and grinned at her snort of disgust.

"I'll tell you what..." Sadie slid a pen across the bar to Shelby. "The idea of giving that old blowhard a run for his money was a whole lot more appealing than actually running against him. Sometimes I think that man hasn't got the brains of a grasshopper."

Trent didn't know the guy, and while he'd always liked Sadie, he couldn't picture her as mayor. But then he'd lived most of his adult life close to Dallas and maybe in a place the size of Blackfoot Falls, Sadie was just the person the town needed.

"I didn't even ask...you two want anything to drink?"

Shelby looked up from the form. "A cola would be great, or anything with caffeine."

Sadie smiled, nodded. "Trent?"

"Much as I'd like a beer, I'll take a soda. We have to hit the road as soon as Shelby finishes. I've got a colt waiting in the trailer."

"You just buy him?"

Nodding, he dug into his pocket. "From the Landers over at the Whispering Pines."

"Good people. I heard they have top-notch stock." Sadie set the colas in front of them. "I haven't seen Violet for a while. How's the old girl doing?"

"Ornery as ever," Trent said, and saw a smile twitch at the corners of Shelby's mouth as she kept writing.

"Tell you the truth, I'm glad you're back and not paying attention to that silly curse," Sadie said. "Violet shouldn't be living out there alone."

Shelby's head came up, her gaze narrowed. "What curse?"

"I'm pretty sure I mentioned it to you," Trent said and took a sip to hide his amusement.

"But I knew you were trying to get rid of me so I didn't believe you."

Chuckling, Sadie traded glances between the two of them. "Don't worry, honey. It's nothing but nonsense anyway."

"I'd still like to hear it."

Sadie shrugged. "It goes back a few generations. Has something to do with anyone trying to make a go of the Eager Beaver being doomed to fail. Don't know who started it. Do you, Trent?"

"I heard it might've been my great-granddad." Trent glanced at Shelby. It only now occurred to him that it could've been her great-grandfather since he'd left angry. But he wasn't about to say anything.

"Of course your pa had horrible luck trying to make a living off the place. And so did your brother, bless his heart." Sadie shook her head. "I'm not saying there's anything to the curse, mind you..."

Trent drained his cola. The subject was closed as far as he was concerned. He couldn't afford to think he might be the next Kimball who failed. "You about finished?" he asked Shelby. "Time to get on the road."

She looked blankly at him, before giving him an absent nod. After checking two more boxes on the form, she passed the paper and pen to Sadie. "Thanks so much for letting me have the booth. I promise not to tell a soul," she said as she slid off the stool.

Sadie snorted a laugh. "Well, you'll never fit in around here."

Although Shelby smiled, something was obviously bothering her.

Sadie stuck the form in the manila folder, then turned back

to see Trent pulling money out of his pocket. "Oh, for pity's sake, all you had were colas. Put that away."

"No, ma'am, we can't have it appear that you're bribing voters." Smiling at her eye-roll, he slid a ten-dollar bill under his glass and noticed Shelby had left something, too. Which was unnecessary but none of his business. "Good luck with the campaigning."

"Thank you again," Shelby said, following him to the door.

He held it open for her, wondering what had her worrying her lower lip and looking plain ol' depressed.

Two cowboys who'd been about to enter the bar stepped aside for them. The taller man tipped his Stetson at Shelby. Both of them stared like idiots. She favored them with a polite smile as she passed, then continued down the sidewalk oblivious to their fascination with her backside.

Trent almost said something. But that would be dumb. Not only did he have no right, but how many times had he done the same thing, himself? Shelby hadn't seen them anyway, so why make matters worse? He did the next best thing and walked directly behind her, cutting off their view.

A minute later she stopped and looked from side to side, before spinning around to face him. "Where were you?"

"Right here." He dug out his keys. "Look, if you'd like to hang around town for a while, I could take the colt and trailer back to the Eager Beaver and pick you up later."

She'd already started shaking her head before he finished. "Thanks, but I have a lot of work to do for the fair." Her smile was for him alone. "If you don't mind, I'd really like to go home."

He didn't miss the slight catch in her voice at the end. He also didn't miss that he might have already crossed from none of his business to very much his concern.

AFTER TAKING A short walk with Mutt, Shelby stopped at the equipment shed for a peek inside. It was definitely roomier than she'd imagined and cleaner, with a raised wood plank floor to keep the contents dry.

On the drive to Castle Ranch two days earlier, Trent had assured her there was adequate space for her belongings. She missed sleeping in her own bed, which she decided would go into her room along with the cherry nightstand and matching dresser. It would be crowded but she didn't mind. Living out of a suitcase was starting to get to her.

"I heard you got movers coming tomorrow."

Startled by Violet's voice, Shelby jerked back and banged her head on the doorframe.

"Ouch." The woman's rusty cackle turned into a brief cough. "Thought you might've heard me come up behind you."

Shelby made sure she'd cleared the doorway before turning around. And caught a nasty whiff of Violet's pipe. Her cough sounded worrisome, yet she was still puffing away.

"The delivery truck should arrive midmorning," Shelby said and rubbed the side of her head. "I don't have much so they shouldn't be here long, but I'll make sure they don't block the driveway."

"Hell, they could be here all day. Won't make no difference to me." Violet moved closer to the shed for a better look inside. "You storing your things out here?" she asked, frowning.

"Some of them... Trent offered the third bedroom."

"Did he now?" Violet looked oddly pleased.

"Yes, he's been very accommodating. He even helped me get a booth at the fair so I can sell my jewelry."

Violet eyed Shelby's ragged jeans and disgraceful finger-nails. "You make the baubles yourself?"

"I do." She plucked at her faded pink T-shirt. "I've been working a lot trying to increase my inventory."

Mutt returned from chasing one thing or another. Sniffing Violet's pocket, he stared up at her with hopeful eyes and a wagging tail.

"Always looking for a handout, ain't you?" There was no

hiding her fondness for the dog. She dug deep in the oversize coveralls and gave him a giant Milk-Bone. "Now git."

Shelby laughed.

"The dog's a pain in the neck just like his master," Violet grumbled.

"Uh-huh. You know I don't buy this act, right? You adore both of them."

"Baloney. Wait till you've been here awhile—"

Shelby sighed. Awhile meant three months tops for her, and if she was any kind of decent human being she wouldn't put Trent through the inconvenience of an unwanted guest for that long.

"What was that sigh for?"

"I should put my things in storage. Trent is being great, and I'm being horrible and selfish. I know I don't have a claim here." Shelby massaged her left temple. "We all know it."

Violet removed the pipe from her mouth and slanted a glance toward the house. "He inside?"

"I think so."

The woman's troubled frown rested on Shelby. "I need to get something off my chest. But before I do, you've got to swear you won't repeat it." Violet paused, her solemn expression making Shelby wary. "I mean it. I want you to swear on your great-granddaddy's grave."

Shelby tensed. What if the woman was ill? What if keeping her secret meant life or death? What if—

"Well, all right," Violet said with a resigned nod. "I respect a person who won't give their word too freely."

"Wait." Shelby couldn't just let her walk away. Violet clearly needed an ear. "You can talk to me. And I promise whatever it is stays between us."

"You sure? It'll be mighty tempting to run straight to Trent."

Now Shelby was just plain curious. "I'm sure."

Violet's eyes bore into hers. "It's about the Eager Beaver. I believe the ranch belongs to you, Shelby Foster. And in ten days I'll be able to prove it."

SHELBY SHOULD'VE BEEN doing a jig. Or grinning from ear to ear. At the very least, she should feel relieved knowing she would have a roof over her head for as long as she wanted to stay in Blackfoot Falls.

Still shocked by what Violet had confided, Shelby entered the house through the front door and glanced around. The leather recliner and couch, the dark wood coffee table, the large wide-screen TV pretty much summed up the living room. And left little doubt a man lived here. Even thinking about where to put her own furniture felt wrong.

Maybe Violet was mistaken. Four generations of Kimballs had lived here, a fact verified by several unbiased townspeople. How weird was it that Shelby almost hoped Violet had gotten confused.

Another thing that didn't add up was the woman's lack of concern for Trent. Those two shared a fondness for each other, and no argument could convince Shelby otherwise. Violet wouldn't want to see him lose out. Maybe she simply expected Shelby to do the right thing, whatever that was.

She heard a low murmur coming from the kitchen. Trent was probably watching a YouTube video on his laptop. He did that a lot when he wasn't working outside. Mostly, though, he kept the computer in his room where she wouldn't walk in and surprise him.

She was fairly certain it was the same video that he'd watched over and over again, and she thought she understood what compelled him to do so.

It was about what had happened in Texas. He hadn't told her about the fateful race. And she hadn't asked. But she knew because she'd looked him up online when they'd come back with the colt. She wasn't proud of being nosy and intrusive, but ever since the meeting with Hank Calhoun, Trent hadn't been quite himself.

Entering the kitchen, she saw him sitting at the table, hunched forward, his attention glued to the computer screen. She made a noise to alert him to her presence. He surprised her by not closing the laptop as he'd always done. After a quick glance at her, he extended his arms over his head and arched back into a serious stretch.

"Man, that feels good," he murmured, his eyes drifting closed.

She let her gaze follow the ridge of muscles defining his arm, trailing the width of his broad shoulders and straining his T-shirt. A flash of memory of him working shirtless provided details of his bare chest and belly. She stopped in the middle of the kitchen, her insides fluttering as though a whole flock of hummingbirds was trying to escape.

Her feet wouldn't move. All she could do was stare. The thick dark lashes, the day's growth of beard covering his chin and jaw, the attractive shape of his lips. She remembered the feel of them against her mouth, as if they'd kissed only minutes ago.

Midway through a long contented moan, he opened his eyes.

She simply stood there, offering a sheepish smile. And doing everything within her power to not make matters worse by looking at the laptop.

"I was about to put water on for tea. Would you like some?" Oh, brother, she knew he didn't drink tea. "Or anything else while I'm up?"

The faint smile he hid made her cheeks warm. But he pulled his arms in and straightened in his seat, his eyes dark and speculative, never leaving her face. "When you're finished, I'd like to show you something."

"Sure." She hurriedly stuck a mug of water in the microwave, set it to heat for two minutes, and brought out an herbal tea bag. "Okay," she said and joined him at the table.

Trent looked her directly in the eyes and asked, "Did anyone tell you about what happened in Texas?"

"No." It was the truth. Also a technicality, because she knew what he was getting at. In spite of herself, she blinked. "But I think I know."

He rubbed his jaw, sighing at the laptop now in screensaver mode. "Damn YouTube."

"And Wiki."

Turning back to her, he snorted a laugh. "You did a search?"

She opened her mouth to deny it, then just pressed her lips together and nodded. "For what it's worth, I read very little."

His wry expression made her wish she'd kept her mouth shut. "I don't know what you found," he said, shrugging. "Basically, I tried to pull a horse from a race. He had a badly bruised sole. I was afraid it might abscess. The vet had given him a non-steroidal anti-inflammatory. But he shouldn't have run. The owner and I had a heated discussion, which unfortunately was overheard. He disagreed with me, let Race the Moon run. Moon placed...that means came in second. I made a wrong call that could've cost the owner forty thousand dollars."

"So he fired you."

"No." Trent touched the screen, bringing it back to life. "I left before the race started."

"Because you knew he would fire you later?" she asked, studying his carefully blank expression. "Or was it because you no longer trusted him?"

He turned away from the screen and met her eyes. "I know for a fact you didn't read that anywhere."

Shaking her head, Shelby smiled. "I think you still believe you made the right call."

His gaze narrowed. "Because?"

"How many times have you watched the video?" She nodded at the laptop. "I doubt it's to punish yourself."

Trent raised his brows. "The thing is, I don't want to think Paul would do anything underhanded or risk injuring a horse. But I really believe he gave Moon an injection to block the nerves...it's for pain. And illegal as far as racing goes."

"How long had you worked for him?"

"Six years." His shrug didn't fool her. A hint of sadness had crept into his voice.

"I'm sorry to say I know nothing about horseracing." She gestured to the laptop. "But may I?"

"Sure." He angled it so she could see the screen just as the microwave dinged. Instead of getting up, she scooted her chair closer to his. "Get your tea," he said. "I'll wait."

"Later." She leaned closer so they could both see, hoping he'd explain what was happening in the video. Her left leg pressed against his right. Their shoulders touched.

The temperature in the kitchen seemed to rise considerably.

Her face and chest felt warm as she tried to get comfortable without doing more touching. She kept her eyes on the screen.

He started the video, then all he said was, "Number 11."

She spotted the chestnut-colored horse right after he left the gate. He was a beauty, shiny and sleek with muscle. She watched him break from the pack along with two other horses. A minute later Race the Moon crossed the finish line a nose behind a gray stallion.

Shelby turned to Trent. "Will you ever know if you made the right call?"

"No. I can't know for sure. You saw it yourself, Moon looked great," he said, shrugging. "A month later he was supposed to run again, but he was scratched at the last minute. After that, there's been nothing. I hope he isn't hurt permanently. I admit, I started watching the video again after he was pulled, hoping to see something that would show me the truth."

"So if he couldn't run that second time, doesn't that mean you were probably right?"

Trent smiled. "Maybe. That doesn't help Moon."

"Can I ask you something?"

"Go ahead."

"What if it had gone the other way? If you'd thought Moon shouldn't race, and you'd kept quiet for whatever reason, and Moon was hurt...could you have lived with yourself?"

He frowned at her as if she'd just asked the stupidest question on earth.

"I'll take that as a no," she said when silence stretched. "That means you made the right call." She scooted her chair back. "You were trying to protect Moon. Personally, I'm glad you're that man."

Trent blinked.

She got to her feet. The water for her tea would be cold by now. She turned to the microwave but stopped when he caught her hand. Startled, she heard his chair scrape back, then he was on his feet, tugging her around to face him.

He released her hand and stared into her eyes. A slow smile curved his mouth as he touched her cheek. His finger trailed to her chin, nudging it up as he lowered his head.

12

THEIR LIPS MET in a warm, soft kiss. A hand cupped the left side of Shelby's waist. Resting her palm on his chest, she lifted herself onto her tiptoes. As the kiss deepened her heart beat faster.

Trent put both arms around her and re-angled his head. The second she parted her lips he slipped his tongue between them and slowly explored the inside of her mouth. She hadn't seen this coming, and she doubted he had, either. Not that she objected.

She slid her hand up to his shoulder, pausing to savor the feel of hard muscles bunching under her palm. He deepened the kiss, his arms tightening around her until she rubbed up against something else that was hard and thrilling.

"Jesus." He moaned quietly against her tongue. On a deep breath, he broke the kiss and, with his head tipped back, briefly closed his eyes. When they finally met hers once more, they were dark with desire and sexy as hell. "This is all wrong," he said.

Regret erased everything in a single heartbeat. Shelby swallowed, confused, and not sure what to do. They were still touching. Her hand stayed frozen on his shoulder, and he'd only loosened his arms but hadn't let go. She moistened her lips. "Why?"

His brows drew together in a slight frown. Once she noticed

that his bottom lip was damp, she couldn't seem to drag her gaze away. That kiss wasn't wrong. Not to her.

"Shelby?"

"What?"

He let go then, and she looked up.

"I know you're hurting," he said, his voice low and careful. "I won't take advantage of you like this."

Even more confused, she stepped back, letting her own hand fall away. "Hurting?"

"Fresh off a broken engagement? It's rough. I know."

"Oh." Her sigh ended with a laugh. "Do I sound like a stone-cold bitch admitting I feel the best I have in three years?" She wrinkled her nose. "No, probably more like four."

Trent looked as though he wanted to believe her but couldn't quite get there.

She probably should feel guilty. And occasionally she did, but only because in her heart she'd known for a while that being with Donald meant giving up too much of herself.

"I do." She shrugged. "If anything, I'm embarrassed for taking so long to man up, so to speak. I stayed too long because I was a big chicken. But that's history. I really appreciate it, though. That you cared enough to stop."

A blush heated her cheeks, and she made herself walk very calmly to get her tea.

"What you said earlier, about how things turned out with Moon...and..."

She'd only made it a few steps before turning back to him.

"...and how you're glad I'm that man." The intensity of his gaze made her toes curl. "I want you to know I appreciate it."

Screw the tea. She moved closer. "Is that why you kissed me?"

Letting out a short laugh, he rubbed his jaw. "Might've started out that way."

"And..." She returned her hand to his shoulder and watched a lazy, arrogant smile tug at his mouth.

"You asking for trouble, darlin'?"

"Really?" She stepped back, narrowing her eyes. "So you don't want me in your bed?" she asked sweetly, darting away when he reached for her.

"Wait." He caught her around the waist and lifted her off the floor until they were eye to eye. "I'll swear on a stack of Bibles never to call you that again."

"Don't bother," she said, leaning in for the quickest of kisses. "We'll just find a notary pub—" She let out a squeak when he lifted her higher and nipped at the stiff nipple straining against her shirt. Heat swept her body. She dug her fingers into his shoulder muscles. "Can Violet see in here?"

His gaze shot to the window. "Depends. How about we—"

"Yes." She expected him to set her down. "Hey, I can walk."

Trent just laughed. "I know. I've admired the view many times."

Still in no apparent hurry to let her feet touch the linoleum, he kissed her jaw, then her chin, holding her in the air as if she weighed no more than a marshmallow. He let her down a couple more inches and brushed his lips across hers.

She felt the hardness behind the fly of his jeans and knew he wouldn't last long. In truth, she doubted she would, either.

All it took was a little strategic squirming, and he set her down. Taking her by the hand, he led her quickly through the living room and straight to his bedroom.

It was a decent size with a king sleigh bed, matching dresser and a single nightstand. Everything was very neat. The bed wasn't completely made but a dark blue quilt had been pulled to the top, smoothed out and partly tucked.

"Bigger bed," was all he said before he tugged up the hem of her faded T-shirt. Too late she remembered what he'd find underneath.

Damn, why couldn't she be wearing one of her pretty lace bras?

"Uh, this doesn't actually work unless you lift up your arms."

"I don't want to," she whined.

He gave her a long look, then laughed. It was cut short when she unbuckled his belt and went for his jeans.

"Hold on." He stopped her, raked a worried gaze down her shirt. "You're really not going to let me take that off?"

She thought of telling him to wait and rushing to her room to change, but... "I'm wearing a sports bra."

"Okay."

"Because I was working...and, well, it's more comfortable..." She sighed. Trent clearly had no idea what she meant. He gave her that slow sexy smile of his, and thumbed her sensitive nipple through the worn material.

Shelby sucked in a breath. "Fine," she said, and pulled the ratty T-shirt off.

He stared at the industrial-strength sports bra. Frowning, he leaned over for a quick glance at the back. "I have no idea what to do with this."

At his adorably bewildered expression, she burst out laughing. "Undress yourself, I'll take care of it."

She didn't have to tell him twice.

He went right to work, yanking off his T-shirt, pulling off his boots and jeans. All that was left were his boxer-briefs when he stopped to stare at her.

Thank goodness for the tiny bikini panties. The way he was looking at them, she kind of hated to take them off. Although his interest shifted the second he noticed her bra was gone. With laser focus he stared at her bare breasts.

His mouth curved in a half smile, he moved closer. "Okay, now I know what I'm doing." He touched a nipple with his finger, then bent and rolled his tongue over it.

At the slight rasp of stubble against her skin, Shelby shivered. She plunged her hands into his dark wavy hair. His musky, thoroughly masculine scent teased her nostrils. He dropped to a crouch and kissed a spot between her ribs while slipping off her panties.

Once he got them off, he reached around and squeezed her butt, pulling her against his mouth, trailing his lips lower, to her belly, then lingering just above the V of her thighs.

The intimate feel of his warm breath sent heat racing through her body. Swaying slightly, she moved her hands from his hair to clutch his shoulders. She'd felt dizzy for a moment. Probably the lack of air in her lungs. One second she'd been inhaling his scent, the next she'd forgotten how to breathe altogether.

After pressing a final kiss to her tingling skin, he rose. "You okay?"

"Yes, except..." She hooked a finger in his waistband. "You still have clothes on."

With a choked laugh, he got down to nothing but a cocky grin and an impressive hard-on. She looked her fill as he yanked back the covers, and got all tingly when he kept looking back at her. He came around the bed, put his hands on her waist and pulled her against him.

His kiss was hot and thorough and scrambled her senses. He was much taller than her now that her feet were bare. As his mouth grew more demanding, her head went back and he moved a hand to cradle her skull as he gentled the kiss.

She pushed her palms up his chest, tunneled her fingers into his hair, and sighed when he wrapped his arms around her and held her tight. He was all hard muscle and smooth skin. His arousal felt hot and insistent pressed to her belly and she couldn't wait. After more kissing, he guided her the few steps to the bed and laid her down, so gently it surprised her.

Not that she'd expected him to be rough or clumsy. She just had never been with a rugged sort of man before. Trent wasn't bulky or anything. But he had calluses on his palms and muscles in places where she'd had no idea...

Instead of lying down beside her, he detoured to the dresser and pulled a box of condoms from the drawer. He took out a packet, then moved the box to the nightstand. She grinned at his optimism. He responded in kind before crawling onto the bed and kissing her shoulder.

"I like your smile," he said in a husky whisper and cupped a breast. He pressed a kiss just above her beaded nipple, then licked it with a slow flat tongue.

Gasping softly, she automatically rolled toward him, seeking more. Needing more. After another leisurely swipe, he sucked the entire nipple into his mouth. She was holding her breath again. This time, she let it out slowly and closed her eyes when he moved a hand down her body, following the curve of her hip, then ending the return trip at the protective seam of her thighs.

He tried to slide in his fingers, but she wasn't ready to come apart yet.

"Hey."

"Patience," she said, liking the way she was making him crazy.

She felt his chest move as he groaned. Oh, she had no doubt he would take her to that place she ached for…and he could accomplish it quickly. But first, she had her own exploring to do.

Starting with his left pec, she skimmed her palm over the swell of flesh and muscle, over his flat nipple. Obviously it wasn't sensitive. She tried the right one…

Trent's low gravelly chuckle stroked every sensitive inch of her body as effectively as if he'd used his hand and tongue on her.

"Ticklish?" With a coy peek through her lashes, she blew on the puckering brown nub.

"Only there."

"Good to know."

"Better think real hard before striking that match." A faint smile touched the corners of his mouth. "Little city girls shouldn't play with fire."

Shelby laughed and pretended the dark intent in his eyes wasn't hot enough to short-circuit her entire system. Wrapping her hand around his erection, she said, "Ready to change your tune?"

His cock jerked. The sound he made was part laugh, but mostly groan. She stroked upward, increasing the pressure, loving the feel of the hot smooth flesh pulsing in her grasp.

On a ragged exhale, he caught her wrist, pulled her hand away, and pinned her shoulders to the mattress. His face loomed just above hers, his eyes glittering with challenge, and his smile utterly wicked when he threw a leg over her, immobilizing her hips. Almost. She still had wiggle room. A slight move to the right brushed his cock and had him clenching his jaw.

"Why don't you want me to touch you?" she asked.

"I never said that." He lowered his mouth to her jaw and kissed his way to her ear.

"You pushed me away when I'd just gotten started."

"Don't pretend you don't know why," he murmured and bit her earlobe.

"Hey," she muttered, even though the light nip felt good.

He shut her up with an openmouthed kiss that made her squeeze her thighs more tightly together. He kneaded her breast gently, then teased it with his fingers while kissing her breathless.

Her skin felt cool from the light breeze sneaking in the open window, yet she felt burning hot wherever their bodies touched. She broke the kiss for some much-needed air.

Trent lowered his head. He took one of her nipples into his mouth and sucked deeply.

She arched off the mattress and clutched at the sheets, only then realizing she had a free hand. He still held the other one captive.

He switched to the other breast, giving it equal attention, before trailing kisses down to her belly. Every time his erection brushed against her hip or leg, he jerked a little. She did her best to make that happen a lot.

His patience was astounding. She wouldn't have guessed he'd

be the type to stretch foreplay out this long. Everything he'd been doing felt amazing. But right now she was feeling needy, greedy and edgy, the hunger inside her going bone-deep. It was a little scary. For God's sake she didn't want to end up begging.

He circled her belly button with the tip of his tongue. He'd moved his hand to her breast, the other molded her hip. She rubbed his shoulder, still in awe of his physique. She traced a muscle over to his back. Whimpered when he thumbed her aching nipple. He shifted and turned away, fueling her frustration.

"Oh, for... Do I have to keep fantasizing about how you'll feel inside me, or are you going to get on with it?"

That's when she realized he was only getting the condom.

He looked at her with an expression of amazement before he laughed. Blushing, she couldn't believe what she'd just said. Out loud. God.

No, she would not cover her face.

"You'll have to unlock Fort Knox first," he said with a nod at her clamped thighs.

"Ha. Funny." She saw that he was as hard as ever. And more beautiful than she'd imagined.

He tore the packet open. "I want to do everything all at once."

"Uh... I don't think that's possible," she said, watching him put on the condom, her breath catching.

"I bet you want to be on top."

"I don't actually care," she said, "as long as I get to see your face."

He lowered his head. "I think I can arrange that," he said and moved between her legs. "Do you have any idea how badly I want you?"

At his raspy admission her whole body tingled. "So I'm not the only one, huh?"

He inhaled deeply, as the look in his eyes softened, grew warmer. "No, you are not." He kissed her lightly, and she could feel how he was trembling. How he was trying to hold back and not overwhelm her.

Seconds later, he slid two fingers inside her, and she spasmed around them, her moan louder than she'd expected.

"You're perfect," he said, using his fingers to tease her and his thumb to drive her crazy.

"Now would be a good time to, you know—"

His fingers slipped out, but his thumb kept circling and circling. "So, you're saying you think now would be a good time for me to—you know. Right?"

"When this is over, I'm going to kill you, Trent Ki—"

He thrust inside her all in one go. And then he kept thrusting, never losing his rhythm as he lifted her left leg and settled it over his shoulder.

Somehow, his thumb had never wavered. He'd even softened the pressure, as if he could read her body like a book.

Her breathing had become panting, her thoughts reduced to begging and her grip on him had to hurt. But none of that mattered because she was going to come any second. Every muscle in her body tightened, and it was clear he wasn't going to last, either.

As hard as she tried to keep her eyes open, to watch him unravel, they closed as she climaxed. As her world became nothing but shimmering sensation, wave after wave of sheer, unrelenting pleasure.

He touched her cheek, then trailed down to her breast with an unsteady hand. She clenched her muscles around his erection, rocked her hips.

His raw, feral groan forced her eyes open.

Trent was arched above her, his neck corded, his muscles straining. He was the most gorgeous man she'd ever seen, and she wanted to remember this forever.

When he finally came down, he pulled out of her before he flopped to her side. She was still learning how to breathe again, as the aftershocks kept surprising the breath out of her.

"I never expected…this," he whispered.

She knew just what he meant. "Me, neither."

"Well, hell," he said.

All Shelby could do was nod.

13

SHELBY WASN'T NEXT to him when Trent woke up shortly after sunrise. He knew she must've left his bed sometime after midnight. They'd been awake until then, making out like a couple of horny teenagers. Hell, he couldn't even remember the last time he'd needed three condoms in one night.

He saw that her bedroom door was slightly ajar when he slipped into the bathroom. He thought he heard her moving around in the kitchen so he listened to be certain before going about his business. It sure would be great if she was making coffee. Normally he got it ready the evening before and programmed the timer. But there'd been nothing routine about last night. They'd barely made it up for air.

Shelby was amazing. Beautiful, smart, kind. Talented. In a lot more ways than he should be thinking about right now. He turned on the shower and pressed the heel of his hand down on his erection. For some reason he decided greeting her with a hard-on might not be the smoothest move.

They'd stayed clear of conversations about the ranch or anything else of importance last night. He didn't regret one minute. But two things hadn't changed. Shelby was fresh off a relationship that had gone sour, and sooner or later she'd discover she had no claim to the Eager Beaver. He dreaded that day as much as he did a trip to the dentist. That was saying something considering his phobia.

He finished his shower and got dressed, hoping like hell that when he entered the kitchen, he wouldn't walk headfirst into a wall of regret. The second he opened the bathroom door he smelled coffee.

Shelby was standing at the sink with damp hair, dressed in jeans and a pink blouse, her back to him.

Hoping not to startle her, he said, "Good morning."

She jumped anyway, before turning with a smile. "Hey."

A part of him wanted to walk right up and kiss her. But instinct kept him in check. She seemed a little stiff. Yet she'd set his mug on the counter for him.

"Thanks for making coffee."

"I don't know if it's strong enough. I used two scoops."

"Great." He liked three, but he'd drink it any way she made it.

She sipped from her own mug and watched him pour the brew into his. He took his time adding some sugar from the white canister next to the coffeemaker. The sudden silence felt awkward. He'd been leery of how things would go between them, but he hadn't expected this.

He gave his coffee a brief stir and left it on the counter. Dammit. This sucked. He looked at her. "I want to kiss you."

Caught in the middle of a sip, she quickly swallowed and blinked at him. "So what's stopping you?"

Trent laughed, mostly at himself. Taking her mug out of her hand, he set it on the counter next to his. A light tug and she stepped into his arms.

Her lips were soft and yielding as he took his time, rubbing a hand down her back, enjoying her warmth and womanly curves. Today she smelled like peaches. That was something new. Probably her shampoo. Her skin just smelled clean and sweet. He waited until she parted her lips in invitation before he used his tongue. And promised himself he wouldn't get carried away.

Not anything he needed to worry about, apparently. Shelby

let him have a little taste, then broke the kiss and stepped back. She lowered the hand that had been placed lightly on his chest.

"I have a lot of work to do today," she said, her gaze flickering.

"We both do." He picked up his coffee and gulped. Damn, it was hot. "After I drink this I'll go tend to Daisy."

"I'm supposed to do the milking—"

"You can have a break."

"No, you don't have to…" She bit her lip. "Look, last night was really—"

"Great," he finished to ease her look of distress. "For me at least. But you don't want it to happen again. I get it." He lifted a shoulder in a deceptively casual shrug. "It's okay."

"No. It's not that." She cleared her throat. "It's just—well, we hadn't talked. You know, before getting carried away and all…" Her voice trailed off and she turned her gaze to the window.

Trent sighed.

"See?" She darted him a glance. "This is exactly what I mean."

"What?"

"That sigh." A blush stained her cheeks. "You think I have expectations. But I don't. Last night *was* great. Better than great for me." A tiny smile teased the corners of her lips and then she slumped. "We should've set the record straight first."

"Shelby, I sighed because you can barely look at me." He set down his mug, his eyes staying on her face. "I hate seeing you uncomfortable. And for that record of yours, not once did it occur to me you'd have expectations."

She blinked, then studied him. "What about you?"

"Me? Expectations? No." He shook his head. "Hopes and dreams? Definitely." She laughed and his mood brightened. He tried for her hand and caught her fingertips. "Better than great, huh?"

She leveled him with a mock glare. "That doesn't mean we're going to screw like bunnies."

"Okay," he said with a solemn nod. It wasn't easy. He tugged on two fingers, urging her closer. She took a step forward, and so did he.

Trent put his arms around her and she looped hers around his neck. He kissed the sweet spot behind her ear, smiling at the predictable shiver rippling through her body. "After I tend to Daisy, I'll make us some breakfast," he said, and brushed another kiss a little lower. "How's that?"

"You must be starving."

"Oh, I am." He bit her earlobe.

"I meant because we skipped dinner."

"That's all I meant, too."

She leaned back to look at him. He made sure he was the picture of innocence. Except he was getting hard and he knew by her raised brows the instant she felt it.

"Ignore everything due south. This will be only a kiss. I promise."

Shelby smiled just before their lips met. He couldn't help grinning in response, which made for a pretty lousy kiss. Neither of them complained. They got right back on track, as if their lips and tongues had been doing the same dance together for a whole lifetime. A troubling thought to some degree.

They were getting warmed up real nice when Shelby stiffened suddenly. "The movers…" she said, drawing back, eyes wide. "They're coming this morning and I'm not ready for them."

"What do you have to do?" he asked, the reminder forcing him to think about something he should've considered before having sex with her.

He didn't try to hold on to her. Without a doubt, he knew he had Shelby's best interests at heart by keeping his promise to Violet. It was possible Shelby wouldn't see it that way. Eventually she'd find out she had no stake in the ranch. And that he'd known before the movers had arrived, before they'd slept together. And when she did find out, he'd damn well better be the one who told her.

AFTER SHELBY EMPTIED the fourth box, she carefully broke down the cardboard and laid it on the pile by her bedroom door. She wouldn't unpack everything, not yet, Just some winter clothes, a few kitchen items and the rest of her jewelry supplies. She hadn't tried to find her grandfather's will. By itself the document meant very little. What Violet had confided about the ranch yesterday still weighed on Shelby. Especially after last night.

While there was no telling if Violet was delusional, or had any ability to determine who owned the Eager Beaver, it still felt wrong not to tell Trent. Thank goodness for the promise Shelby had made. At least she could fall back on that if things got dicey. Of course that made her somewhat of a coward. But after the glorious night they'd shared, it was going to kill her to see the look on his face if he learned the ranch didn't belong to him or his family. Another eight or nine days without being sure would be torture enough, but then they'd have to get through three months together. Boy, that had certainly sounded like a better deal a couple of days ago.

Why couldn't Violet have waited until she had proof before saying anything? Somehow Shelby felt quite sure Violet wasn't trying to cause trouble.

But she had to stop thinking about Violet, the ranch and even Trent if she could. It was great to have her things within reach. Most of it was stored in the shed, but only because she'd started working in the third room. Trent had insisted she use the space and even moved the few boxes he'd kept in there.

They'd found a spot in the living room for her overstuffed reading chair but her couch was outside. The shed was the most logical place to store the big items. She'd even decided to put her bed in there. But only after she was certain Trent understood the decision was not a statement about their new sex life. Using the smaller daybed simply made more sense.

Remembering his feeble attempt to control a smile while she'd explained her reasoning made her shake her head. How could a man be so irritating and endearing at the same time?

The way he slid back and forth between the professional horse trainer and the simple cowboy still amused her. Trent was one of a kind. She really liked him, dammit. Twice she'd made a special trip to the kitchen just to peek out the window and watch him work with Solomon.

That baloney had to stop. She had so much of her own work to do.

The county fair would be opening before she knew it, and with only two dozen pairs of earrings and fifteen necklaces in her inventory she was right to be concerned.

God, what if she couldn't sell a single piece?

Her stomach knotted. She shoved the harmful thought aside. She didn't know the area or the people who lived around Blackfoot Falls. Her work might not appeal to them so it wasn't wrong to be prepared for the worst. Of course she'd be disappointed but she couldn't afford self-doubt. Her jewelry had been popular right up until Donald's family had made her stop making them. There had to be a market for her designs somewhere. Her best bet might end up being to sell the jewelry online.

She hung up a few sweaters, glanced at her dresser standing in the corner and did a little happy dance. Who would've thought she could be so excited about having real drawers? Her gaze caught on the digital clock sitting on top. Midafternoon already and she hadn't gotten to work yet.

"Shelby?" Trent stood at her door. His voice alone sent her heart into a somersault. The way he smiled at her curled her toes. "Can you come for a minute?"

"Sure." She stepped over bags of toiletries and miscellaneous items she needed to go through later. "What's going on?"

"I'll show you," he said, holding out his hand.

"Can't you tell me?"

"Nope."

"You're being cryptic."

"Yep."

She laughed at his lopsided smile and let his hand close

around hers. It felt weirdly right and safe to be led all the way to the barn without him letting go even once. Safe, and perhaps a little too comfortable.

This wasn't her standing on her own, forging a new path into the future.

Oh, for God's sake. Sometimes she drove herself crazy. In the grand scheme of things, the two of them were the proverbial ships in the night. Her new life had begun the day she'd left Denver. Trent was a bonus she hadn't expected. And she needed to shut up and enjoy him for as long as things lasted between them.

"We'll have to be quiet," he whispered as they disappeared into the shadows at the far back.

She heard something. Soft yet high-pitched, almost a whine.

"Wha—?" A silencing finger touched her lips.

A few more feet and they stopped. He slipped behind her and wrapped her in his arms, so that she leaned back against his chest. He ducked his head to her level and pointed to a short stack of hay bales.

Mostly it was dark and her eyes were still adjusting. Seeping through narrow gaps in the wall the dappled sunlight helped. Shelby squinted, listened. Was that a cat between the wall and the hay? With a whole bunch of tiny kittens?

A soft gasp escaped her. She clamped her mouth shut.

Trent pressed his cheek to hers, and she felt him smile.

Mama had spotted them, her eyes green and glowing in the murky light, piercing them with a warning glare. Her tail shot high and twitched. Probably the feline version of giving them the finger for disturbing her babies. Shelby really didn't know much about cats.

"They're only a few hours old," Trent said, keeping his voice low.

"I didn't know you had a cat. What's her name?"

"She's not mine."

"Then whose?"

"She's feral. I might've fed her a few times," he said, straightening. "Hell, I've been calling her Tom. Should've known it was another female."

Shelby turned to grin at him. "Oh, poor Trent. Surrounded by women. You have Mutt."

"Yeah, right. The traitor."

"Mutt?"

"He's been wanting to sleep with you since the day you showed up. At least I beat him to it."

"You did not just say that."

He smiled and motioned with his head for them to leave. "I'll check on them throughout the day," he said, keeping an arm around her shoulders as they exited the barn. "They should be okay."

"Could you tell how many kittens?"

"Five, I think. You going to finish unpacking?"

"Maybe this evening. I have to get to work." She sensed his disappointment. "So I can knock off at a decent hour."

He didn't react as she'd hoped. Just lowered his arm and nodded. "Me, too. I have some repairs to make on the east corral. I heard we might be getting some cold temperatures."

"Oh, no. What about the fair?"

"The weekend's supposed to be fine. They're predicting the cold front to hit on Monday."

"Snow?"

"I hope not. I might have to buy a new winter jacket. Living in Texas for ten years spoiled me."

"That's one reason I was so relieved to get my things. I have a ton of sweatshirts and sweaters. It would've killed me to spend a penny on clothes." They stopped at the porch steps. "It's not that I'm a cheapskate," she said, looking up into his steady gaze, her heart beginning to pound. "I'll be putting a lot of money into supplies. Beads are cheap, but silver isn't. I ordered a soldering iron online yesterday, which will probably take at least ten days to arrive. Plus I need a new torch, a good backup supply of soldering picks and silver wire… Sorry, I don't know why I'm rambling. Too much on my mind." They both just stood there. "Are you coming inside?"

"Not unless you need my help moving something."

"No, not really." She should be glad he was staying outside. Otherwise he'd be a distraction. "I can make coffee so you can fill your thermos."

"I still have some." He pressed his lips together, something hot and unmistakable flaring in his eyes. Trent wanted to kiss her. She'd bet he wanted to do more than that, and holy crap, she doubted she could refuse. "Call if you need me," he said, his voice and expression too neutral to not mean something. So what was he trying to hide? "I'll be in the stable or the corral."

"Thanks." She smiled, and as soon as he made a move to go she stepped onto the porch, telling herself she wouldn't look back.

Her willpower carried her into the house. Once inside she peered out the screen door, watching him walk to the stable. Even his stride seemed a bit off. His demeanor had shifted in a matter of seconds. Shelby was pretty sure something important had just happened. She just didn't know what it was.

14

WHEN SHELBY'S GLUE gun died on her, she decided to call it quits for the day. She had another one somewhere but this was her favorite. Working without a spare made her nervous so she'd have to check with the variety store in town or place another order online. Also, discovering that she'd outgrown working with beads, colored glass and the occasional feather or shell was dampening her enthusiasm.

She should've known better. Back in college, earrings made from those kinds of materials had been her bread and butter. But after working for the Williamsons, she'd come too far from her early days of experimenting with cheaper supplies.

And she had to admit she'd become accustomed to cushier work. Designing expensive baubles was a whole lot easier than getting her hands dirty and bending over a work table all day.

She pressed a hand to her lower back, applying pressure in increments, and glanced at the clock. It was so late she forgot about the slight ache. How could she have worked five hours straight?

Oh, well, she was still itching to get her hands on the bigger torch she hadn't been able to afford in college. With it she'd be able to work with hard-grade silver, something she hadn't done yet.

She washed her hands in the bathroom sink before heading for the kitchen. Trent sat at the table watching something on his laptop. A quick peek told her it wasn't the same video of Race the Moon. However, she caught a glimpse of a different horse and rider on a racetrack.

But it was the breadth of Trent's shoulders that held her attention. And the way his thick dark hair tended to curl at his nape. The silky texture had surprised her, and now the memory had her fisting her hands to keep from touching him.

Hoping she wouldn't disturb him, she continued quietly to the fridge. Not counting the apple she'd gobbled earlier, she'd missed lunch and hadn't given a single thought to dinner.

"Hey, you." Trent leaned back in his chair, his head angled toward her. "Are you finished working?"

"Yep, the staff mutinied." Nothing quick and easy in the fridge, but she noticed a pot sitting on the stove. "My glue gun quit on me. Think I can find one at the variety store?"

"Maybe." His gaze roamed her face, lowered to her chest and hips, his mouth curving in a faint smile. Because of her Tweety Bird T-shirt, perhaps, but she didn't think so. Wrong sort of smile, judging by her accelerated pulse. "If not, try the fabric shop."

"Have you eaten?"

"I was waiting for you. There's chili from the freezer in the pot on the stove," he said, and followed her gaze to the computer screen. "Calhoun emailed me this video."

"Oh." Weird. "Did you change your mind about working for him?"

"Nah. He's still trying to sell me on the Arabian. I'm just drooling over his setup. The guy might be a jerk but his stables and racetrack are primo."

"You have a lot of land for a track. Can't you—" She remembered the precise thing she'd been trying to forget. For the time being, anyway. Why had Violet told her? Surely the woman could've waited for confirmation on who owned the

Eager Beaver. Knowing what little she did, Shelby somehow felt as if she was betraying Trent. He was giving her a curious look, so she shrugged. "Ignore me. What do I know about horses and racetracks?"

"Ignore you?" He snorted a laugh. "Sure, I'll just go grab a pair of blinders from the stable."

Grinning, she got a glass out of the cabinet, then paused. "Want anything?"

He stared long enough for her to get that he had sex on the brain, before refocusing on the laptop. "A training facility is more complicated and costly than you might think. Racehorses are valuable animals. Some of them are insured for millions. You gotta treat them with kid gloves." He looked back at her. "You visit the stable yet?"

"Only once, briefly." She'd been amazed at the pristine condition inside.

"You won't find a single hinge or latch with a sharp edge or a bolt sticking out. I had the stall doors custom-made and so far I've replaced half the barbed-wire fence in the north pasture with solid wood. Even with all the money I've sunk into the place and work I've done myself, I couldn't board and train horses yet. Still too many hazards around here. Solomon's mine and he's safe. I paid a nice sum for him out of a bonus a couple years back. And Jax, it's looking as if he'll never race. Good all-around horse, though."

"What about Griffin?"

He smiled at the name she'd given the colt. "His training is coming along fine. He's got potential. It won't be long before I can take him to the track outside of Kalispell, the same one I use for Solomon." He shrugged. "I start making some good money again with Solomon or training, and who knows? I can get this place up to standard."

Shelby's stomach churned. Listening to how much time and money Trent had invested made her sick. Even if Violet was right about the Eager Beaver, Shelby would never ask him to leave. Surely, they could work something out.

No. Even after a brief acquaintance, she knew Trent had too much pride. He wouldn't stick around. The best she could do would be to repay him for the improvements he'd made. Though it would probably take her years.

"Why the sad face?"

She shrugged it off and poured herself some water.

His expression troubled, he stood. He took her glass, set it on the counter and put his arms around her. Held her close. "It's about the Eager Beaver, isn't it?"

Her whole body tensed. "What do you mean?"

"It's a touchy subject for both of us. I say we ban any mention of the ranch." He rubbed her back, and she hid her face against his chest. "What happens, happens. We'll deal with it when the time comes. No matter what, we have a grace period agreement. Right?"

What else could she do but nod?

He leaned back. "I make a mean chili," he said, and nudged her chin up. "How about it?"

Shelby met his sympathetic eyes. "I thought you couldn't cook."

"I can't. That's why there's leftovers." He smiled that damn cute-boy smile. It got to her almost as much as the sexy version. "I figure we're both hungry enough it won't taste too bad."

She couldn't help laughing. "I'm in."

His eyes had already begun to darken. He'd lifted his hand to stroke her hair. Clearly he had dessert planned, as well. Fine with her. She'd grab some of that good loving while he was still offering.

And try not to dwell on their looming expiration date.

"UNPACKING OR RELAXING?" Trent asked the second he dumped the clean pot on the draining rack.

They'd worked together, he washing and she drying, only

because she'd insisted. He didn't see the point—he usually just let the dishes air-dry—but he hadn't argued. Though now, he blocked her reach for the pot.

"We're gonna let that one dry all by itself," he said, taking the towel from her and tossing it on the counter.

Shelby opened her mouth to object and he swooped in for a kiss. She sputtered in surprise but settled quickly, and let him have his way with her. Giving as good as she got, and then some.

He couldn't believe he'd gotten so hard so fast. Jesus, there was nothing remotely hot about a sudsy pot. But knowing what came next had lit a fire in his belly before he'd so much as touched Shelby. He figured her pretty lips and laughing green eyes might've played a small part.

He skimmed a hand over the curve of her firm, round backside and deepened the kiss. The little moaning sound she made was sexy as hell, tempting him to pick her up and carry her caveman-style straight to his bed. Suspecting she might have a problem with that, he kept kissing her instead.

She slid her hands up to his shoulders and pressed her soft breasts against his chest. He could almost taste the ripeness of those perfect rosy tips. Damn, the woman was responsive. He'd bet she was good and wet already, and sweet as honey.

Their tongues tangled. She pressed closer, rubbing her belly and hips against his fly, forcing his cock to take notice. As if it wasn't already standing at attention. He tensed, resisting the urge to lift her onto the counter and strip off her jeans. But if she kept at it, he wasn't sure he could trust himself. He grabbed a handful of her hair. Pure silk.

Ignoring his slight tug at her scalp, she kept kissing him with an eagerness he found arousing, but also curious. Something was different about her tonight. Damned if he was going to analyze it now. She rocked her hips against him and seemed to make it her mission to taste every inch of his mouth. He released her hair and slid his hands down her spine. No way he'd last long. He squeezed her butt, the pressure inside him building…

Shelby pulled back suddenly. "We're in the kitchen again," she said, her voice a breathless whisper.

"I know." He tightened his arms, needing to feel her against him.

"Must be a fetish."

He paused to look at her. "Me?"

Trying to catch her breath, she laughed. "Same problem as last night. Violet, remember?"

Trent fixated on her distracting lower lip. It was Tuesday. For sure Violet was glued to the TV. "We'll move. In a minute." He cupped her face between his hands and paid homage to her lips.

"Or Jimmy," she murmured against his mouth. "He could—"

Jimmy?

The thought cooled him. Yeah, he didn't need the kid popping up unexpectedly and getting an eyeful. Especially with Trent not being at his smoothest. It was Shelby's fault. She had him so turned on he hadn't felt more awkward since his first time at sixteen.

He patted her fanny. "Let's go."

Shelby made no move. Humor shined in her eyes. "You're more worried about Jimmy seeing us."

"No, I'm not." Trent backed her to the door and turned her around.

She grinned over her shoulder at him. "Why?"

Trent just shook his head.

"Huh. Must be a guy thing."

"Probably." He tried to give her backside another tap but she scrambled out of reach.

Mutt barked at the kitchen door.

Shelby turned around.

"Keep going," Trent said. "He's staying outside."

"But—"

"Just for now."

She nodded, walked briskly to the hall and turned left to his bedroom without a word. Following behind, he couldn't help noticing the stack of cardboard outside her door and wondered if she'd dug out her grandfather's will.

Hell would freeze over before he'd ask. Not a subject he wanted to visit. He'd seen her pawing through sweatshirts like it was Christmas. Learning she was counting pennies to support her new business had felt like a two-by-four to the gut. Was she just being frugal? Or did Shelby need the ranch as much as he did?

The eagerness he'd sensed earlier had held a trace of desperation. She knew something had to give soon. And maybe she'd decided, just as he had, that they'd enjoy their time together while they could. Not the ideal situation, but probably the best he could hope for.

She stood at the foot of the bed, her eyes shining, her head tilted a bit to the right. "Did you get lost?"

"I knew you were about to ravage me, so I took a breather."

Her throaty laugh cranked up the heat. "You wish."

Smiling, he tugged up the hem of her shirt. "Am I going to find another weird contraption under here?"

"Maybe." She lifted her arms without him asking.

He drew the shirt over her head and tossed it against the wall. His gaze stayed on the lacy black bra. "Pretty," he said. "Pity it's gotta come off."

"Wait." She clutched his arm, forestalling his bid for the back hook. After shoving his hand away, she unzipped her jeans and pushed them down her hips. She kicked them aside and stood there, waiting.

He studied the black bikini panties. Remembering vividly what they were hiding, his cock was ready to explode through his fly. His gaze moved up to the bra. "They match. Is that what you wanted me to see?"

Shelby pursed her lips, then slumped on a sigh. "Yes. I was trying to redeem myself after last night. But now I just feel stupid. Thank you."

Trent laughed. "Ah. Sweet, warm, sexy Shelby," he murmured, drawing her into his arms and inhaling her skin and hair. "I'll let you in on a secret. You didn't have to do a damn thing for me to want you like crazy." One flick freed the bra's clasp.

When she yanked up his shirt, he was more than happy to give her a hand. They were both naked in less than a minute.

Flushed and warm, her skin was a soft pink, all except for her small tight nipples. He rubbed both thumbs over the darker, rosier tips, and felt her tremble. Placing a hand on his forearm to steady herself, she tried to stand still, barely moving when he bowed his head for a taste. He licked both nipples, then sucked the left one until she wouldn't stop squirming.

He brushed a kiss across her lips as he straightened. Her eyes looked almost black.

Not bothering with the quilt, he walked her backward until she bumped into the bed. A gentle hand on her shoulder was all it took for her to sink to the edge of the mattress.

"Condoms," she reminded him, her breath hitching.

"We don't need them yet." He crouched and spread her legs.

With a soft gasp, she fell back, supporting herself on her elbows while she watched him kiss the inside of her thigh. Her skin was as smooth and soft as satin. He switched to her other thigh, planted a quicker kiss there, too anxious to get to the wet heat in between. He parted her lips with his fingers, then followed with his tongue.

She bucked against his mouth. Her breathy moans drove him crazy. He sucked and licked and thrust his tongue as far as he could, unable to get enough. She kept moving, breaking contact with his mouth, finally going still when he inserted two fingers inside her. He repositioned himself and when she began bucking again, he stayed with her. Within seconds she climaxed, her orgasm quaking through her flushed body.

Cursing himself for not having the condom closer, he got up to grab the packet. He forced himself to unwrap it carefully while he watched Shelby. The way she was arching and moaning only made him more impatient. But she was watching him, too, and she dragged herself back toward the pillows, getting ready for him.

Trent propped himself on one arm and caressed her cheek. Her eyes fluttered closed and with a single thrust, he entered her, fast and deep. He caught her gasp in his mouth and kissed her as thoroughly as possible, considering he was about to explode. Lifting his head, he looked into her dazed eyes.

He pulled out, shifted, hoping to make every move count, give her as much pleasure as possible. Bringing her leg up higher around his waist he sunk into her. By her moan he knew he'd found the perfect angle. Keeping control of himself was the problem.

Arching up to reach him, she raked her fingernails down his chest. The way she'd moved drove him deeper, making her moan louder. He stilled, cupped her breast, then leaned down to kiss her parted lips. On his way back up he stopped briefly to suck her nipple.

Then he tried out their new position with another hard thrust.

Her shoulders came up off the mattress again. She murmured something he didn't catch, then shifted her hips to the right and nearly set him off.

He slowly withdrew, smiling at her cute pout.

"Don't you dare," she panted, clutching at his arms, trying to pull him back to her. "Trent, please."

For a long time they stared into each other's eyes, and then he entered her again and started moving. Slowly at first, before thrusting harder, deeper until she writhed and whimpered, and then bucked up against him as she came. He bent to kiss her and she squeezed him so hard it triggered his own explosive release.

15

THE WEATHER WAS PERFECT the first day of the fair. With the cooler temperatures, it finally was beginning to feel like fall, Shelby's favorite season. Good for long sleeves, but no jacket needed during the day. The gorgeous blue sky stretched all the way to the distant Rockies where most of the clouds hovered. She was lucky her booth faced that direction.

A line of cars turning off the highway caught her attention and she checked her watch. The fair officially opened in fifteen minutes. Trent had set up the tables and secured the awning for shade while she'd unpacked her jewelry and laid everything out, so she'd been ready for an hour. She appreciated his help, but it had given her extra time to fret.

Sighing, she glanced at the earrings and necklaces she'd placed on the center table. At first she'd worried about her meager inventory. The booth on her left overflowed with homemade baked goods and to her right a friendly older woman was selling beautiful porcelain dolls. Considering Gladys had made each intricate doll herself, she offered quite a variety.

But then it occurred to Shelby that having less jewelry on display meant she wouldn't be so mortified when she didn't sell squat. People might think she'd sold out quickly. The rationale had cheered her some. Though she was still tense. And

Trent telling her all morning not to be nervous didn't make her any less so.

Wondering what was keeping him, she poked her head out. She spotted him in front of the cotton-candy wagon, holding the drinks he'd gone to get them and talking to a young couple. She swore the man knew everyone.

She got a whiff of popcorn and pressed a hand to her roiling tummy. Other food smells were beginning to permeate the air. Great. She tried to distract herself by scanning the kiddie rides being tested just past the row of food vendors. Not a good idea. She was terrible at fairs and festivals, wanting every fried and sugar-coated treat in sight. And she usually gave in.

"Sorry I took so long. I kept running into—" Trent lowered the cup he'd been about to pass her. "You don't look so hot."

"Just nerves." She waved dismissively and peered at the cup. "What did you get?"

"Hot chocolate."

"Ah." No, she'd have to wait on that. Her stomach would rebel for sure.

He set the two cups aside. "Shelby." He placed his hands on her shoulders and gave her a warm smile. "It's going to be fine."

"I know." She shrugged. "I'm being ridiculous."

"I didn't say that." He ran his hands down her arms and pulled her close. Obviously he didn't have a problem with people seeing them together like this.

She didn't, either, but she still glanced around.

"Even giving myself a ten-percent margin for bias, your jewelry is terrific. I don't understand where this insecurity is coming from."

Her eyes burned a little at his praise. She wanted to stay right where she was, her face half buried in his chest until they could leave. "I wish I'd had the time and supplies to make better stuff. Some of this goes back to my college days. I only brought them because I was desperate." She drew back. "Sadie was so nice to rent me a booth. I couldn't sit here with nothing.

But honestly, I really should've thrown some of this junk out or donated it by now."

Frowning, he took a long considering look at her, and then at the displays. "You're not seeing clearly. I don't see any junk here." He sounded a bit put-off. Probably sick of her self-pity, and she didn't blame him.

Clearing her throat, she straightened, smiled. "You're right. I told you I was being ridiculous."

He obviously wasn't buying her born-again act. A scowl darkened his face. "I'd sure like five minutes alone with the person who did a number on you."

"What? No. I'm a very good designer. I know that. For God's sake, I've designed rings and necklaces for celebrities from all over the country. It's just—" She sighed. "I haven't done this sort of work in a while."

Still troubled, he opened his mouth to say something but someone called out to him.

"Trent Kimball. I thought that was you. It's been a long while." The stout graying woman displaying lovely handmade quilts down the way from them strolled over. "How are your folks doing?"

"Fine," he said. "Just fine. And yourself, Mrs. Stanley?"

"Can't complain. Retirement has its ups and downs."

"I imagine so." To Shelby he said, "Mrs. Stanley was my sixth-grade teacher." He made a quick introduction, and Shelby managed to get out a hello before a throng of people coming toward them sent Mrs. Stanley scurrying back to her booth.

The crowd swelled and thinned for the next three hours. Trent stayed with her a good deal of the time, when he wasn't being pulled away to the cavernous warehouse-looking building where horses and other livestock were being judged for one thing or another.

A cute girl in her early teens challenged him to enter the pie-eating contest. He'd only laughed. When her pushing went from cute to bothersome he'd told her, in no uncertain terms, it wasn't going to happen. Shelby would never tell Trent, but she understood why the girl had been so insistent. Or that half the women at the fair had given him a twice-over. And the other half needed glasses.

Shelby heard there would be a junior rodeo later in the evening. At the same time tomorrow was the much-anticipated demolition derby with a five-thousand-dollar prize going to the person who took first place. The event was sold out, Gladys had told her, so the crowd would be bigger tomorrow evening. Apparently Gladys's sales were in line with Shelby's, as in pathetic.

The good news was, her stomach had settled down. In the bad news column—out of boredom, she'd eaten a hot dog, half an order of disgusting nachos, a frozen lemonade and three chocolate-chip cookies from the booth on the other side of her. Now she was contemplating a funnel cake. If all that food made her sick, at least she'd have an excuse to go home.

"Here you are. How are you doing?"

Shelby turned, pleased to see it was Sadie. "Okay. Did you just get here?"

"Nah, a couple hours ago." She inclined her head toward the building. "Putting out fires. You'd think some of those cocky hotheads were putting their private parts on display instead of their livestock."

Shelby laughed. "Men."

"Amen, sister." Sadie reached for a pair of earrings and held them up. Dangling from a brass crescent moon, three strings of glass beads caught the late sun. "This is pretty."

Biting her lip, Shelby said nothing. The three times she'd seen the woman, Sadie hadn't worn jewelry. She was just being nice. It made Shelby feel worse.

"Oh, look at these." She held up another similar pair, only with a brass sun, and the longer beads a mix of purple and gold. "I'll take them both," she said and pulled out money from the neckline of her yellow knit top.

"You don't have pierced ears," Shelby said.

Sadie snorted. "They aren't for me. I don't wear jewelry. My daughter and granddaughter will love 'em in their Christmas stockings. Purple and gold are Julie's school colors. How much do I owe you?"

Shelby forced a smile. "The price should be on the back of the card."

Sadie turned it over and frowned.

"Too much?" Shelby searched her pockets for the pen. "I can reduce it."

"Had to cost you more than this for the material." Sadie passed the earrings to her. "Better check the others. Make sure you didn't make a mistake with them, too."

Shelby stared at the price. "I guess I wasn't thinking," she murmured. "Please. Pay me what's marked. That's fair." She quickly wrapped the earrings in white tissue paper. "I'll check the other prices."

"Be sure that you do," Sadie said, with a glance toward the parking area. "These first few hours are always slow. People are knocking off work about now and trust me, pretty soon they'll be here in droves." Sadie accepted the wrapped earrings and passed over the money. "It's the correct amount. No change. See you later, hon."

Shelby fisted the bills, knowing full well that Sadie had paid her too much. But calling her on it would likely create a scene. Last thing Shelby wanted. The sun was sinking, leaving her to decide on a new spot for her folding chair.

She thought about Sadie's advice on the pricing, and admitted she was probably right. Shelby was out of touch with the real world. People who had money rarely cared about what baubles cost, especially if they were meant to impress.

First she found her pen, then quickly scanned the stickers and tried to make reasonable price adjustments. Something made her look up. Trent was headed toward the booth, tall, posture straight and looking ridiculously hot in dark jeans, a tan Western-cut shirt and brown Stetson.

Of course someone stopped him to talk, but in less than a minute he was walking right to her, a smile on his handsome face. Just watching him made her skin tingle.

"Better be careful, young lady," he said, his voice low and gravelly, moving in so close he forced her to tilt her head back to look at him. "Eyeing a man like that could give him the wrong idea."

"Or the right one."

Grinning, he pushed back the rim of his hat and briefly kissed her. "How've you been doing?" Without waiting for an answer, he swooped in for another brush across her lips.

Sighing, she drew back, her gaze fastened to his. "People are probably watching."

"Let 'em."

She ducked back, placing a refraining hand on his chest. "I should tell you... I signed you up for the chili cook-off."

His confused frown quickly turned into a smile. "Very funny. I seem to remember you cleaning your plate."

"I'm not complaining. But you're a much better kisser than a cook."

"There you go." Their lips barely touched.

"Trent Kimball, quit bothering that poor woman and let her sell her wares."

Evidently he recognized the voice. "Rachel McAllister," he said, before turning to the woman with gorgeous auburn hair. "Still causing trouble."

"It's not McAllister anymore, smart-ass." She was about Shelby's age, close to the same height. Her laughing eyes and friendly smile made Shelby like her instantly.

"That's right. I heard you roped some poor bastard into marrying you."

"Poor bastard," Rachel repeated in a deadpan voice. "Matt's the luckiest guy in the world." She jerked a thumb at the building. "Go ask him."

The blonde woman accompanying her smiled, but kept sifting through the necklaces.

"He must be helping out with the junior rodeo tonight," Trent said, then as an aside to Shelby, "I don't know if you follow rodeo. Matt Gunderson is a champion bull rider." He introduced her to Rachel.

Then Rachel introduced the blonde woman as Jamie. She was married to Cole, Rachel's older brother. Trent seemed to know the whole family. They mentioned the Sundance, which sounded familiar, and then Shelby remembered it was the dude ranch Abe at the variety store had mentioned. Had it really been two weeks already? Wow.

"I would've invited you to the wedding, but I didn't hear you were back until a week later." Rachel was saying when Shelby rejoined the conversation. "Why didn't you tell anybody?"

"I got here in March, just in time for that last snow. The Eager Beaver needed a lot of work before I could settle in. I barely had time to breathe."

"You should've called," Rachel said. "You know my brothers. They would've been right there to give you a hand."

Shelby felt her chest knotting. She didn't know how much longer she could last keeping Violet's claim from Trent. Aware of Rachel's gaze on her, Shelby wasn't sure if she'd turned as green as she suddenly felt or if it was just curiosity on Rachel's part.

"These are really nice," Jamie said, holding up a necklace. "Did you make these, Shelby?"

She nodded, glad for the diversion. "That's an older piece. I didn't know about the fair in time or I would've had a better selection."

"Are you kidding? These are great." Jamie set the necklace aside and picked up another one.

Rachel's attention turned to the jewelry. "Turquoise." She reached around Jamie for the silver heart-shaped earrings with the turquoise center. "I went to school in Dallas. I love all the turquoise and silver they have in Texas. Wow, these are heavy but really terrific."

Jamie glanced over at them, looking seriously interested.

"Sorry," Rachel told her. "I'm buying them." She scanned the other two tables and picked up another turquoise-and-silver combination.

"Okay, now you're just being a pig," Jamie said, and Rachel laughed. Though Jamie seemed a bit annoyed.

While they continued looking, Shelby slanted a glance at Trent. He stood back, arms crossed, a satisfied smile on his face. Catching her gaze, he winked. If he'd orchestrated this whole thing she was going to kill him.

The two women attracted more shoppers. Within minutes all three tables were crowded with lookers, most of them sifting through the jewelry and asking questions about the different material and stones Shelby used. Whether they bought anything or not, the women all had very nice things to say about Shelby's work.

She kept casting glances at Trent. Most of the time he was engaged in conversation, sometimes with a guy he'd gone to school with or a friend of his parents. Even an old girlfriend of his had stopped to chat. She had a baby on her hip, and two more little ones trailing after her.

The whole time they spoke Trent kept unconsciously loosening his collar, looking more and more like a man relieved he'd dodged a bullet. When the woman finally moved on, he stared after her with an expression of mild shock.

"Do you want kids?" Shelby asked before she'd considered how the question would sound.

He blinked at her, then narrowed his eyes.

She felt a blush and gestured vaguely in the direction of the woman and her children.

"Oh." He removed his hat and ran a hand through his hair. "I think two would be enough."

His gaze intensified when he met her eyes, and she was really, really glad to hear someone say, "Excuse me, miss. I have a question."

For the next two hours, the crowds steadily increased. Trent had wanted to help but there was nothing for him to do except handle the money. He knew so many people, several he hadn't seen in years, so Shelby encouraged him to go catch up with his old friends.

As soon as the rodeo started, the crowd thinned. Shelby had sold a lot and was deciding on whether to follow Gladys's lead and shut down the booth for the night when Rachel showed up.

"Oh, I think Trent's inside," Shelby told her.

"I know. I saw him." She pursed her mouth, looking hesitant. "I have a favor to ask, and if you say no it's fine. I promise. No pressure."

"Okay." Shelby maintained a blank face, convinced things were about to get awkward. Of course this had to do with Trent. "Ask away."

"Would you mind giving me a peek at the rest of your stuff? You know, the jewelry you're putting out tomorrow." Rachel gave her a sheepish smile.

"Um, I—"

"I'm really not being a pig." She rolled her eyes. "It's for Christmas presents. For Jamie and my other sister-in-law. Or I wouldn't ask."

Shelby was speechless. Was this Trent's doing? While she appreciated his good intentions, she would kill him.

Rachel sighed. "I'm sorry. Pretend I didn't open my big mouth."

"No. Wait." What if she was wrong about Trent? "I'm hesitating only because I don't have anything else. This is it."

Rachel glanced at the dozen or so pairs of earrings, the lone necklace that was left on the table. The other two tables had already been folded up and put away thirty minutes ago.

"Are you kidding?" Rachel seemed genuinely shocked. "You have nothing else. The fair runs two more days."

"I wasn't prepared," Shelby said, miserable and embarrassed. "I had no business taking up a booth when I didn't know a thing about this fair."

"Oh, no, it doesn't matter." Rachel waved away the concern. Nose wrinkled, and staring off, she gave the impression she was thinking hard. "This is your main business, right? How you make your living?"

"Now." Shelby nodded. "Yes."

"I have an idea. How about you hang onto whatever you have left here... I'll even loan you the pieces I bought. I'll get Jamie to do the same," she said, waving a hand as if it was a done deal. "So you can at least take orders and make the jewelry after the fair. What do you think?"

Stunned and seriously touched, Shelby gaped for a moment. "That you're brilliant," she said finally.

Rachel laughed. "We'll get along just fine." She held out her bags. "Feel free to pass around the part about me being brilliant."

Her thank-you came out choked.

"Oh, Shelby." Rachel dropped the bags on the table and came around to give her a hug. "It's nothing. We're a small, friendly town. We help each other. Well, most of us do. I can think of a few people I would love to kick in the tush, but hey..."

Shelby laughed and blinked several times before she embarrassed herself. No tears had actually fallen and she wanted it to stay that way.

Rachel released her. "I'll talk to Jamie, but I'm sure she'll be on board. She's inside with Cole and my other two brothers. Maybe you'll meet them later. If not, someday."

Shelby nodded. "You really are brilliant."

"I know." Rachel grinned. "Don't look now but the kissing bandit's coming." She stepped back. "Trent's one of the good guys. I'm glad he's come home. And that he has you. I bet you and I will be friends."

Shelby just nodded. Her eyes still burned and if she tried to

speak she'd be toast. Rachel was right. This was Trent's home.
And Shelby was nothing but an interloper looking for an easy
way out of her old life.

_16_

THE FAIR ENDED after three successful days. Shelby had seemed to enjoy herself, and hadn't minded a bit when he'd had to run home to take care of Griffin. Trent had made it a point to be there for the tear-down, but enough people had volunteered that he didn't feel guilty leaving early to get Shelby home. Poor woman was exhausted.

They weren't too far from the Eager Beaver. Neither of them had spoken in a while. Thinking she might've dozed off, he glanced over at her snuggled down in the passenger seat.

She had her whole body turned toward him, her cheek resting against the back of the seat. "I have a confession to make," she said.

He felt his gut clench. She hadn't been quite herself the past two days. He'd chalked it up to exhaustion. After a jarring silence, he took a curve in the road, then glanced back at her. She was yawning hugely. He smiled.

"You know that first day when I met Rachel and Jamie?" she said, and he nodded. "I thought you put them up to it."

Trent frowned. "Put them up to what?"

"Saying all those nice things about my jewelry. Buying all that they did."

"Why would I have done that?"

"Because you felt sorry for me. You knew I was worried my jewelry wasn't any good."

"Yeah, but I also knew that wasn't true. And that you'd see for yourself soon enough." He reached across the console for her hand. "Tell you the truth, I was a little worried. I knew people would snap up your stuff fast and then you'd be upset when you sold out."

Her hand felt cool and limp, and she didn't respond. Even though the road was tricky for a couple of miles, he had to take a quick look at her.

She blinked and turned her head.

"Shelby?"

"Careful. There's a deer up ahead on the right."

"I see her." He watched the doe hover at the side of the highway, then bound into the woods. He was more concerned with the suspicious glassiness in Shelby's eyes. And the fact that she'd pulled her hand away. "Something bothering you?"

"You mean other than I've been sleepwalking for two days and I have a ton of orders and no idea how I'll ever complete them before Christmas?"

"You will. I have faith in you."

She sniffled. Turned sharply to look out her window.

What the hell? He pulled the truck over to the shoulder and cut the engine.

"What are you doing?" She straightened, glanced at him, looked away and dabbed at her eye.

"Tell me what's wrong." He swore, if she said "nothing," he would lose it. He'd heard enough "nothings" from his ex to last him a damn lifetime.

"We're almost home. Can't we talk then?"

"We could."

"Okay." She glared at him. "You're not driving."

"I said we could, not that I agreed."

"Trent." Her shoulders slumped against the seat. "Please."

"Are you telling me nothing's wrong?"

"No. I'm telling you I want to get home. Before the first snowfall if possible. Please."

Trent started the engine. He let her be for the ten minutes it took to arrive at the Eager Beaver and park. But then she opened her door and jumped out so fast he wondered if she planned to dodge him all night. Fine. He wouldn't say another word.

Shit.

Mutt came running from behind Violet's trailer straight toward him. He stopped to scratch behind the dog's ears. "How are you doing, boy? Have you been taking care of those kittens and their mama?"

He barked and led Trent to the kitchen door.

Trent sighed. Animals were so much easier to understand than women.

He let Mutt in behind him, scooped kibble out of the bin and dumped it into his bowl. Without a single complaint or cross look Mutt chowed down. Didn't take much to make an animal happy, either, unlike women. Trent should've learned that lesson by now.

Irritated with himself for giving a damn, he walked through the house to see if Shelby had closed herself off in her room. Just as he got to the hall she stepped out of the bathroom.

"Was that..." He closed his eyes for a second. "Better?"

"Much," she said with a regal lift of her chin. "Thank you."

"You could've just told me."

"I could've." She tried keeping a straight face. "But I didn't."

He lunged for her and missed. Laughing, she did a taunting little shimmy and danced out of his reach.

"Okay. I see how you are. Now that you're a mini tycoon you think you're too good for me."

She stopped and stared at him.

He expected her to laugh. Maybe flip him off. Or play along by sticking her nose in the air.

Trent never thought she'd burst into tears.

And damned if he knew what to do. He froze, a bunch of stuff flipping through his mind, afraid he'd make a wrong move and chase her off. He could only do one thing—trust his instincts.

He grabbed a box of tissue from the bathroom, then he pulled Shelby into his arms.

She cried louder.

Holy hell.

She didn't push him away, though, so he hugged her a little closer and rubbed her back, letting her cry with her face buried against his chest. He lightly kissed the top of her head, hoping she hadn't noticed. She might not like it at the moment, but he'd needed the small comfort.

Wanting Shelby to call the shots, he stayed quiet and completely still, even when Mutt barked at the door.

She drew back, pulled out half the tissues in the box, and kept her head bowed while she wiped her eyes and blew her nose. "We better let him out."

Mutt probably just wanted to go chase evening critters. But Trent went ahead and opened the door to give Shelby a moment. After that... Hell, he didn't know.

"Can I get you something?" he asked. "Water? A sandwich? How about a beer?"

She gave him a watery smile and shook her head. "Thanks."

Realizing he was still wearing his hat he yanked it off and spun it around in his hands. "Guess you're just tired, huh?"

"I am," she said, "but that's not it." She cleared her throat. "Maybe I will have some water."

They both turned to the kitchen at the same time.

"I think I can manage," she said with a soft laugh. "May I get you anything? A beer?"

"I don't know. Will I need one?"

Her expression faltered. "I don't think so."

Goddamn it, he wanted to kick himself. What a jackass thing to say. He'd given her an out. It would've been easy for her to blame exhaustion. But she seemed willing to talk, and what did he do?

Halfway to the kitchen she turned around. His gut clenched. She walked back to him, got up on tiptoes and kissed him before continuing to the kitchen.

Shit. He really did want that beer. But he wouldn't follow her. "Shelby?"

"Got it." Less than a minute later she returned with water for her and a bottle for him.

"Thanks," he said, and twisted off the cap. "This is not a commentary on anything. I just feel like a beer."

"Got that, too." She smiled. "Let's sit on the couch for a change, huh?"

She sat first, in the middle, which helped him out. Hard for him to make a wrong move. His ex would've plastered herself to one corner and silently dared him to overstep. Hell, why had he been thinking of Dana lately? He wasn't even that pissed at her anymore. Setting his beer on the coffee table, he sat in his normal spot. Shelby inched a bit closer. The warmth flooding his chest made him a little tongue-tied, so he just smiled and put a loose arm behind her on the couch.

She shifted to face him and sighed. "Thank you," she said. "For helping me get the booth at the fair. For having faith in me. For liking my jewelry. For…putting up with me. I showed up out of the blue, turned your life upside down and you still—" Her voice caught. She took a quick sip, her gaze lowered. "I guess I'm just trying to say thanks for everything."

Part of him thought he should just keep his mouth shut. The other part had him scared to death she was working up to a goodbye. "You're tired," he said, taking her free hand in his. "Now isn't the time to make any big decisions if that's where you're going with this."

Her eyes widened in genuine surprise. "I'm not. I honestly just wanted to tell you how great you've been and how much it matters to me." She took another sip then put her glass on the coffee table. "It's been a long time since anyone has been in my corner. That's why I'm emotional. I just—"

He squeezed her hand, wanting to hold her. But something told him there was more to be said first. "You don't have to thank me. Look how supportive you've been of me. What you said about Moon and that last call. Hey, we're—" His throat closed some when she warily looked up. "We're friends." When the hell had that word become inadequate? She felt it, too, and yet what else were they if not friends. "That's what friends do. Support each other."

She nodded. "You're right," she said with a short laugh. "Who woulda thunk it, huh? That we'd ever reach across that blue duct tape and—"

Trent groaned. "Okay, not a shining moment. Can we forget about that?"

"Well, what about me?" She winced. "Coming out wrapped in just a towel."

"Oh, well, that's completely different. Feel free to do that anytime."

Shelby laughed. "See? You make me laugh. Before meeting you, do you know how long it had been since I really laughed, or felt like myself?" She sighed. "Of course you don't. The other night I was trying to remember and I honestly couldn't."

"Ah, Shelby…"

She leaned another inch closer. "I'm not done thanking you." He opened his mouth and she put a finger to his lips. "Rachel and Sadie and Jamie, I like them all so much and they seem to like me. One word from you about why I came here in the first place and they'd hate my guts. Things would've gotten too icky for me to stick around…"

"I would never have done that." His heart pounded. He should tell her right now how much he wanted her to stay. Call them friends, whatever. It didn't matter.

"I know." She touched his face. "You're a real sweetheart. Even when you pretended to be a meany there were a lot of tells that said otherwise. And now that I know a bit about your world, I'd say every one of your friends knows what a good man you are."

Trent wasn't very comfortable with all this. "I think you're being over-generous, but thank you." He brushed her cheek with the back of his hand. How easy it was to get lost in that beautiful smile of hers. He could stare at her lips forever.

Damn, he needed to say something. Fast. Shelby needed to hear how much he cared for her and wanted her to stay. Now. Once Violet showed them proof that the ranch was his, Shelby might think he was only being a softie by letting her stick around, that she was extra baggage.

He cleared his throat. "What I said about being friends—" Why was this so hard? "You know I care about you...right?"

Shelby nodded, but she was worrying that lush bottom lip of hers.

Hell, his getting all serious could chase her away. He had only known Shelby for a little over two weeks. His feelings for her were strong, stronger than was wise. For both their sakes, they should take whatever was happening between them slowly. He hoped this wasn't just a rebound thing...for both of them.

When she drew closer and kissed him, he went with his gut and pulled her onto his lap. They'd had a long, full weekend and were both tired. Now wasn't the time for words.

SHELBY CURLED UP in Trent's lap, soaking in his warmth and caring. She'd never had a friend like him before. In fact, she had a pretty strong feeling they were a lot more. Everything seemed better when his arms were around her.

He was so different from Donald; Trent made it hard to remember why she'd ever loved Donald.

Trent tilted her chin up. His lips brushed hers softly, back and forth in a gentle rhythm as he stroked her hair. Her eyes closed and with his hypnotizing touch, she felt the stress of the weekend fade away.

If she could just stay right where she was for the next ten hours or so…

She pulled away for just a few seconds, far enough to see the way he looked at her with his beautiful gray eyes. Oh, yeah. They were more than friends. When she found his lips again, she wasn't nearly as tender as he'd been. Neither was the way she held on to him. She wanted to stop the world. Right here in this perfect moment.

At first sight, she'd thought he was just a hot cowboy. A pretty damn rude hot cowboy. But even as he'd tried to bully her off the ranch, she'd seen enough to know he would never do anything to harm her. That his grouchy routine with Violet was just a ruse to let two stubborn people take care of each other.

His tongue slipped between her lips, and she was back in the present, in the safety of his arms. She needed to remember everything. The soft groan he made when she followed his tongue back into his mouth. How fast he could make her heart pound while the rest of her was as relaxed as Mutt in front of the fireplace.

Making out with Trent should be included among the wonders of the world. Not that she wanted anyone else to prove her point. The thought of someone else kissing him…

She pulled back and met his gaze again. He seemed surprised, a little worried. It was nothing compared to how she felt.

"You okay?" he asked.

She nodded. "If I ask you to take me to bed, just to cuddle, would that be all right?"

His slow smile made her melt inside. "Anything," he said. He helped her up and they walked to his bedroom in no hurry. When they got there, he turned down the bedding, then took off Shelby's clothes. The whole time, she just smiled. Memorizing his gentle touch, his reverent looks. Pity she'd probably be asleep by the time he could join her.

She slipped between the cool sheets and lay on her side, both hands underneath her head as she watched him strip bare. He was mostly hard when he walked around to the other side, but all he did was scoot in back of her and tuck her in close. He made a perfect big spoon.

He cuddled like a champ, and yeah, there was no mistaking his condition. But when his hand moved down her tummy and snuck in between her thighs, he whispered, "Don't worry. This is all about you. All you have to do is close your eyes and enjoy. Okay?"

She nodded. No one had ever...

His talented fingers knew exactly what to do. The key was slow and steady. Circling her clit until she was moving her hips, breathing deeper. Clutching his arm and the bottom sheet as he patiently drove her nuts.

"Come on, baby," he said, kissing her shoulder. "That's it. Just let go."

She nearly tore the sheet as her climax started deep inside. Like swirling clouds about to become a tornado, all the ripples started coming together, swelling underneath his fingers.

"I've got you," he whispered. "I'm right here. Let go, honey. I've got you."

It hit her hard, not just between her legs, but all over. He held her as she trembled. Not just because of her orgasm, but because she completely believed him.

As soon as the quaking subsided, she turned to face him. He smiled, until she drew away and sat up.

"Where are you going?"

"Nowhere." She pushed at his shoulders and he fell back.

"No, Shelby, that's not what I was trying to—"

"I know." She swung a leg over his hips and straddled him. "This is what I want."

"You're tired."

"Shut up," she said and leaned down to kiss him. It took little to get him to respond.

While their tongues explored and mated, she reached between them. He was hard. Incredibly hard, the silky head smooth and moist. She firmed her grasp and slid down the length of him. His breath stuttered in her mouth. She only teased him for a few seconds before she grabbed a condom from the nightstand, sheathed him, then positioned him to enter her.

She sank down all the way and his moan filled the room. He cupped her breasts, his hands shaking as he gently kneaded. Rocking against him, she fought the stunning surge of pressure building in her own body.

"Ah, Shelby." He was gazing up at her, the tenderness in his face nearly her undoing.

She lifted slightly and came down harder.

He bucked up squeezing his eyes shut. "Take it slower," he whispered. "Please."

No, not this time. She wanted him to explode just as she had done.

It barely took any movement at all. She rocked once, twice, and they both trembled.

Froze.

He whispered her name the same instant she whispered his. She started to move again. In a matter of seconds the world shattered around them.

17

SHELBY STARED AT the bags littering her workroom and groaned. After digging through every one of them she still couldn't find the special wire cutters and polished hammer she'd bought in Kalispell yesterday. They weren't in her trunk, either. She'd checked. Twice. She really had to do something about organizing her work space.

"What's wrong?"

She looked up to find Trent leaning against the doorframe, a steaming mug in his hand and a telltale smile on his face. "Don't even—"

"What?"

"You think I don't know that smile by now? Please. We are both too busy to start having—"

He pushed off the doorframe and walked into the room, with an expression of faint amusement. "Go ahead and finish. Having what?"

Oh, he was going to make her insane. She met him partway, grabbed the front of his shirt and gently pulled him down so their lips were inches apart. "You're lucky you're holding that coffee."

"I can put it down."

Shelby laughed and gave him a quick kiss. "I really can't."

Trent chuckled. "Hey, I came in to get a refill and was minding my own business when I heard you shriek. I'm just here to investigate, ma'am. That's all."

"I don't think I shrieked." She sighed and, stepping back, glanced around the floor. "I really am an organized person. It's just— I'm glad for this room. It's wonderful. But I need to get better set up or I'll never fill all those orders in time. Jeez, what a nightmare."

"In time? You mean for Christmas?"

She shrugged. "I know some of the jewelry is for gifts."

"It's been only three days since the fair and this is Blackfoot Falls. You meet a deadline or do anything too quickly and everyone will start talking. By day two word will have spread that you're an alien."

"Fine. If people start hounding me about their orders, I'll send them to you."

He smiled. "Come here."

"See? I knew it." She couldn't help her own grin as she took the four steps back to him.

The kiss began light, a brush of lips, a tiny nip, a quick taste. As usual, within seconds they gave in to it. She wouldn't let them get carried away, though. Not so much because she was busy, but she knew Trent was rushing to beat winter, and he was tired from all the sheet-tangling lasting into the wee hours.

She broke the kiss. "We need to talk," she said, putting up a finger. "Not now. Later." The late nights really had to stop. It wasn't as if either of them were going anywhere...

A sudden painful awareness squeezed her chest. Ten days, Violet had said. Which meant D-day would be...

Shelby sucked in a deep breath. It was no wonder she couldn't hold on to the looming date she'd calculated a hundred times. The whole thing was stressing her out. It wasn't today and not tomorrow. No, wait. Maybe it was tomorrow. And she hadn't done anything about it. She'd thought about visiting Violet, but the woman had practically disappeared.

"A talk?" Trent pushed a hand through his adorably rumpled hair. "Am I gonna hate it?"

"Possibly." She gave him a deceptively bright smile. "For now I have to run into town since I can't seem to keep track of a darn thing." She swept a gaze over the ridiculous number of packages. "Need anything?"

He relaxed. "Condoms."

Yes, they had more to discuss than she'd thought initially. But no point in making him tense—

"What? Condoms?"

"Get the big box."

The Food Mart and Abe's Variety were the only two places she'd find them. "You couldn't have told me yesterday when I was in Kalispell?"

Trent laughed. She glared, and he only laughed harder.

"You're a sophisticated city woman. I didn't think you'd have a problem with—" he lowered his voice to a whisper "—*s-e-x*."

She blushed, but couldn't say why. Well, except…small town. No anonymity.

Pretty good reasons why she was a smidge embarrassed. "Fine." She scooped her purse off the floor. "I'll buy the biggest box they have."

"I was just teasing." He lowered his chin and gave her a contrite puppy-dog look. "We're okay until I go in to pick up my feed order on Friday."

"Nope. Already on my list. A supersize box. Just so long as you can live up to the order."

He laughed again, put an arm around her waist and planted a noisy kiss on her cheek. "Darlin', I'll do my best."

Trent had asked for the large box, she thought, smiling all the way to her car. Look at her, making plans, looking forward to a future with Trent. Was she…falling in love? With the man who might lose his ranch, his home, because of her?

God, very scary thought.

Unfortunately, that didn't make it less true.

TRENT HAD JUST swapped out the rusty metal fence post for a sturdy cedar pole when he heard a car. It didn't sound like Violet's truck—he'd been praying she'd come home before Shelby so he could speak with her in private. No, this engine was smooth, the rich purr similar to Shelby's sedan.

He rounded the barn just as a black car pulled to a stop. A Mercedes? Sweat trickled down his forehead into his eye. Damn weather was being fickle. Yanking up his T-shirt, he blotted the sweat from his eye as he approached the sedan.

The driver had climbed out. A tall thirty-something man with dark blond hair was staring at Trent as if he was part of a freak show. He pulled down the hem of his shirt, grabbed his hat off the wheelbarrow and watched the stranger pan the house and stable with a critical frown.

"Afternoon," Trent said, setting the Stetson on his head and pulling down the rim against the sun. "Can I help you?" The second the words left his mouth he noticed the Colorado plate.

Shit.

"I'm not sure." The man checked his phone, glanced back toward the house. "Do you know Shelby Foster?"

"I do."

His faintly patronizing smile stuck in Trent's craw. "Is she here?"

"Nope."

"Do you know where she is?"

Trent was tempted to just say *yep*. "Who's asking?"

"Donald Williamson. Her fiancé."

"Huh. Sorry." Wiping his palm on his jeans, he walked around the hood with his grime-streaked hand extended. And thoroughly enjoyed watching Donald's look of disdain turn to dread. "I thought you two split up."

The man's gaze shot up to meet Trent's. He seemed barely mindful of Trent firmly pumping his hand. "Is that what Shelby told you?"

"She didn't tell me you were coming." Trent stood back, folding his arms across his chest, feet planted shoulder-width apart.

"She wouldn't have. It's a surprise." To give him credit, he didn't inspect the grime Trent left on his palm. "Would you mind me asking how you two know each other?"

He scratched his jaw, trying to act perplexed. This was tricky. Trent had no idea what she'd told the guy. Obviously she'd told him something, though, or he wouldn't be standing here making Trent sweat. The guy was good-looking, he supposed. Rich. And he'd come running after her. Women liked that shit.

Jesus. Trent wasn't feeling so smug all of a sudden. "Haven't you two talked since she's been here?"

"Once. Briefly."

Trent's gut knotted. Time to decide which road to take. The low road was looking mighty good. "We're friends. Old family friends. Our great-grandfathers knew each other."

"Ah." Donald seemed vaguely relieved. "And this is the Eager Beaver ranch?"

"Correct."

"How long has she been staying here?"

No. No way. He wouldn't discuss Shelby. "Tell you what… It's Donald, right?" Trent waited for the nod. "Why don't you come inside, have something cold to drink. She should be back at any minute."

Donald didn't look overjoyed with the suggestion. He brushed something off his tailored navy blue sports jacket, turned and glanced back at the road, probably hoping to see Shelby's car turn down the driveway, then said, "Thank you."

Waiting while Donald pressed his key fob and locked the Mercedes's doors, Trent held in a snort. "So, Donald," he said, clapping the guy on the back and steering him to the porch, "you like beer?"

SHELBY NEEDED TO be smarter about planning her trips to town. Now that she knew a few people, there was no such thing as dashing in and out of a store. Some of the folks in Blackfoot Falls liked to chitchat about absolutely nothing. For goodness' sake some of them already recognized her car.

It was sort of nice, so she wasn't really complaining. But it would be much nicer when she didn't have a gazillion orders to fill, or a giant box of condoms to buy. She just had to laugh as she turned down the driveway. This sure *wasn't* Kansas anymore.

She saw a black car and couldn't remember Trent mentioning that he was expecting company. As she got closer, and recognized the familiar Mercedes, her heart leaped into her throat. How was this possible? Donald couldn't know she was here. She'd spoken to him only once and had never said a word about the Eager Beaver, or Montana for that matter.

Her cell buzzed. She parked, read the text. It was Trent, warning her about Donald. A little late. Could mean he'd just arrived. God, she really hoped so.

She got out and went around to the passenger side for her packages. Her hands shook, so she hefted the bags into her arms. The stupid box of condoms was sitting right on top. She threw everything back on the seat, not caring that the contents spilled onto the floor. She drew in a deep breath and took only her purse with her.

Dammit. Dammit. Dammit.

How long had Donald been here? What were he and Trent talking about? How had Donald even known she was here? He had no right to track her down, much less show up without warning.

This was bad.

Okay, she needed to calm herself. Slow down her heart rate. Anger and nerves, not a good combination.

God, she wished she knew if they'd seen her. She lingered on the porch, away from the living room window, drawing in long deep breaths.

Finally, she opened the front door.

Trent was lounging in the recliner, his expression unreadable. Donald was sitting on the couch, leaning forward. Looking out of place in his sports jacket. Both men turned toward her.

Donald smiled, and got to his feet.

She closed the door behind her. "What are you doing here?" she asked, annoyed when he approached to kiss her cheek. No need to make a scene, she reminded herself. And stood still as a statute for the light peck.

He reached for her hand, but she moved it back. Too bad Trent couldn't see her reaction from where he sat. God, she hoped he didn't think she'd invited Donald.

"You haven't told me why you're here," she said, unsmiling. "Or how you found me."

"Shelby, honey, I think we should have this conversation in private, don't you?"

Frankly, she couldn't imagine that they had anything to say to each other, period. Her resentment and disappointment toward him had started to fade since leaving Denver. But showing up unannounced and uninvited? She was pissed all over again.

But she needn't be rude, or make Trent feel uncomfortable. That was the last thing she wanted to do. She gave Donald a stiff nod.

"Guess that's my cue to leave. I got a lot of work to do outside, anyway." Trent stood and stretched. "I offered Donald something to drink when he got here ten minutes ago. You might want to get him something now that he's had to listen to me go on about our families being friends for three generations."

"Four," she said without thinking. She wanted to kiss him for sliding in the heads-up. That was so like Trent. What a wonderful, caring man. She should kiss him. Right now. In front of God and Donald. "Thanks." She gave him a small smile. "I shouldn't be long."

With a slow nod and lingering look he walked past her to the door. "Nice meeting you, Donny."

"Yes, likewise." Donald's troubled eyes stayed on her. He waited until Trent had left and said, "What the hell's going on with you, Shelby?"

She huffed a laugh and evaded the hand he extended. "What the hell's going on? That's what I want to know. How did you find me?"

"Your mom. Between the two of us we figured out you must have come here."

Shelby did a quick mental replay of the two conversations she'd had with her mom. Montana might've been mentioned, but— It didn't matter. "That you had to figure out where I was should have been your first clue. Why on earth would you think you could just show up like this?"

"Because I love you," he said with a hint of impatience, a dash of arrogance.

"Donald…" She sighed, suddenly so drained she could weep. "Let's sit." She waited until he was reseated on the couch and then took the recliner. It was obvious he didn't like it. But she didn't particularly care. "Because you love me isn't enough. I hope that doesn't hurt your feelings, but it's true."

Donald stood up, and she recognized his frown and his pacing. He'd been all ready to sweep her off her feet, forgive her silly tantrum and win her back with his heartfelt plea. As if.

"Look," he said. "I know why you left, okay? I get that now. But you didn't even give me a second chance."

"A chance for what?"

"To convince you we deserve to try again." He stilled in front of her. "You have to admit we had a lot of good times together, Shel. And you've got your job just waiting for you. Along with a nice raise, of course."

"Of course."

"We'll start fresh." He pulled a familiar box from his jacket pocket. The diamond was an extraordinary three-carat round solitaire, nearly flawless, mounted on 18k white gold. And it could be hers, just for marrying Donald—right after she signed a document stating it would go back to the family if they should ever split up.

"Put that away, Donald," she said. "Please."

He sighed. "If we can't work it out, then okay. But we have to at least try," he said, gripping the velvet box in his hand. "I meant it. I do love you. I never stopped loving you."

It was her turn to stand. Aside from giving him a pop in the nose for showing up here without an invitation, she didn't want to hurt him. He'd grown up in a world of wealth and privilege and she was sure he had no idea why she would choose anything else. "You said you understood why I left."

He nodded, moving closer, but stopping before she had to rethink popping him. "I didn't understand how important your hobby was to you, all right? We can work around that. I swear. Besides," he said, lowering his voice as he touched her arm, "You shouldn't have to live in this godforsaken place."

Hobby? He so didn't get it. He didn't get her. And he never would. Despite everything, it made her a little sad. Still, it was tempting to tell him to just go back home and lose her number and address. But she really couldn't. After signing over a quitclaim deed to Trent, it was possible that she wouldn't have a place to live, or a job. Trent was still recovering from his divorce. They hadn't even known each other for a whole month. And one county fair did not a successful business make.

Her and Donald? That was over. But if she had to work for his parents for a while, it wouldn't kill her.

Then again it might.

"Tell you what," she said, taking Donald's hand. "I'll think about it, okay?"

He looked slightly appeased. "I knew you'd be reasonable about this."

She didn't bother pointing out that she was only agreeing to think about it. "I won't take too long to make up my mind."

His sigh this time was one of relief. She felt somewhat guilty for giving him false hope because she honestly couldn't see them fixing anything. But he'd caught her off guard and that wasn't fair, either.

TRENT WANTED TO kick himself across three states. He'd known eavesdropping was a bad idea when he'd walked over to the side window. Though technically the window was on his list of chores. It needed new grout, which meant he could hear pretty much everything from the living room.

He couldn't see them, of course, which was the only part that worked in his favor. Because if he'd seen them kiss or do anything, he surely would've lost it.

As he crossed to the stable to disappear for a while, he cursed himself for being every kind of fool. He passed the stable and kept walking.

She was going to think about it. About going back to that rich bastard and his rich bastard family. Why wouldn't she? She'd have it made. And she wouldn't have to live in this "god-forsaken place."

He kicked a bush and it didn't do him a damn bit of good, so he picked up the nearest rock he could find and threw it with all his might. He should go back to the stable, saddle up Solomon and ride until the sun went down. He wasn't about to go back to the house.

She was going to think about it.

How could she? When they made each other laugh, and she was proud of him and he was proud of her. She'd already made friends here, and her business was off to a flying start, so what had he done wrong?

Goddammit, how could she think about going back to Denver when he was gonna give her the ranch?

When he'd already fallen in love?

_18_

TRENT HAD CAUGHT a glimpse of Violet's rusted-out pickup turning off the driveway and felt equal parts relief and irritation. She was trying to sneak back and park on the other side of her double-wide before anyone saw her. The hell with that.

He headed toward her parking spot at a fast clip, slowed so she wouldn't see him between the barn and her trailer. Then as soon as it was safe, jogged the rest of the way. That's when he saw the rearview mirror was gone, and there was another dent in the front bumper. Fender benders twice in two months. She was damn lucky nothing worse had happened.

She'd barely shut off the engine when he opened her driver door.

"Where the hell have you been for two days? Dammit, you can't just take off like that, Violet."

She glared at him. "I can, and I did."

He scowled right back. "I swear to God I'm gonna make you carry a cell phone from now on."

"That'll be the damn day." With a snort, she stuck her pipe in her mouth. Normally he would've backed up. She wouldn't hesitate to blow smoke in his face if it served her purpose. "Move."

He made his disgust known with a grunt and stepped back. She wasn't as spry as she had been just a few months ago. It was hard watching her climb down so slowly. He had to convince her to quit driving. It wasn't safe.

"You have bags you want me to carry inside?"

"I carry my own things. You know that." She shouldered past him.

"Jesus," he muttered under his breath. "I have to worry about you. Worry about Shelby. My life has gone straight down the tubes."

Violet stopped, her face creased in a frown. "What about Shelby? Why are you fretting about her?"

He glanced at the house. She'd been working last he knew. Except it was becoming more and more obvious he didn't know jack shit. Ever since Donald had gone, the two of them had hardly spoken. She'd grabbed food and drink when she needed it, then gone right back to working. "Can we go inside?"

"Come on." She had a Food Mart bag in one hand, a legal-size envelope in the other and a worried look on her face.

He followed her up the steps to her porch, wondering if the deed to the Eager Beaver was in the envelope. Tomorrow was supposed to be the day of reckoning, which was something he needed to discuss with her.

Reaching around her frail body, he opened the door. She didn't object. Something else worrisome. He followed her inside, his gaze catching on the small wood-burning stove. "I left a stack of firewood for you in the back," he said absently.

Watching him closely, Violet set down the bag and envelope. "Well, go ahead and talk, seems you've got something you wanna get off your chest."

"I do. First, you're gonna be mad, but so be it. You can't drive anymore, Violet. You just can't. You can barely see over the wheel. And your eyes aren't so good. You've been lucky so far, and haven't hurt yourself or someone else, but luck can't hold out forever. Besides, even as ornery as you are, I don't think you want to worry me like you did these past two days."

With a leathery hand she gestured for him to sit. "Next."

Shocked, Trent stared at her a moment then took a seat.

"It's Shelby." Sighing, he rubbed his closed eyes. "I want her to have the Eager Beaver. I'll sign whatever it is I need to sign."

"Why would you do a damn fool thing like that?" she muttered. "And you think *I'm* senile."

He opened his eyes just as she lost a smile. "I never said you were senile." He groaned when she walked away. "We're not done. Where are you going?"

"To get you a beer, you damn cry baby."

"Okay." He slumped back. "Good. Thanks."

She brought two bottles out of the refrigerator and let him twist the caps off. They took swigs at the same time.

"Explain to me why you want to sign the ranch over," Violet said, settling into her plaid recliner.

"Shelby needs a place to call her own. A place that won't cost her an arm and a leg while she gets her business off the ground. She needs to feel independent. You of all people should understand." He looked at the big envelope she'd brought in. "I assume that's the deed. Just, she can't know I signed the ranch over to her. That's important."

Violet's narrowed eyes bore into him. She gulped some beer without taking her gaze off his face. "Ever consider that what she needs is you?"

"Come on, Violet, don't start meddling in that area. You know I'm recently divorced. And Shelby was engaged until a few weeks ago. She needs space, and time to think. We can't just— Look, I'm trying to do the right thing here."

"So?"

"So it's complicated. We don't even know each other all that well."

She snorted. "You know her well enough to hand over the Eager Beaver."

Trent clamped his mouth shut. Hard to argue that point. After another pull of beer, he said, "If I don't, I'm afraid she'll go back to Denver. To her old job. Maybe even marry her ex-fiancé." There. He'd voiced his biggest fear. The thought alone was killing him.

Violet frowned. "What would you do if she doesn't want you to stick around?"

His gut clenched at the possibility. "I don't know yet. But I have more options than she does."

"Good God in heaven. You've always been my favorite, Trent. Don't be a dummy." Violet shook her head. "Fretting over my poor eyesight, when you can't see what's plain as day."

"Dammit, Violet—"

"Go on. Get. I missed my nap." She pushed to her feet.

"You know what, why don't you just give me the paperwork, and I'll go down to the county office and make things official."

Violet smirked. "You got any idea how old that piece of paper is? It ain't in just your name." She sighed with disgust. "If you want the girl to have it, I'll take care of it." Her face softened. "But I'm telling you, it's not the Eager Beaver that'll keep her here."

Trent felt as if his feet were planted in cement. A few days ago, he might've believed that Shelby felt strongly enough about him to stay. But now, after he'd overheard her talk with her ex? Hell, she'd slept in her own room last night. If that wasn't a sign, he didn't know what was.

"Feel like going out for dinner?"

Shelby looked up at Trent standing in the doorway. He must have just finished working outside and washed his face because his damp hair was slicked back. Smiling, she set aside her glue gun. "What brought this on?"

"What? I can't ask my favorite girl out on a date?"

She raised her brows. "Your favorite *girl*."

"I knew you'd like that."

She doubted she'd be able to eat. Her stomach was acting up, and she'd pricked her fingers a million times on stupid silver wire. She'd slept terribly, wanting badly to crawl into bed with Trent. But by the time she'd finished working it had been almost 2:00 a.m. and she hadn't wanted to wake him.

It wasn't enough that she was panicked about getting out her orders. Tomorrow was the *day*. And Violet had been AWOL. Shelby couldn't rest until she'd told the woman she wanted Trent to have the Eager Beaver.

"You're thinking about going back to Denver, aren't you?"

"What?"

"It's okay." Trent shrugged, as if he was commenting on the weather. "I mean, I'd understand. Not that you'd need my permission."

"You're right about that." It was about the only thing he was clued in to from where she sat.

"What I'm trying to say, and doing a very bad job of it, is that I wouldn't try and stop you."

Speechless, hurt to the bone, she could only stare at him. She'd been praying for a sign he wanted her to stay. She'd really thought...

Oh, God.

"Donald seems like an okay guy." He glanced at the mess she'd made of the room. "You wouldn't be working so hard for peanuts."

Money didn't mean anything to her. He knew that. "So, tonight is supposed to be a goodbye dinner?"

"No, Shelby." The mask of indifference slipped. He finally looked like himself again. For a few seconds, anyway. "No. You've been edgy all day. I figured— I thought maybe you were dreading having to tell— I don't know." He scrubbed at his face. "Guess I'm still tired."

She had been edgy, cursing under her breath every time she'd nicked herself or dropped the tweezers. So, okay, she could cut him some slack. Still, tired or not, she hated that he could look so okay with her leaving.

"How about sandwiches?" she said, and tried to smile. "I

don't really want to go anywhere until Violet comes home. Aren't you worried? Does she do this often?"

"She's home," he said, his expression a mixture of caution and concern. "We already had a talk."

Her heart pounded so hard she jumped to her feet hoping to slow it down. "A talk?"

"Yeah." He eyed her warily. "About not taking off like that."

"I should go check on her." She tried to skirt him, but he caught her arm.

"She's fine, Shelby. I told her she shouldn't drive anymore so she's not in the best of moods."

"Oh, so now you know what's best for everybody, is that it?"

"Whoa." Frowning, he let go her arm. "You don't agree that Violet shouldn't be behind the wheel?"

Shelby swallowed. "Of course I agree, but don't think you know what's best for me. Because I can assure you, you're clueless." She tried to squeeze past him. "Absolutely clueless." She'd tossed and turned last night, thinking about Donald and Denver, and what would happen once she relinquished her rights to the Eager Beaver. How foolish she'd been to spend so much of her salary on the right clothes, the right car, trying to belong in Donald's world. Now, her savings wouldn't take her far. It would be hard to turn down working for his family.

Just thinking that made her sick to her stomach. Dammit, no matter what happened she wouldn't return to Denver. She'd rather live in her car than settle for a man, or a job. In fact, she was done with settling for anything. She was better than that.

And if Trent didn't love her? She'd be fine. Okay, maybe not fine, but she'd survive. Right?

That last part made her a little shaky.

"Excuse me, please. I want to check on Violet."

"She's taking a nap," he said.

"How convenient."

Trent looked confused at first, and then uneasy as he stepped aside. "If I swear to you Violet's fine, will you leave it alone?" he asked quietly as she passed him.

Shelby froze. He knew. Violet had already told him the ranch was hers, and the first thing he'd said to her was about how he wouldn't stop her from going back to Donald? How could it be that after everything they'd been through, Trent hadn't changed at all? He still wanted her to go back where she'd come from so he could have his precious ranch.

It hit her hard. So hard, she could barely breathe. Trent was supposed to tell her he didn't care about who owned what. That all he wanted was for the two of them to be together. Instead, he wanted to pack her off to Denver so he could have the Eager Beaver to himself.

She nearly choked on a sob and hurried on through the house. No. She wouldn't cry. Not again. Not in front of him, or because of him. Why had he been so great the night after the fair? How could he have looked at her as if he cared...as if he might even love her back. It made this so much harder.

For a split second she thought about changing her mind. But keeping the ranch would be spiteful and so not her. At heart Trent was a good man. One of the best she'd ever known. He only wanted to keep his home, continue with his new life. She understood that bone-deep need. God, how she understood. But dammit, she loved him. Which was turning out to be a huge mistake. One of many. But this one would be incredibly hard to get over.

She paused in the living room, looked toward the kitchen. Where was she going? She had no idea where she was headed. Oh, Violet.

Shelby stopped again in the kitchen. Filled a glass with water and downed half of it. When had her mouth gotten so dry? She drained the glass, set it in the sink. Pushed her hands through her hair as she composed herself on the way to the back door.

"Shelby, wait." Trent was standing at the doorway to the living room. "Come on, honey, can't we talk?"

"Don't—" She whirled around with a finger in the air. How dare he? "Do not call me that. Not now. Not ever."

His stricken expression faded, hardened. "Okay." He shoved his hands into his pockets, his mouth a firm thin line. "Got it."

This was the image of him she needed to keep in her head. And not cry, she told herself again. Crying would be bad. She still had to see Violet. Pack.

Oh, God.

She pulled open the screen door and almost trampled the poor woman.

Violet jerked back. "Where's the damn fire?"

Shelby glanced over her shoulder. Trent was still there. "Can we go to your trailer and talk?" she whispered.

"Nope." Violet pushed past her. She walked straight to the kitchen table and laid down an envelope. "We're talking right here. All of us."

Trent eyed her, his expression a warning. "You aren't going to do anything foolish now, are you, Violet?"

"Nah, I'll leave that to you. Being so good at it like you are."

He slowly walked to the table, looking pale under the kitchen light. "Violet, I'm begging you."

He looked scared, desperate and angry all at the same time. Shelby had never seen this expression on him before. Her stomach clenched painfully.

"Actually, Violet, I really need a minute alone with you," Shelby said in her most persuasive voice.

"Tough. Sit down. Both of you. I'm missing my nap and my TV shows so I ain't in a good mood."

Trent folded his arms across his chest, his mouth clamped tight. Shelby tried not to notice how his biceps bunched. Or that he still looked a bit scared. She did as Violet asked and took a seat. But Trent, he wasn't having it. He stayed right where he was.

Violet dragged a chair from the table and sat. "I'm only going to say this once—"

"Fine. I already know." Trent cut in, staring at Violet so hard it had to hurt. "Shelby owns the Eager Beaver."

"What? No." Shelby shot to her feet. "You do. Tell him, Violet." She silently pleaded with the woman, staring just as hard as Trent. She crouched next to Violet. "Tell him," she whispered, her eyes burning. She willed the tears to remain unshed. "Please."

Violet blinked back a suspicious sheen of moisture. "I don't have the stomach for all this nonsense. You both own it." She slapped a hand on the envelope. "And I got this here legal document to prove it."

"What?" Trent and Shelby said at the same time and gave each other quick glances, as if they were opponents in a ring.

"But you told me I owned the—" Trent plowed a hand through his hair. "Goddammit, Violet."

"Wait." Shelby rose. "You told me I owned the Eager Beaver."

"I know what I said." She looked from one to the other. "I ain't senile."

"You sure about that?" Trent muttered something else but Shelby couldn't hear it.

She was too angry with Violet. "Trent warned me about you, and I didn't listen. Do you have any idea what you've done?" Outwardly she tried to look calm, but her voice was shaking like crazy. "How your meddling—"

Suddenly Trent was behind her, pulling her back against his strong chest, whispering, "It's okay, honey. We'll straighten things out."

She spun out of his grip. "How are we going to work things out when you want to pack me up and send me back to Donald?"

"What? I never said—"

Violet got to her feet. "Be mad as polecats at me. Not each other," she said. "I was young when they named me trustee, just a foolish girl. Hell, I've outlived the lawyer who drew up the paperwork. Had to deal with his grandson who took over. Explaining to that young upstart what needed doing 'bout gave

me a stroke. But now everything's put to right. Harold and
Edgar shoulda—" Her voice cracked. "Your two great-grand-
daddies were too stubborn for their own damn good." Without looking at either of them, she slid the envelope across the
table. "Here's the deed. Both Kimball and Foster names are on
it. So, figure it out."

She turned and left the kitchen without another word.

"I have no idea what just happened," Shelby said.

Trent shrugged. "I'm clueless, remember?"

She looked down, not ready to admit to anything until she
understood.

"One of the things I really, really love about you is that you
aren't afraid to talk," Shelby said, then raised her head and met
his gaze.

"I haven't always been that way," he admitted without wa-
vering. "But I'm trying." He quietly cleared his throat. "Shelby,
I don't want you to go back to Denver. I honestly don't understand how you got that idea. Jesus, it's the last thing in the
world I want."

"But you said if I decided to go back you wouldn't try to
stop me."

"I did say that." Trent nodded once. "When Donald showed
up and I thought you might still have feelings for him. I—I don't
know. I wanted to kick his ass all the way back to Colorado."

He sighed. "You are a smart, capable woman and you know
better than anyone what's best for you. Now, if you did decide
to leave, I'd like to think I'd keep my word and let you go like
a real gentleman. But the way I feel about you? There's no telling what I'd do to keep you."

She stared at him, shaking her head, stunned silent not by
the words so much as the way he said them. Okay, so he hadn't
used the *L* word. It came hard to some people. If he needed
time, she was willing to wait. Because this was the man she'd
dreamed about long before they'd met. So she'd be brave. Be
the first to say it...

"Want to know what I really, really love about you?" he asked, his eyes dark with emotion.

She could only nod.

"Pretty near everything," he said, pulling her into his arms, where he kissed her for a very long time.

Epilogue

Eight months later

LYING ON HER SIDE, Trent's warm, naked body pressed against her back, Shelby squinted blearily at the bedside clock. "Please tell me it's not seven thirty."

His arm tightened possessively around her. "It's not seven thirty," he murmured into her hair, then kissed the side of her neck.

"Oh, good." Smiling, she turned over. They both shifted so that her breasts pressed against his chest and they could look into each other's eyes. "You've been awake for a while," she said, feeling something hard nudging her tummy.

"Not too long." He brushed the hair away from her face and gave her that special smile reserved for her alone. "I have an idea."

"Which is...?"

"Let's take the day off."

"Really?" It was the middle of spring and they still had so much to do in the three weeks before the two horses he'd been hired to train arrived. "Are you sure you mean the whole day? Or were you thinking we should stay in bed awhile longer?" Just to make her point, she rubbed against his erection.

"Both." He scooped her into his arms and rolled over so that she was lying on top of him. "How about it?" he asked, leisurely stroking her back.

Shelby grinned. "What did you have in mind?"

"Now, I know you can guess the first part."

She laughed, and Trent joined in.

"So," she said, nudging him again right where it counted. "What's the second part?"

"We need to give Violet her present. She's gonna try to hide out in that old trailer of hers, so we'll need to double-team her."

"Once she learns she can watch *Duck Dynasty* on her new smartphone, she won't give us any grief."

"Of course she will." He chuckled. "Just not for too long. Okay, so after, we could go to Kalispell for corned beef hash at the Knead Cafe, then drop off your necklaces at the Noice, go by the hardware store, get married, see if we can get in for the sunset champagne deal at the Conrad—"

"Wait." Shelby sat up, the covers falling down around her waist, and his gaze dropped to her naked breasts. "What was that last thing?"

"The hardware store?"

She socked him in the arm.

Trent grinned, looking her in the eye again. "Okay, okay. I thought maybe you'd like to, you know, get married. But if you'd rather not—"

"Wait."

"Again?"

She flopped down next to him so they were eye to eye. "We don't have a license. Or a certified copy of your divorce decree."

He gave her an innocent look. "Well, to tell you the truth, we have both of those... Hey, wait. How'd you know I needed a certified copy of my divorce decree?"

She just smiled, then wiggled against him until he growled and rolled her beneath his body, pinning her to the bed.

There was no place she'd rather be...

* * * * *

NEW RELEASE!

Rancher's Snowed-In Reunion

The Carsons Of Lone Rock

Book 4

**She turned their break-up into her breakout song.
And now they're snowed in...**

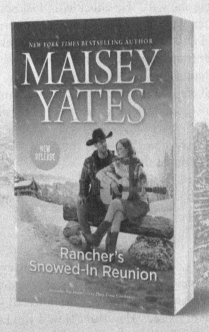

Don't miss this snowed-in second-chance romance
between closed-off bull rider Flint Carson and Tansey
Sands, the rodeo queen turned country music darling.

In-store and online March 2024.

MILLS & BOON

millsandboon.com.au